STEPHEN BOOTH

Stephen Booth was born in the Lancashire mill town of Burnley, and has remained rooted to the Pennines during his career as a newspaper journalist. He lives with his wife Lesley in a former Georgian dower house in Nottinghamshire and his interests include folklore, the internet and walking in the hills of the Peak District. *The Dead Place* is the sixth in the series featuring Derbyshire detectives Ben Cooper and Diane Fry. The second, *Dancing with the Virgins*, was nominated for the coveted CWA Gold Dagger Award.

Visit www.AuthorTracker.co.uk for exclusive information on Stephen Booth

www.stephen-booth.com

By the same author

STEPHEN BOOTH

The Dead Place

HARPER

This novel is entirely a work of fiction. The names, characters and incidents portrayed in it are the work of the author's imagination. Any resemblance to actual persons, living or dead, events or localities is entirely coincidental.

Harper
An Imprint of HarperCollins*Publishers*
77–85 Fulham Palace Road,
Hammersmith, London W6 8JB

www.harpercollins.co.uk

This paperback edition 2011
1

First published in Great Britain by
HarperCollins*Publishers* 2005

A catalogue record for this book
is available from the British Library

ISBN 978-0-00-789660-8

Typeset in Meridien by
Palimpsest Book Production Limited,
Grangemouth, Stirlingshire

Printed and bound in Great Britain by
Clays Ltd, St Ives plc

'For what is it to die,
But to stand in the sun and melt into the wind?
And when the Earth has claimed our limbs,
Then we shall truly dance.'

Kahlil Gibran (1883–1931), 'The Prophet'

*For everyone who has ever
had to deal with death.*

The Death Clock really exists,
but try it at your own risk!
You can find it at: http://www.deathclock.com

1

Soon there will be a killing. It might happen in the next few hours. We could synchronize our watches and count down the minutes. What a chance to record the ticking away of a life, to follow it through to that last, perfect moment, when existence becomes nothing, when the spirit parts with the physical.

The end is always so close, isn't it? Fate lurks beneath our feet like a rat in a sewer. It hangs in a corner of the room like a spider in its web, awaiting its moment. And the moment of our dying already exists inside us, deep inside. It's a dark ghost on the edge of our dreams, a weight that drags at our feet, a whisper in the ear at the darkest hour of the night. We can't touch it or see it. But we know it's there, all the same.

But then again . . . perhaps I'll wait, and enjoy the anticipation. They say that's half the pleasure, don't they? The waiting and planning, the unspoiled thrill of expectation. We can let the imagination scurry ahead, like a dog on a trail, its nostrils twitching, its tongue dribbling with joy. Our minds can sense the blood and

1

savour it. We can close our eyes and breathe in the aroma.

I can smell it right now, can't you? It's so powerful, so sweet. So irresistible. It's the scent of death.

Footsteps approached in the corridor. Heavy boots, someone pacing slowly on the vinyl flooring. Here was a man in no hurry, his mind elsewhere, thinking about his lunch or the end of his shift, worrying about the twinge of pain in his back, a waistband grown too tight. An ordinary man, who rarely thought about dying.

The footsteps paused near the door, and there was a rustle of papers, followed by a moment's silence. An aroma of coffee drifted on the air, warm and metallic, like the distant scent of blood.

As she listened to the silence, Detective Sergeant Diane Fry rubbed at the black marks on her fingers with a tissue. The fax machine invariably did this to her. Every time she went near the damn thing, the powder ended up on her skin. There always seemed to be a spill from a cartridge, or fingerprints left on the casing. But tonight she felt as though she were trying to wipe a much darker stain from her hands than fax toner.

'He's seriously disturbed,' she said. 'That's all. A sicko. A Rampton case.'

But she didn't expect a reply. It was only a tactic to delay reading the rest of the transcript. Fry scraped at her fingers again, but the marks

2

only smeared and sank deeper into her pores. S̶
would need soap and a scrubbing brush later.

'Damned machines. Who invented them?'

On the other side of the desk, Detective Inspector Paul Hitchens waited patiently, rotating his swivel chair, smiling with satisfaction at a high-pitched squeal that came from the base at the end of each turn.

Fry sighed. Waiting for her in the CID room was the paperwork from several cases she was already up to her neck in. She was due in court tomorrow morning to give evidence in a murder trial, and there was a conference with the Crown Prosecution Service later in the day. She didn't have time to take on anything else, as her DI ought to know.

She'd also slept badly again last night. Now, at the end of the day, her head ached as if steel springs had been wound tight across her forehead and driven deep into the nerves behind her eyes. A growing queasiness told her that she ought to go home and lie down for a while until the feeling passed.

And this will be a real killing – not some drunken scuffle in the back yard of a pub. There'll be no spasm of senseless violence, no pathetic spurt of immature passion. There's no place for the brainless lunge of a knife, the boot in the side of the head. There'll be no piss among the blood, no shit on the stones, no screaming and thrashing as a neck slithers in my fingers like a sweat-soaked snake . . .

'll be none of that sort of mess. Not this
's the sign of a disorganized brain, the
to an irrational impulse. It's not my kind of

*My killing has been carefully planned. This death
will be a model of perfection. The details will be precise,
the conception immaculate, the execution flawless. An
accomplishment to be proud of for the rest of my life.*

TRANSCRIPTION NOTE: BRIEF PAUSE,
LAUGHTER.

A cold worm moved in Fry's stomach. She
looked up from the faxed sheets, suppressing a
feeling of nausea that had risen as she read the
last sentence.

'I need to hear the original tape,' she said.

'Of course. It's on its way from Ripley. We'll
have it first thing in the morning.'

'What are they using – a carrier pigeon?'

Hitchens turned to look at her then. He
smoothed his hands along the sleeves of his jacket,
a mannerism he'd developed over the past few
weeks, as if he were constantly worrying about
his appearance. Tonight, he looked particularly
uncomfortable. Perhaps *he* wasn't sleeping well,
either.

'Diane, I've heard this tape,' he said. 'This guy
is convincing. I think he's serious.'

When the footsteps outside the door moved on,
Fry followed their sound and let her mind wander
the passages of E Division headquarters – down
the stairs, past the scenes of crime department,

the locked and darkened incident room, and into a corridor filled with muffled, echoing voices. By the time the sounds had faded away, her thoughts were aimless and disoriented, too. They were lost in a maze with no way out, as they so often were in her dreams.

'No, he's laughing,' she said. 'He's a joker.'

Hitchens shrugged. 'Don't believe me, then. Wait until you hear the tape, and judge for yourself.'

Fry regarded the DI curiously. Despite his faults as a manager, she knew he had good instincts. If Hitchens had heard the tape and thought it should be taken seriously, she was inclined to believe him. The printed words on the page weren't enough on their own. The caller's real meaning would be captured in the sound of his voice, the manner of his speech, in the audible layers of truth and lies.

'He seems to be hinting that he's killed before,' she said.

'Yes. There are some significant phrases. "Not this time", for a start.'

'Yet in the same breath he's disapproving of something. Disapproving of *himself*, would you say?'

With a nod, Hitchens began to smooth his sleeve again. He had strong hands, with clean, trimmed fingernails. A white scar crawled all the way across the middle knuckles of three of his fingers.

'He could turn out to be an interesting psychological case for someone to examine,' he said.

The DI's voice sounded too casual. And suddenly Fry thought she knew why he was looking so uncomfortable.

'Don't tell me we've got a psychologist on the case already?'

'It wasn't my decision, Diane. This has come down to us from Ripley, remember.'

She shook her head in frustration. So some chief officer at Derbyshire Constabulary HQ had got wind of the phone call and decided to interfere. That was all she needed. She pictured one of the ACPO types in his silver braid strolling through the comms room at Ripley, demonstrating his hands-on approach to visiting members of the police committee, hoping they'd remember him when promotion time came round.

'OK, so who's the psychologist?' said Fry. 'And, more to the point, who did he go to school with?'

'Now, that's where you're wrong,' said Hitchens. He pulled an embossed business card from the clip holding the case file together. As she took the card, Fry noticed that it was a pretty slim file so far. But it wouldn't stay that way, once reports from the experts started thumping on to her desk.

'Dr Rosa Kane,' she said. 'Do you know anything about her?'

The list of accredited experts and consultants had recently been updated. Someone had wielded a new broom and put his own stamp on the list, bringing in people with fresh ideas.

'Not a thing,' said Hitchens. 'But we have an appointment to meet her tomorrow.'

Fry took note of the 'we'. She made a show of writing down Dr Kane's details before handing back the card. If the psychologist turned out to be fat and forty, or a wizened old academic with grey hair in a bun, Fry suspected that she'd become the liaison officer, not Hitchens.

She stood up and moved to the window. The view of Edendale from the first floor wasn't inspiring. There were rooftops and more rooftops, sliding down the slopes to her right, almost obscuring the hills in the distance, where the late afternoon sun hung over banks of trees.

Whoever had designed E Division's headquarters in the 1950s hadn't been too worried about aesthetics. Or convenience either. The public were deterred from visiting West Street by the prospect of an exhausting slog up the hill, and the lack of parking spaces. Because of its location, Fry missed the sensation of normal life going on outside the door. There had always been that feeling when she served in the West Midlands – though maybe not since they'd started building their police stations like fortresses.

'You haven't finished the transcript,' said Hitchens.

'I think I'll wait for the tape, sir, if you don't mind.'

'There isn't much more, Diane. You might as well finish it.'

Fry bit her lip until the pain focused her mind. Of course, even in Derbyshire, all the darkest sides of human experience were still there, hidden beneath the stone roofs and lurking among the hills. This was the smiling and beautiful country-side, after all.

The transcript was still in her hand. Holding it to the light from the window, she turned over to the last page. The DI was right – there were only three more paragraphs. The caller still wasn't giving anything away about himself. But she could see why somebody had thought of calling in a psychologist.

Detective Constable Ben Cooper watched the dead woman's face turn slowly to the left. Now her blank eyes seemed to stare past his shoulder, into the fluorescent glare of the laboratory lights. The flesh was muddy brown, her hair no more than a random pattern against her skull, like the swirls left in sand by a retreating tide.

Cooper was irrationally disappointed that she didn't look the way he'd imagined her. But then, he'd never known her when she was alive. He didn't know the woman now, and had no idea of her name. She was dead, and had already returned to the earth.

But he'd formed a picture of her in his mind, an image created from the smallest of clues – her height, her racial origins, an estimate of her age. He knew she had a healed fracture in her left forearm. She'd given birth at least once, and had particularly broad shoulders for a female. She'd also been dead for around eighteen months.

There had been plenty of unidentified bodies found in the Peak District during Cooper's twelve years with Derbyshire Constabulary. Most of them had been young people, and most of them suicides. In E Division, they were generally found soon after death, unless they were dragged from one of the reservoirs. But this woman had been neither.

In profile, the face was cruelly lit. Shadows formed under the cheekbones and in the eye sockets. Creases at the corners of the eyes were picked out clearly in the lights. He could see now that it was a face with a lot of character, marked by life and formed by experience. A woman in her early forties. Someone's daughter, and someone's mother.

But the human remains found by walkers in the woods at Ravensdale had lain there a long time, exposed to the weather and the attention of scavengers. The body had decomposed beyond recognition. It had begun to disappear under the growth of moss and lichen, its shape concealed by the blades of coarse grass that had grown through the eyes of the skull.

The head continued to rotate. It travelled through three hundred and sixty degrees, revealing the back of the neck then the opposite profile, finally coming to a halt facing forward again.

'What about the eyes?' said Cooper. 'Are those her proper eyes?'

'We'll try a couple of different colours. Blue and brown, perhaps.'

Suzi Lee had cropped dark hair and long, slender hands. She was a forensic artist who worked with the Pathology department at Sheffield University. Cooper watched her fingers stroke the sides of the reconstructed head, as if feeling for the shape of the skull that lay beneath the clay.

'Blue and brown? We don't know which?'

'The eyes are one of the first parts of the body to decompose. There's no way we can tell what colour they were in life.'

'It was a silly question,' said Cooper.

'Don't worry about it.'

'OK. Here's another one, then – just how accurate is this reconstruction?'

'Well, like the eyes, the appearance of the nose and mouth can't be predicted with any confidence, so they're largely guesswork. If I use a wig for her hair, that will be a stab in the dark, too. But the overall shape of the head is pretty accurate. That's the foundation for a person's physical appearance. It's all a question of bone structure and tissue depth. Look at these –'

She showed him a series of photographs of the skull, first with tissue depth markers glued to the

10

landmark locations, then with a plasticine frame-work built up around them. The numbers of the markers still showed through the plasticine like a strange white rash.

'Let's hope it's good enough to jog someone's memory, anyway,' said Cooper.

'I take it this is a last resort?' said Lee. 'Facial reconstruction usually is.'

'The clothes found with the body had no iden-tification. There was no jewellery, or other posses-sions. And no identifying marks on the body, obviously.'

'The remains were completely skeletonized?'

'Pretty much,' said Cooper. But it wasn't entirely true. He still remembered the partially fleshed fingers, the thin strips of leathery tendon attached to the bones. Some parts of the woman's body had clung together stubbornly, long after her death.

'By the way, I've been calling her Jane Raven,' said Lee. 'Jane, as in Jane Doe. Raven after where she was found. That's right, isn't it?'

'Yes, Ravensdale, near Litton Foot.'

'Apart from the basic facts and a few measure-ments, that's all I know about her. But I don't like to leave a subject completely anonymous. It's easier to interpret a face if I give the individual a name.'

'I know what you mean.'

'So I named her Jane Raven Lee. Then I could think of her as my sister. It helps me to create the

11

details, you see.' Lee smiled at his raised eyebrows. 'My English half-sister, obviously.'

Cooper looked at the file he'd been holding under his arm. It contained a copy of the forensic anthropologist's report in which the dead woman had been assigned a reference number. This was her biological identity, all that was officially known about the person she had once been. A Caucasian female aged forty to forty-five years, five feet seven inches tall. The condition of her teeth showed that she'd been conscientious about visiting the dentist. There would be useful records of her dental work somewhere, if only he knew which surgery to call on.

But perhaps it was the detail about the width of her shoulders that had given him his mental picture of the dead woman. He imagined the sort of shoulders usually associated with female swimmers. By the age of forty-five, after at least one pregnancy, her muscles would have become a little flabby, no matter how well she looked after herself. Living, she might have been generously built. A bonny lass, his mother would have said.

'Facial reconstruction is still an art as much as a science,' said Lee. 'The shape of the face bears only limited resemblance to the underlying bone structure. It can never be an exact likeness.'

Cooper nodded. A reconstruction couldn't be used as proof of identification, but it did act as a stimulus for recollection. The accuracy of the image might not be as important as its power to attract media attention and get the eye of the public. Any ID would have to be confirmed from dental records or DNA.

'There's a fifty per cent success rate,' said Lee. 'You might be lucky.'

Cooper accepted a set of photographs from her and added them to the file. It immediately felt thicker and more substantial. Reference DE05092005, also known as Jane Raven Lee, five feet seven, with shoulders like a swimmer. A bonny lass.

'Thank you, you've been a big help,' he said.

Lee smiled at him again. 'Good luck.'

But as he left the laboratory and went out into the Sheffield drizzle, Cooper wondered if he was imagining too much flesh on the unidentified woman now. It could be an emotional reaction to compensate for what he had actually seen of her, those last few shreds of skin on the faded bones.

Her biological identity had been established, at least. Now the anthropologist and the forensic artist were passing the responsibility back to him. He had to find out who Jane Raven really was.

Twenty-five miles away, in the centre of Edendale, Sandra Birley had stopped to listen. Were those footsteps she could hear? And if so, how close?

She turned her head slowly. Echoey spaces, oil-stained concrete. A line of pillars, and steel mesh covering the gaps where she might hurl herself into space. A glimpse of light in the window of an office building across the road. But no movement, not on this level.

Sandra clutched her bag closer to her hip and followed the stairs to the next level. At night, multi-storey car parks were the scariest places she knew. During the day, they were made tolerable by the movement of people busy with their shopping bags and pushchairs, fumbling for change, jockeying for spaces amid the rumble of engines and the hot gust of exhaust on their legs. But after they'd gone home, a place like this was soulless and empty. Drained of humanity, even its structure became menacing.

She pushed at the door to Level 8, then held it open for a moment before stepping through, her senses alert. Not for the first time, Sandra wondered whether she ought to have worn shoes with flatter heels, so she could run better. She fumbled her mobile phone out of her bag and held it in her hand, gaining some reassurance from its familiar feel and the faint glow of its screen.

This was a night she hadn't intended to be late. A last-minute meeting had gone on and on, thanks to endless grandstanding from colleagues who wanted to show off, middle managers who didn't want to be seen to be the first going home. She'd been trapped for hours. And when it was finally over, the Divisional MD had taken her by the elbow and asked if she had a couple of minutes to go over her report. Why hadn't he taken the trouble to read it before the meeting?

But then, why should he, when he could eat into her personal time, knowing that she wouldn't say no?

Her blue Skoda was parked at the far end of Level 8. It stood alone, the colour of its paintwork barely visible in the fluorescent lights. As she walked across the concrete, listening to the sound of her own heels, Sandra shivered inside the black jacket she wore for the office. She hated all these ramps and pillars. They were designed for machines, not for humans. The scale of the place was all wrong – the walls too thick, the roof too low, the slopes too steep for walking on. It made her feel like a child who'd wandered into an alien city. The mass of concrete threatened to crush her completely, to swallow her into its depths with a belch of exhaust fumes.

And there they were, the footsteps again.

Sandra knew the car park well, even remembered it being built in the eighties. Some feature of its design caused the slightest noise to travel all the way up through the levels, so that footsteps several floors below seemed to be right behind her as she walked to her car.

She'd experienced the effect many times before, yet it still deceived her. When it happened again tonight, Sandra couldn't help turning round to see who was behind her. And, of course, there wasn't anyone.

Every time she heard the sound of those footsteps, she turned round to look.

15

And every time she looked, there was no one there.

Every time, except the last.

Wasn't it Sigmund Freud who said that every human being has a death instinct? Inside every person, the evil Thanatos fights an endless battle with Eros, the life instinct. And, according to Freud, evil is always dominant. In life, there has to be death. Killing is our natural impulse. The question isn't whether we kill, but how we do it. The application of intelligence should refine the primeval urge, enrich it with reason and purpose.

Without a purpose, the act of death has no significance. It becomes a waste of time, a killing of no importance, half-hearted and incomplete. Too often, we fail at the final stage. We turn away and close our eyes as the gates swing open on a whole new world – the scented, carnal gardens of decomposition. We refuse to admire those flowing juices, the flowering bacteria, the dark, bloated blooms of putrefaction. This is the true nature of death. We should open our eyes and learn.

But in this case, everything will be perfect. Because this will be a real killing.

And it could be tonight, or maybe next week.

But it will be soon. I promise.

2

Melvyn Hudson had decided to do this evening's removal himself. He liked a fresh body in the freezer at the end of the day – it meant there was work to do tomorrow. So he called Vernon out of the workshop and made him fetch the van. Vernon was useless with the grievers, of course. He always had been, ever since the old man had made them take him on. But at least he'd be where Hudson could keep an eye on him.

The vehicle they called the van was actually a modified Renault Espace with black paintwork, darkened windows and an HS number plate. Like the hearses and limousines, the van's registration number told everyone it was from Hudson and Slack. *Your dependable local firm.*

They were dependable, all right. *Bring out your dead* – that might be a better slogan. Sometimes Melvyn felt like the council refuse man arriving to pick up an old fridge left on the back doorstep. Nobody worried about what happened to their unwanted rubbish. Their disused fridges could pile up in mouldering mountains on a landfill site somewhere and no one would be bothered, as long as they didn't have to look at them. Most people were even more anxious to get a corpse off the premises.

A few minutes later, Vernon drove out on to Fargate, hunched over the steering wheel awkwardly, the way he did everything. Hudson had sworn to himself he'd get rid of Vernon if he messed up one more thing, no matter what old man Slack said. The lad was a liability, and this firm couldn't afford liabilities any more.

Hudson snorted to himself as they drove through the centre of Edendale. *Lad?* Vernon was twenty-five, for heaven's sake. He ought to be learning the business side of things, ready to take over when the time came. Some chance of that, though. Vernon was nowhere near the man his father had been. It had to be said that Richard had done a poor job of shaping his son. Not that there'd be a business much longer for anyone to run.

When they reached the house in Southwoods, Hudson asked the relatives to wait downstairs. There was nothing worse than having distressed grievers watching the deceased being manhandled into a body bag. If full rigor hadn't set in, the corpse tended to flop around a bit. Sometimes, you'd almost think they were coming back to life.

This corpse was an old man, shrunken and smelly, with a bubble of grey froth on his lips. He

18

wasn't quite cold yet, but his skin felt like putty, flat and unresisting. Hudson thought that if he poked a finger hard enough into the man's stomach, it would sink right in until it touched his spine.

Vernon was standing by the bed like an idiot, his arms hanging at his sides, his mind on anything but the job.

'What's up with you?' said Hudson.

'Melvyn, when you do a removal like this one, don't you ever notice the little things in a person's bedroom?'

'Like what?'

'Just the little things. Look, there's a glass of water he's only half drunk. There's a razor here that somebody used to shave him with this morning. It's still got some of his hairs on it, even though he's dead.'

'Of course he's bloody dead,' said Hudson, struggling to keep his voice down. 'What do you think we're doing here?'

'Don't you look at those things, Melvyn?'

'No. It's just a job. We're professionals.'

'But don't you sometimes think . . . Well, while all this stuff is lying around, it's as if he's not really dead at all. He's still here in the room.'

'For God's sake, leave off the thinking, Vernon, and get a grip on this stiff.'

Hudson took the knees of the corpse, while Vernon grasped the shoulders. An arm lifted and a hand flapped, as though waving goodbye.

19

'Watch it, or he'll end up on the floor,' said Hudson. 'The family down there are doing their best to pretend they don't know what's happening. An almighty thump on the ceiling will ruin the illusion.'

They got the body on to the stretcher and began to negotiate the stairs. These old cottages were always a problem. The doorways were too narrow, the stairs too steep, the corner at the bottom almost impossible. Hudson often thought that people must have been a lot smaller when they built these houses – unless they lowered corpses out of the window on the end of a rope in those days.

They loaded the stretcher into the van, then Hudson went back into the house, smoothing the sleeves of his jacket. It wasn't his funeral suit, of course, just his old one for removals. But appearances mattered, all the same.

'Now, don't worry about a thing,' he told the daughter of the deceased. 'I know your father was ill for some time, but it always comes as a shock when a loved one passes over. That's what we're here for – to ease the burden and make sure everything goes smoothly at a very difficult time.'

'Thank you, Mr Hudson.'

'There's only one thing that I have to ask you to do. You know you need to collect a medical certificate from the doctor and register your father's death? The registrar will issue you with a death certificate and a disposal certificate. The disposal certificate is the one you give to me.'

'Disposal?' said the daughter uncertainly.

'I know it seems like a lot of paperwork, but it has to be done, I'm afraid.' Hudson saw she was starting to get flustered, and gave her his reassuring smile. 'Sometimes it's best to have lots to do at a time like this, so you don't have time to dwell on things too much. We'll give your father a beautiful funeral, and make sure your last memories of him are good ones.'

The daughter began to cry, and Hudson took her hand for a moment before leaving the house.

Back in the van, Vernon reached for the pad of forms under the dashboard.

'Leave the paperwork,' said Hudson. 'I'll do it myself.'

'I know how to do it, Melvyn.'

'I said leave it. You just concentrate on driving.'

'Why won't you let me do the forms?'

'Oh, shut up about it, Vernon, will you? You get the best jobs, don't you? I let you drive the van. I even let you drive the lims.'

'I'm a good driver.'

Hudson had to admit that Vernon was quite a decent driver. But everyone liked driving the limousines. You got to hear some interesting stuff from the grievers in the back. They didn't care what they said on the way to a funeral, and especially coming back. They gave you a different view of the deceased from what the vicar said in his eulogy. Vernon was the same as everyone else – he liked to earwig on the grievers. But if he was

21

going to go all moody and yonderly on a removal, it was the last straw.

A few minutes later, they drew up to the back door of their own premises, got the body into the mortuary and slid it into one of the lower slots of the refrigerator. Even Vernon would have to admit a corpse was just a *thing* once it was removed from the house, away from the half-drunk glass of water and the hair on the razor. There was no other way to think about it, not when you did the things you had to do to prepare a body – putting in the dentures, stitching up the lips, pushing the face back into shape. It never bothered Hudson any more. Unless it was a child, of course.

'Watch it, don't let that tray slide out.'

Vernon jerked back into life. His attention had been drifting, but so had Hudson's. Even at this stage, it wouldn't do to spill the body on to the floor.

Vicky, the receptionist, was in the front office working on the computer, but there were no prospects in, no potential customers. The last funeral was over for the day, though the next casket was waiting to go in the morning, and one of the team was already attaching the strips of non-slip webbing to hold wreaths in place.

Hudson knew that some of the staff thought he fussed too much. They sniggered at him behind his back because he got obsessed about timing, and was always worrying about roadworks or traffic jams. But he wanted things to be just right for every funeral. It was the same reason he spent his evenings on the phone to customers, advising them on what to do with their ashes, getting feedback on funerals, hearing how the family were coping.

It was all part of the personal service. And personal service was Hudson and Slack's main asset. Probably its last remaining asset.

Ben Cooper drove his Toyota out on to the Sheffield ring road, just beating a Supertram rattling towards the city centre from Shalesmoor. Technically, he was off duty now, but he plugged his mobile into the hands-free kit and called the CID room at E Division to check that he wasn't needed. He didn't expect anything, though. In fact, it would have to be *really* urgent for somebody to justify his overtime.

'Miss is in some kind of meeting with the DI,' said DC Gavin Murfin. 'But she didn't leave any messages for you, Ben. I'll tell her you checked in. But I'm just about to go home myself, so I wouldn't worry about a thing.'

'OK, Gavin. I've hit rush hour, so it'll take me about forty minutes to get back to Edendale anyway.'

Brake lights had come on in front of him as scores of cars bunched at the A57 junction. A few drivers were trying to take a right turn towards the western suburbs of Sheffield. But most seemed intent on crawling round the ring road, probably heading for homes in the sprawling southern townships, Mosborough and Hackenthorpe, Beighton and Ridgeway. Some of those places had been in Derbyshire once, but the city had swallowed them thirty years ago.

'Gavin, what's the meeting about?' said Cooper, worried that he might be missing something important. Everything of any significance seemed to happen when he was out of the office. Sometimes he wondered if Diane Fry planned it that way. As his supervising officer, she wasn't always quick to keep him informed.

'I've no idea,' said Murfin. 'She didn't tell me. I've got some files to give her, then I'm hoping to sneak away before she finds another job for me to do.'

'There's no overtime, Gavin.'

'Tell me about it.'

Cooper had come to a halt again. Clusters of students were standing near him, waiting for the tram to re-emerge from its tunnel under the roundabout. They all wore personal stereos or had mobile phones pressed to their ears. The main university campus was right across the road, and he could make out the hospital complexes in Western Bank. The one-way system in central Sheffield always baffled him, so he was glad to be on the ring road. He didn't want to stay in the city any longer than necessary.

'I don't suppose you fancy going for a drink tomorrow night?' said Murfin.

'Don't you have to be at home with the family, Gavin?'

'Jean's taking the kids out ice skating. I'll be on my own.'

'No, I'm sorry. Not tomorrow.'

'You're turning down beer? Well, I could offer food as well. We could have pie and chips at the pub, or go for an Indian. The Raj Mahal is open Wednesdays.'

'No, I can't, Gavin,' said Cooper. 'I've got a date.'

'A what?'

'A date.'

'With a woman?'

'Could be.'

At last, Cooper was able to take his exit, turning right by the Safeway supermarket and the old brewery into Ecclesall Road. Ahead of him lay a land of espresso bars, Aga shops and the offices of independent financial advisors. In the leafy outer suburbs of Whirlow and Dore, the houses would get bigger and further away from the road as he drove into AB country.

'Are you still there, Gavin?'

Murfin's voice was quieter when he came back on the phone.

'I'm going to have to go. Miss has come out of her meeting, and she doesn't look happy. Her nose has gone all tight. You know what I mean? As though she's just smelled something really bad.'

'I know what you mean.'

25

'So it looks as though I've blown it. I just wasn't quick enough.'

'Good luck, then. Speak to you in the morning.'

Cooper smiled as he ended the call. Murfin's comment about Diane Fry had reminded him of the forensic anthropologist's report on the human remains from Ravensdale. The details in the document had been sparse. Like so many experts' reports, it had seemed to raise more questions than it answered. But he'd made a call to Dr Jamieson anyway, mostly out of optimism. In the end, there was only one person whose job it was to find the answers.

'The nasal opening is narrow, the bridge steepled, and the cheekbones tight to the face. Caucasian, probably European. An adult.'

'Yes, you said that in your report, sir.'

'Beyond that, it's a bit more difficult. We have to look for alterations in the skeleton that occur at a predictable rate – changes in the ribs where they attach to the sternum, or the parts of the pelvis where they meet in front. We can age adults to within five years if we're lucky, or maybe ten. So you'll have to take the age of forty to forty-five as a best guess.'

'And the chances of an ID?' Cooper had asked.

'To a specific individual? None.'

Dr Jamieson had sounded impatient. Probably he had a thousand other things to do, like everyone else.

'Look, all I can give you is a general biological

profile – it's up to you to match it to your missing persons register. I'm just offering clues here. I don't work miracles.'

'But it's definitely a woman?' Cooper persisted.

'Yes, definitely. That should narrow it down a bit, surely? You don't have all that many missing women on the books in Derbyshire, do you?'

'No, Doctor, we don't.'

And Jamieson had been right. The problem was, no one had ever filed a missing person report answering the description of Jane Raven.

Fry got herself a cup of water from the cooler and waited a few moments before she went back into the DI's office. She was vaguely aware of Gavin Murfin lurking rather furtively in the CID room, sitting down again when she looked his way. But the rest of the place was already deserted. It smelled stale, and ready for the arrival of the cleaners.

She walked back in and put her water down on Hitchens' desk.

'He was on the phone for more than three minutes,' she said. 'Why haven't they traced the call?'

'They have. He was in a public phone box.'

'Of course he was. No doubt in some busy shopping centre where no one would notice him. And I suppose he was long gone by the time a patrol arrived?'

Hitchens looked at her with the first signs of

27

impatience, and Fry realized she'd gone a bit too far. She blamed it on the headache, or the fact that she felt so exhausted.

'Actually, Diane, the phone box was in a village called Wardlow.'

'Where's that?' She screwed up her eyes to see the map on the wall of the DI's office, making a show of concentrating to distract him from her irritability.

'On the B6465, about two miles above Monsal Head.'

Fry kept the frown of concentration on her face. She thought she had a vague idea where Monsal Head was. Somewhere to the south, on the way to Bakewell. If she could just find it on the map before the DI had to point it out . . .

'Here –' said Hitchens, swinging round in his chair and smacking a spot on the map with casual accuracy. 'Fifteen minutes from Edendale, that's all.'

'Why there?'

'We can't be sure. At first glance, it might seem a risky choice. It's a quiet little place, and a stranger might be noticed – or at least an unfamiliar car parked by the road. Normally, we'd have hoped that somebody would remember seeing a person in the phone box around that time.'

'So what wasn't normal?'

'When a unit arrived in Wardlow, a funeral cortege was just about to leave the village. There had been a burial in the churchyard. Big funeral,

28

lots of mourners. Apparently, the lady who died came from Wardlow originally but moved to Chesterfield and became a well-known business-woman and a county councillor. The point is, there were a lot of strangers in the village for that hour and a half. Unfamiliar cars parked everywhere.'

Hitchens drew his finger down the map a short way. 'As you can see, it's one of those linear villages, strung out along the road for about three-quarters of a mile. While the funeral was taking place, every bit of available space was occupied, including vehicles parked on the grass verges or on the pavement, where there is one. Some of the villagers were at the funeral themselves, of course. And those that weren't would hardly have noticed one particular stranger, or one car. On any other day, at any other time. But not just then.'

'So it was an opportunist call? Do you think our man was simply driving around looking for a situation like that to exploit and took the chance?'

'Could be.'

Fry shook her head. 'But he had the speech all prepared, didn't he? That didn't sound like an off-the-cuff call. He either had a script right there in front of him in the phone box, or he'd practised it until he was word perfect.'

'Yes, I think you're right.'

'Either way, this man is badly disturbed,' she said.

'That doesn't mean he isn't serious about what he says, Diane.'

Fry didn't answer. She was trying to picture the

caller cruising the area, passing through the outskirts of Edendale and the villages beyond. Then driving through Wardlow and spotting the funeral. She could almost imagine the smile on his face as he pulled in among the mourners' cars and the black limousines. No one would think to question who he was or why he was there, as he entered the phone box and made his call. Meanwhile, mourners would have been gathering in the church behind him, and the funeral service would be about to get under way.

'The recording,' said Fry. 'Have Forensics been asked to analyse the background noise?'

'We'll make sure they do that,' said Hitchens. 'But why do you ask?'

'I wondered what music was playing. "Abide With Me", perhaps. Or "The Lord's My Shepherd". We might be able to tell what stage the funeral service had reached, whether he was already in the phone box as the mourners were going in, or waited until the service had started to make the call. Maybe there were some late arrivals who noticed him. We'll have to check all that. If we can narrow it down, we might be able to trace the people who were most likely to have seen him.'

'That's good.'

'And another thing –'

'Yes?'

'I wonder if he just drove away again as soon as he'd finished the call.'

'Why?'

'Well, that would make him stand out, wouldn't it? Someone might have wondered why he left without attending the service. If he was really so clever, I'm guessing he'll have stayed on.'

'Stayed on?'

'Joined the congregation. Stood at the back of the church and sung the hymns. He might have hung around the graveside to see the first spadeful of dirt fall on the coffin. He probably smiled at the bereaved family and admired the floral tributes. He'd be one of the crowd then.'

'Just another anonymous mourner. Yes, I can see that.'

'One of the crowd,' repeated Fry, struck by her own idea. 'And all thinking about the same thing.'

'What do you mean, Diane?'

'Well, we know nothing about him yet, but I bet he's the sort of person who'd love that idea. All those people around him thinking about death while he made his call.'

She paused and looked at Hitchens. He turned on his chair and met her eye, his face clouded by worry. Fry saw that she'd reached him, communicated her own deep uneasiness. The caller's words in the transcript were bad enough. Now she found herself anticipating the sound of his voice with a mixture of excitement and dread.

'Except that *his* death,' said Hitchens, 'the one he was talking about in his call, was nothing to do with the deceased councillor who was being buried in Wardlow churchyard. It was a different death altogether.'

'Of course it was,' said Fry. 'But we have no idea whose.'

The DI looked at his watch. It was time to call it a day. Unlike some of his officers, he had good reasons for wanting to get home on time – an attractive nurse he'd been living with for the past two years, and a nice house they'd bought together in Dronfield. But it'd be marriage and kids before long, and then he might not be so keen.

'It's the Ellis case in the morning, isn't it?' he said. 'What time are you on, Diane?'

'Ten thirty.'

'Is everything put together?'

'DC Murfin is doing a final checklist for me.'

'Good. Well, the undertaker who conducted the funeral at Wardlow is based right here in town,' said Hitchens. 'You'll have time to drive round and speak to him in the morning before you're due in court.'

Fry wasn't looking forward to her court appearance next morning. But at least she'd done everything she could to make it as straightforward as possible and give the CPS a solid case. With a bit of luck, there'd be another long-term resident occupying a bunk in Derby Prison by the end of the week.

Many of the details of the Micky Ellis case were

depressingly predictable. Whenever officers of E Division got a call-out to a body on Edendale's Devonshire Estate, they expected it to be another domestic. A killing in the family, a Grade C murder.

'You know, it never ceases to amaze me how often the offender calls in the incident himself in a case like this,' said Fry, checking through the files Gavin Murfin had gathered for her. 'They can't think what else to do when they see the body on the floor, except dial 999.'

'Well, I think it's very considerate of them to worry about our clear-up rate at a time like that,' said Murfin.

'Is everything there, Gavin?'

'All tied up with a neat bow. Fingers crossed for a short hearing, then,' said Murfin as she closed the top file. 'I hear Micky is pleading guilty, so it should all be over by Christmas. Not that he had much choice in the matter.'

'It was just a walkthrough,' said Fry.

'The best kind. I hate the whodunits, don't you? All those computers thinking they can tell me what to do, and every bugger in the building complaining about my paperwork.'

'I presume you're referring to the HOLMES system.'

'HOLMES – who thought up *that* name? Some Mycroft down in Whitehall, I suppose. One day they'll sack all the dicks and let the computers out on the streets.'

'When is your tenure up, Gavin?'

Murfin said nothing. He worked in silence for a while. Out of the corner of her eye, Fry could see his mouth still moving, but no words came out.

'Only a few months left now, aren't there?' she said.

'Could be.'

'Back to core policing for a while, is it?'

'Unless I get promoted,' said Murfin bitterly.

'Let's hope for the best, then.'

Fry was aware of the look that Murfin gave her. Of course, they might have different ideas as to what the best might be.

Ben Cooper was still smiling as he cleared the outskirts of Sheffield and dropped a gear to start the climb towards Houndkirk Moor. At the top of this road was the Fox House Inn, where he crossed back into Derbyshire and entered the national park. As soon as he passed the boundary marker at the side of the road, Sheffield seemed to fall away behind him quite suddenly. And when he saw the moors opening out ahead of him, burning with purple heather, it always filled his heart with the pleasure of coming home.

Cooper looked again at the file on the passenger seat. In all likelihood, the area he was entering had been home for Jane Raven Lee, too. Somewhere in the valleys and small towns of the White Peak would be the place she'd lived, a house full of her possessions, perhaps a family who still missed her and wondered what had become of her. But a family who loved and missed someone reported them missing, didn't they?

The previous weekend, Cooper had spent a couple of days walking in the Black Mountains with his friends Oscar and Rakesh. There had been plenty of fresh air to blow away the cobwebs, and a chance to forget the job for a while. But there had been an undercurrent of unease that he hadn't been able to identify until they were on their way home, driving back up the M5 from South Wales.

It had been Rakki who dropped the first bombshell. He was due to get married next April, and he'd started to talk about moving back to Kenya. His reasons had seemed impractical, even to Cooper – something to do with the smell of lemon chilli powder, tiny green frogs in the grass, and the moonlight on the beach at Mombasa. But Rakki had been five years old when his family emigrated to Britain in the late seventies, and those were the only memories he had. Later, when they stopped off at Tamworth Services, he'd mentioned Gujarat, the Indian province his grandparents came from. Rakki had never even seen it, but his brother Paresh had visited last year. There were endless opportunities for the educated Gujarati, apparently.

And then it had occurred to Cooper that Oscar had been in a serious relationship for almost a

35

year. He could sense his old High Peak College friendships slipping away, a process that had started when they went their separate ways and took up different professions – Oscar to become a solicitor and Rakki to go into IT. Points of contact were becoming difficult to maintain. And one day soon, as they stood on top of a hill somewhere in the country, they would quietly agree. It would be their last weekend together.

Cooper put his foot down a little harder on the accelerator as the Fox House came into view, outlined against the evening sky. He sensed the Toyota surging forward, eager to cover the ground. An irrational feeling had come to him, one probably born of relief at getting out of the city. It was a sudden burst of confidence, a certain knowledge that he was going to achieve his task.

The facial reconstruction had given him the chance he needed, and he was sure it was going to work. Once he crested that hill, Jane Raven Lee would be coming back home, too.

With a sharp backwards kick of her right foot, Diane Fry slammed the street door of the house. But the noise from the ground-floor flat didn't even falter. Disco-house with urban drum loops at full volume. No matter how hard she slammed it, the damn students wouldn't hear the sound of the door over the din of their stereo system.

For a moment, she thought of ringing their bell and complaining. It might give her a brief feeling of satisfaction to shout at them. But she knew she'd be wasting her time, and she'd only get herself wound up unnecessarily. Coming home from work was supposed to help you relax, not pile on more stress. Wasn't that right?

Fry looked up the stairs at the door of her own flat. Yeah. Some hopes.

Inside, there was no noise but for the thud of the drum loops through the floor. So Angie was out. There was no note, nothing to indicate when she might be back. Fry opened the door of her sister's room and looked in. If it was anyone else, she might have been able to tell by what clothes were missing whether the person who lived there had gone to the pub, gone out for a run, or set off for a job interview. But not in Angie's case. One T-shirt and one pair of jeans would do as well as any other, whatever the occasion.

Since her sister had moved into the flat with her, Fry found herself worrying about her almost as much as she had when Angie was missing. Perhaps more. During all those years when they were separated, Angie's whereabouts had been a generalized anxiety, deep and nagging, but an aspect of her life she had learned to accept, like an amputated finger. Now, the worry was sharper and more painful, driven in by daily reminders. By her sister's presence in the flat, in fact.

Fry found a cheese-and-onion quiche in the freezer compartment and slid it into the microwave. Then she opened a carton of orange juice, sat down at the kitchen table and turned to the Micky Ellis file. She'd appeared in crown court to give evidence many times, but always found it a difficult experience. Defence lawyers would be waiting to pounce on her smallest slip, the slightest hint of doubt in her manner, the most trivial inconsistency between her oral evidence and written statement. A case could so easily be lost on a suggestion of failure in procedure. Forget the question of innocence or guilt. That was yesterday's justice system.

And yet this defendant was certainly guilty. There couldn't truly be any doubt.

There was an old joke on Edendale's Devonshire Estate that you had three options when someone in your family died. You could bury them, cremate them – or just leave them where they fell when you hit them with the poker. Micky Ellis had chosen the Devonshire Estate third option.

When Fry had arrived at the scene, the body of Micky's girlfriend had still been sprawled right where she'd fallen, half on the rug and half under the bed on the first floor of their council semi. She remembered that the bedroom had lemon yellow wallpaper in pale stripes, and a portable TV set standing on the dresser. She'd noticed a series of cigarette burns on the duvet cover close to the pillow on the left-hand side of the bed, where a personal stereo and a half-read *Bridget Jones* novel lay on the bedside table. Fry had looked up at the ceiling for a smoke alarm then, but there wasn't one. And she remembered thinking that maybe Denise Clay had been lucky to live as long as she did.

In this case, it had been the uniforms who made the arrest. The first officers to arrive had found Micky Ellis in the kitchen washing the blood off his hands and worrying about who would feed the dog. It was a walkthrough, a self-solver. Somebody had the job of doing the interviews, of course, as well as taking statements, gathering forensic evidence and putting a case together for the prosecution. And that was down to CID. The DI would be able to add the case to his CV, notching up a successful murder enquiry. It was all very predictable, but at least it didn't tie up resources the division couldn't spare. No one wanted the cases that stayed on the books for months, or sometimes years – the cases that Gavin Murfin called 'whodunits'.

Fry heard a sound and looked up from the file. But it was only one of the students leaving the house. She could tell by the way the music increased in volume as a door opened, then reverted to its normal mind-numbing thud.

The microwave pinged, and she realized she'd forgotten to get out a plate for the quiche. But first she put the orange juice back and opened a bottle of Grolsch instead. There was a shelf full of swing-tops in the fridge. Maybe she'd get a bit drunk on her own tonight. It would ruin her fitness programme, but she needed something to help her sleep. Come the morning, she would have a chat with a funeral director to look forward to before her court appearance in a grubby little murder trial that might drag on for days. And then, if Ripley finally got their act together, she could expect to spend a bit of quality time listening to the voice of a sick, disturbed individual with violent fantasies and intellectual pretensions.

Fry stabbed a fork into the quiche. The outside was hot, but the centre was stone cold. Some days, this was about the best that it got.

3

Hudson and Slack was one of the oldest established funeral directors in the Eden Valley. A dependable family firm, according to the sign over the entrance. Diane Fry pulled her Peugeot into the car park next to the chapel of rest. The company might be long established, but the premises dated from the 1960s, flat-roofed and square, with a modern plate-glass frontage. The place had been built discreetly out of sight in a side street off Fargate.

Fry got out of the car and stood at the gate, looking at the houses in Manvers Street. There were stone terraces on both sides, with no gardens between their front doors and the roadway. She wondered what sort of people would choose to live where death passed their windows every morning. How many times must they look up from a meal or a TV programme and see the long, black limousines creeping by? How often did they try to enjoy a moment's peace, only to catch a glint of chrome from the handles of a coffin out of the corner of one eye?

She turned back to the entrance of Hudson and Slack. She was sure that living here wouldn't suit her at all. But there must be many ways of shutting out the sight of death passing by, or pretending it didn't exist.

'I presume you want me to come in with you, Diane?' said a voice from the other side of the car.

For a moment, she'd forgotten Ben Cooper. As usual, he'd been the only DC she could find in the CID room when she needed company. If there was anything to follow up from this visit, she wouldn't be able to do it herself, because she'd be tied up in court.

'Yes, of course. You're not here to enjoy the scenery.'

Cooper followed her into the funeral director's, where they found Melvyn Hudson to be a dapper man in his late forties, with neat hair greying at the temples. He was wearing a black suit and black tie, and he seemed to slip effortlessly into character as he came through the door into the waiting room and held out his hand.

'Come through, come through. And please tell me exactly how I can help.'

Beyond the door was a passage, and two men walking towards them. Like Hudson, they were in black suits, though neither of them carried it off so well. The larger man had a shaven head and a prominent jaw, like a night-club bouncer, while the younger one was slender and ungainly, his suit barely concealing the boniness of his shoulders and wrists. They stopped in unison when they saw the visitors, and their faces fell into serious expressions.

'Sergeant, these are two of our bearer drivers,' said Hudson. 'Billy McGowan – and this is Vernon Slack.'

The two men nodded and moved on, closing a door quietly behind them.

Hudson's office felt like a doctor's consulting room, with soothing décor, interesting pot plants and certificates framed on the wall. Who did funeral directors get certificates from, Fry wondered. Were there classes in undertaking at night school? A diploma in coffin manufacture at High Peak College?

'You realize there are quite a lot of people like that?' said Hudson, after Fry had explained what she wanted.

'Like what?'

'People who make a hobby of going to funerals. We see them all the time. Sometimes we joke to each other that a funeral isn't complete without our usual little bunch of habitual mourners.'

'You mean they go to the funerals of people they never knew?'

'Of course,' said Hudson. 'They watch the church notice boards, or read the death announcements in the *Eden Valley Times* to see what funerals are coming up. And then they plan their diaries for the week ahead. For some people, funerals are their favourite type of outing. They become social occasions. Perhaps even a place where they meet new people.'

Hudson must have noticed the shocked expression on Fry's face.

'It's perfectly harmless,' he said. 'These are people who simply like funerals.'

'And you recognize these individuals when they turn up?'

'Oh, yes. Many of them are familiar faces to staff at Hudson and Slack, as they are to all my colleagues in this area.'

Fry saw Cooper open his mouth as if about to join in, but she gave him a glance to shut him up. As he dropped his eyes to his notebook, an unruly lock of hair fell over his forehead. She ought to suggest it was time for a haircut again.

'I don't suppose you could let me have some names, Mr Hudson?' she said.

'As it happens, yes. The *Eden Valley Times* used to publish lists of mourners on its obituary page until quite recently, and it was usually our job to collect the names. We did it as part of our service to the bereaved family, you see. The names wouldn't be hard to find, anyway. You'd only need to look through a few back copies of the newspaper and check the obituary pages, and you'd see them listed as mourners at almost every funeral in the area.'

'No addresses, though?'

Hudson shrugged. 'I can't help you with that.

The only thing I can say is that they tend to stick to funerals on their own patch. They don't travel very much for their hobby.'

Fry nodded. 'What about Wardlow?'

'Well, that's different,' said Hudson. 'A small village, a few miles out of town – there aren't many funerals in a place like that, as you can imagine. Hudson and Slack are one of the busiest funeral directors in the valley, but we don't do more than one job a year in Wardlow, if that. So if there were habitual mourners in Wardlow, I wouldn't recognize them.'

He smiled, a sympathetic smile that suggested he cared about everybody, no matter who they were.

'And I don't suppose they get much outlet for their interest, either,' he said. 'They'd be all dressed up with nowhere to go. Rather like a dead atheist.'

'Sorry?'

'Just my little funeral director's joke.'

Fry raised her eyebrows, then looked at Cooper to make sure he was taking notes. 'Mr Hudson, you said a minute ago that the *Eden Valley Times* published lists of mourners until quite recently?'

'Yes. But they've stopped doing it now. A new editor arrived, and he thought it was rather an old-fashioned practice. Well, I suppose he was right. The *Times* was one of the few local newspapers left in the country that still did it, so it was bound to go the way of all traditions eventually. But our customers liked it.'

'Why?'

'Well, locally, it became an indicator of status – an individual's popularity and success in life were measured by how many mourners they had at their funeral, whether the mayor attended or only the deputy mayor, that sort of thing. Also, people would look to make sure they were on the list and their names had been spelled right. Of course, there was often a lot of gossip about who'd turned up and who hadn't – especially if there had been some kind of family dispute. You know what it's like.'

'Not really,' said Fry.

Hudson looked at her more carefully. 'You're not from around here, are you?' he said. 'I should have noticed.'

She tried to ignore the comment. It wasn't the first time she'd heard it. The traces of her Black Country accent normally betrayed her straight away, but apparently Melvyn Hudson wasn't quite so observant as he claimed to be. Nevertheless, Fry found herself unreasonably irritated by the implication that he ought to have been able to tell at a glance she wasn't local.

'Wouldn't it be true to say there's another factor?' she said.

'What's that?'

'That it isn't enough just to show your respects when somebody dies, you have to be seen to be doing it. That's the whole point of getting your name in the paper, isn't it? So that everyone can see you were doing the right thing, no matter what you thought of the deceased person?'

'I think that's a little unfair.'

'And it's the purpose of all the money spent on floral tributes too, isn't it? After all, they don't do the person who's died much good, do they?'

Cooper stirred restlessly and snapped the elastic band on his notebook, as if he thought it was time to leave. Hudson's smile was slipping, but he stayed calm. Of course, he had to deal with much more difficult situations every day.

'Have you had some kind of unfortunate personal experience?' he said. 'If something is troubling you, we can offer the services of a bereavement counsellor.'

'No,' snapped Fry. 'It was a general observation.'

'Well, your view might be considered somewhat cynical, Sergeant,' he said. 'But I won't deny there's an element of truth in what you say.'

'All right. Do you conduct all the funerals here, Mr Hudson?'

'My wife Barbara does some of them.'

'And I suppose the fact that the *Eden Valley Times* stopped printing lists of mourners means your staff no longer collect the names,' said Fry.

'That's correct. We don't do it as a matter of course any more. Only if a customer specifically asks us to.'

'And at Wardlow church yesterday?'

Hudson shook his head. He accompanied the gesture with his sympathetic smile, suggesting

47

that he understood her distress, and she had his condolences.

'No names at all,' he said. 'I'm very sorry.'

Back in the CID room after his unexpected trip to the funeral director's, Ben Cooper wondered why Fry looked so distracted. Worried, even. But whatever was bothering her, at least she had time to take an interest in his forensic reconstruction, shuffling through the photographs he'd brought back from Sheffield.

'They're not bad,' she said. 'Are we going to get these into the papers?'

'I delivered them last night. Media Relations have already set it up.'

'Good. You might get an early result. Have you got any other ideas, Ben?'

'I thought I might take copies round to show Mr Jarvis.'

'Who?'

'The owner of the property nearest to where the remains were found. His name is Tom Jarvis. We don't know how she ended up down there, but it's possible Mr Jarvis may have seen her around the place while she was still alive.'

'No indication of how she died, right?'

'Not so far.'

Fry handed the photos back. 'Bear in mind, if it turns out she was killed, this Mr Jarvis might become a suspect.'

'Of course,' said Cooper. 'But in that case, if he

denies all knowledge of her now, it could be the thing that catches him out later on.'

'Forward planning. I like that.'

For a moment, Cooper thought she was going to pat him on the head or give him a gold star. But she began to move away, already thinking about something else. She went back to her desk and began to open a package that had arrived from Ripley, suggesting she'd forgotten about him already. Cooper called across the office.

'Have you got something interesting on, Diane? The visit to Hudson and Slack this morning – and I heard there was a tape of a call to the Control Room . . .'

'It's probably nothing,' she said. And she picked up her phone, a sign that the conversation was over.

Cooper laid his photographs alongside the forensic anthropologist's report. There were also a series of scene photos from Ravensdale. They showed the remains half-concealed by vegetation that had grown up around them, the long bones turning green with moss, like the roots of some exotic tree. When the tangles of bramble and goose grass were cut away, they revealed the skeletal hands folded carefully together, the legs straight, the feet almost touching at the heel, but turned outwards at the toes.

Dr Jamieson had an opinion on the feet. He felt it was only the tugging of scavengers at decomposing flesh that had moved them from their original position. They had been neatly closed together at the moment of death, or some time after.

It was the 'some time after' that worried Cooper. The location and position of the body were so carefully chosen that they gave the appearance of ritual. In fact, the foliage winding its way through the bones might even suggest an offering to nature, a human sacrifice that was slowly being claimed by Mother Earth. But that was pure fancy, surely.

He looked up the number and called the anthropologist again. Sometimes, you just had to hope for a bit of luck.

'Any chance of a cause of death?' he said.

'You're joking.'

'Nothing at all?'

Dr Jamieson sighed. 'I've looked for signs of any skeletal trauma that might suggest the manner of death, or indeed tell us something about what happened to the body *after* death.'

'And?'

'Nothing. No cut marks, no visible trauma, other than a certain amount of postmortem damage. Some gnawing of the bones at the extremities.'

'Scavengers,' Cooper said. 'Foxes, rats.'

'Or some kind of bird. We're missing two of the carpals – the hamate and capitate. If you happen to come across them, one is a cuboid bone with a hooklike process, and one is a bit like a miniature half-carved bust. They're small, but quite distinctive. We've also lost some of the tarsal bones from the left foot, but otherwise the extremities are mostly intact. And of course the hyoid bone is gone.'

'Why "of course"?'

'The hyoid is located just above the larynx, where it anchors the muscles of the tongue. It's the only bone in the body that doesn't touch any other bone. So when the tissue around it disappears, the hyoid drops away and can be lost completely. You're lucky to have the incisors, since they have only one root. When the soft tissue decomposes, there's nothing to hold them in the jaw.'

'Doctor, isn't the hyoid bone the one that sometimes gets broken when a victim is strangled?'

'Yes, that's correct.'

'And with skeletonized remains, damage to the hyoid bone might be the only indication we have that the victim died of strangulation?'

'I shouldn't really comment on that. But it's true that, without any soft tissues present, we can only look for trauma. Unless there are signs of fractures or nicks to the bone from knife wounds, the condition of the hyoid might well be crucial to an assessment of the cause of death. But only if the cause was manual strangulation.'

Cooper recognized the hopelessness of the thought that came into his mind then. But he said it anyway.

'We'd have to organize another search of the scene, if we're going to find that bone.'

'It *is* a very small bone,' the anthropologist said. 'Given the nature of the location, you'll be looking for a needle in a haystack. And, don't forget, the hyoid could have disappeared from the scene completely.'

'That doesn't sound very hopeful.'

'Well, I can give you an estimate of the time of death, based on plant growth. We got a botanist to have a look, and his report has just landed on my desk.'

'And?'

'Well, she probably died during the spring. Her body was already partially skeletonized by this summer, when vegetation began to push its way through the remaining tissue and between the ribs.'

'February or March?'

'Yes. But the botanist also found some dead vegetation – the previous season's growth.'

'You mean she died in the spring of *last* year?'

'I'm just summarizing the report. I'll send a copy through later today so you can see the details.'

'Does that fit with the skeletonization?'

'Oh, yes. You might want to get someone to check the weather during the relevant period. If it was cold, it would have delayed decomposition.'

'Last summer was warm and wet,' said Cooper. 'It was like that for months.'

'Hence the degree of skeletonization, then. An exposed body in warm, humid conditions. Decomposition must have advanced pretty fast. There's a rough-and-ready formula, based on the average temperature of the surrounding area. In a reasonably warm summer, you'd get a temperature of around fifteen degrees Celsius perhaps?'

'Yes.'

Cooper could almost hear him doing the mental calculation. 'So during the summer, an exposed corpse could be skeletonized within around eighty-five days.'

'Just eighty-five days? And this one could have been out in the open for eighteen months?'

'Yes. If the body was left a few weeks earlier, skeletonization would take a little longer. But given the exposed position, you're looking at a matter of months, not years. The botanist's report will suggest an upper end of the time scale.'

'What about a toxicological analysis?' said Cooper.

'Well, we could do that,' said the anthropologist, 'if you want us to.'

Cooper knew that 'if you want us to' translated as 'if you're prepared to pay us'.

'I'll check,' he said, because budget decisions weren't his to make.

Diane Fry sat for a while in her car outside the courthouse in Wharf Road. People were streaming down the steps and heading for their own vehicles – lawyers and court officials in one direction, members of the public in another. She was aware of the security cameras on the building watching her. Cameras were everywhere in the new riverside development – it was amazing how much crime took place in the precincts of the court.

Fry lifted the package from the passenger seat beside her. She ought to have taken it into court with her, but security would have asked awkward questions. When she'd seen the tape on her desk that morning, she'd known that the first time she listened to it couldn't be in the office, surrounded by a bunch of cynical DCs. Nor in the DI's office, with Hitchens watching her for a reaction. She needed to hear it alone.

She wasn't sure what she would have done if her car hadn't been old enough to have a cassette player. But now she slid the tape in and pressed the 'play' button. She rested her head on the back of the seat and waited until the hiss faded away.

Soon there will be a killing. It might happen in the next few hours. We could synchronize our watches and count down the minutes . . .

As she expected, the voice was distorted. The caller had done something to disguise it – not just the old handkerchief over the mouth, but some kind of electronic distortion that gave the voice a metallic sound, vibrating and echoey. The accent was local, as far as she could tell. But she hadn't yet worked out the subtle differences between Derbyshire people and their neighbours in Yorkshire, let alone between North and South Derbyshire. There were some who claimed they could pin down an accent to within a few miles, but that was a job for an expert.

One of the most worrying things about the tape was that the caller seemed completely calm and under control. His delivery was very deliberate, with no signs of agitation that she could detect. As Hitchens suggested, he sounded convincing. In fact, he would come over well in the witness box.

... What a chance to record the ticking away of a life, to follow it through to that last, perfect moment, when existence becomes nothing, when the spirit parts with the physical ...

Fry glanced at the courthouse again. Her appearance seemed to have gone well, and the CPS were happy. Barring any major disasters during the rest of the hearing, Micky Ellis would be going down for a few years. It wouldn't do much good for Denise Clay, who had lain dead in her nightdress with her personal stereo on the bedside table and cigarette burns on the duvet. For her, justice would come too late. Denise was long since buried by now.

But it didn't do to personalize things too much. Sometimes, the processes of the law needed victims to take a back seat.

... We turn away and close our eyes as the gates swing open on a whole new world – the scented, carnal gardens of decomposition. We refuse to admire those flowing juices, the flowering bacteria, the dark, bloated blooms of putrefaction. This is the true nature of death. We should open our eyes and learn.

Fry's eyes had started to close, but a few minutes later they came wide open again. She looked at the cassette player in bewilderment. She stopped the tape, rewound it and played it again from the section about Freud and the death instinct. There were a few seconds of silence, then the voice started again, filling the car with its metallic echoes.

'Damn it,' said Fry. 'Why did no one tell me there were *two* calls?'

And you can see the end for yourself. All you have to do is find the dead place. Here I am at its centre, a cemetery six miles wide. See, there are the black-suited mourners, swarming like ants around a decaying corpse.

We fill our dead bodies with poison, pump acid through their veins. We pollute the atmosphere with the smoke from their flesh. We let them rot below ground, in coffins bursting with gas or soaked in water like minestrone soup. But true death is clean and perfect. Lay them out in the sun, hang their bones on a gibbet. Let them decompose where the carrion eaters gather. They should decay in the open air until their flesh is gone and their bones are dry as dust. Or, of course, in a sarcophagus. Clean and perfect, and final.

Yes, you can see it for yourself. You can witness the last moments. Follow the signs at the gibbet and the rock, and you can meet my flesh eater.

It's perfectly simple. All you have to do is find the dead place.

4

There was a motorbike parked outside the Jarvis house, and several lumps of metal rusting in the paddock. The rain that had been falling all morning made sporadic rattling sounds in the long grass, as if hitting something metallic and hollow, like a car roof.

Ben Cooper stopped halfway up the path to take a closer look. Yes, the largest lump had been a car once – maybe an old Datsun Sunny, judging from the chocolate brown paintwork. Nearby were the remains of a chest freezer and a pig trailer with a broken chassis. None of them had served any useful purpose for a long time, except as homes for insects and rodents. Tongues of pale bracken were breaking through the floor of the Datsun, and nettles had folded themselves into its wheel arches, clutching the deflated tyres in tangles of spiky leaves. Now that summer was nearly over, the nettles, like everything else, were starting to die.

Cooper could feel the dampness penetrating the hems of his trousers as he brushed through the grass. Even when it wasn't raining, it would be permanently wet down here on the low-lying ground at Litton Foot. White bracket fungus flourished wherever it could find an inch of surface soft enough to plant its spores. Layers of it grew from the rubber seal on the lid of the abandoned freezer, and from the crumbling foam insulation behind the dashboard of the car.

He saw that there were other rusted hulks lying in the paddock, and more of them hidden in brambles growing around a gate that led down to the woods. But it was too wet, and Cooper didn't feel interested enough to explore.

A man in jeans and a thick sweater stood watching him from a wooden porch built on to the back of the house. Cooper hoped he hadn't looked too interested in the wrecked Datsun. The man had the expression of a used car salesman spotting an approaching customer. Predatory, yet ready to turn on the charm. Cooper could feel himself being assessed.

'Mr Jarvis?' he called.

'Aye. What can I do for you?'

Before he answered, Cooper moved a bit closer. He had to watch where he was putting his feet to avoid stepping on shards of rusted metal lying in the grass.

As he got closer, he saw that the porch itself seemed to have been made out of old timber salvaged from a converted chapel or schoolroom. The boards Mr Jarvis was standing on were massive planks of weathered oak, full of knot-holes and the heads of six-inch nails embedded in the wood and painted over. Here and there, patches of black paint still showed through a layer of varnish. The whole structure must weigh a ton – no modern pine decking from Homebase for Tom Jarvis.

'Detective Constable Cooper, sir. Edendale CID.'

Cooper was used to a variety of reactions when he identified himself. He was rarely a welcome visitor, even to someone who'd been the victim of a recent crime. Then, he was often the target of their frustration. But there was no anxiety or surprise from Tom Jarvis, only a slight disappoint-ment that he hadn't found a customer for the old Datsun after all.

'Did you want something?' he said.

'Could I ask you a few questions, sir? Nothing to worry about – just routine.'

'Come up on to the porch, then.'

The deck of the porch was quite a long way off the ground, and Mr Jarvis was looking down on him from a height of about nine feet. Cooper could have scrambled up, but he thought he might lose dignity doing it. Instead, he walked around to the side to reach a set of wide wooden steps that led down to a path into the trees.

Going up the steps, he felt as though he was mounting a stage. That was something he hadn't done for a long time, not since he went up to collect his certificates at his school prize-giving. For a moment, Cooper felt as vulnerable as he had when he'd been convinced he was going to trip over the top step and fall flat on his face in front of eight hundred pupils and parents.

'How are you, Mr Jarvis?' he said.

'Sound. I'm sound.'

'This porch is a solid piece of work, sir. Did you build it yourself?'

'With a bit of help from my sons. Joinery used to be my trade, but this was a challenge. I wanted something that'd last, not some rubbish that would blow down in the first gale.'

'It won't do that.'

Jarvis kicked a post reflectively. His boot connected with a dull thud. 'No, I reckon it won't.'

Cooper grasped the rail to help himself up the last step. The wood felt smooth and comfortable, and he saw that it was turned in decorative patterns, like the end of a church pew. It was the sort of smoothness that resulted from the touch of many hands over centuries of use, wherever it had originally come from.

'You'll be all right,' said Jarvis from the end of the porch. 'They won't bother you. They always sleep at this time of day, and it'd take Armageddon to wake 'em up.'

Puzzled, Cooper looked up. Four huge mongrel dogs lay in a tangled heap on the porch, like a badly made rug. At least, he *thought* there were four. There could have been another shaggy head or two somewhere in the middle of the heap, without making much difference.

'What are their names?' he said, knowing it always went down well with the punters to show an interest in their pets.

Jarvis grimaced at the dogs. 'Feckless, Pointless, Graceless and Aimless.'

'Really?'

'Don't ask me why. It was *her* idea.'

'Whose?'

He jerked his head towards the house. '*Hers*. The wife's.'

'Well, I don't need to ask why. Mrs Jarvis must be a fan of *Cold Comfort Farm*. The Starkadders and Aunt Ada Doom.'

'Aunt who?'

'"Something nasty in the woodshed."'

Jarvis shrugged, his expression unreadable. 'If you say so.'

Cooper stepped carefully over the dogs. None of them moved, or even opened an eye to look at him. There seemed to be an awful lot of muddy paws and scruffy tails protruding from the heap and sprawling across the oak boards. But Mr Jarvis said there were only four dogs, and Cooper had to believe him.

'Just routine,' said Jarvis. 'That's what you all say, isn't it? Do they teach you that in police school?'

Cooper laughed. 'Yes. But I do mean it for once.'

Jarvis gave him a brief nod. 'You've time for a brew then, if it's just routine.'

'No, sir. Thank you.'

'Suit yourself.'

'Actually, it's about the human remains that were found at the edge of your property,' said Cooper.

'Bloody hell, that was weeks ago. Have you found out who the poor bugger was?'

'Not yet.'

'Some dropout, I reckon,' said Jarvis.

Cooper smiled at the old-fashioned term. It was what his grandfather had called anyone with long hair, an expression he'd picked up in the sixties and never stopped using.

'Why do you say that, sir?'

'Well, it was a skeleton. That person must have been there for years. Yet nobody missed them.'

'Perhaps.'

Cooper produced the photographs he'd been given by Suzi Lee. 'This is a facial reconstruction. Does it remind you of anyone you might have seen around this area at any time?'

'The dead person?' said Jarvis, making no attempt to reach for the pictures.

'Yes, sir. We've had them done by a forensic artist, so the likeness won't be exact. We're hoping it might jog someone's memory.'

Rather reluctantly, Jarvis took the photos. He frowned at the appearance of the face, perhaps noticing the inhuman aspects of it first before focusing on the features that might be recognizable.

'A woman,' he said.

'Yes, sir. We know that much, at least. She was white, aged between forty and forty-five, five feet seven inches tall. The hair and eyes may not be quite right.'

Jarvis was silent, staring fixedly at the photos. Cooper waited patiently, conscious of a trickle of dampness in his collar and a pool of water forming at his feet as the rain ran off his clothes on to the porch.

'Do they ring any bells, sir?' he asked.

But Jarvis shook his head. 'Strange to think she was lying dead as a doornail just down there. It makes me feel a bit peculiar.'

'I understand.'

'She doesn't look like a dropout, though.'

'No,' agreed Cooper. 'She doesn't.'

Jarvis handed the photos back. 'I never thought it would be a woman. No bugger told me that.'

'While I'm here, would you mind if I had a look at the site where the remains were found?' asked Cooper.

'If you like. There isn't much to see.'

As Cooper turned, he caught a movement out of the corner of his eye. One of the dogs was loping across the grass towards the woods. Matted lumps of hair bounced on its sides, and legs flew in all directions as its tongue sprayed saliva into the air. The dog had a curious gait – it ran almost

63

sideways, with one shoulder pointing in the direction it was going, but its head turned to the side, like a circus clown grinning to the audience. Cooper had no idea which of the dogs it was, but he knew which name would fit perfectly.

'Yes, that's Graceless,' said Jarvis. 'The only bitch in the bunch. Lovely nature, she has. Ugly as sin, though.'

'Yes, I can see.'

Graceless seemed to be the only one of the dogs with enough energy to reach the woods. Feckless, Pointless and Aimless lay on the porch and watched her with weary, patronizing expressions. One of them yawned deeply and dropped his head back to the floor with a thump, rolling his eyes at the two men.

'They're hoping it'll be dinner time soon,' said Jarvis. 'Idle buggers, they are. I don't know why I give them house room.'

'Are they any good as guard dogs?'

Jarvis snorted. 'Guard dogs? Well, if I could train them to sleep in the right places, they might trip somebody up in the dark. But that's about the strength of it.'

'Still, they're big enough,' said Cooper. 'The sight of them alone might deter burglars.'

'Aye, happen so.'

But Jarvis didn't seem convinced. Perhaps living at the damp end of the valley for so long had given him an eternally sceptical view of life. The outlook was always rain at Litton Foot. He would probably react the same way if Cooper told him the sun would break through one day. *Aye, happen so.*

Jarvis descended the steps and headed down the path, not looking to see if Cooper was following.

'Graceless, now, she really likes people,' he said. 'Whenever somebody new comes to the house, she always wants to . . .'

'What?'

'Well, she likes to sniff their trousers, if you know what I mean.'

'Their trousers?'

'If you know what I mean.'

'Oh, yes.'

'Not everybody likes it,' said Jarvis.

'No, I can imagine.'

'But she's only being friendly. I'm wasting my time trying to stop her. She's a big lass, and if she wants to go somewhere, she goes. She doesn't mean any harm by it, but some folk get the wrong idea when they see her coming.'

'Yes.'

'*She* hates it,' said Jarvis, with that jerk of his head again.

'Your wife? Well, it must be a bit embarrassing when you have visitors.'

'What visitors?'

'Business not good, sir?'

Jarvis gave him a sour look and wiped the moisture from his hands on the legs of his jeans.

It had been dry on the porch, but now Cooper was glad he'd put on his jacket before he left the car. It was the one he'd taken to the Black Mountains with him for the weekend, so the pockets were full of all kinds of odds and ends, but it kept him dry as he waded through the long grass in the rain.

Litton Foot lay deep in Ravensdale, above Cressbrook village. Ash woods hung above the stream here, deep and dank. Ivy had wrapped itself around the tall, slender trunks of the trees, spiralling high into the canopy, seeking a bit of sun. Everything at ground level was covered in moss so thick that it was difficult to tell what was stone, what was wood, and what was something else slowly rotting in the damp air.

Just downstream, he knew there were two rows of cottages built for the workers at Cressbrook Mill, but they weren't visible from here. Stepping stones crossed the water down there to help climbers reach the limestone pitches on Ravenscliffe Crags. On the wet margins of the stream grew clumps of a plant that Cooper didn't recognize – something like a ten-foot-high cow parsley with purple stems and spotted leaf stalks, furred with tiny spines.

'There's a footpath at the bottom of your land, isn't there, sir?' he said.

'It isn't the footpath that's the problem,' said Jarvis. 'That's been there for centuries, as far as I know. It's this new law they brought in. This . . . what is it? . . . right to roam. Some folk think it gives them the right to go traipsing all over the shop. There was a bunch of them came right down through the paddock and tried to walk across the weir. I don't mind admitting, I were fair chuffed when one of them fell in the stream. She were near to drowning, judging by her noise.'

Finally, they reached the patch of ground that had been dug out around the remains of the unidentified woman. Blue-and-white police tape still clung to the trunks of nearby trees, some of it trailing on the ground now in sodden strands, one loose end rattling sporadically in the breeze. Cooper couldn't tell now how wide an area the search had covered.

He hadn't brought any of the scene photos with him, but could remember them well enough to picture the position of the skeleton. The skull had been at the far end of the excavation, close to the roots of an ash tree; the arms had been slightly bent at the elbow, so that the fleshless hands rested somewhere in the pelvic region, while the legs were laid out straight and close together, with the feet near to where he was standing now.

Cooper looked up through the canopy of trees to locate the sun. The cloud cover wasn't heavy, and a gleam of brightness was visible, despite the rain. Higher up, on the moors, he could always orient himself if he could see the sun. But down here, among the winding dales and shelving banks of woodland, it was easy to lose his sense of direction.

Most of the available sunlight seemed to be coming from beyond the trees to his left. Since it was morning, that should be approximately south-east. Cooper patted the pockets of his jacket. Somewhere here, he was sure . . . ah, yes. He pulled out a small Silva compass and swivelled it until he'd oriented the needle to the north. He looked at the grave again. Head there, feet here. He nodded. But it probably meant nothing.

'What are you doing?' said Jarvis.

Cooper had almost forgotten him. The man had been so silent and so still that he might as well have merged into the trees. He was standing under the boughs of an oak, with water dripping on to his sweater. He hadn't bothered to put on a coat before they came down to the stream. In a few more minutes, he'd be as wet as the ground he was standing on.

'Nothing important, sir,' said Cooper. 'Just checking some details.'

'Routine?'

Jarvis said the word as if it summed up everything that was wrong with the world. This was a world that wouldn't leave him alone to sit in peace on his porch with his dogs.

'What's on the other side of these woods?' asked Cooper, pointing across the stream to the east.

'It's part of the Alder Hall estate.'

'I've never heard of it.'

'It's not exactly Chatsworth – though they say it belongs to the Duke again now. The house has been empty for the last two years, anyway. This stream is the estate boundary.'

'But there's a fence up there above the trees. That looks as though it ought to be the boundary.'

'That fence is new. It marks the end of the access land.'

'Of course.'

The walkers who found the human remains at Litton Foot had been here only as a result of their new freedom under the Countryside and Rights of Way Act. The so-called 'right to roam' legislation had opened up a hundred and fifty square miles of private land in the national park to public access for the first time. Otherwise, the remains might have lain undiscovered for years yet. In a different location, they'd probably have been found months ago, before they deteriorated beyond hope of identification.

'Bad business, it being a woman,' said Jarvis.

'Yes.'

'*She* doesn't know. The wife, I mean. She gets upset about stuff like that. Hates these ramblers coming across our land. But I suppose I'd better tell her.'

'It'll be in the papers anyway,' said Cooper.

'Aye.'

Cooper almost slipped on the stones, and put his hand on to the wall to keep himself upright. The moss covering the wall was thick and fibrous to the touch, like a cheap carpet that had been soaked in a flood and never dried out. It held water as effectively as a sponge, and no air could penetrate it. When he raised his hand from the wall, Cooper's fingers smelled dank and woody.

'Well, thank you for your time, sir,' he said. 'I think I've got what I need for now.'

'Aye? You don't need much, then.'

As they walked back towards the house, Cooper noticed an enclosure next to the paddock. A row of old pigsties stood on a concrete apron surrounded by muddy ground and a stone wall, mortared to give it extra stability.

'Do you raise livestock, Mr Jarvis?' he said.

'No. These dogs are enough livestock for me.'

Cooper dug into an inside pocket for one of his cards.

'If you do happen to remember anyone, sir – I mean if the facial reconstruction rings any bells later on – you will let us know, won't you? The photographs should be in the papers in a day or so, too. You can contact me at the office on this number, or leave a message.'

Jarvis took the card and glanced at it before tucking it away somewhere in his clothes.

'Cooper. That's you, is it?'

'Yes, sir.'

Cooper braced himself for the inevitable question. Tom Jarvis was local. He would surely know all about Cooper's father and how he'd met his death. Memories were long in these parts, and he didn't expect he would ever escape it, no matter how long he lived.

But Jarvis just gave him a quizzical look, no more than the lifting of an eyebrow and a momentary understanding in his dark eyes. And Cooper suddenly found himself liking the man much more.

He walked back through the overgrown garden, the only sounds the swish of his own footsteps in the wet grass and the rattling of raindrops on rusted metal. The place had an air of dereliction, a sense of things that had been left to rot in peace.

Tom Jarvis didn't come with him to the gate but stood and watched him from the top of the porch steps, with the dogs sprawled at his feet. When Cooper reached his car, he turned to say goodbye.

'Well, Graceless hasn't bothered me at all while I've been here,' he said.

'No, you're right,' said Jarvis. 'The old bitch must not fancy you, then.'

Diane Fry watched DI Hitchens tapping a pen against his teeth and swivelling in his chair. Some of his mannerisms were starting to annoy her, but she tried not to show it too much.

'The two calls weren't linked straight away,' said Hitchens. 'I didn't know about the second one myself until this morning, and there was no chance to tell you about it.'

Fry hadn't bothered looking at the transcript yet. She felt too angry. 'Where was the call made from? Wardlow again?'

'We don't know, Diane. It was too brief to be traced. But they were only a few minutes apart, so it's a good bet.'

She looked up at the map, finding Wardlow easily this time. 'It's an entirely different kind of message, isn't it?'

'Yes. The similarities between them are the voice distortion and the timing, otherwise the connection might not have been made at all.'

'He's being very specific: "a cemetery six miles wide." And what does he mean by "the dead place"? Or "a flesh eater"?'

'We'll analyse it later,' said Hitchens. 'Was your funeral director any use?'

'Mr Hudson did manage to remember who a few of the mourners were at Wardlow. There's the family, of course. And they had some local dignitaries and business types in the congregation, people who'd worked with the deceased councillor, so I've got a decent list to be going on with. And when we talk to the family, we can get more names. That would be a good start.'

'Yes,' said Hitchens, without enthusiasm.

Fry took off her jacket. 'I appreciate we're talking about over two hundred people, sir. But if we put a couple of enquiry teams on to it, we can add more names with each interview until we build up a picture of the whole congregation. We should be able to narrow the possibilities down to a few individuals who nobody knew. And one of those will be our man.'

'That probably won't be necessary,' said the DI. 'But we'll bear it in mind.'

Fry looked at him. 'Why won't it be necessary?'

'It's a lot of effort for potentially little result, Diane. There are other major leads we can be following up.'

'Such as?'

'Such as the possibility that our caller has already committed his murder.'

5

'She never liked using that car park,' said Geoff Birley. 'But it was the only place near enough to the office, without her having to walk a long way.'

He stared down at his large pale hands where they lay helplessly on his knees. He'd given his age as forty-one, three years older than his wife. He was a foreman on the despatch floor at one of the big distribution centres just outside town. Hard physical work, no doubt, but never any sign of sun.

'That's the trouble with this town, you know. Not nearly enough parking spaces.'

He looked at DI Hitchens for understanding. Always a mistake, in Diane Fry's view. But Birley's face was pale and set in an expression of shock, so maybe he knew no better at the moment. A family liaison officer had been appointed, a female officer who might make a better job of sympathizing with Birley and getting him to talk once the detectives had gone.

'They keep opening more shops, and encouraging more and more tourists to come in, but they don't give people anywhere to park.'

Hitchens didn't answer. He left it to Birley's sister, Trish Neville, a large woman wearing an apron, who had insisted on making tea that neither of the detectives had touched.

'Geoff, I'm sure the inspector doesn't think that's worth fretting about just now,' she said. 'He has more important things to talk to you about.'

She spoke to her brother a little too loudly, as if he were an elderly relative, senile and slightly deaf.

'I know,' said Birley. 'But if it hadn't been for that . . . If there had been somewhere nearer to park her car, and more secure. If the company had provided parking for its staff . . .'

They were sitting in a low-ceilinged room with small windows, like so many of the older houses in the area. Peak Park planning regulations wouldn't have allowed the owners to knock holes in the walls and put picture windows in, even if they'd wanted to. It wouldn't have been in keeping.

The room might have been dark and gloomy, if it hadn't been recently decorated with bright floral wallpaper and dazzling white gloss on the woodwork. Somebody, presumably Sandra Birley, had arranged mirrors and a multi-faceted glass lamp to catch what light there was from the windows and spread it around the room. Fry found herself seated in an armchair with a chintz cover, facing the windows. Normally, she disliked the fussiness of chintz intensely. But in this room it seemed to work, softening the crude lines of the stone walls.

Geoff Birley had stopped speaking. He licked his lips anxiously, as if he'd forgotten what he was saying. He seemed to know they were expecting something of him, but wasn't sure what it was. He looked up at his sister, who was standing over him like an attentive nurse.

'Well, I'm just saying, Trish,' he said. 'About the car park.'

Trish Neville sighed and folded her arms across her chest. She looked at the two detectives. *Over to you*, she seemed to say.

'Despite that, your wife used the multi-storey car park regularly, didn't she, sir?' said Fry.

'Yes, she did,' said Birley. 'But she always tried to get a space on the lower levels, so she wouldn't have to go up to the top to fetch her car if she worked late at the office. Only, you have to get there early, you see. You have to be there at seven o'clock, or you've had it for the rest of the day.'

'And she was late yesterday morning?'

'She got held up by a phone call as she was leaving the house. It was only her mother, mithering about nothing as usual. But Sandra always has to spend a few minutes listening to the old bat and calming her down. Sandra is like that –

if she cut her mother off short, she'd have felt guilty about it all day. So she made herself late because of it. By the time she got to Clappergate, the bottom levels of the car park would already have been full. A few minutes make all the difference, you see. And when that happens, you have to go up and up, until you're on the bloody roof.'

'Her car wasn't quite on the roof level, in fact,' said Fry. 'It was on the one below, Level 8.'

'She was lucky, then. She must have nipped into a space.'

Fry and Hitchens exchanged a glance. The fact that Mr Birley should still be describing his wife's actions as 'lucky' told them that reality hadn't sunk in for him yet. The one thing Sandra Birley hadn't been last night was lucky.

'Mr Birley,' said Hitchens. 'When your wife went back for her car, we think she used the stairs to get to Level 8, instead of the lift. Yet the lift was working. Would that have been her usual habit, do you think?'

The question seemed only to confuse Geoff Birley. 'How do you mean?'

'Would your wife normally have used the stairs to go up eight floors, rather than take the lift?'

Birley hesitated. 'It depends. What did it smell like?'

Now it was Hitchens' turn to look puzzled. 'I'm sorry, sir?'

'The lift. What did it smell like? Did anyone open it and have a smell inside?'

Fry had been present when the lift was examined. Even now, she had to swallow a little surge of bile that rose to her throat as she remembered the stink.

'Yes, it smelled pretty bad.'

'Like somebody had thrown up in there, then pissed on it?'

'Those smells featured, I think.'

Birley shook his head. 'Then Sandra wouldn't have gone in it. She might have pressed the button and opened the doors. But if the lift smelled as bad inside as you say it did, she wouldn't have used it. No way. She couldn't stand bad smells in an enclosed space. It made her feel sick.'

'So you think she'd have used the stairs, even though the lift was working?'

'Yes, I'm sure she would. You can count on it.'

Trish put her hand on her brother's shoulder, perhaps detecting some sign of emotion that Fry had missed. She left it there for a few moments, while Birley breathed a little more deeply. The two detectives waited. Fry noticed that Trish's arms were broad and fleshy, yet ended in surprisingly small, elegant hands with long fingers, as though the hands had been transplanted from someone else.

'I'm fine, really,' said Birley at last.

'Your wife was late leaving the office too, wasn't she, sir?' said Fry.

'Yes, she was. There was a late meeting, and then she had some work she had to finish. She's done very well for herself at Peak Mutual, you know. She's an account executive.'

'Did you know she'd be late?'

'She rang me just before five thirty to let me know, and told me not to wait for her to get home before I had something to eat. I got a pizza out of the freezer and left half of it for her. Hawaiian-style. She likes pineapple.'

Fry saw Trish's hand tighten on his shoulder in an affectionate squeeze. She was anticipating Birley's realization that the five-thirty phone call was the last time he would ever speak to his wife, that Sandra would never come home to eat her half of the pizza. But the moment didn't come. Or at least, it didn't show on Geoff Birley's face.

'When Mrs Birley called, you were already home, sir?' asked Hitchens.

'Yes, I was on an early shift.'

'Your wife didn't happen to say what the work was she had to finish?'

'No, she didn't often talk about her work. She told me about the people in her office – little bits of gossip, you know. But she didn't bring her work home. She was good at her job, but she liked to keep the two halves of her life completely separate, she said.'

It was a good trick if you could do it. Fry glanced at Hitchens, who nodded.

'Mr Birley, we have to ask you this,' she said. 'Can you think of anyone who might want to harm your wife?'

He frowned and shook his head. 'No, not at all. Everybody liked her. She wasn't the sort of person to get into arguments. She hated upsetting people. If there was someone at work she didn't get on with, she would just try to avoid them.'

'I see.'

'It wasn't somebody Sandra knew, was it? Surely it was one of these lunatics who prey on women? She was a random victim. She was in the wrong place at the wrong time.'

'Most likely, sir,' said Hitchens. 'But we have to cover all the possibilities.'

Geoff Birley looked up at his sister again. It seemed to Fry that it was Trish he was talking to now, as if the police had already left his house.

'Only, I'd hate to think it was someone Sandra knew that attacked her. I couldn't bear the thought of that. It had to be a stranger, didn't it? That's the only thing we can cling to. It's some consolation, at least.'

'What time did you first try to call your wife's mobile, sir?'

'About eight, I suppose.'

'And it was already off then?'

'Yes.'

Hitchens leaned forward in his chair, as if about to leave.

'Would it be all right if we take a look around while we're here, sir?' he said.

'What for?'

'Anything that might help us find your wife.'

Puzzled, Birley looked at his sister, whose face had set into an angry expression. 'I suppose it'll be all right,' he said.

The Birleys lived in a detached limestone cottage with an enclosed garden. Fry guessed there were probably three or four bedrooms upstairs. From outside, it was obvious that the property had been created by combining two cottages whose roofs were at slightly different heights. An external chimney stack at one end suggested there might have been a third cottage in the row at some time.

Fry looked first into the kitchen and saw an enamelled range, the kind that provided central heating and hot water as well as cooking. She'd never be able to manage one of those herself. In the sitting room, the focal point had been a cast-iron stove with a carved surround, which looked equally impractical.

In the dining room, Fry paused to admire a carving of a leaping dolphin on a table near the fireplace. There was much more light at the back of the house, thanks to a sliding door that led into a conservatory, with pine floorboards covered in raffia matting. She walked straight through it and out into the garden, past a lawn and a series of raised borders, until she found a brick store place and a garden shed that had been painted bright blue. Neither of them contained the body of Sandra Birley.

Re-entering the house, Fry saw Hitchens descending the stairs from the bedrooms. She shook her head, and they both went back into the sitting room, where they were met with a glare from Trish Neville. Geoff himself was gazing at the carved surround of the stove, as if searching for a meaning in its decorative curlicues.

'Is that your car parked outside, sir?' said Hitchens. 'The green Audi?'

'Yes. Why?'

'Do you mind if DS Fry takes a look?'

Birley found the keys to the Audi without argument. Either he'd cottoned on by now, or his sister had explained it to him while they were out of the room.

Fry went outside and checked the interior and boot of the car. It contained nothing more incriminating than half a roll of blue stretch wrap that looked as though it might have come from the despatch department at a distribution centre.

'I don't know what I'll do without Sandra,' Birley said, as the detectives prepared to leave.

'We don't know that your wife is dead, Mr Birley,' said Hitchens.

'What? You think he might be keeping her prisoner somewhere?'

'It's quite possible. Until we know one way or the other, we're keeping an open mind.'

Birley had begun to look hopeful. But now he dropped his eyes again.

'You're just saying that. You'll find her dead, won't you? You know you will. Why else would he have snatched her from that car park?'

'Until that happens, we can still hope for the best, sir.'

As soon as he'd spoken, Fry remembered having said something similar quite recently. But she couldn't quite recall when and where.

Detective Chief Inspector Oliver Kessen leaned against the side of the crime scene van and thrust his hands into his pockets. 'Well, this place must be dead overnight,' he said. 'Do many people leave vehicles in here until morning?'

Fry assumed that the DCI was talking to her, though he gave no sign of it. Scenes of crime had almost finished with Sandra Birley's Skoda, and were moving away along the retaining wall towards the ramps.

'Very few,' said Fry. 'It's too expensive.'

She looked around for Ben Cooper to get confirmation.

'This is a shoppers' car park,' he said. 'It's meant for short stay. But some of the office workers use it, if they need to. The other parking facilities get full.'

'That's what Mr Birley told us, too,' added Fry.

Kessen kept his eye on the Skoda, as if it might do something. Perhaps he expected it to crack open its bonnet and make a confession.

'The attacker must have known it would be empty by that time.'

Fry nodded, though she knew Kessen wouldn't see her gesture. He'd barely looked at her yet.

83

'Yes, he certainly seems to have known his way around. There are eleven CCTV cameras in here – one on each level, and two at the entrance and exit. But he must have known exactly where they were, because none of them seem to have caught him, so far as we can tell from the attendant.'

One of the SOCOs, Liz Petty, glanced over towards them and smiled. Fry thought she'd found something significant, but she went back to dusting the edge of the wall near Sandra Birley's car. Elsewhere, DI Hitchens was supervising a search on the stairs and in the lift, followed by the concrete parking bays between them and the car. The whole of Level 8 had been sealed off, which meant no one could reach the roof level of the car park either. Apart from the Skoda, the only vehicles here now belonged to the police team.

'Just one attendant?' said Kessen.

'At that time of night, yes. He has a little office on the first level, and he monitors the cameras from there.'

'Someone will have to go through every bit of footage.'

'Yes, sir.'

Looking at the vehicles lined up in the multistorey car park reminded Fry that her Peugeot was due for its MoT this month. She ought to check the date on the certificate – she suspected there were only a few days left before it expired. It didn't do a police officer's reputation any good to be caught driving an illegal vehicle.

Sealing off the two top levels of the car park was undoubtedly causing problems. The 'full' sign at the entrance had already been illuminated when the first police officers arrived to look at Sandra Birley's car. Now, frustrated motorists were continually pulling up to the barrier at ground level and reversing away again.

'What about the lifts?'

'They're cleaned out every day,' said Cooper. 'The interiors are specifically designed for easy washing and disinfecting. It's a familiar problem, apparently.'

'And here I was thinking it was only a problem in high-rise flats on council estates in Birmingham,' said Fry. 'You've imported some dirty habits into Derbyshire, haven't you?'

'Well, I got on to the cleaning contractors a few minutes ago. They swear the lift at the Hardwick Lane entrance was thoroughly cleaned early yesterday morning. So it shouldn't have smelled of anything but industrial disinfectant with a hint of pine forest when Mrs Birley arrived.'

'When she *arrived*, yes. But somebody had been up to their dirty tricks by the time she came back for her car that night.'

'Do you think she'd have been safer using the lift?'

Fry strode in front of the DCI and gestured at the Skoda, the SOCOs in their scene suits still clustered round it. It wasn't a murder enquiry, not without a body. So Kessen would disappear soon.

He needed to know who had the ideas at an early stage.

'Well, look at the layout of this level,' she said. 'If Sandra Birley used the lift, she'd have had only a few feet to walk before she reached her car. In fact, I think it's likely she chose that parking space precisely because it was near the lift. But the exit from the stairs is fifty yards further on, and it meant she had to pass the bottom of the down ramp from Level 9 on the way to her car.'

'Where her attacker may have been waiting behind the concrete barrier.'

'Exactly.'

'So it seems her own fastidiousness led her into danger.'

DI Hitchens trotted towards them from the stairs, red in the face and puffing slightly. He was followed by the crime scene manager, Wayne Abbott, who was about the same age as Hitchens but looked much more fit.

Abbott had recently been appointed senior SOCO for the area after finishing a scientific support management course at the training centre near Durham. Fry didn't much like having to deal with him at a crime scene. There was something about his aggressively shaved head and permanent five o'clock shadow that suggested too much testosterone. From the first time she set eyes on him, she'd wondered why Abbott was a civilian. He ought to be kitted out in full public-order gear, wielding a baton and breaking down doors.

'Sir, the bad news is that only half the CCTV cameras in this place are operational,' said Hitchens. 'The others are dummies.'

Kessen cursed quietly. 'And Level 8?'

'One of the dummies.'

'Damn and blast.'

'The camera at the exit is working, sir. We can get registration numbers for any vehicles that left the car park after the attack.'

'He wouldn't have been so stupid,' said Kessen. 'Ten to one he was on foot.'

'That would make the job much more difficult than just bundling someone into a vehicle.'

'But it would be the only way to avoid the cameras. So what about pedestrian access?'

'Two flights of stairs, one at either end. Lifts at the entrance into the shopping centre. Also, the attacker could have made his way down through the levels via the car ramps. That would be a dangerous thing to do during the day, when it's busy. But after seven o'clock it would be so quiet that he could do it easily. And he'd have heard any car coming a long way off. Noises really travel in here, have you noticed?'

'Yes, I have.'

'But wouldn't the operative cameras pick him up on some of the levels, at least?' said Fry.

'Yes, you're right, DS Fry.' Kessen looked thoughtful. 'Who's talked to the attendant?'

'The FOAs. He's got his supervisor here with him now, too. He called his head office as soon as we arrived.'

'We need to talk to him again,' said Kessen. 'If it was so quiet in here last night, it makes me wonder what exactly the attendant was doing down there.'

Hitchens wiped his face with a handkerchief. He was getting very unfit if he couldn't walk up a few flights of stairs without risking a heart attack.

'At least he heard the scream,' he said.

'Oh yes, the scream.'

'It helps us with the timing.'

'Well, it's a pity he wasn't quicker off the mark getting up here, instead of staring at his little screens wondering if he was on the wrong channel.'

'According to his initial statement, there was no one around when he did come up to check, so he thought it must be kids messing around outside.'

'And then he went back to his tea break, no doubt,' said Kessen.

Hitchens shrugged. 'Also, the mobile phone network recorded the logging-off signal from Mrs Birley's phone. But I don't think that will help us much, in the circumstances.'

The smashed phone had been bagged by the SOCOs, along with the bits of broken plastic scattered across Level 8 by the tyre of a Daihatsu 4x4 that had driven over it. The SIM card would identify the phone definitely, but it matched the description given by Geoff Birley – a Nokia with a soft leather case and a red fascia.

Fry walked to the outside wall of the car park and looked over the ledge at the buildings in Clappergate. Far below, a group of youths wearing rucksacks went by with their skateboards, whistling between their teeth as they entered the shopping precinct. She tugged at the wire mesh, but it didn't shift an inch.

A movement caught Fry's attention, and she saw Liz Petty again, walking across to the crime scene van to speak to Abbott, who was now her supervisor. She had pushed her hood back from her face, and she looked flushed. SOCOs didn't like wearing the hoods of the scene suits if they could help it, especially the female officers. Petty brushed her hair back and tried to confine it in the clip behind her head. She saw Fry watching her, and smiled again.

'I'll get everything under way, sir,' Hitchens was saying. 'DS Fry and I have an appointment with the psychologist.'

'The phone calls?' said Kessen.

'Yes, sir.'

'I don't suppose we've had a call since Mrs Birley disappeared?'

'No. And it's difficult to know whether we should hope for one or not.'

'At least we'd know where we stand. You need to make the right call on this one, Paul.'

Fry felt a little sorry for Hitchens. Nine times out of ten there were other reasons why people went missing, especially adults. They usually turned up alive and well, with surprised looks on their faces at all the fuss they'd caused. That could waste a lot of time and resources if a hasty decision was made.

For now, Hitchens was the man who had to make that judgement. He'd want firm evidence of a serious crime before he pressed the alarm button. A vague message from a disturbed individual wasn't adequate justification – not enough to look good on paper when the DI's handling of the case was reviewed. But add a scream in the night, a dropped mobile phone and a missing woman, and the equation became much more difficult. All Fry could hope for was that it added up on the right side for Sandra Birley.

6

Dr Rosa Kane wasn't what Fry had expected at all. New experts with fresh ideas were fine, but they weren't supposed to be young and attractive, with Irish accents and the shade of red hair that DI Hitchens had a weakness for. These were factors that distracted Fry from the start, and somehow interfered with her ability to listen to what Dr Kane was saying with serious attention.

'We can make some tentative deductions from the language he uses, of course,' said Dr Kane, some time after the introductions had been made and the content of the calls summarized.

'Can we?' said Fry.

Then she realized immediately that her surprised tone might give away the fact that it was the first comment from the psychologist she'd really heard.

'For a more detailed analysis, you'll need the services of a forensic linguist. But some of it is fairly obvious. If you'd like my opinion, that is . . .?'

'Please go ahead, Doctor,' said Hitchens, smiling as he saw an opportunity to save on the expense of another expert.

'Well, for a start, there's his tendency to make grammatical switches from first person singular to first person plural, and then to third person. That's very interesting. When he says "I", "me" and "my", he's almost certainly telling the truth. But when he switches to the plural or third person, or to a passive form, that's when he's concealing something. It's an unconscious sign of evasion.'

Intrigued now, Fry hunched over the transcript. She ran a yellow highlighter pen through some of the phrases. *Perhaps I'll wait, and enjoy the anticipation . . . I can smell it right now, can't you? . . . I promise . . . My kind of killing . . .* And then there was a change halfway through a sentence: *as a neck slithers in my fingers . . .*

There were a few more sentences with 'me' and 'my'. But then the entire final section was couched in the first person plural, as if to draw his listeners into a conspiracy. *The question isn't whether we kill, but how we do it.* That section contained all the stuff about Freud and Thanatos, too. No 'I' in it anywhere.

'I see what you mean,' Fry said, reluctantly.

She pushed the highlighted transcript across to the DI, who smiled. A cheap result.

'As for the second message, some of the phrases don't fit at all,' said Dr Kane.

Fry was taken aback. In a speech written by

someone so disturbed, it hadn't occurred to her there might be some phrases that didn't fit. Because none of it fit, did it? Not with anything rational.

'Yes, of course,' said Hitchens. He pulled his reading glasses out of his pocket and looked at the transcript with an intelligent smile. 'Which phrases were you thinking of in particular, Doctor?'

'"A cemetery six miles wide", for example. What does that have to do with anything? It's too specific.'

'Anything else?'

'Yes. "Here I am at its centre." Also "the signs at the gibbet and the rock". The most significant thing about these phrases is that all three of them occur in the second message, the one which is obviously scripted. In my opinion, he was making sure that he included those phrases. They were important, for some reason.'

'"Six miles wide",' said Hitchens. 'Do you think . . .?'

'They're clues,' said Fry suddenly. 'He's left us some clues to a location. It's a location within a six-mile radius of . . . Well, of what?'

'His own position?' said Dr Kane. 'The place where he was making the call from?'

'Of course. "Here I am at its centre."'

She took off her glasses, and Hitchens did the same.

'That would suggest he knew in advance where he was going to make the call,' said the DI.

'Is that a problem?'

'Well, it isn't the scenario we had in mind. We think he had the speech prepared, but not the location.'

'It could be that he simply inserted an appropriate figure according to where he eventually made the call,' said Dr Kane. 'A six-mile radius? He might have driven around a specific area until he found somewhere suitable that he knew was within that range.'

Hitchens looked worried. 'Damn it, he might just have been guessing at the three miles, in that case. How many people know even the approximate distance from one spot to another across the countryside? I don't suppose he's using GPS.'

'And that's only if he meant the distance as the crow flies, rather than the distance by road, which people might be more familiar with.'

Fry saw from the DI's expression that he was starting to lose faith in his expert. Dr Kane seemed to be setting up more obstacles than she was helping to overcome. But experts loved to make things look more complex than they really were, didn't they? It helped to justify their fees.

'So what about the dead place?' said Fry. 'And the gibbet? The flesh eater?'

But the psychologist had begun to gather her papers together. 'That's your job, I believe. You have an individual here who's trying to draw attention to himself, perhaps because he knows subconsciously that he needs help. Right now, he's doing his best to assist you. His clues are a little obscure and ambiguous, certainly. That's because he has to appear to be demonstrating his superior intelligence. But if you listen properly to what he's telling you, I'm sure it will help you far more than I can at this stage.'

Dr Kane stood up ready to leave, then paused. She was looking at Fry, not at Hitchens, when she delivered her parting advice.

'It's generally true,' she said, 'that you can learn a lot by listening to what other people have to say.'

The regional manager for PNL Parking was called Hicks. Cooper found him in a cramped office on the street level with an attendant in a yellow fluorescent jacket.

'We're bound by all the rules, you know,' said Hicks. 'We have to register the CCTV system and make sure we're compliant with the Data Protection Act.'

'No one is suggesting you've broken any rules,' said Ben Cooper for the third time.

But Hicks barely blinked. 'Apart from anything else, footage won't be accepted as evidence in court if we don't comply with the rules,' he said. 'And registering the system means we have to deal with requests from people for copies of film.'

'Do you get many requests?'

'Some. A lot of them are too vague, though. They have to give us an idea of what time they might have been filmed, where they were and what they look like.' He shrugged. 'Most of them give up when they're asked for details. They're just fishing. And then there are some where we have to admit we didn't film them at all, because the camera they saw was a dummy. Well, we don't say dummy. We just say the camera wasn't functioning at the time.'

'And the camera on Level 8 would be one of those dummies?' asked Cooper.

'Yes.'

'Has it always been non-functioning?'

'For as long as I can recall.' Hicks hesitated. 'Yes, I'm pretty sure it was installed like that. It's a bit ridiculous really, but at the time it was considered more economical. Cameras were supposed to be a deterrent, as much as anything else.'

'I'd like to see any requests you have on file for copies of film from the camera on Level 8.'

'As I said, we don't give out copies of film from that camera, because it's non-functioning.'

'Exactly,' said Cooper. 'You know that, and I know that. And anyone who's ever requested film from it must know that, too.'

Hitchens got up to escort Dr Kane out of the building, leaving Diane Fry on her own. She watched them walking away down the corridor, the DI's hand lightly touching the doctor's elbow as he chatted to her about his student days in Sheffield.

Fry knew that seeing visitors off the premises would normally be a job the DI delegated to somebody more junior. But for Dr Kane, Hitchens was making an exception. Probably because she was an expert and had to be treated with respect. Probably.

To prevent herself from thinking about it any more, Fry lowered her gaze and found herself staring at the yellow highlighter marks on the transcript in front of her. She wished she hadn't used yellow. Now that the colour had dried, it looked faintly rancid and unhealthy, like a four-day-old bruise or a urine stain. Pink or orange would have been much more cheerful.

But who was she kidding? Whatever colour she chose wouldn't make a bit of difference to the sly, evil look of the words themselves.

I can smell it right now, can't you? It's so powerful, so sweet. So irresistible.

She left the DI's office and walked slowly back to the CID room. Ben Cooper wasn't at his desk, but Gavin Murfin and a couple of other DCs were in, and they looked up as she entered.

As usual, there was a whiff of pastry from Murfin's direction. Steak pie or Cornish pasty, she wasn't sure. Right now, she wouldn't have been able to identify it. Another, more elusive smell was in her nostrils, something rancid, unhealthy, yellow and evil. It was a smell she knew would only get closer and couldn't be dispersed by the ventilation system.

I can smell it right now, can't you? . . . It's the scent of death.

'Let's get the map out,' said Hitchens, almost before he could get back into the CID room. 'We need the Ordnance Survey map, Diane – White Peak.'

'We could use the mapping system on the computer,' said Fry.

'That's no good for a six-mile radius. We won't be able to see enough detail at that scale.'

He cleared a table while Fry found a copy of the right map and they spread it out.

'Wardlow is here,' said Hitchens. 'Now we need a ruler to measure three miles in each direction. Damn it, the village is too close to the edge of the map – we'll have to turn over to the other side. Why is everything you want to look at on an OS map always too close to the edge?'

Cooper came in as they were finding a ruler, and Hitchens called him. 'Ben, just the lad we need. You know this area, I'm sure.'

'Yes, sir. What is it you're looking for?'

The DI explained, while Fry checked the scale of the map and used the ruler and a pen to draw a rough circle around the location of the public phone box in Wardlow, helpfully marked by the OS with a capital 'T' and a little blue handset.

'Why the six-mile radius?' asked Cooper.

'We've got some clues from the tape. Or we think they're meant as clues.'

Continuing the westward arc of her three-mile

circle on to the other side of the map was tricky, but finally Fry managed it.

'We'll get somebody to do a proper job of it, but this will do for now,' said Hitchens, oblivious to the exasperated look that Fry gave him. 'What do you make of it?'

Cooper bent over the map. 'Well, you've got an area that includes a dozen villages and one small town. Several dales on the western side, including part of the Wye Valley. The main A6 between Bakewell and Buxton is down here, and near the top there's a smaller trunk road that cuts right across the A623.'

'A busy area, would you say?'

'Only parts of it, sir. The two main roads carry a lot of traffic. And there are some popular tourist spots, such as Tideswell and Monsal Head. And Eyam of course, on the eastern side.'

'That's the plague village, isn't it?'

'Plague?' asked Fry.

'Oh – Ben will tell you the story some time.'

'I'll look forward to it.'

Cooper moved a hand across the map, spanning his fingers over tight clusters of contour lines and long bands of green woodland. 'But there are much quieter corners here, too. This is part of the Derbyshire Dales Nature Reserve. Only walkers can get into some of these smaller dales, and the woods on the valley sides are quite dense. What roads there are tend to be single track and too narrow to take a vehicle of any size. On the other hand, the eastern and northern parts are limestone plateau. That's farming country, with a few small villages and the odd abandoned quarry thrown in.'

Fry watched Cooper and Hitchens poring over the map. They looked like two schoolboys marshalling their armies of toy soldiers to act out a desktop battle.

'We're looking for somewhere within this area that might be referred to as "the dead place",' she reminded them.

Cooper stood up and drew a hand across his forehead. 'The possibilities are endless.'

Fry sighed. 'Ben, that isn't what we wanted to hear.'

'I'm sorry.'

'It's not your fault,' said Hitchens. 'Let's think about this logically. What are the possibilities.'

'"The dead place" . . .' said Fry. 'Well, does he mean the place itself is dead, or is he referring to a place *for* the dead.'

'As in a cemetery?' said Cooper.

'Hold on, let's take the first option,' said Hitchens. 'What did you say – where the place itself is dead?'

'Yes. It depends what sort of bee he has in his bonnet.'

'What do you mean?'

'Well, it could be some kind of anti-quarry protest, or some farmer driven to the end of his tether by Foot and Mouth Disease. Are there any disposal pits for incinerated cattle around here?'

'Not that I know of. Foot and Mouth never reached these parts, but there were some farms affected down on the Staffordshire border.'

'Factory closures, then. Any major employers gone under?'

'Not since the pits closed in the east of the county. Lots of communities almost died out there. But not here.'

'Toxic waste dumps?'

'OK, wait . . . yes, there's one near Matlock.'

Hitchens shook his head. 'Too far. It's way outside of the six-mile zone.'

'What about a place *for* the dead, then?' said Fry. 'A cemetery. What better place to hide a dead body than among hundreds of others?'

'He'd still have to bury it, or conceal it in some way,' said Cooper. 'People visit cemeteries all the time. I'm sure they wouldn't be used to seeing a fresh body left lying around.'

'There must be some abandoned cemeteries,' said Fry.

'Well, plenty of closed churchyards. Most of the older ones are full now and don't have room to expand. In a lot of villages they have to send you to the municipal cemetery, or to the crematorium.'

'Mostly the crem these days, isn't it? I don't think I've ever been to a burial in my life. Everyone I've known who died has been cremated.'

'But the churchyards are still there.'

'OK. Anywhere else you can think of, Ben?'

'It depends what you mean by a cemetery. There are plenty of burial places, some of them thousands of years old – Neolithic sites, remains of chambered cairns. A lot of them are in fairly remote locations, but hikers like to visit the more historic sites. You couldn't leave a body in full view for long without it being discovered.'

'Like the Nine Virgins,' said Fry.

'Exactly.'

Cooper remembered the Nine Virgins well. The body of a murdered mountain biker left inside the stone circle had been found within minutes of her death. No such luck in this case, though.

'Some sites aren't so well known, of course,' he said. 'There's the Infidels' Cemetery, for example.'

'The what?'

'The Infidels' Cemetery. Oh, it's really a tiny, neglected nineteenth-century graveyard on the road between Ashford in the Water and Monsal Head. Last time I saw the place, it was waist high with nettles and weeds. And it's in the middle of nowhere – you'd drive right by without knowing it was there.'

'And why *is* it there?'

'I think it was actually the graveyard for a community of Baptists. They weren't regarded very highly by their neighbours, I suppose.'

'Why "infidels"?'

'Well, the story is that the inscriptions were recorded by a local historian, who noticed that none of the epitaphs contained references to the

Bible, God or Jesus. That was so unusual at the time that it was considered very suspicious.'

'Between Ashford in the Water and Monsal Head?' Fry remembered the DI mentioning Monsal Head. 'It's not far from Wardlow, then.'

'Very close.'

'Let's go take a look. I'd like to get the lie of the land around Wardlow anyway.'

She looked at Hitchens, who nodded. 'I can handle everything here. It's going to be a question of waiting at the moment.'

'Do you have time, Ben?' asked Fry. 'You're the obvious candidate for a guide.'

'I'll get my coat.'

In the CID room, Gavin Murfin had seen Dr Kane leave after the meeting.

'You know, I didn't realize they made profilers so young,' he said.

'Actually, she doesn't call herself a profiler,' said Fry.

'Oh no, of course not. Not since the Washington Snipers, and the Rachel Nickell case. Not to mention Soham, when the SIO took the wrong advice. Even profilers start to get themselves a bad name after too many disasters. So obviously they have to change their name to something else.'

For once, Fry didn't try to shut him up. It was DI Hitchens who started to look annoyed. 'As a matter of fact, DC Murfin, the real professionals have always tried to play down the hype that the press generate around psychological profiling. Dr

Kane has asked us to refer to her simply as a specialist advisor because she wants to avoid publicity.'

'To keep a low profile, in fact,' said Murfin, and laughed.

Hitchens went a bit red around the ears. It was interesting to watch, because the DI was known as a man who found amusement in winding up his own senior officers. Some people said it was why he hadn't made chief inspector by now.

'Dr Kane is an investigative psychologist,' he said. 'She's trained in behavioural science and criminology, so she can provide a useful insight into the investigative process. She's been an advisor on a number of cases for other forces.'

Fry gave Murfin a warning glance, and he tried hard to look chastened. 'No offender profile then, sir?'

Hitchens shook his head, still edgy. 'We don't have enough information at this stage. We don't even know what sort of offence we're looking at, if any.'

Murfin seemed to think about what else to say, then changed his mind and kept quiet. Hitchens waited for more comments, fidgeting a little, before turning to go back to his office.

'Besides,' he said, 'she isn't all that young. Thirty-three.'

7

Twenty minutes later, Cooper's car was climbing out of Ashford in the Water. The River Wye took a sharp turn here as it came down from the north, so an observer standing at Monsal Head seemed to be looking up two separate valleys. A small road dropped down from a Bavarian-style hotel and an adjoining café before running north into the woods of Upperdale and Cressbrook Dale. To the south there was no road, only a footpath that clung to the slope for a while before slithering down to the river and crossing a bridge to the opposite bank.

A few walkers were on the five-arched viaduct that spanned the valley. The Wye narrowed as it ran underneath, and less adventurous visitors could be seen sitting on the banks of smooth grass enjoying an hour of September sunshine. But the walk down to the river was steep, and many people stayed to have lunch at the café or eat an ice cream while they enjoyed the view.

Fry shaded her eyes against the sun in the south-west. 'What's that place on the side of the hill up there? It looks like the ruins of a house.'

'Hob Hurst's House,' said Cooper. 'It isn't really a house.'

'And I suppose there was never really anyone called Hob Hurst?'

'Well, no.'

'How did I guess?'

'It's the name of a character in local folk stories. A goblin or a giant, I'm not sure which. What you can see there is actually the result of a landslip, but it does look like a ruined house from a distance, if you have a bit of imagination.'

'Whoever built that hotel certainly had a bit of imagination,' said Fry. 'Some romantic Victorian, I suppose, fresh from a trip to the Alps.'

'Probably. You know, when this viaduct was built for the railway line, there was a campaign against it. Everyone said it would ruin the view, just for the sake of getting from Bakewell to Buxton more quickly. Now it's one of the most popular sights in the area.'

They almost passed the Infidels' Cemetery without seeing it, although it was right by the roadside. Cooper had driven a few yards beyond it before he braked suddenly and reversed. Part of the wall that had once protected the graveyard had been knocked down. A wire fence was all that barred the gap, though the deep beds of stinging nettles behind it looked pretty hostile.

It was much quieter here than at Monsal Head. Across the valley they heard a shepherd calling to his dog, his voice a high, harsh cry like a moorland bird. Somebody was shooting on the opposite hill. As always in the countryside, the sound of gunfire didn't seem out of place, let alone worth commenting on.

'Well, nobody has been in this cemetery for months,' said Fry. 'Even I can tell that.'

'They didn't venture beyond the first couple of yards, anyway.'

Most of the ancient gravestones had fallen flat and were smothered with tangled goose grass and brambles. The stones that had stayed upright were coated in yellow lichen and shrouded in ivy that masked their familiar graveyard shapes. The only exceptions were the two stones nearest the road. Someone had cleared the ivy from them, revealing their inscriptions.

With difficulty, Cooper read the name and dates on one of the stones.

'I don't think this person was much appreciated in his day,' he said. '"Though man's envy may thy worth disdain, Still conscious uprightness shall fill thy breast." I might suggest that one to Gavin for his epitaph.'

'Why? Is he feeling under-appreciated?'

'I think so.' Cooper moved a few yards to the side. 'Diane, look at this one.'

Only a small patch had been cleared in the ivy covering the second stone. It had been done quite recently, too. The broken stems were still shredded and oozing a little sap when Cooper touched them.

'That's a bit odd,' he said.

'Why?'

'Well, I was assuming that whoever cleared the ivy from these stones was an amateur historian, trying to confirm the names of people buried here. Or maybe a relative who wanted an ancestor to be remembered, not just lost in the undergrowth.'

'Seems reasonable,' said Fry.

'But look at this – the name and dates haven't been exposed, just the inscription after them. It's only a short one, too. *Caro data vermibus*. What does that mean?'

'I've no idea.'

'You're the educated one.'

'Ben, I took a degree in Criminal Justice and Policing at the University of Central England. It didn't make me fluent in Latin.'

Cooper walked backwards and forwards in front of the stones, but beyond the first few feet of ground from the road the blanket of nettles and brambles was dense and unbroken. He watched a butterfly flit among the nettles.

Impatiently, Fry walked back to the entrance and looked up the road. 'How near is this to Wardlow, did you say?'

'Only a couple of miles.'

In the language of Derbyshire place names, 'low' always meant 'high'. So this particular village must have been named after the lookout hill, Wardlow Cop, whose flattened conical shape appeared on their left as they began the descent from Monsal Head.

Wardlow itself was just as DI Hitchens had described it – a series of farms and houses scattered along one road. It was bordered on both sides by long, narrow strips of pasture land, preserved in their medieval patterns by drystone walls, networks of them strung across the fields and climbing the hills. Some parts of the White Peak plateau were said to have twenty-four miles of wall for every square mile of farmland. Instead of regular field patterns, the eye was likely to see a confusing geometry of stone, long courses of wall exaggerating every contour in the landscape.

Some of the farms at Wardlow had been converted into homes, but others were still working. A tractor turned out of a yard as they reached the start of the village, where two Union Jacks were flying. Cooper noticed that the village pub was closed during the day, like so many in places without much tourist trade. The Church of the Good Shepherd was just beyond a cattery operating from a cluster of surplus farm buildings. It was a small stone church with a slate roof and leaded windows, but no tower. Anything bigger would have been out of place.

They finally found space wide enough to park alongside someone's hedge without blocking the road completely, and they crossed to the church. Through double gates they walked into a grassed area, where a pair of stocks stood near the rear wall. Cooper didn't think they were medieval – more likely erected for a village fête some time in the last few decades. A chance to throw wet sponges at the vicar, rather than rotten eggs at a convicted felon. Ritual humiliation, all the same.

Behind the church was the graveyard itself, small and under-used. There'd be no need to close this one to burials for a few years yet.

'Melvyn Hudson said there were very few funerals in Wardlow,' said Fry.

'He's from the funeral directors, Hudson and Slack?'

'That's right.'

'Well, I'm sure Mr Hudson is right. A lot of these graves date back to Victorian times.'

Several large sycamores and beeches darkened the top end of the graveyard, and nothing grew underneath the trees. Even their own seedlings had sprouted and died in the barren ground. Dead branches, beech nuts and small stones crunched under their feet as they walked among the gravestones. Swallows swooped around them, diving almost to the ground in pursuit of the small flies that hung in clouds over the graves. The Victorian graves were surrounded by low iron railings, rusted and falling apart in the damp air.

'Here's the deceased councillor,' said Cooper. 'Mrs Sellars, right? It's by far the newest burial here.'

'OK. Now, where's the phone box?'

'The other side of the church.'

A small parish room was attached to the church, a kitchen visible through a window piled with jars, cutlery and old newspapers. As they walked past it towards the phone box, Cooper saw a movement inside a house directly across the road. It was no more than a shape against the light, but he knew they were being watched.

'Has anyone spoken to the neighbours?' he asked.

'All those who had a view of the church or the phone box,' said Fry. 'Uniforms did it yesterday.'

'The residents directly opposite have a good view.'

'Unfortunately, they were attending the councillor's funeral themselves.'

'Pity.'

'As you can see, there aren't many others to talk to.'

Cooper looked at the red phone box itself, twenty yards away from where he was standing. It was more than a pity, wasn't it? It was a big stroke of luck for the individual who'd made the phone call. There was no way he could have known that the occupiers of that property opposite weren't watching every movement he made.

Although he hadn't heard the tapes himself yet, Cooper was starting to have a sneaking doubt about the caller's intentions. On the surface, he appeared to have taken care to conceal his identity, as might be expected. But some of this individual's actions looked almost reckless – as if he wanted to be identified. Maybe the whole thing was no more than a cry for help. But there was no point in suggesting the idea to Fry.

Behind the churchyard, Cooper could see a sprawl of farm buildings and trailers, and a wandering pattern of drystone walls. A cockerel crowed somewhere nearby, though it was already afternoon. The phone box stood close to a foot-path sign, its fingerpost so weathered that the lettering had worn away completely, and now it seemed to indicate a path that led nowhere.

Then the sun came out, and the limestone walls formed themselves into a bright tracery running across the landscape. Cooper wondered what he might find if he followed those white pathways. The instinct to pursue the light rather than return to the gloomy churchyard was almost irresistible.

Half a mile north, at the junction with the A623, there was a smaller collection of houses called Wardlow Mires. A petrol station and another pub called the Three Stags' Heads sat among farms and some derelict buildings covered in honeysuckle.

The A623 took traffic through sheep pastures and across the plateau towards Manchester. Almost as soon as Cooper turned on to it, he sensed the landscape opening out on his left. In a gap between the hills stood a strange, isolated outcrop of limestone. Its distinctive shape looked almost artificial – straight, pillared walls of white rock split by crevices and fissures, and a rounded cap grassed over like a green skullcap. The slopes of short, sheep-nibbled grass around it seemed to be gradually encroaching on the limestone, as if reaching up to pull it back into the ground.

The rock looked familiar. Searching his memory, Cooper thought it might be called Peter's Stone. He had no idea what the name meant, but guessed it was probably some biblical reference to St Peter, the reasons for it lost in the passage of time and the mists of folklore.

'Can I listen to the tapes some time, Diane?' he said.

'Don't imagine you'll recognize the voice. It's electronically disguised.'

'I might have some ideas, though.'

'Yes, OK. Remind me when we get back.'

'Thanks.'

Fry tapped a finger on the map. 'Ben, we should be going the other way. Eyam.'

Cooper pulled over and reversed into the Litton turning. 'By the way,' he said, 'my unidentified remains were found at Litton Foot, in Ravensdale.'

'Yes? What about them?'

'Litton Foot is less than three miles from Wardlow across country. It falls within your circle.'

Fry looked at the map. 'But your body is eighteen months old, Ben.'

'I know.' Cooper shrugged. 'I just thought I'd mention it.'

'Tell me about Eyam.'

'For a start, it's pronounced "Eem". The village

113

was infected by the plague from some infected cloth, but the villagers quarantined themselves so they wouldn't spread it to the rest of Derbyshire.'

'When was this?'

'Seventeenth century.'

'OK.'

'Well, three hundred and fifty people died in Eyam. The names of the victims are recorded on some of the cottages. Plague victims couldn't be buried in the churchyard, so their graves are in the fields around the village. Whole families together sometimes.'

'Are these places well known?'

'Well known? They're a tourist attraction.'

Back at West Street, Diane Fry disappeared for a meeting with the DI before the evening briefing, and Cooper didn't get a chance to remind her of her promise. So instead of listening to the tapes, he took the opportunity to spread out the photos of the human remains found in Ravensdale.

The quality of crime scene photography had improved tremendously since the photographic department spent money on replacing its printing equipment. Colours had started to bear some relationship to reality, instead of looking like snaps taken by a passing tourist with a Polaroid. Now you could see that the stuff on the floor near a body was actually blood, not the corner of a donkey-brown rug.

Outdoors, they sometimes managed to get quite

interesting lighting effects. In one of the Ravensdale photographs, Cooper could make out the dappling effect of sunlight through the canopy of trees. The sun had swung round to the south by the time the shots were taken, so it must have been around the middle of the day. The photographer would have been wondering when he'd get a chance for his lunch.

There was also a sketch plan done by one of the SOCOs, complete with arrows indicating the points of the compass. It confirmed what Cooper had noticed at the site: the feet of the victim had been pointing to the east and the head to the west.

He had a feeling there was some significance in that alignment. It was one of those half-remembered things, a vague superstition in the back of his mind. He couldn't have said who had put the idea in his head, or when. Maybe it was only something he'd overheard as a child, a whispered conversation among elderly relatives at a funeral, a bit of local folklore.

East to west. Yes, there was some significance, he was sure. But the alignment of the body was just as likely to be a coincidence, wasn't it?

From the fragments collected at the scene, the dead woman seemed to have been wearing a rather plain, light blue dress, underwear, tights and blue strappy shoes with one-inch heels. No coat, nothing worn outside the dress. It was unlikely that she'd walked down to the stream at Litton Foot herself, but not impossible.

The skeleton had been incomplete when it was found, with several small bones missing. And there was no jewellery that might have been used for identification. No engraved bracelets, no wedding ring. This woman had been someone's daughter and mother. But had she been someone's wife, too?

Cooper knew he might never be able to get a lead on how the woman had died. Not from the remains, at least. Forensics could perform wonders, but not miracles.

And there was the question of what had happened to Jane Raven Lee's body *after* her death. The possibilities were bothering him. The dead woman hadn't been buried, she'd been laid out and exposed to the elements. The whole thing had too much ritual about it. Cooper wished there was someone on hand who could tell him whether he was discerning a significant fact, or just imagining things again.

The evening briefing didn't last long. There wasn't much to report, after all. A forensic examination of the scene had found no signs of a struggle near Sandra Birley's car, which suggested her abductor had given her no chance to make a run for it, and had probably used a weapon to subdue her quickly. The Skoda had still been locked, and there was no sign of the keys.

The concrete floor of a multi-storey car park was hell for a fingertip search. Who could say whether an item found on the oil-stained surface had been dropped by Sandra Birley, her attacker, or one of a thousand other people who had used Level 8 in the past few weeks? Scores of fibres had been recovered from the retaining wall and the ramp barrier. Partial footwear impressions were numberless. And the SOCOs had collected enough small change to pay their coffee fund for a week.

'One question I'd like answered,' said DCI Kessen, 'is whether our man knew which CCTV cameras were dummies, and which weren't. And if so, how? There's no way of telling just by looking at them, is there?'

'I don't think so,' said DI Hitchens. 'Maybe he'd worked there himself, or he knows somebody who does. Anyway, DC Cooper is already on to the employees angle.'

'What do we make of the husband? What are the odds we'll find a green Audi on the CCTV footage?'

Hitchens shrugged. 'He seemed genuine enough to me. He says he was at home when his wife phoned him. We should be able to confirm that from phone records.'

'So not much to go on at this stage.'

'We do have two confirmed sightings of Sandra Birley prior to her abduction,' said Hitchens. 'She was seen leaving her office and walking down Fargate in the direction of the multi-storey car park between seven fifteen and seven thirty. Even allowing for a margin of error on the part of the witnesses, she ought to have reached her vehicle by around seven forty.'

'Hold on,' said Fry. 'When was the last sighting of her exactly?'

Hitchens consulted his notes. 'No later than seven thirty. A shopkeeper in Fargate saw her passing his shop.'

'He was in his shop at seven thirty? What sort of shop is this? I thought everything in Edendale closed by six at the latest.'

'It's a shoe shop. And yes, it was closed. As luck would have it, the proprietor was in the store room stock-taking – he's closing down and selling up soon, so he's doing a full stock check. But he could see through the shop on to the street. He said he'd seen Sandra Birley many times, and he knew she worked at Peak Mutual, though he didn't know her name. We showed him the photos, and he's positive about the ID.'

'OK.'

Fry picked up the transcripts of the two phone calls. The fax sheets had been sitting on her desk only since this morning, but already they were getting smudged and creased at the corners. It was a plain paper fax, and they were supposed to be a lot better than the old thermal rolls. Maybe it was something to do with her hands. Too much heat.

She checked the information at the top of the first page, though she knew both messages almost by heart. *Soon there will be a killing . . . All you have to do is find the dead place.*

'This second call was received by the control room at Ripley shortly after three thirty yesterday afternoon,' she said.

'What of it, DS Fry?'

'He appears to be warning us of his intentions. "Soon there will be a killing." That's what he says.'

'Yes.'

Fry dropped the sheets. 'If Sandra Birley was the victim he was talking about in his phone calls, it means he had four hours to drive into the town centre and either set up an abduction he'd already planned in advance – or choose a victim.'

'Still, it's possible.'

'What we don't want to face is the possibility that Sandra Birley isn't the victim he was warning us about. That *his* killing is yet to take place.'

'We'll probably get another call from him, Diane. He's obviously an attention seeker, so he'll want us to know this is him. No doubt he'll think he's being very clever.'

'What did the psychologist say?' asked Kessen.

'She told us to listen to the phone calls,' said Fry.

Hitchens scowled. 'Actually, that wasn't quite all Dr Kane said. She gave us some useful ideas about what the caller is trying to tell us.'

'Are we expecting miracles from her?' asked Fry.

Kessen looked at her for the first time that day.

And Fry knew that he'd seen everything, heard everything, and taken it all in. She found herself fooled by his manner every time.

'We can always hope, DS Fry,' he said.

Then the DCI turned back to Hitchens.

'By the way,' he said, 'let me make one thing clear. Nothing goes from us to the media about these phone calls. Not a word. Otherwise we'll have every lunatic in the country calling in. And one lunatic at a time is quite enough.'

A few minutes later, Cooper knocked on the door of the DI's office to explain his problem. With the briefing over, Hitchens was already getting ready to go home. Cooper caught the chink of bottles, and saw that the DI was checking the contents of a carrier bag. From the frown on his face, he was wondering whether he'd bought the right wine for dinner tonight.

'I could use some advice on the Ravensdale human remains case, sir,' said Cooper. 'If I might be allowed to consult –'

The DI held up a hand. 'If you're going to mention anybody who charges for their services, Ben, the answer is "no". We've already met the cost of a facial reconstruction on your case. Forensic artists don't come cheap, you know. Unless you can come up with enough evidence to turn the case into a murder enquiry, you're on your own.'

'But, sir, there could be unusual areas of significance – subjects I don't know anything about.'

'I'm sure everyone understands that, Ben. But you'll have to cope for a while. We have other priorities at the moment.'

'Well, mightn't there be . . .?'

But the DI shook his head. He tucked the bag under his arm and rattled his car keys impatiently.

Cooper went back to his desk. He separated one of the photographs of the facial reconstruction from its stack and clipped it on to the copy holder attached to his PC screen. The room was emptying, and no one paid any attention to him, or noticed that Ben Cooper was talking to himself again. It was just one sentence anyway, spoken resignedly to the photograph next to his screen.

'It's just you and me then, Jane,' he said.

The face of Jane Raven Lee gazed back at him silently – the muddy brown flesh, the random streaks against her skull, the blank eyes awaiting an identity.

8

When Cooper got back to his flat that night, the light on the answering machine was flashing and the cats were demanding to be fed. One was always more urgent than the other, so it was a few minutes before he pressed the button to play back his messages. There were three of them.

'Ben, it's Matt. Give me a call.'

The first one was a very short message, but it made Cooper frown. His brother didn't usually call him unless it was really necessary. In fact, Matt was always scrupulous about not phoning his mobile because he knew he used it for work. He supposed he'd have to call back and see what was wrong. But there were two more messages to listen to yet.

'Ben. Matt. Give me a call as soon as you can. It's important.'

Now Cooper began to feel uneasy. He pressed the button for the third message.

'Ben, please give me a call. It's very important.' Then a pause. 'It's about Mum.'

Turning her Peugeot from Castleton Road into Grosvenor Avenue, Diane Fry finally pulled up at the kerb outside number 12. The house had once been solid and prosperous, just one detached Victorian villa in a tree-lined street. Its front door nestled in mock porticos, and the bedsits on the top floor were reached only by hidden servants' staircases. But now most of the occupants were students at the High Peak College campus on the west side of town.

Fry often found her flat depressing, especially when it was empty. But she'd found Wardlow depressing, too. The very ordinariness of the place had made the calls from the phone box near the church seem even more disturbing.

Though Wardlow had been bad enough, at least it wasn't the real back of beyond, the area they called the Dark Peak. Up there was only desolation – bleak, empty moorlands with nothing to redeem them. She recalled the road sign she'd seen last time she was there: SHEEP FOR 7 MILES. Seven miles. That was the distance all the way across Birmingham from Chelmsley Wood to Chad Valley, taking in a population of about a million people. But here in Derbyshire you could find seven miles of nothing. That just about summed it up.

She'd transferred from the West Midlands as

an outsider, the new girl who had to prove herself. It had been a struggle at times, just as she'd expected. But she'd been focused, and she'd worked hard. And now she got a lot of respect, though it was mostly from people she despised.

Fry went to the window, thinking she'd heard a car in the street. But she could see no vehicles, not even pedestrians passing on their way home for the night. All she could see out there was Edendale.

No, wait. There *was* someone. Two figures parting on the corner, so close to the edge of her field of view that she had to press her forehead to the window pane to see them. A second later, one of the figures came into focus, walking towards the house. Angie.

Fry pulled away from the window before she was seen, and went into the kitchen. Two minutes later, she heard Angie's key in the lock.

'Hi, Sis.'

'Hi. Had a good day?'

'Sure.'

'What have you been doing?'

Angie had that secret little smile on her face as she took off her denim jacket. It was hard for Diane to know how to feel towards her sister. She knew she ought to be glad that Angie looked so much better than when she first moved in. Her skin was less pallid now, her eyes not quite so shadowed, her wrists and shoulders less painfully thin and bony. Anyone who didn't know them might not be able to guess which sister was the recovering heroin addict.

Yet Diane was unable to suppress a resentment that was there every day now, barely below the surface of their relationship. No sooner had she been reunited with Angie than her sister had started to drift away from her again, and this time it seemed more personal. Would it have been different if she'd found Angie herself, without the interference of Ben Cooper? She would never know.

'Actually, I've got myself a job,' said Angie.

'What?'

'Did you think I was going to sponge off you for ever, Di? I'm going to pay you some rent.'

Angie kicked off her shoes and collapsed on the settee. Diane realized she was hovering in the doorway like a disapproving parent, so she perched on the edge of an armchair.

'That's great,' she said. 'What sort of job?'

There was that smile again. Angie felt among the cushions for the remote and switched on the TV. 'I'm going to work in a bar.'

'You mean you're going to serve behind a bar,' said Diane carefully.

Angie looked at her, and laughed at her expression. 'What did you think, I was going to be a lap dancer or something? Do they have Spearmint Rhino in Edendale?'

Diane didn't laugh. She tried to force herself to relax. 'What pub are you going to work in?'

'The Feathers. Do you know it?'

'I've heard of it.'

'I've done a bit of barmaid work before, so I'll be fine. A few tips, and I'll even have some spending money. Aren't you pleased, Sis?'

In her head, Diane was running through the wording of Police Regulations. Regulation 7 restricted the business interests of police officers and any members of their family living with them, including brothers and sisters.

'As long as you're not going to be a licensee, or I'd have to get permission from the Chief Constable.'

She tried to say it lightly, but Angie flicked off the TV and stared at her in horror.

'You've got to be bloody joking.'

'No.'

'Your chuffing Chief Constable can't run *my* life. So what if he didn't give permission? What does he think he could do to me?'

'Nothing,' said Diane. 'But I'd have to resign from the force.'

'Oh, tough.'

Angie bounced back on to her feet and picked up her shoes as she went towards her bedroom. Diane began to get unreasonably angry.

'Angie –'

Her sister turned for a second before she disappeared. 'Quite honestly, Di, resigning from that bloody job of yours would be the best thing you could do. And then maybe I'd get back the sister I remember.'

Diane remained staring at the door as it slammed behind Angie. She didn't know what else to think, except that she'd never got a chance to ask who the man was she'd seen on the corner of the street.

Ben Cooper felt as though he'd been walking through hospital corridors for half an hour. He was sure he'd turned left at a nurses' station a hundred yards back, yet here was another one that looked exactly the same. Had hospitals always been so anonymous, or was it just a result of the latest improvements at Edendale General?

And then, in the corridor ahead, he saw a familiar figure wearing worn denim jeans and a thick sweater with holes at the elbows. Cooper smiled with relief. His brother Matt looked totally out of place in a hospital. For a start, Matt was built on a different scale to the nurses who passed him. His hands and shoulders looked awkward and too big, as if he might break anything fragile he came near. He wasn't a man you'd want to let loose among hypodermic needles and intravenous drips.

He also looked far too healthy to be inside a hospital, even as a visitor. Constant exposure to the sun and weather had given a deep, earthy colouring to his skin that contrasted with the clinical white, the pale pastels of the newly painted walls.

Matt looked up and began to move towards

him. He put his arm round his brother's shoulder, a rare gesture of affection that made Ben's heart lurch with apprehension.

'I've spoken to the doctor,' said Matt. 'Not the top man, just some houseman or whatever they call them. Come down to the waiting room. We can get a cup of tea.'

'I want to see Mum.'

'She's asleep, Ben. They say she needs to rest. Actually, I think they gave her something to put her out.'

'Matt –'

'Come on, it's this way. I think the WI still do a canteen for visitors, so the tea should be all right.'

Ben felt he was being swept along by his brother, dragged in his wake. Almost the way it had been with their father for so many years.

'Matt, never mind the tea. I need to know how Mum is now. What happened?'

Instead of answering, Matt began to move along the corridor again. He was a couple of inches taller than his brother, and much heavier. Ben knew it was pointless trying to dig in his heels, and tried to keep up with his brother's stride instead. He felt a warm flush of resentment starting, a rush of anger that he knew was born of fear.

'Tea,' said Matt. 'And then I'll tell you everything I know.'

*   *   *

Matt Cooper walked carefully back across the hospital cafeteria balancing two cups of coffee. He looked terrified of spilling liquid on the polished vinyl tiles, in case someone slipped and broke a leg. An accident in a hospital would seem worse than one that happened anywhere else, somehow.

Ben wrapped his hands around the cup, needing only the warmth and the comfort of watching the movement of steam – anything to settle his impatience.

'Kate says she saw you earlier today,' said Matt. 'Your car was parked on Scratter.'

'Where?'

'Scratter. The road between Wardlow and Monsal Head. That's what they call it.'

Ben frowned. 'Come on, Matt, get on with it.'

His brother sighed as he eased himself into a chair. 'It seems Mum had a bit of a fall at the nursing home.'

'What do you mean "it seems"?'

'Well, all right – she had a fall. But the staff at Old School aren't sure how it happened. And you know how confused Mum gets. I managed to speak to her before they sedated her, and she hadn't a clue where she was.'

'How badly is she injured?'

'She's broken her hip.'

'Shit.'

'I know. And they think she might have banged her head when she fell, too. She was very dazed, and couldn't really remember anything.'

'Somebody from the nursing home ought to be here,' said Ben. 'Why aren't they here? It's their responsibility.'

'Ben, calm down. The senior nurse came to the hospital with her and stayed for two hours until I sent her back. The manager's been on the phone twice to see how Mum is. They're all concerned about her.'

'So they should be. They've got some questions to answer.'

Matt took a drink of his coffee, but Ben didn't even lift his cup. He found that his hand was shaking with anger, and he knew he would only spill it.

Someone had left a copy of the evening paper on the table, folded to the top half of the front page. Ben could see only the first inch of a photograph above the fold, but he recognized it straight away. He'd been looking at it for a large part of the day. At least Media Relations had done their job properly.

'When will Mum be awake?' he said.

'They want to keep her sedated until they can do the X-rays and get her into theatre. Tomorrow we can talk to her, perhaps. But we can go and sit with her for a few minutes, if we ask the sister.'

Ben stared at his cooling coffee. It looked particularly unappealing now that the steam had vanished.

'Let's do that, then.'

'It's just a fall, Ben. A broken hip sounds bad at first, but she's not all that old.'

'Don't you know what head injuries are like? Even a minor knock –' Ben stopped, took a deep breath. 'OK, I'm sorry. You think I'm over-reacting.'

'Yes, you are.'

'Sorry, Matt,' he said again. 'Work, you know . . .'

'Getting you down again?'

Ben didn't like the 'again' part. As they walked back down the corridor towards the ward, he felt another surge of anger. He put his hand on Matt's arm.

'What's the name of the manager at Old School?'

'Robinson. Why?'

'When I leave here, I'm going to go and see him.'

'Ben, you wouldn't do any good.'

'I need to know exactly how this happened, and what they're going to do about it.'

Matt took hold of his arm, gripping a little too tightly. His face was flushed a deeper red than usual, and he was breathing too heavily.

'I'm warning you – don't start lashing out at everyone you can find, Ben. You can't get rid of your guilt feelings this way.'

Broken earth lay under her feet, like shards of glass. Two days of rain had splashed her legs with

131

mud, and now it lay dark and damp in the cracks between her toes and in the line of an old fracture on her left thigh. Ants had emerged from the leaf mould on the woodland floor to wander among the stiff folds of her dress and crawl across her hands. One of them paused at her scentless flowers before climbing upwards. But it didn't seem to know what to do when it reached her head. It wasn't aware of the sky, or even of Alder Hall Woods. The ant saw only its own tiny patch of her body – an inch of her neck, its surface white and hard, and smooth to the touch.

That afternoon, someone had come into the woods. It was a figure wrapped in a coat and scarf against the wind, hands thrust into pockets, a canvas bag over one shoulder. The visitor had followed the path from the bottom of Alder Hall Quarry, crossed the stream and climbed the slope through the trees. At the edge of the clearing, the figure stopped for a few moments before moving into the open, then forced a way through the tall swathes of willowherb, oblivious to fragments of stem that caught on sleeves and clung to jeans.

Reaching the plinth, the visitor opened the canvas bag, took out a spray of flowers and placed them at the feet of the statue, then stood back to admire the arrangement. The sight brought a smile of satisfaction. The flowers were white chrysanthemums, suitable for a death.

*   *   *

MY JOURNAL OF THE DEAD, PHASE ONE

No one told me that the worst nightmares would come while I was still awake. No one ever warned me that I'd lie in my bed in the darkness, eyes wide open, praying for sleep. Those were the hours I spent counting faces in the wallpaper, seeing the shape of a monster where my clothes lay strewn on a chair. Those were the times I listened to the noises outside the house, listened as hard as I could, hoping I might make the noises inside go away. Finally, as the hours went by, there would be nothing left but the sounds of the night – the slither of the darkness as it crept across my roof.

Something lives in that darkness. It's our greatest fear, and it's called the unknown. Everyone knows this fear, but few of us dare to think about it. We'd never be able to go on living our lives if we really saw the grinning presence that waits behind our shoulder. It's far better to pretend we don't see the beast. We turn away our eyes and convince ourselves it's just a shadow cast by the sun. It's only a draught from an open window, a rustle of dead leaves on the other side of the door.

It's the same fear for the child whose bedroom door has to stand open at night for a glimpse of light and for the old woman whose hand trembles as she draws back the bolts. In the end, we're all destined to fall into the claws of that darkness we glimpse in our dreams. The great snatcher of souls, the unseen lurker on the threshold. What threshold would he lurk on, if not on the threshold of death?

Do you see that shadow now? Do you feel the chill, and hear the rustling?

These days, my dreams are different. Sometimes, in my nightmares, I see bodies moving inside their coffins. Their mouths twist, their limbs writhe, their hands open and close like claws as they reach towards the light. I try to make them settle down, to lie still so they can be buried. But it never does any good. In my dreams, the dead just won't stop squirming.

9

Next morning, Diane Fry found two middle-aged DCs occupying desks in the CID room. They wore almost identical navy blue suits, and they were both a bit too meaty around the shoulders, so they hardly seemed to have any necks. One had a tie with blue stripes, and the other black-and-white checks. They could have been visiting sales executives from a pharmaceutical company.

'Who are those two?' asked Gavin Murfin.

'CID support,' said Fry.

'What?'

'They retired from D Division last year. But they've come back to help out for a bit, while we're short-staffed. Mr Hitchens says they're very experienced. They both put in their full thirty.'

'Yes, I can tell.'

At the morning briefing on the Sandra Birley enquiry, Ben Cooper was the first to raise a hand. Keen to get noticed, no doubt.

'Sir, do you think Mrs Birley's attacker might

have watched her for some days beforehand and worked out her habits?'

'What habits?' said DI Hitchens.

'For a start, the location she chose to park her car. And her practice of not using the lift when it smelled.'

'What, and pissed in the lift to discourage her from using it?'

'It was just a thought.'

'It would be too good to be true, wouldn't it? A suspect who covered the floor of the lift with his DNA for us to find?' The DI considered it. 'No, it won't work, Ben. He couldn't possibly have known Sandra Birley would work late that night.'

'No? Well, not unless –'

'Unless?'

'Unless he worked in the same office.'

'We have to look at all her colleagues, then,' said Hitchens. 'How many are there?'

'About forty people work at Peak Mutual,' said Fry. 'Male and female.'

'Male and female? Good point, DS Fry. We mustn't assume we're looking for a male offender at this stage.'

'The phone call, sir?' said somebody.

'The phone call may turn out to have nothing to do with the abduction.'

DCI Kessen was present at the briefing, but sitting to one side and letting DI Hitchens take the floor. Fry wasn't surprised to see the acting head of CID. If the Birley case became a murder enquiry,

Kessen would be appointed Senior Investigating Officer. But for now, they had no body, no evidence that there had been a serious crime. The possibility that Sandra Birley had been abducted from the Clappergate car park was just that – a possibility.

'Are we going to get the husband to make an appeal, sir?' asked Cooper, raising his hand. Fry nodded reluctantly to herself. At least that was one tactic they could use without committing themselves to anything.

'We think it's too early yet,' said Hitchens. 'Besides, he isn't in any condition at the moment. I spoke to the family liaison officer first thing this morning, and it seems Mr Birley's emotional state has deteriorated considerably since yesterday.'

Then it turned out that the two retired DCs had been working an early shift, too. They'd already been through the CCTV footage from the Clappergate multi-storey. That wasn't anybody's favourite job. Feelings in the room began to warm towards them.

'First of all, we've eliminated the owners of the other two vehicles that were left in the car park overnight,' said the one with the black-and-white tie. 'The first bloke had drunk too much in the pub and sensibly decided to get a taxi. He turned up to get his car next morning, so we got a statement from him. He didn't see anything. But how would he, when he was in the pub at the time?'

'OK,' said Hitchens. 'And the other one?'

'Even more innocent. He works in the IT department of a company with offices in Buxton Road. That afternoon, he dropped a computer monitor on his foot and broke two toes. He was in A & E at the relevant time. His girlfriend turned up to collect the car.'

'They never really looked like contenders anyway. Why would Sandra Birley's attacker leave his own vehicle in the car park as well as hers?'

'Exactly, sir. But we had to eliminate them. We've also been through every bit of tape from the functioning cameras, and we've managed to trace all the vehicles that left the car park later that night – in other words, after Mrs Birley was abducted. There were only four of them, because the place was practically empty. In fact, we've matched all but one of those vehicles to CCTV footage of the owners returning to their cars. Two were lone males, and there was one couple – but older, in their early sixties. It's clear from the tape that the woman isn't Sandra Birley. She's the wrong age, wrong height, wrong clothes, everything. All of these people have been spoken to, and they seem to be genuine.'

'And none of them saw anything suspicious?' asked Fry.

'That's right, Sergeant.'

Fry sighed. That was the trouble with law-abiding members of the public – they never saw anything. She'd lost count of the number of times she'd attended a serious incident, only to be met by members of the public with helpful smiles and short-term memories.

'If my maths are correct, there was one more vehicle.'

'Unfortunately, the fourth vehicle seems to have been parked on Level 2.'

'Where there's a non-functioning camera?'

'You've got it, Sarge. We do have footage of the vehicle exiting the car park at the barrier. It's a blue Saab. There appears to be a male driving, no one visible in the passenger seat.'

'And has the owner been interviewed?'

'He lives in Sheffield. There's a team on the way there now to talk to him.'

'So if the Sheffield driver is eliminated,' said Fry, 'the only other possibility is that our man didn't have a vehicle of his own in the car park.'

'Well, he had to have a vehicle somewhere close by,' put in the DC with the striped tie. 'He must have been parked on the street.'

'More CCTV footage, then. The town centre cameras?'

'Right.'

Fry turned back to the DI. 'And what are we doing about the phone messages, sir? The clues he left . . .?'

Hitchens had his map pinned up on the board – or at least, an adaptation of it, showing the whole six-mile circle around Wardlow, with labels marking a scatter of locations.

'We've passed on a list of potential locations for

the uniforms to check out when practicable,' he said. 'By that, I mean any locations that might possibly be referred to as "the dead place". Otherwise, unless his clues get any clearer, there's nothing concrete for us to act on. Meanwhile, if you've got any reasonable theories, let's hear them. If you haven't heard the tapes and you want to listen to them, speak to DS Fry.'

'When practicable? That could mean never,' said Cooper.

Hitchens shrugged. 'As you said yourself, DC Cooper, the possibilities are endless. We need something more substantial.'

'We're hoping he'll phone again?'

'Well, it would help, wouldn't it?'

DCI Kessen had been listening quietly to the discussion. When the meeting had finished, he stood up and put his hand on Hitchens' arm.

'Keep me in the loop, won't you, Paul?' he said. 'Regular updates.'

Ben Cooper was about to leave the briefing with everyone else, when the DI called him over. He thought at first he'd misheard, and Hitchens had to speak to him again – a bit louder this time, as if Cooper was daydreaming at the back of the class.

'Oh, Ben. Have you got a minute?'

'Yes, sir?'

Cooper left his jacket over the back of his chair and walked to the front of the room, moving against the flow of bodies and conscious of the glances he was getting. But perhaps he was being over-sensitive. He still felt ashamed of his outburst at the hospital last night, and this morning he couldn't seem to concentrate on anything for more than a few minutes. His thoughts kept drifting back to the image of his mother's pale, helpless body lying in that side room off the ward, amid the smells of disinfectant and the constant slapping of heels in the corridor outside the door, back and forth, back and forth, until he thought it would drive him mad. When he'd phoned the ward first thing this morning, he'd been told that Mrs Cooper was 'satisfactory'.

'There's something for you, Ben,' said the DI, fiddling with some papers on his clipboard. 'It looks as though you've had a bit of early luck. A member of the public called in to say she recognized the facial reconstruction.'

'Already?'

'It was in the evening paper last night, and it got a couple of minutes on the local TV news, too.'

'Brilliant.'

Hitchens looked at him critically, as if detecting something not quite right. Cooper wondered if he'd forgotten to shave properly, or had his tie on crooked. Both were perfectly possible.

'The lady's name is Ellen Walker. She believes the deceased is her cousin, Audrey Steele. Here's the address, Ben.'

'I'm on my way, sir.'

Cooper grabbed his jacket from his chair and

tried to straighten his tie. It was best to look professional when meeting law-abiding members of the public.

'One more thing, Ben . . .' Hitchens was holding out a sheet torn from a message pad.

'What's this?'

'Another bit of luck for you. This gentleman is a retired forensic anthropologist with a special interest in Thanatology. Apparently, we've consulted him now and then in the past, and he's been living in this area since his retirement. He's willing to do a little consultancy work for us at no cost.'

'At no cost? Who says?'

Hitchens smiled. 'The vice-chairman of the police committee, who's a member of the same Rotary Club as Professor Robertson.'

Cooper took the sheet of paper and looked at the contact details. 'Is he ACPO accredited?'

'Of course. Give him a try, Ben. He might be exactly the person you need.'

'Yes, I suppose he might.' And he thought: *Especially since he's free.* But he didn't say it out loud.

'OK then, Ben, that's it.'

Cooper was aware that the room had emptied round him, and the DI was impatient to get on. But his father had taught him he should never pretend to understand something when he didn't. It always led to disaster, he'd said.

'Er . . . just one thing, sir,' he said.

'Yes?'

142

'What on earth is Thanatology?'

Hitchens looked flustered for a moment, then snapped his clipboard shut and headed rapidly towards the door, as if he didn't have a second to spare for inane questions.

'For heaven's sake, Cooper – if you don't know, look it up.'

As he was getting ready to leave the office, Cooper noticed a book on Gavin Murfin's desk. Gavin never had books on his desk. Pies and cakes, yes. Chocolate, obviously. Anything edible, in fact. So unless this book was made of iced sponge, it was a historic first.

Murfin saw him looking. But before he could move the book, Cooper picked it up. Dozens of bits of paper protruded from it, marking specific pages.

'*A Promotion Crammer for Sergeants, Part One.* I thought there must be some reason why you were suddenly talking like a training manual. What's going on, Gavin?'

'I'm just trying to improve my performance, like,' said Murfin.

'Your *what*?'

'It's something we should all stop and think about now and then, in my view. If we're going to make any progress in our careers, that is.'

Cooper stared at him. 'But this is a crammer, Gavin – you're surely not thinking of going for promotion?'

143

'As a matter of fact, I am.'

'You're going to put in for your sergeant's exam? Are you serious?'

Murfin snatched his book back. 'Why shouldn't I? Nobody around here seems to appreciate the depth of my experience. I was in CID when you were still in short pants. I've seen it all, I have. So it's time I shared the benefit of my knowledge and expertise in a supervisory capacity.'

'You've been practising your answers for the interview,' said Cooper in amazement.

'Go ahead, take the piss. I don't care. One of the advantages of my years of experience is that I remain cool and unflappable, even in the face of extreme provocation.'

'Hold on,' said Cooper. 'How many years exactly?'

'What?'

'How many years' experience, Gavin? How long have you been in CID?'

Murfin didn't answer. He opened his crammer and pretended to be studying a page.

'Come on, Gavin – how many years?'

'Eleven,' said Murfin casually.

Cooper let out a long breath. 'Ah. Tenure. That explains everything. You've only got a year left, at most. And you don't want to go back into uniform. Gavin, you're getting desperate.'

'Do you find the idea of me being promoted to sergeant inconceivable?'

'Well, yes.'

'Thanks a lot.'

Cooper laughed, then instantly felt guilty – not for laughing at Gavin, but because it didn't seem right that he should have something to laugh about right now.

They both looked up as Diane Fry came into the room. Her face was dark with irritation.

'Hey up,' said Murfin quietly. 'Are we in for another go at boosting morale?'

'Shh. You'll just wind up her again,' said Cooper.

'Well, these team-building exercises are wearing me down, Ben. I'm getting emotionally exhausted from all the love I feel for my colleagues.'

Fry approached Cooper immediately. 'Ben, the DI says he's given you the name of some old professor to talk to.'

'Yes. I'm hoping to see him this afternoon.'

'When you get back, have a word with me, will you? I need to make a judgement on whether he might be of use in another enquiry. So I'll be interested in your opinion of him.'

'You're not usually very keen on outside experts, Diane,' said Cooper.

'Personally, I wouldn't touch him with a bargepole. But I need a reason to justify my decision not to use him. Follow?'

'You want me to come back and tell you he's useless, right?'

'Frankly, I expect you to come back and tell me he's some barmy retired academic who drinks too

145

much and has long hair, a smelly dog and holes in his cardigan, but likes to be visited by nice young police officers. Anything like that will do.'

As Fry walked off, Murfin pointed at a page in his sergeant's crammer, marked with a yellow Post-it. '"A supervisory officer should always be prepared to justify any decision,"' he said. 'See – I could do that.'

'Hey,' said Cooper, 'if you've been raiding the reference library, did you happen to see that big dictionary?'

'It's on the shelf over there.'

'Thanks.'

Cooper lifted the book down and flicked through the pages. There it was – Thanatology: *The scientific study of death and the phenomena and practices relating to it. From the Greek* Thanatos, *meaning death.*

Lovely. His professor was the genuine Dr Death.

Ellen Walker's home was a double-fronted stone villa in the middle of a nineteenth-century terrace near the parish church. The very last house in the row had been converted into a shop at some time, but now the shutters were down and there was no sign of what had once been sold. By the look of the lace curtains at the first-floor windows, somebody still lived in the flat above the shop. A retired greengrocer or ironmonger, perhaps, driven out of business by Tesco or the massive B&Q store on the outskirts of town.

Through panes of frosted glass in the door of number 15, Cooper had a distorted glimpse into the hallway. All four windows at the front of the house had their blinds pulled down far enough to cover the upper sashes.

'Mrs Walker?' said Cooper when a middle-aged woman answered the door.

'Are you from the police?'

'Detective Constable Cooper, Mrs Walker.'

'It's Ellen.'

'Thank you very much for calling us. You understand the circumstances? Why we had the facial reconstruction done?'

'Well, I saw the photograph in the newspaper. My neighbour showed it to me. I didn't really understand why it was there, but I was fairly sure . . .'

'Let's just take a look at it again first, shall we?'

Cooper didn't like the sound of 'fairly sure'. It would be better to let the witness come to her conclusion more slowly.

Ellen Walker seemed nervous at being visited by the police. It was so refreshing that Cooper forgot for a moment that it was so often a sign of guilt. He looked at the Victorian-style fireplace with its raised slate hearth. Disappointingly, it contained a coal-effect gas fire that had nothing Victorian about it. The windows faced on to the street, but through the kitchen he saw a conservatory leading on to a patio area enclosed by low gritstone walls.

'The newspaper reproduction might not have been of very good quality. This is the original, Ellen. Take your time and have a good look at it. Bear in mind some of the details might not be exactly accurate. The hairstyle, for example.'

Mrs Walker obediently studied the picture. 'The hairstyle isn't too far out, not really.'

'You're sure it's your cousin?'

'Fairly sure.'

Cooper sighed. Fairly sure wasn't much, but it would have to do for now.

'The other details fit,' said Mrs Walker. 'Audrey was forty-two, and an inch or two taller than me.'

'Was Audrey married?'

'For a while. She met a bloke called Carl, who worked offshore on the oil rigs. He was all right, but they drifted apart after a bit. I think he went to Germany after the divorce went through.'

'Would you have his address, if we needed it?' asked Cooper.

'I expect so.' Mrs Walker frowned. 'Audrey and I were always very close, you know. Her mother is Auntie Viv, my mum's sister. Audrey was my chief bridesmaid when I got married.'

'Excellent. So we could say that you knew her very well.'

'That's what I said.'

'And when did Audrey Steele go missing?' said Cooper.

Ellen Walker stared at him. 'Missing?'

'When was she last seen? We don't have her

recorded as a missing person. But it seems she must have been missing since at least February or March last year.'

'She isn't missing. She died.'

'Yes, we know she died,' said Cooper patiently. 'We know *now* that she died. But before anyone knew what had happened to her, she must have been missing.'

'I don't know what you mean,' said Ellen Walker nervously. 'Audrey died. She had a brain haemorrhage and died.'

Now it was Cooper's turn to stare. 'How do you know what she died of?'

'It was on the death certificate.'

'What?'

'Her mother will have it put away somewhere, if you want to see it.'

With an effort, Cooper tried to focus his thoughts and figure out what Mrs Walker was telling him. 'We *are* talking about Audrey Steele?'

'Yes, of course.'

'Ellen, when did your cousin die exactly?'

'The second week of March last year. She was cremated at Edendale. An awful day, it was, too. It sleeted all afternoon.' Ellen Walker shivered at the memory. 'There's nothing worse than sleet, is there? It makes you feel cold and damp right through to the bones.'

10

Liz Petty was already waiting in the DI's office when Fry entered. She looked cheerful, as though she might have good news to share. But Fry watched her uncertainly as she took a chair. SOCOs were civilians, and therefore unpredictable, in her view.

'We've had an initial technical analysis of the two phone calls,' said Petty. 'I thought you'd be interested in what we've come up with.'

DI Hitchens turned and raised an eyebrow at Fry. 'Was there anything interesting in the background?'

'The background noise has been enhanced. Technical Support say they need a bit more time to work on it, but they've sent a few notes through, in case they're any use.'

'Anything might help us at this moment.'

Petty tugged at her sweater and fiddled with her hair as she looked down at the papers she'd brought. Watching her closely, Fry was reminded of some of the suspects she'd interviewed over the years, who gave away their nervousness with little mannerisms. After all, Petty couldn't really care all that much about how she looked at work. That navy blue sweater worn by scenes of crime officers wasn't intended to be flattering – though it looked better on Liz Petty than on some of her middle-aged male colleagues.

'I'll try not to take up too much of your time,' said Petty, and handed round copies of the analysis.

Fry took the copy she was offered. She saw references to traffic noise, bird song, a barking dog. And there was a puzzling reference to a loud, echoey voice, like someone shouting in the background, but inside a building – and not really shouting as such.

'Do the boys in Technical Support never go to church?' she said.

'Sorry?'

'The shouting they refer to would be the eulogy for the deceased councillor, delivered by the vicar from his pulpit. That means the funeral service had already started when the call was made.'

'It has to give us a better chance of identifying him, if we decide to follow that route,' said Hitchens.

Fry sighed as she recognized one of the phrases the DI used to avoid commitment.

'They've done well to bring out that amount

of detail from the tape,' she said. 'I didn't notice any of it. The quality of the recording is too poor.'

'But how is he disguising his voice?' asked Hitchens. 'Don't you need special electronic equipment to do that? How did he manage it in a public phone box?'

'I'm coming to that,' said Petty. 'Technology makes it a lot easier these days. He used a telephone voice changer. Probably something like this –'

She produced a tiny aluminium device no bigger than a pocket watch, with a couple of buttons on top. It looked almost like a miniature computer mouse.

'This is a voice changer?' asked Hitchens sceptically.

'It has six voices to choose from. You select the one you want by using the button on the casing. Then you simply hold it over the telephone mouthpiece and speak into the microphone on the top. There are more sophisticated devices on the market, but for most ordinary purposes this is sufficient. You can pick one up for less than twenty pounds on the internet.'

'It's easily small enough to carry in a pocket,' said Hitchens.

'Certainly. There's even a little chain, so you can attach it to a key-ring.'

'And most people would take it for a garage door remote.'

Petty laid two small handheld dictation machines on the table. 'This one has a tape of the original phone call in it,' she said, pressing a button. A familiar voice filled the silence, metallic and vibrating with artificial echoes.

Soon there will be a killing. It might happen in the next few hours.

'That's enough, I think. Now listen to the second recording. I borrowed this from one of my colleagues.'

She pressed the 'play' button on the second machine.

Soon there will be a killing. It might happen in the next few hours.

'What do you think?' she said, turning it off.

'They sounded identical.'

'If we'd recorded a longer piece, you would probably have noticed the difference. Actually, the second voice was mine.'

'You're kidding.'

Petty held up the voice changer again. 'It was pretty close, wasn't it?'

'Close? It was uncanny.'

Petty passed the voice changer round.

'How is it powered?' said Fry.

'An ordinary three-volt lithium button cell battery, exactly the same as you might use in an electronic keyfob or a watch. I can't confirm the battery life yet, but the manufacturer says an hour. More than enough for the calls made so far, anyway.'

'So we can't even hope that he's going to run out of batteries,' said Hitchens.

But Petty just smiled as she put away her dictation machines.

'I think there was a particular reason you recorded the trial message yourself, Liz,' said Fry. 'You wanted to make the point that our caller could be a woman, didn't you?'

'I'm afraid so. We wouldn't want to start out with closed minds, would we?'

Ben Cooper leaned back on his desk, wondering when it would be reasonable to phone the hospital again. He'd only just come in, and was waiting for Fry to finish talking to the two support officers. It looked as though she was making sure they knew who was boss.

'Well, keep trying, Ben,' she said when he explained the outcome of his visit to Ellen Walker. 'You'll get a better result, given time.'

'You think so, Diane?'

'Mrs Walker was obviously misled by a superficial resemblance. These facial reconstructions are an art, not a science – no matter what the experts might try to tell you. It doesn't matter whether they're done by hand or on a computer. A lot of it is guesswork.'

'Yes, as a matter of fact, that's exactly what –'

'So it's hardly surprising that you'll get a false hit now and then. Just put it down to experience. And, like I say, keep trying.'

'Right,' said Cooper. 'Keep trying.'

'What else have you got there?'

'I've had the dental mapping done by the odontologist. Now I need a dentist who can match the chart to his records.'

Cooper had found a copy of the postmortem dental chart on his desk. Most of the dark areas where work had been done seemed to be in the sides of the mouth, in the molars and pre-molars. The front teeth were almost free of fillings, and were described by the odontologist as 'regular'.

'I wish it was as easy as they make it look on TV,' he said. 'Like all we had to do was enter details for any set of teeth into some huge database and get an instant identification.'

Fry was no longer listening, but Gavin Murfin looked up from his desk.

'You mean it isn't like that?' he said. 'The BBC has been lying to me, then.'

Cooper remembered the moments that Ellen Walker had spent staring at him while he tried to recover from his surprise at hearing Audrey Steele had been cremated. All he'd been able to think of to do after that was to ask her for a recent photograph of Audrey.

'You mean, from not long before she died?' she'd said.

'Preferably.'

'I wouldn't have one normally. Nothing since we were in our twenties, anyway. But her mum had some cards done for the funeral. They were like a memorial tribute, with a bit of a poem on them. Do you know the sort of thing I mean?'

'Yes, I think so.'

'Well, I kept mine, so it should be around here somewhere. The quality isn't too bad. I think Auntie Viv spent quite a bit of money on having them done. But then, she would do. She thought the world of Audrey.'

'Viv is her mother, I take it?'

'Vivien Gill. Auntie Viv is my mother's sister.'

'Would you be able to find the memorial card for me, Mrs Walker?'

Ellen had hesitated. 'I don't know why you want to see it. What use can it be to you?'

'I'm not really sure myself. But, all the same, if it isn't too much trouble . . .?'

'All right. But it might take me a minute, so sit yourself down while you're waiting.'

'Thank you.'

She'd gone through into the next room, and Cooper had heard her opening a drawer.

'Here we are. It didn't take long, after all.'

'Thank you.'

The photo of Audrey Steele had been in colour, with a little too much red tone, but printed on good quality card, with a gloss finish. Audrey was smiling, enjoying herself somewhere in the sun, with a cocktail on a table in front of her and a patch of blue sea in the background. She was wearing a white, sleeveless T-shirt with thin straps that revealed her shoulders, pink from the sun.

'Audrey always had boyfriends when she wanted them,' Ellen Walker had said. 'Men liked her.'

'Yes, she looks . . . Well, she looks fun.'

'That's exactly right. That's what she was. Everybody liked Audrey, because she was such fun.'

'Was she an only child?'

'No, she has a brother and sister.'

Cooper had hesitated, more questions burning in his mind that he was almost afraid to ask.

'I don't suppose she ever had any children?'

'She had a little girl when she was with Carl – that's the oil-rig man. But the child was born premature and died before they could get her home from the hospital. It was a real shame. I think those two would have settled down together if Corinne had lived.'

'Can you remember if Audrey ever broke her arm?'

'She might have done. Or was it her leg? No, I'm not sure.'

'Or had a head X-ray?'

'I've no idea.'

Ellen Walker had started to look uneasy then, and Cooper had known she would either clam up, or demand an explanation.

'One last thing. Could you let me have an address for your Auntie Viv, please?'

'Yes, if you like.'

Finally, Cooper had stood up, still troubled. 'Ellen, are you certain?'

'Certain?' Mrs Walker had looked at him as if he'd challenged her on her prediction for the weather. 'Of what?'

'Are you certain your cousin was cremated?'

'Well, I didn't think there was much doubt. Why else would they have taken her to the crematorium?'

'We could try a different eye colour,' said Suzi Lee reluctantly, when Cooper phoned her at the university later that morning. 'I can do that on the computer, if you like. Or a change of hair-style. Glasses, perhaps.'

'Would that make a lot of difference?' asked Cooper.

'As I said before, it's the bone structure and tissue depth that decide the shape of the face. And I'm confident that's accurate.' She paused. 'Why do you think it isn't?'

'A wrong identification.'

'I see.' She sounded unreasonably disappointed. But Cooper knew how she felt.

'I'm not suggesting there's anything wrong with your reconstruction,' he said.

'No, of course not. You're just saying it looks like the wrong person.'

Cooper studied the photograph for a moment. Its eyes were fixed on the middle distance, and the face held no expression. But it didn't need to. He wondered if Suzi Lee was doing the same thing at the other end of the line.

158

'I'll see what I can do,' she said.

'In your own mind,' said Cooper, 'do you feel the first reconstruction is as accurate as you could have got it?'

She was silent for a moment. 'Yes, I am. Not in my mind, but in my heart. I feel sure that's Jane Raven Lee.'

Cooper nodded. 'Yes,' he said. 'That's my feeling, too.'

Audrey Steele's mother lived on the Devonshire Estate, in a cream – rendered semi that had a washing line full of sheets billowing in the back garden. You didn't see many washing lines these days, but maybe Vivien Gill was the old-fashioned type.

Inside, a rustic-effect brick fireplace had been set into one wall of the sitting room, and a central heating radiator on another. Above the picture rails, the ceiling was coved and artexed. At the back of the house was a kitchen smelling strongly of disinfectant. When he followed Mrs Gill into it, Cooper became aware of a sickeningly sweet scent that might have several sources he didn't want to think about. A baby sat in a high chair at the table, its mouth smeared with something sticky and yellow. Doidy Cup and Bickiepegs were set out on the counter.

'This is my granddaughter,' said Mrs Gill. 'Isn't she gorgeous?'

'She's beautiful,' said Cooper, giving the child

a brief wave. He might learn the attraction of babies one day, but for now the appeal was lost on him. Once they could walk and talk, and look after their own toilet arrangements, he had no problem with children. But babies made him a bit nervous.

In the sitting room, Vivien Gill made him sit down in one of the armchairs, though he told her he couldn't stay long.

'Mrs Gill, I don't know whether you've spoken to Ellen Walker today . . .'

'I talked to Ellen last night. She had some idea about a picture in the paper. An artist's impression, or something.'

'A facial reconstruction, yes.'

'I thought it was a daft idea myself.'

'Did you see the picture?'

'No. I don't get the evening paper.'

Cooper looked out of the window and saw a man watching the street from a house opposite. Maybe that was why Mrs Gill had wanted him to sit down, so that he couldn't be seen by nosey neighbours. She hadn't otherwise seemed particularly hospitable. Of course, this was the Devonshire Estate, where residents were practised at recognizing a police officer, even out of uniform.

'It was on the TV news, too,' he said.

'I've got the child to look after. I don't spend all my time watching telly.'

'May I show you a copy of the photo?'

Mrs Gill squinted at the picture he handed her,

held it up to the light, then put it down while she found her glasses. 'It doesn't look human,' she said. 'It's just a clay model, painted up.'

'Does it bear any resemblance to your daughter?'

'No. It's daft.'

She handed the photograph back dismissively. But Cooper noticed that her hand was shaking a little more. The baby was snivelling and getting ready to start crying, but Mrs Gill ignored it.

'What about these items of clothing?' said Cooper gently. 'I'm sorry about the condition of them. Do they look familiar at all?'

Mrs Gill barely glanced at the second set of photographs. They had been taken in the mortuary after the remnants of clothing had been removed and laid out on a table. They were stained and partially rotted, and they had an air of squalor despite the mortuary lights.

The old woman turned pale, but shook her head, perhaps a little too vigorously. She looked at Cooper, then out of the window.

'No, they mean nothing to me.'

'One more thing,' said Cooper, 'and then I'll get out of your way. Could you tell me what doctor your daughter went to?'

Mrs Gill breathed an audible sigh of relief. Now she was on safer ground, and she didn't question why Cooper wanted to know such information.

'Doctor? Well, the same one as me. Crown House Surgery, here in Edendale.'

161

'And a dentist?'

'Moorhouse's in Bargate. He's NHS, so you have to go for a check-up every six months or you get kicked off his list. Audrey always went regularly. She was a nurse – she knew about looking after her health.'

Cooper smiled as he gathered the photographs together. 'I bet she took regular exercise, too.'

Mrs Gill stood and gazed out of the windows as she waited for him to leave.

'She swam as often as she could,' she said. 'Audrey competed in the county championships when she was a youngster. Her brother was a good swimmer, too – this is his child I'm looking after.'

'Audrey also has a sister, doesn't she?'

'Oh, *her*. She doesn't live around here any more.'

There was something about the way Mrs Gill said 'her' that reminded Cooper of Tom Jarvis, as though there was a name that mustn't be spoken. But there had been a gruff affection in Jarvis's voice when he referred to his wife. There was none in Mrs Gill's when she spoke of her daughter.

'Has there been some kind of rift in the family?'

'Eh?'

'You've fallen out with your other daughter?'

'We just don't see as much of each other, not since she re-married. I don't trust that new husband of hers. A leopard doesn't change its spots so easily – no matter what *she* says.'

* * *

162

Cooper just had time to call in at West Street before he was due to meet Professor Robertson. But the moment he walked into the office and sat down, the phone rang on his desk. It was Tom Jarvis.

'The old girl's dead,' said Jarvis. 'Somebody shot her.'

Cooper sat bolt upright.

'Dead? Have you called 999, Mr Jarvis?'

'Nay. But I thought you'd want to know.'

'Where – ? I mean, where's the body?'

'I laid her out on the porch. But I'll bury her by and by. I thought I'd put her in the orchard. She always liked it there.'

'No, Mr Jarvis, don't touch her. Just wait until someone gets there. I'll send the paramedics, and a doctor. We need to get scenes of crime there. And she was shot, you say? My God, we need the armed response unit as well. You really should have called 999 straight away.'

Jarvis breathed down the phone at him for a few moments in puzzled silence.

'Well, I didn't think you'd be all *that* bothered,' he said. 'Not for a dog.'

11

Professor Freddy Robertson's home stood on rising ground in a cluster of newer houses on the outskirts of Totley. It had a flat, brick face broken by bay windows and an oak front door. Its gardens were reached from a broad gravelled driveway that ran past a detached garage with a dark blue BMW drawn up outside.

Cooper had been given the impression that the professor had retired to Derbyshire, but this wasn't strictly true. Totley was an outer suburb of Sheffield, and it lay in South Yorkshire. But the county boundary was only a stone's throw away across the fields, and the national park a few hundred yards further on. The rural setting was one of the attractions for those who could afford to live here.

Cooper had spent the drive to Totley listening to a Runrig CD. 'The Edge of the World' didn't quite describe his journey across Froggatt Edge and the eastern moors, but it came close.

'This is an Edwardian gentleman's residence,' said Robertson, meeting Cooper at his car. 'As you can see, we had it refurbished in a manner sympathetic to the Arts and Crafts movement. Four bedrooms on a galleried landing, original beams, a wine cellar. And look at these gardens –'

The professor was a big man in his early sixties, his hair greying and rather too long at the sides to compensate for the bald patch at the front. He wore a rather baggy pinstripe suit like a lawyer's, and moved a little stiffly, as if suffering from the first symptoms of arthritis.

They entered an L-shaped reception hall with mosaic tiles on the floor and a staircase with mahogany balustrades. On the wall was the ugliest coat rack Cooper had ever seen. It was covered in imitation deer hide, and had four real hooves turned upside down to act as hooks.

Robertson took him through into a study lined with books, the floor space almost filled by an oak desk and a set of deep leather armchairs. The professor sat at his desk, with his back to a window looking out on to the garden. He offered Cooper a drink, which he refused, but poured himself a whisky from a bottle of Glenfiddich he took from a cupboard. Then he linked his fingers, like a headmaster with an errant pupil on the carpet.

'I'm sorry to have messed you around, sir,' said Cooper. 'I hope I haven't disrupted your afternoon too much.'

'Oh, I'm glad you could make it. I was worried

that you'd decided you didn't need to call on my services after all. But I suppose you were detained on urgent police business?'

'You might say I had to speak to a man about a dog.'

'Oh, dogs,' said Robertson. He sniffed suspiciously, as if Cooper might have smuggled one into the house, or at least brought in the smell and a few stray hairs. 'Now I'm really wounded, Detective Constable. I'd have been happy to come in second to anybody or anything, except a dog.'

Cooper smiled hesitantly, not sure whether the professor was joking.

'You don't like dogs, sir?'

'I find their form of domestication offensive, on an ethical basis.'

'I'm sorry?'

'Well, dogs are basically animal slaves, aren't they? People find them useful for certain menial tasks, or for massaging their egos. Dogs fawn on their owners shamelessly. Don't you find it so? No, I expect you disagree with me.'

'Many people would value dogs for their loyalty,' said Cooper.

'Oh, you're thinking of the dog that will dive into the river to save its master when he's drowning? Well, the fact is that nine dogs out of ten would sit on the bank and watch you drown. And then they'd go off to see where their next meal was coming from. Loyalty is skin deep, you know.'

Cooper shifted uneasily under the professor's gaze, but didn't argue.

Robertson smiled. 'Now, I presume there was something you wanted to ask me about. Which case is it, now? Somebody mentioned skeletonized remains . . .?'

'That's correct, sir.'

Briefly, Cooper explained the background to his enquiry and showed Robertson photographs of the scene at Litton Foot.

'You see, sir, the feet were pointing to the east and the head to the west. For a start, I wondered if that might have any significance.'

'That was very observant of you,' said Robertson. 'Well, it certainly reflects the Christian cemetery tradition. The practice was based on the belief that the Lord's Second Coming would be from the east. When you rise from your grave on Judgement Day, you want to be facing your God, not turning your backside to him.'

'I see.'

'Burials in Roman Britain were already east–west oriented by the end of the second century AD, so the tradition lasted a long time. But this isn't an ancient burial, or you wouldn't be here, surely?'

'That's correct, sir.'

Robertson waved a hand. 'It's all right – you don't have to tell me more than you want to. I can see you're not sure whether you can trust me.'

'It isn't that, sir. We don't know a great deal at the moment.'

'Are you sure you wouldn't like a drink? Something non-alcoholic, of course, since you're so very much on duty.'

'No thank you, sir.'

Robertson took a gulp of his whisky. 'There are other practices you may be familiar with. In some of our older churchyards, it's still possible to see the traditional pattern of burials. At one time, a person's place in the social hierarchy was preserved for posterity by the location of their grave. The better class of people were buried on the south side of the church, in the sunniest position. The poor were planted on the west, and the clergy on the east.'

'And the north?'

'Ah, the fourth side of the church was known as the Black North because it was always out of the sun. It was reserved for suicides and murderers, who were denied Christian burial rites. Those poor souls were condemned to the darkness, both literally and spiritually.' The professor pursed his lips as he looked at Cooper. 'Normally, a funeral procession would enter the churchyard from the eastern gate and follow the direction of the sun to the newly dug grave. On the other hand, a murderer or suicide would be brought in at the west gate and carried against the sun.'

Robertson lifted his shoulders and let them drop again, as if shrugging off any personal responsibility for such practices. But Cooper was thinking of the dark woods in Ravensdale, the dripping canopy of ash trees, the dank moss coating everything, never drying out because it was hidden from the sun.

'Do you have a complete skeleton?' asked the professor suddenly.

Cooper was startled. 'Why do you ask?'

'It could be significant.' Robertson smiled. 'That's what detectives say when they're interviewing a witness, isn't it?'

'On TV it is, anyway.'

Robertson's face changed, but he hid his expression behind his whisky glass.

'There *are* some bones missing,' said Cooper. 'It may mean nothing, though. The forensic anthropologist's report suggests the activity of scavengers.'

'It's quite possible. But if you're thinking along ritual lines, you should bear in mind that there have been many different attitudes to death, and some of our ancestors' practices have caused problems for archaeologists.'

'Problems?'

'Animals and birds do tend to carry off the smaller skeletal parts, so it was usually only the larger bones that survived excarnation – that's the technical term for leaving the corpse out in the open air. But after the animals and birds had taken their pick, the long bones and skull were often taken for use in ceremonies.'

Robertson looked at him expectantly. When Cooper asked the next question he felt as though he was responding to a cue, like one of Pavlov's dogs.

'What kind of ceremonies?'

'Any ceremony in which it was useful to have the assistance of one's dead ancestors. Skulls are considered particularly powerful. But other bones have their significance, too. They relate to the continuing influence of ancestral spirits.'

Robertson stood up and walked to the window, clasping his hands behind his back and staring at the ground like an Oxford don in his college quad.

'You must think about death quite a bit, sir?' said Cooper.

But the professor just laughed, his mouth opening wide to show strong teeth and a glimpse of a moist tongue.

'Try reading Ecclesiastes.'

'Sir?'

'Old Testament, dear boy. "As one dies, so does the other. They all have the same breath, and man has no advantage over the beasts. All are from the dust, and all to dust turn again."'

Cooper was starting to feel much the way he had at school during lessons from one of his more pedantic history teachers.

'I'm sorry,' said Robertson, studying his expression. 'I'm afraid I miss my little group of students, and I can't resist an opportunity to lecture.'

'That's all right, sir.'

'Anything else?'

Cooper still hadn't been given a chance to hear the tapes of the phone calls that Fry was so worried about. But her hunt through the area for locations had left him turning over in his mind the possible meanings of the phrase the caller had used.

'Yes. What does "the dead place" mean to you?'

Robertson gazed out of the window thoughtfully, took a sip of his Glenfiddich, and shook his head, stirring the wings of grey hair over his temples. He repeated the phrase silently to himself a couple of times, his lips glittering with drops of whisky as they moved.

'It could mean anything, couldn't it?' said Cooper finally.

The professor jerked as if woken from a daze. 'Yes, I'm afraid so.'

Cooper closed his notebook. 'Well, I think that's about it for now, sir.'

'Please don't hesitate to get in touch if you need to talk again. It all sounds most intriguing.'

As he made his way back through the tiled hallway, Cooper passed under the coat rack. He wondered if the professor had shot the deer himself and taken its feet instead of its antlers as a trophy.

'Fashions change,' said Robertson, his voice echoing in the hallway. 'But our deepest instincts don't, I'm afraid. We're fascinated by death, yet afraid of it. The enclosed coffin is a symptom of

171

our refusal to accept the reality. Did you know the word "burial" derives from the Anglo-Saxon *birgan*, meaning to conceal. Personally, I've always felt the sarcophagus was a rather more civilized option.'

'A sarcophagus?' Cooper's head was suddenly filled with images of Egyptian mummies, and a half-remembered kaleidoscope of pyramids, pharaohs and golden effigies of Tutankhamen.

'At least we'd enjoy a bit of light and air,' said Robertson as he opened his front door.

And Cooper was still shaking his head at the professor's non-sequitur as he drove past the new houses, out of Totley, and back towards the Derbyshire border.

It was Graceless who lay dead on the boards of Mr Jarvis's porch. As Ben Cooper walked up the steps, the first thing he noticed was the blood-stained patch of hair on the dog's side, just behind her front leg.

'Did you see anybody, Mr Jarvis?'

'No. They were off in the woods somewhere. But I heard the shot.'

It was immediately obvious to Cooper that the dog had been killed by a rifle bullet, not by a discharge from a shotgun, as he'd expected. He'd seen dogs killed by shotgun pellets before. In fact, a few weeks ago, Matt had shot a stray Doberman that had been worrying his sheep. A cartridge full of pellets caused a very visible mess. But in this case, the blood seemed to have come from a single wound, close enough to the heart and other vital organs to be instantly fatal.

When he bent to examine the injury, Cooper saw that the blood had already darkened and begun to dry. It had matted the hair even more and made it difficult to find the exact entry point of the bullet. He forced apart two hanks of sticky fur and glimpsed a neat black hole in the dog's skin.

'Only one shot?'

'That's all I heard. I thought there must be folk out rabbiting.'

'Maybe there were. And a stray shot . . .'

'Oh, aye. A stray shot that hit the old lass right in the heart. That'd be what it was, no doubt.'

Jarvis threw a blanket over the dog and turned away.

'Where are the other dogs?' said Cooper.

'Down in the paddock.'

Everything was soaking wet, including the boards and the dog. Jarvis took off his cap, revealing a patch of white scalp where his hair had receded but the sun had never reached his skin.

'You'd best get moving if you're going to stand a chance of catching them,' he said.

'We'll be following the incident up, sir.'

'Bloody amazing.'

He reached down to the dog's neck and unfastened the collar. When Cooper followed him to the door of the house, he saw Jarvis drop the strip of worn leather into a drawer of the kitchen dresser. He thought he glimpsed other collars in there, perhaps mementos of previous dogs he'd owned. A little private collection of memories.

'If you could just show me exactly where you found the dog, sir?' said Cooper.

They walked through the overgrown paddock and down towards the stream. The three remaining dogs were pacing restlessly backwards and forwards in the grass. One of them crept behind the abandoned trailer and waited out of sight for Cooper to pass. But it only wanted to sidle up to him and push its wet muzzle into his hand. He patted the dog's head and rubbed its ears.

'Why did you come down here in the first place?' asked Cooper as he stood looking at the stream running through the damp shade of the ash trees.

'I heard a noise in the woods during the night.'

'What sort of noise? Voices?'

Jarvis frowned. 'No, not that. A metallic thump, like they'd walked into something in the dark.'

Cooper glanced up at the paddock, with its lumps of rusting metal hidden by the long grass.

'More than likely,' he said. 'And what did you do, Mr Jarvis?'

'I went out to have a look, of course.'

'What time was this?'

'It must have been about midnight, and it were siling down.'

'Not a good time for someone to be taking a midnight stroll, then.'

Jarvis gave him a sour look, but didn't bother to reply.

'When you went outside, did you see anybody?' asked Cooper.

'No. There was just a bag on the ground near the porch. A game bag – like shooters and poachers use sometimes, you know what I mean? So I picked it up. I thought maybe somebody had left me a bit of a present.'

'Has that happened before?'

'I know a few lads who go shooting,' said Jarvis evasively.

'OK. So what was in the bag?'

'Cack. It were full of cack.'

For a moment, Cooper didn't understand. 'You mean dung? It was full of animal excreta?'

Jarvis shook his head and screwed up his face, as if remembering all too clearly the distinctive smell as he opened the bag.

'Human,' he said.

'Are you sure?'

Jarvis gave him a derisive look, but didn't answer. Some questions were too stupid to waste breath on.

'Do you have any idea who might have a reason to do that?'

'Somebody I've pissed off, I suppose. That doesn't take much working out.'

'And have you pissed off many people? Have you had a dispute with someone recently?'

'Ramblers, now and then. They're a bloody nuisance, some of them.'

'Have you still got the bag?'

'I burned it.'

Cooper sighed. 'I don't suppose Mrs Jarvis saw anything?'

'She was fast asleep. She sleeps through anything.'

The three dogs sprawled on the porch steps now, their huge heads hanging over the edge as they watched the men walk towards the gate. Cooper recalled the motorbike he'd seen outside the house the first time he'd visited. It wasn't here now, and he wondered who rode it. Probably one of Mr Jarvis's sons. Or maybe even the mysterious Mrs Jarvis herself. Perhaps he should have taken more notice of the bike at the time, but he'd been too intrigued by the abandoned hulks in the paddock, and too keen to get out of the rain.

'Oh, the bag of cack,' said Jarvis.

'Yes.'

'*She* doesn't know anything about it. The wife, I mean.'

'I see.'

'She gets upset about stuff. No point in telling her.'

'I don't think that'll be a problem, sir.'

Cooper coasted to the corner of the track and stopped the car. He turned towards the driver's window, as if having difficulty adjusting his seat belt. From here, the roof and upper storey of the Jarvis house were still visible through the trees. But the movement he'd seen in an upstairs window failed to resolve itself into more than a pale blur. It was the face of a person standing too far back from the window to be recognizable in the shadows. Was it Mrs Jarvis? Or just her husband, anxious to see whether Cooper had left the premises? Of course, it could be someone else entirely. There was no way of telling.

Cooper closed the window, pressed the accelerator and bumped the Toyota back up the track from Litton Foot. When he was fifty yards from the house, he pushed a CD into the player and filled the car with the sound of Runrig's 'Hearthammer'.

As a result, he just missed hearing the grumble of a motorcycle engine as it moved hesitantly through the damp woods of Ravensdale.

When Cooper walked back into the CID room, Fry was listening to the tapes again, with her headphones over her ears and an expression of concentrated loathing on her face.

'What's that, Diane?' Cooper asked as he took off his coat, shaking a few drops of water on to the carpet.

She paused the tape and slipped off her headphones. 'Our talkative psycho. These clues he's given us in his second call have *got* to be his big mistake.'

'Is he a man who makes mistakes, do you think?'

'No,' said Fry. 'Bastard.'

She began to put the headphones back on, but Cooper stopped her.

'Hold on. Can I listen? I haven't had a chance to hear it yet.'

Fry nodded. She unplugged the headphones and started the tape again. Cooper listened to it for a few moments, trying to filter out the words from the distortion that robbed them of any recognizable humanity. Then he remembered Audrey Steele's dental records. If they hadn't arrived, he'd have to make another call to Moorhouse's. He checked the fax machine, and gave a murmur of satisfaction.

'Diane, I've got the dental records for Audrey Steele.'

'Are you going to send them to Sheffield?'

'It's already done. I got the dentist to send them direct, and this is just a copy. Trouble is, all this stuff doesn't mean anything to me.'

'You'll have to wait until we hear what the experts have to say.'

Cooper was looking at the fax when the voice coming from the tape machine penetrated his concentration.

'What was that bit?' he said.

Fry looked up in surprise. 'What?'

'What did he say just then?'

The tape was still running, and Cooper waved his hand urgently. 'Wind it back a bit, Diane. Let me listen to that last part again.'

'If you want, Ben. There's nothing in it, though.

178

Only a lot of pretentious drivel he likes to spout.'

But she did as he asked, and replayed the last couple of minutes.

'Well, if that isn't pretentious, I don't know what is,' she said.

'Not that part,' said Cooper. 'Shh.'

They should decay in the open air until their flesh is gone, said the metallic voice.

Then there was a pause. And to Cooper it seemed a perfectly drawn-out pause, like the skilful timing of an experienced actor.

Or, of course, a sarcophagus.

12

Melvyn Hudson forced himself to smile sympathetically at a passing griever. He was afraid his expression might come out as a grimace and give the wrong impression. As soon as he could, he took the old man by the arm and encouraged him gently towards the limousines.

'It was nothing, Abraham,' he said. 'Nothing to do with us.'

'Why did the police come, then?'

'It was only one officer. Just routine enquiries, I expect.'

Abraham Slack was a little more frail than he used to be, and paler. But he still had a strength and dignity that made Hudson feel uncertain when he had to deal with him.

The old man took a deep breath. 'It's damaging to the firm's reputation, Melvyn.'

'Yes, yes, I know. But nothing will come of it.'

'There would never have been anything like this in your father's day.'

'Abraham, you know damn well there wouldn't still be a company if it weren't for me – so don't start telling me what it was like in my father's day.'

Hudson realized he was losing his composure. He looked around anxiously, and saw some of the mourners watching him. This was the last funeral of the afternoon, and the crematorium staff would be getting impatient if the family weren't shepherded off the premises soon.

'This is not the time,' he said.

'We need to talk, Melvyn,' said Abraham.

'Later, later.' Hudson brushed nervously at his black jacket as he strode back towards the chapel, his face returning automatically to its professional expression.

Tom Jarvis put on his boots and collected a spade from the workshop. He walked slowly away from the house, past the empty pigsties and down to a small paddock at the edge of the woods. They called this place the orchard because it contained two apple trees. But the fruit had suffered from blight for years, and now the windfalls already starting to litter the ground looked more like wrinkled plums than apples. Even the birds wouldn't touch them, unless the winter weather got really bad.

The ground was damp here, but it was the only part of the property where the soil was deep enough, without hitting rock. Jarvis settled his cap firmly on his head, spat on his hands, and began

181

to dig. His mind seemed to switch off when he was involved in physical work. It helped him to avoid thinking about things too much.

He had been digging for about half an hour and had built up a good sweat, when he stopped for a moment to wipe his forehead. Across the stream, someone was watching him. The person was partly hidden by the trees, and was given away only by a slight movement. Jarvis stared at the figure for a while, until it slipped away into the woods, back towards the Alder Hall estate.

With a sigh, Jarvis took up his spade and began to dig again. The grave needed to be a bit deeper yet, and the soil was heavy. There was no need for him to call out, or go after the person who had been watching him. He already knew exactly who it was.

'Well, this *is* nice,' said Professor Robertson. 'And such a surprise. I really hadn't anticipated an outing this evening. I think I'm going to like you, Detective Constable Cooper. You bring a little excitement into my life.'

The professor stood on the grass between the graves in St Mark's churchyard. His hands were thrust into the pockets of his coat, as if he was afraid to touch anything. Long strands of hair hung over his ears, flapping in the breeze that blew down from the hillsides above Edendale. Below the church, the River Eden could be seen snaking its way through the town.

'I'm really sorry to drag you all the way out here, sir,' said Cooper. 'But it could be important.'

'Not at all, not at all. It's good to get out of the study and away from the books now and then. Very stimulating.' Robertson nodded, and smiled slyly. 'Besides, I'm thrilled to get a chance to meet your colleague.'

Behind Cooper, Fry was leaning against a tomb-stone, listening but saying nothing. He tried to avoid her eye.

'And these things are actually sarcophagi, you say?'

'Certainly.'

There were five of them, standing upright against a wall of the church, near the bell tower. Someone had arranged them in descending order, from six feet in length down to one the size of a small child. There were deep cracks in the stone and some of the corners had been sheered off. Pale green lichen had spread across the lower surfaces, like a shroud of cobwebs.

Cooper reached out a hand to touch the nearest one. He ran his fingers over the rough stone, and felt the chisel marks made by the mason. Despite the occasional bits of damage, the sarcophagi were remarkably intact for their age. Whatever their age was, exactly. They seemed to belong to that murky period of history beyond the medieval.

'Roman?' he said. 'They'd be about two thou-sand years old, I suppose.'

'Oh, perhaps of that era,' said the professor. 'It's

impossible to date them with any accuracy. Their design never really changed. It was so simple and functional that there wasn't much you could do to tinker with it.'

'But they're just stone coffins, aren't they? Old churches often have them in their graveyards.'

Robertson shook his head. 'Most people think of them as stone coffins. And I can understand how they might give that impression, at first glance.'

The sarcophagus nearest to Cooper was one of the bigger examples, its upper end at eye level against the church wall. It tapered towards the foot, and the mason had hacked a vaguely human shape out of the stone, including the outline of a head and shoulders.

'There's no mistaking that they're designed to contain a body.'

'Ah, but there are differences. For a start, these sarcophagi never possessed lids. They were always open to the air like this.'

For some reason, Cooper felt reluctant to examine the smallest sarcophagus, so he concentrated on the bigger ones instead.

'Of course, the distinctive feature is the hole in the bottom. I wouldn't expect that in my coffin.'

Robertson nodded encouragingly, as if to a student who was none too bright but was making an effort. 'Exactly.'

Moving closer, Cooper tilted his head. The base had been shaped more carefully from the stone than at first appeared. Despite the crudeness of its construction, the surface showed a distinct dip towards the centre, where a hole a couple of inches across had been drilled through the stone.

'The hole must be there for drainage. If these things didn't possess lids, there had to be some way of letting the rain run out, or they'd be full of water.'

'No, no,' said Robertson. 'Sarcophagi were kept under cover. They had to remain dry. It was essential to the process.'

'But . . .?'

'Well, you're partly right, DC Cooper. However, rainwater wasn't involved. Yes, sarcophagi were designed to provide drainage – but it was the drainage of body fluids.'

'Ah.'

The professor flapped his coat like the wings of a bird as he stood back and looked up at the church. Underneath the coat, he was still wearing the baggy pinstripe suit. 'You see, the sarcophagus dates from a time before the practice of shutting up a corpse in a box and burying it. At that time, there was the charnel house and the sarcophagus. A charnel house was known as the "dead place", or the "place of the dead".'

Fry stirred for the first time at the mention of the phrase, and Robertson saw that he'd finally got her interest.

'It was your mention of the dead place that put the idea of a sarcophagus into my mind,' he explained. 'But I wasn't aware at the time of the significance. There could be other interpretations, of course.'

'What happened in this dead place, Professor?' asked Fry.

'A corpse was left exposed to the air until decay had done its work, the flesh had dried and the bones were clean enough for disposal. Periodically, a priest would enter the charnel house to check if the corpse was ready.'

'Ready?'

'Our ancestors considered decomposition a perfectly natural stage of the body's evolution,' said Robertson. 'It marked the passage from earth-bound spirit to a soul free to ascend to Heaven. They thought it was only the flesh that kept the soul trapped in the body. The soul had to be released to achieve real death. Looked at in that way, decomposition was a positive development. I imagine they might have wanted to observe this process taking place, much as we watch our children growing up.'

As they walked back down the flagged path through the churchyard, Cooper heard the professor muttering to himself. He caught the sound of a familiar phrase and realized the historian was quoting Shakespeare. *Hamlet*, if he wasn't mistaken.

'"Oh that this too, too solid flesh would melt, Thaw, and resolve itself into a dew."'

Robertson caught Cooper's eye and smiled.

'Appropriate, I think. More so than "dust to dust" and all that. Trust the Bard. He always had the right phrase for the occasion.'

'But that word – sarcophagus,' said Cooper. 'Where does it come from?'

'It's derived from the Greek. A compound of two words – *sark* and *phagos*. We doctors do so love our Latin and Greek.'

Cooper looked at the professor and raised his eyebrows to indicate that he was none the wiser. Robertson beamed with satisfaction and allowed himself a small dramatic pause before he explained.

'Loosely translated,' he said, 'the name means "flesh eater".'

Before either of the detectives could react, Robertson began to amble around the flagged paths, casting backwards and forwards as if trying to pick up a scent.

'If you're interested in old graveyards, you'd like those in Perthshire, where I hail from,' he said. 'Near Pitlochry, there's a churchyard where some of the graves were protected by mortsafes – a kind of iron cage over the grave, to prevent body snatching. A pernicious activity, which we Scots were particularly good at, it seems.'

Cooper looked at him in surprise. 'Body snatching? Yes, a particularly unpleasant crime.'

'Ah, that's where you're wrong. I'm surprised to find myself putting you right on a matter of law, Detective Constable.'

'What do you mean, sir?'

'Body snatching wasn't an offence. Once you were deceased, your physical remains couldn't be owned by anyone, and therefore couldn't be stolen. A body snatcher was only committing a crime if he stole other items with the body, even the shroud. It was popular opinion that turned against the resurrection men, not the law.'

'But Burke and Hare . . .?'

'A different case altogether. They weren't content to wait for a supply of dead bodies to become available, so they decided to procure their own from among the living. Murder was their crime. It was all a question of market forces at work. The demand for bodies for dissection was enormous.'

'There are probably other reasons people might want to obtain a dead body,' said Cooper.

'Undoubtedly.'

Robertson followed Cooper's gaze as he looked around the graves in the churchyard.

'Oh, there are no records of body snatching taking place in Derbyshire,' he said. 'People feared it, nevertheless. They had a superstitious dread of the body being removed from its last resting place. It meant they wouldn't be able to rise from the grave on Judgement Day.'

'So I believe.'

Robertson glanced up at him. 'Perhaps I shouldn't have called it superstition. I don't want to be offensive.'

It sounded almost like an apology. Cooper waved it away. 'It doesn't matter.'

The professor straightened up with a sigh. 'Nobody can be sure when society developed its distaste for death. But for centuries it's been kept out of sight. Few people ever see the process of decomposition now. Only those whose profession is death have that privilege.'

'Pathologists, funeral directors?' said Cooper. 'Police officers?'

'All our good friends,' agreed Robertson. 'God bless them.'

Cooper looked at Fry, and knew it was time to leave. Dusk was falling, and the churchyard was filling up with shadows. They softened the edges of the tombs, obscured the inscriptions, and made the stone slabs look a little less cold. Too much daylight didn't suit the dead.

'The "flesh eater", Professor,' he said. 'What did the Greeks mean by that name?'

'Well, the original phrase was *lithos sarkophagos*: "flesh-eating stone". It reflected a belief that a certain type of limestone consumed the flesh from the body, and was therefore the perfect material to be used as a receptacle for the dead.'

Cooper laughed, and gestured at the hills on all sides. 'Limestone? This is the White Peak. Everything is limestone here.'

'Yes,' said Robertson doubtfully. 'Of course, we only have the word of Pliny the Elder. Pliny said limestone could consume a body in forty days.

189

Personally, I wouldn't rely on it too much as a forensic theory.'

As Fry lifted the latch on the churchyard gate, she turned towards them, and Cooper saw that her face was set into an expression of impatience and scorn.

'Thank you for the history lesson, Professor,' she said. 'I'm sure you've improved DC Cooper's education immensely. He'll be a much better detective from now on.'

Fry moved off towards the car, but Robertson touched Cooper's sleeve to hold him back as they reached the gate.

'There's one more word that I'm sure you know,' said the professor.

'What's that, sir?'

'Sarcasm. Another figurative expression handed down to us from the Greek. It means tearing or biting at the skin, like an animal. The Greeks didn't like sarcasm very much.'

Fry was waiting by the Toyota, tapping her fingers on the roof as she watched people walking by on the street. Cooper unlocked the car, and she slid quickly into the passenger seat.

'Oh yes, we doctors do so love our Latin and Greek,' she said, fastening her seat belt. 'It's so, so fascinating – but only for those with a little knowledge of the classical world. Not for the ignorant plebs who studied useful subjects, instead of some ancient dead language.'

'Diane . . .'

She looked at him with irritation. 'A real bloody Aristotle we've got there, haven't we? I bet he can't get in the bath without jumping out again and shouting "Eureka!"'

'I think that was Archimedes,' said Cooper, waving to Freddy Robertson as they pulled away from the church. Standing by his BMW, the professor gave a little bow.

Fry stared out of the window at the streets of Edendale.

'Lawyers are just the same. Why do these people have to make their jobs sound like some kind of arcane mystery the rest of us couldn't possibly understand?'

'Maybe it's insecurity . . .' Cooper paused. 'Why didn't you let me listen to the tape of the phone calls before I went to see the professor?'

'You never asked.'

'It would have helped a lot. As it was, I only had partial information.'

'Yes, OK, Ben.'

The BMW closed up behind them as they stopped at the traffic lights before the relief road.

'Those sarcophagi he showed us,' said Fry. 'They're not even in our target area.'

'Yes,' said Cooper. 'I know.'

Robertson was right about one thing, though. Cooper had seen the watch house built at Bradfield to guard against men who might come by night to dig up freshly buried bodies from the churchyard. And here in Edendale was that

191

massive block of sandstone carved in the shape of a coffin. There was no logical reason for its size and weight, except to prevent access to the grave beneath. And yet the body snatchers had never come to Edendale, or to anywhere else in Derbyshire.

Then Cooper remembered Audrey Steele, and corrected himself. Body snatchers had never come to Derbyshire – until now.

MY JOURNAL OF THE DEAD, PHASE TWO

And the biggest unknown is death. We'd rather not think about death at all. We fear our own dead, we believe that corpses pollute the living. To acknowledge death is to accept our own mortality, so the dead have to be hidden away, shielded by rites, prayers and superstitions. Even in death, we fear the final battle with evil. We're afraid to face our angry gods.

That's why we've produced all our myths and folklore, all our rituals and deceptions. It means the thing we have to face is only a fiction of our own creation, and not the inconceivable reality. We're like a flock of chickens running around a yard until the day the axe falls on their necks. The only difference between us and the chickens is that we know the axe is there from the start. If you think about that too much, you might start to envy the chickens.

What happens after death is unspoken, and sometimes unspeakable. But we have to see the truth. We can close our mouths and ears, but we can't avert our eyes. Remember those visions of death that cross your mind as you enter into sleep? Your subconscious is trying to share the knowledge that you deny.

From the Buddhist Sutra on Mindfulness – Nine Cemetery Contemplations:

And further, a bhikkhu sees a body thrown on to the cemetery reduced to disconnected bones, scattered in all directions – here a bone of the hand, there a bone of the foot, a shin bone, a thigh bone, the pelvis, spine and skull. So he applies this perception to his own body thus: 'Verily, my own body, too, is of the same nature. Such it will become, and will not escape it.'

13

A manila envelope lay on Ben Cooper's desk on Friday morning. At first, he didn't want to touch it. It reminded him too much of the envelopes he saw at the hospital. There were always stacks of them behind the nurses' station, full of medical records and test results. A manila envelope would contain a patient's diagnosis and prognosis, a plan for their discharge or their disposal after death, the discreet arrangement of their living and dying, all wrapped up in brown paper.

He got himself a coffee from the machine in the corridor and finally felt able to rip open the sealed flap. The contents slid out on to his desk. Dental records, and it was good news. Or at least, he supposed he ought to consider it good news. He had a confirmed ID for his human remains.

Cooper tried to feel elated as he looked at the photographs of Audrey Steele again. But it seemed very tough on Audrey that she should have ended up like this.

There was a lot of talk these days about the dead speaking from beyond the grave. People usually meant the remarkable amount of forensic evidence that could be collected from a dead body. It was a way that murder victims could help investigators to achieve justice against their killers. But in Audrey's case, her voice was silent. The examination of her remains had revealed nothing useful, as far as he could tell. And how could it, when she'd died of natural causes? Audrey's mother had the death certificate. Brain haemorrhage, confirmed by a second doctor prior to disposal by cremation.

But that didn't feel right to Cooper. From the moment he'd seen Suzi Lee's reconstruction in the Sheffield laboratory, he felt as though he'd been able to hear Audrey Steele speaking to him from the woods at Ravensdale. The fact that she hadn't told him anything crucial to the enquiry seemed to be his fault, not hers. From now on, he ought to listen a bit more carefully.

A few minutes later, DI Hitchens was rubbing his fingers together thoughtfully as he listened to Cooper run through the available facts.

'This woman was supposed to have been cremated eighteen months ago?' he said. 'Is that what you're saying?'

'Yes, sir. As far as her family are concerned, she *was* cremated.'

'And yet her remains turn up in the woods ten miles from the crematorium. I've never heard anything like it, Ben.'

'There seems to be no doubt she died of natural causes. I've got copies of the certificates.'

'All done properly? Signed by two doctors?'

'Yes.'

'OK. Then we're looking at an offence of un-authorized interference with a body. God knows what the penalty is for that. I've never come across a case of this kind before.'

'I'll get some checks done and see if similar incidents have been recorded anywhere.'

'Yes, that's a good first step. And you'll be talking to the family again, I suppose?'

'Of course.'

Hitchens swivelled his chair away from Cooper, a sign that something was worrying him.

'And then there's the question of when and where the theft of the body took place. You said that Audrey Steele was in hospital when she died?'

'Yes.'

'Identified by the family, and all that?'

'I think so, but I'll get a statement from her mother, or whoever saw her in hospital last.'

'Right. Then the obvious places where the opportunity might have arisen would be the funeral director's premises, and the crematorium itself.'

'I'd have thought those were the *only* places,' said Cooper. 'The family didn't take her body home for a wake. The funeral director's preparation room and chapel of rest seem most likely, as regards an opportunity for interfering with the body.'

'And the funeral directors in this case are . . .?'

'Hudson and Slack.'

The DI nodded. 'Tread carefully, Ben. Be discreet. We don't want a scare on our hands, with bereaved relatives panicking about the fate of their dearly departed. Nor do we want to wreck the good name of a reputable company without cause.'

'I'll be careful, sir. In fact, I thought I might start with the crematorium and work backwards.'

'From the point of departure, so to speak? OK, that sounds like a plan.'

'Meanwhile, I wondered . . . well, what about a new search at Litton Foot?'

'In case we missed something the first time?'

'For one thing, there are some bones missing from Audrey Steele's remains,' said Cooper. 'There might be other evidence lying around the scene, too. Now that we have an angle on how she got there, I think we ought to take a fresh look, perhaps extend the area of the search.'

'It would only be on a limited scale, Ben.'

'I understand that, sir.'

Hitchens made a note. 'I'll get something set up.'

'Thank you.'

The DI turned back towards the window, as if he believed the meeting was over. 'At least Mrs Steele died of natural causes,' he said. 'So we're not looking at a murder enquiry here.'

Cooper thought of Vivien Gill at home on the Devonshire Estate, sitting in her smelly kitchen with her Doidy Cup and Bickiepegs.

'Well . . .' he said.

Hitchens spun round on his chair to face him. 'What? What?'

'It's just . . .' Cooper hesitated a moment under the DI's gaze. 'Well, sir, there *is* another question to be answered. If Audrey Steele's remains ended up in the woods in Ravensdale, then who was cremated in her place?'

Cooper sat down at his desk and ran a check on the Criminal Intelligence System, but without result. Apparently, unauthorized interference with corpses wasn't a common offence in Derbyshire. Who'd have guessed it? He requested a flag on any reports of similar incidents collated by intelligence officers on other forces, though he knew it would take time before there was any response.

Then he wondered what law the offence came under, and tried the legislation index. The Anatomy Act and the Human Tissues Act covered the anatomical examination of dead bodies and the removal of a dead person's organs respectively. Not really applicable. In any case, the maximum penalty under either act was three months' imprisonment, and hardly worth bothering about. He did locate a definition of a 'person lawfully in possession of the body', but even that wasn't very clear or helpful. And the only other reference he found was in Section 70 of the Sexual Offences Act – sexual penetration of a corpse. Best not to think about it.

Besides, if it turned out that Audrey Steele had been evicted from her coffin to make way for a body that hadn't died of natural causes, the minor charge might become irrelevant. The case would escalate instantly into a murder enquiry.

Cooper felt a surge of excitement when he thought of it. Everything depended on what he did in the next few days. He'd have to trawl through missing persons again, dating back eighteen months at least. If he could narrow down the list and start making some connections, he'd be getting somewhere.

First, he phoned Eden Valley Crematorium to make an appointment with the manager. It was a private sector operation, built by a company in East Anglia to meet the increasing demand for cremations. The manager's name was Lloyd, and he was available in his office all morning. Cooper picked up his car keys and notebook.

'Where are you going, Ben?' said Fry.

'The crem.'

She stopped what she was doing and stared after him as he went through the door.

'Why?' she said.

Cooper heard her, but kept going. As he closed the door behind him and set off down the corridor, he thought he could still hear her voice somewhere behind him. He'd explain to her later. She'd have to make do with partial information for a while.

* * *

Fry didn't really have time to worry about Ben Cooper. When her phone rang, it was Gavin Murfin suggesting that she come over to the CCTV control room.

'We've got something you'll want to see,' he said.

The control room staff monitored cameras covering the streets in the centre of Edendale. These cameras were mounted on high poles or on the sides of buildings, swivelling to cover a three hundred and sixty degree field of vision and capable of zooming in on suspicious individuals. Unlike the private security system at the Clappergate car park all of these cameras were functional and constantly monitored.

When Fry arrived, one of the monitoring staff was printing out some screen shots for Murfin, who looked pleased with himself.

'We've been trawling through all the CCTV footage,' he said. 'Not the car park cameras, the town centre ones. Remember we eliminated all the vehicles in the multi-storey itself? And we reckoned our man must have taken Sandra Birley out on to the street . . .'

'Yes?'

'Well, we got a possible sighting at the corner of Hardwick Lane and New Street.'

'Let's see it.'

They played back the tape for her. It had been recorded by a camera high above New Street, close to the traffic lights at the start of the pedestrianized section of Clappergate. Seven forty-five. It was pretty much dark, of course, but the street lighting was on and the quality of the image was surprisingly good. At first, there seemed to be no one in the street, only the brake lights of a car moving away from the camera position.

Then a dark shape appeared from the corner of Hardwick Lane. It seemed to be one person. But a second later, Fry realized there were two people, one much heavier and taller than the other. They were unnaturally close together, the larger with his arm around the smaller.

'Is that Sandra Birley on the left, do you think?'

'We estimate she's about the right height to fit the description,' said one of the operators. 'Dark-haired, too. And she's wearing a skirt, as you'll see in a moment.'

The smaller figure seemed to stumble, or try to pull away. As they separated, it became clear for the first time that she was a woman, wearing a dark skirt with a hem just above knee length. Then she was pulled back towards the tall man, seemed to stumble again, but regained her footing.

'There's no indication that he's threatening her with a weapon,' said Fry.

'No, sorry.'

'Maybe he didn't need to,' said Murfin. 'He's twice her size at least.'

'Why didn't she scream, though? There must have been people within earshot.'

'OK, he could be holding a knife close to her

201

body. We wouldn't see it from this angle, nor would any passers-by in the street. She wouldn't dare scream with a knife in her ribs.'

'That's possible.'

The couple made slow progress up the street. This was no quick getaway. At one point, the woman seemed to turn towards the man and speak to him. No, she was arguing with him, trying to turn back the way she'd come. He shook his head, said something, pulled her roughly along with him again. This time, the violence was more overt.

'We eliminated the Sheffield man, didn't we?' said Fry, watching the jerky footage.

'Yes. Dad's Army checked him out,' said Murfin.

'Who?'

'Oh, the temporary CID support staff.'

'Right.'

'And remember, his car was parked in the multi-storey. This one is in New Street, look –'

Then Fry saw the car. It was a light colour, barely picked out by the streetlamps on the upper edge of the camera's field of view. She peered closer, squinting at the boot and the rear wings.

'Is that a Vauxhall?'

Murfin gave her a smug smile. 'We've already blown up the screen shots and identified the model,' he said.

'Well done, Gavin.'

'It gets better. The guys here read off a partial licence plate number for me, and I ran it through the PNC just before you arrived. We've narrowed it down to two possible owners.'

Fry felt her fists clench with excitement. It was the moment of breakthrough that sometimes came when you knew you were close to making an arrest.

'Come on, Gavin. Don't hold it back.'

'It turns out that one of the possible owners of this vehicle works at Peak Mutual Insurance. A gentleman by the name of Ian Todd. He's a colleague of Sandra Birley's.'

'Where does he live?'

'In the Hathersage Road area – 28 Darton Street.'

'Excellent.'

'Darton Street isn't inside the famous six-mile zone,' said Murfin. 'It's way out.'

'Yes, Gavin.'

'So much for our profiler.'

'She's not a profiler,' said Fry automatically.

'So much for our special advisor, then. I guess her advice was just too special for me to cope with.'

As Cooper arrived at the crematorium, a hearse was creeping down the access road towards the chapel, followed by two black Daimler limousines, their gleaming paintwork streaked with raindrops. All three vehicles had personalized number plates starting with HS, indicating they belonged to Hudson and Slack.

Mourners who had already gathered under the porte-cochere to be out of the rain moved to one side to allow family members to disembark on the chapel side. By the time Cooper had parked and got out of his car, he could see Melvyn Hudson himself moving among the family, grey-haired and solemn, offering a few words of consolation.

At the side of the chapel, near the car park, was an area where the floral tributes from mourners were displayed. The day's cremations were announced by a line of name cards on metal stakes, like place markers for an absent queue. *Shirley Bramwell 10 a.m., Billy Booker 10.30 p.m., Lilian Outram 11 a.m.* Each person's slot in the schedule lasted half an hour. A cremation service was hardly an elaborate ritual, after all. It was more of a gesture, a quick farewell wave as the body passed through on its way to the flames.

Cooper noticed that the display of flowers included hearts and crosses, arrangements wired together to spell out 'Dad' or 'Nan', and a huge tribute in the shape of the Pearly Gates, with one of the gates invitingly cracked open an inch to welcome a new arrival to Heaven.

To get to the crematorium office, he'd have to pass through the porte-cochere, where the cortege had just pulled up. Rather than trying to push his way through, Cooper stood and watched as four drivers and bearers gathered at the rear of the hearse. Billy McGowan and Vernon Slack were among them, but he didn't recognize the other two. No doubt they'd be on the staff list when he eventually got around to asking Mr Hudson for one.

McGowan and the others all seemed to have flat shoulders, like shelves designed specially for carrying a coffin. Were bearers made that way, or did they develop flattened shoulders as an occupational hazard, like a police officer's bad back?

Cooper watched one of the bearers open the tailgate to reveal the coffin and its covering of flowers. None of them spoke to the mourners. Instead, they stood looking at each other, or at the ground, shuffling their feet a little, uncomfortable in their black suits and ties. McGowan looked particularly out of place. His shaved head and prominent jaw gave him an aggressive look that didn't fit the occasion at all. The collar of his white shirt was too big, and it made him seem to have no neck. Yet when a late mourner arrived with an armful of flowers wrapped in cellophane and didn't know what to do with them, it was McGowan who went across to relieve him and put his flowers into the hearse with the others.

Then began those awkward few minutes while the party waited outside for the previous service to finish and the chapel to be vacated. Everyone knew that someone else's coffin was just sliding through the curtains into the cremation suite, but they all tried to look as though they weren't aware of it. A female relative began to cry. A mourner smoking a cigarette by the roadway threw it down

205

and stubbed it out with the toe of his shoe. A thin trickle of blue smoke rose from the butt until it was dampened by the rain and died.

Cooper started to feel as though he was intruding. He didn't always find it possible to be a detached observer, unaffected by other people's grief. But it would seem odd and disrespectful just to walk away now, so he waited until the bearers had slid the coffin out of the hearse. Hudson stepped forward to help the four men raise it on to their shoulders smoothly. Then they lowered their heads in a practised movement and entered the chapel. Gradually the mourners followed them, until they had left Cooper standing on his own in the rain.

He began to walk towards the office block behind the chapel. But he was barely halfway there when the music started, and his pace slowed instinctively until he had to stop. Cooper could never hear the first hymn of a funeral service without being pierced by that sudden sense of loss. It seemed to come from nowhere, entirely unexpected, and unrelated to any thoughts that had been in his head. The feeling was somehow bound up in the music, buried deep in the raw sound of untrained voices faltering into the opening verse of 'Abide With Me'.

But it was ridiculous to be standing alone outside a crematorium chapel feeling like this. He tried to recall whose loss was being mourned. Was it Shirley Bramwell or Billy Booker? Their names had stayed in his mind, but the order of their disposal was already a blur.

In the office, he announced himself to a secretary, who told him that Mr Lloyd was engaged in a meeting, but would be with him shortly if he cared to wait. Cooper looked at his watch. It was his own fault – he was a bit early. He'd been too eager to get out of the office, even if the alternative was the crematorium.

'I'll take a walk round and come back in a few minutes,' he said. And the woman looked relieved to have him out of the building.

At least the rain was easing off a bit. The cool air felt quite refreshing as Cooper walked up the roadway to the other end of the chapel. Mourners from the previous service were still milling around in the exit, and a few of them were inspecting the floral tributes. Someone exclaimed in admiration at the Pearly Gates, even though they were from a cremation earlier in the day, a tribute to a stranger. This party was in a completely different mood from the one that had just gone in. They were chatting and laughing with relief at being outside, despite the rain. Their laughter seemed odd when another service had begun behind them, the tears and the music just starting over again for someone else.

Two limousines had been waiting here to take the family mourners away, even as the next hearse rolled into the porte-cochere. Cooper watched the two men in black frock coats who seemed to be in charge. They were a discreet presence, taking a party of mourners each, one coming in and one going out. Crematorium attendants, presumably.

As the crowd dispersed into the car park, they left only Cooper, the two Hudson and Slack limousines and their drivers, who were taking the chance to have a break. They were standing in their black suits near the cars, smoking cigarettes and chatting. Or, rather, three of them were – Billy McGowan and the other two whose names he didn't know. The exception was Vernon Slack, who'd lifted the bonnet of the leading limousine and was tinkering with something inside the engine compartment, checking the oil level or testing the tension of the fan belt.

Cooper began to walk towards him. Slack didn't look up, though he was aware of somebody approaching. He surreptitiously disposed of his cigarette in the nearest flower bed and moved back towards his limousine, pulling a yellow cloth from the pocket of his jacket. If he kept that sort of thing in his pockets, it was no wonder his suit didn't fit too well.

By the time Cooper reached him, Vernon had put the bulk of the limousine between them and was bending down to rub at the bodywork, wiping off the raindrops. He seemed to be trying to hide his face behind the wing mirror, as if afraid to look anybody in the eye.

'Mr Slack?'

From the other side of the car, the young man's

head came up. He looked worried, but he didn't answer immediately. His hand kept moving automatically over the bodywork, rubbing at the same patch with his cloth.

'Vernon, isn't it?' said Cooper. 'Vernon Slack?'

'Yes.'

The hand stopped at last. Vernon let it fall by his side, still holding the cloth.

Cooper held out his warrant card. 'There's nothing to worry about. I'm here to make some enquiries with the crematorium manager, Mr Lloyd. But I thought I recognized you from the other day. I was at Hudson and Slack with a colleague, DS Fry. Do you remember?'

'You were talking to Melvyn. It wasn't anything to do with me, was it?'

'Of course not.'

Vernon was standing in front of a back door to the chapel, or possibly it was a staff entrance to the cremation suite, which stood at right angles to it. On the door was a notice warning that anyone caught taking floral tributes would be prosecuted. Cooper wondered what sort of person would want to steal flowers from a crematorium. He hoped no one would make a mad grab for the Pearly Gates and run off with them right under his nose.

'You must spend quite a bit of time here in your job, Mr Slack,' said Cooper, smiling in an effort to put Vernon at his ease.

'Here, or at Brimington or Sheffield. It depends where they want to go.'

'I realize Hudson and Slack is a family firm from your point of view, but how long have you actually been working for the company? Would you have been around about eighteen months ago?'

Vernon's lips moved slowly, as if he was counting up to eighteen and trying to work out how long ago that was.

'March of last year,' said Cooper helpfully.

'Yes. Well, I've always helped out a bit. My dad, you know . . .'

'Yes, of course.'

Vernon's reluctance to meet his eyes made it easy for Cooper's gaze to slide past him and land on something more interesting. The door behind Vernon had glass panels, and through them Cooper could see some kind of store room. The item that had caught his attention was a brand-new microwave oven, still in its box. Presumably the cremation suite staff used it to make their lunch. With a faint queasiness in his stomach, he pictured them watching a pie turn slowly in its dish as the meat bubbled inside.

'Do you know the other bearers very well, Mr Slack?'

'Some of them. They come and go, you know how it is.'

'What about Billy McGowan?'

'Billy? I've known him for yonks. Yonks.'

'Has he worked at Hudson and Slack for a long time?'

'I can't remember how long exactly, but I know

he worked for Granddad. Billy was casual for quite a few years, then Dad gave him a full-time job.'

'Your father gave him the job, not Melvyn Hudson?'

Vernon looked down at the car, as if embarrassed at being tricked into an admission.

'Yeah.'

'Is your father still with the company?'

Vernon didn't answer, but fiddled with his cloth, itching to get polishing again. But no doubt it had been drummed into him to be courteous to people at funerals, and he seemed reluctant to make an exception, even for a police officer.

'He's dead.'

'Your father died?'

The only response was a brief nod. Vernon was starting to remind Cooper of Tom Jarvis, another man who didn't believe in wasting words. He'd seemed sullen at first, but now Vernon was just smiling and smiling. Not with pleasure, but with anxiety. His expression was a perpetual grimace of apology.

Suddenly he looked past Cooper and his expression changed to one of relief, as if the cavalry had arrived.

Cooper hadn't heard any footsteps behind him. He hated it when his alertness slipped so much that someone was able to creep up on him. As a result, he hadn't even begun to turn round when a hand landed on his arm.

14

An unmarked car was already in position in Darton Street, parked a few doors down from number 28 to keep surveillance on the front door.

DI Hitchens picked up the radio handset. 'Is he still at home?'

'The suspect entered the house about twenty minutes ago, and we haven't seen him come out again.'

'What about a rear exit?'

'He'd have to go over the garden wall, sir. But there's a unit in the back alley, just in case.'

'Good. Remember, this individual could be armed, so no one goes near him without a vest on. Understood? Just stay out of the way and let the arrest team deal with him.'

'Understood.'

'Here's the van now,' said Diane Fry, as a police Transit pulled into the end of the street and officers in bulletproof vests deployed from the rear doors.

In a few more minutes, the scene would be contained, and ready for the execution of a safe and uneventful arrest. With Ian Todd removed from the scene, they could bring in the SOCOs and search teams. But would Sandra Birley still be alive somewhere?

It was more than sixty hours since Sandra had been taken from the multi-storey car park. Two days and three nights – more than enough for her abductor to carry out whatever he had in mind. Although his supervisor at Peak Mutual confirmed that Todd had been working as normal during those two days, his job involved spending several hours on the road each day, visiting clients across North Derbyshire.

In any case, the nights had been entirely free for him to pursue his activities. He was unmarried and lived alone, so there was no one at home demanding an account of his whereabouts, or to question the condition of his car or his clothing. He could have taken his victim anywhere during that first night, before she was even reported missing. She could be at the other end of the country.

But Fry didn't think that was the case. She thought Sandra Birley would be found within a few miles of Edendale, in a six-mile radius of Wardlow. Ian Todd had been ideally placed to make the phone calls. He had been on the road in his light green Vauxhall Vectra when both those calls had been made.

That Vectra stood on the drive of number 28 now. Shortly, it would become a crime scene and Forensics could give it a going-over.

Then the radio crackled back into life.

'He's out of the house, sir, going for the car. He must have seen us.'

'Who the hell blew it?' shouted Hitchens. 'Never mind – get moving. Block him in and we'll take him now, before he gets his vehicle on to the street.'

The unmarked car started up and pulled away from the kerb with a squeal of tyres. The surveillance team were only yards from the driveway of number 28 and within seconds they had blocked Ian Todd's exit. He looked up and saw them coming just as he reached his Vectra and thumbed the remote on his keyfob.

Fry was out of her door and standing in the road. She had a good view of Todd as he momentarily froze in his garden. He was tall, about six feet two, she guessed, and strongly built. But right now he looked scared.

'He's going to leg it,' she said.

'Diane, don't go near him,' said Hitchens. 'You're not wearing a vest.'

But in the end, she didn't have to go near Ian Todd at all. He glanced from one end of the street to the other, taking in Fry and the police vehicles. And then he ran towards the marked van, where four officers in uniforms and bulletproof vests were advancing towards him. He met them a few

214

yards down the road, and two of them took hold of his arms, turned him round and handcuffed him. Fry saw his face then. He looked more surprised than frightened.

'Well, he must have thought you looked really scary,' said Gavin Murfin, arriving at Fry's shoulder. 'He took one look at you and ran the other way.'

'You shouldn't be here, Gavin,' she said. 'You're not wearing a vest.'

'He's handcuffed. What's he going to do, kill me with his evil stare?'

Fry scrutinized Ian Todd's house. It looked ordinary enough, but what killer's home didn't?

As Fry walked up the drive to the house, the front door opened. She stopped, suddenly conscious that Todd might have had an accomplice. If there was a second person involved and they were armed, she was completely exposed. She was appalled at herself for making such an elementary error.

Then, from the shadows of the hallway, a woman emerged and stood on the step. She was dark-haired and attractive, with a startled look in her eyes. They stood frozen, staring at each other, until Fry felt the initial surge of shock give way to anger. She stepped forward and held out her warrant card.

'Detective Sergeant Fry, Edendale Police,' she said. 'And you, I believe, are Mrs Sandra Birley.'

*　　*　　*

215

'Excuse me. Detective Constable Cooper?'

Cooper turned to find a man in a dark suit standing behind him. Another funeral director's assistant? But no . . .

'I'm Christopher Lloyd, the crematorium manager.'

'Oh, Mr Lloyd. Thank you for taking the time to talk to me.'

Lloyd looked at Vernon Slack. 'Come inside. It'll be a little less public.'

Another funeral party was gathering, even while the previous one was less than halfway through its service. Because they couldn't go into the chapel, the mourners were milling about outside near the porte-cochere. They'd be in the way when the hearse arrived, but no doubt there would be someone whose job it was to herd them in the right direction.

The cremation suite itself stood at right angles to the chapel, with frosted windows under its square chimney stack. Inside, it had an inevitable industrial feel. The main room was dominated by two giant stainless-steel ovens with sliding doors just wide enough to take a coffin.

Cooper had only ever seen one cremator before, and that had been in Germany – a huge thing, fed by a machine built into the floor with an overhead crane to lift coffins into place, while others waited in line, as if on a conveyor belt. But the one he was looking at now was smaller. The only way of loading the coffins was by hand from a hydraulic bier.

To one side, he saw a computer control desk and a cremator operator wearing heat-resistant gloves and an aluminium apron. There was very little smell, except for the aroma of hot brick and metal from the ovens and the heat exchanger behind them.

'Now, what would you like to know?' said Lloyd. 'Would it help if I began with a brief description of the way we operate?'

'Yes, sir. For a start, does the body always stay with the coffin after it arrives here?'

'Without exception. Our code of practice requires the coffin to be placed in the cremator exactly as received. When a coffin arrives in the committal room, it's labelled with a card that accompanies the body right through until final disposal.'

'How long does that process take?'

'A modern gas-fired cremator can deal with the average body in half an hour.'

'And the ashes?'

'The cremains,' corrected Lloyd. 'Well, when they come out of the chamber, they consist mostly of bone residue. Sixty per cent of bone is non-burnable material, so at that stage there'll be a number of bone fragments.'

Cooper was shown a cooling tray where bone residue was run under a magnet to sift out wedding rings and scraps of melted jewellery. When Lloyd lifted the lid, the cremated bones inside looked the colour and consistency of meringue – pale grey, granular and brittle. In places, their shape was still visible, but Cooper felt sure they would crumble at a touch.

They passed through into what Lloyd called the preparation room, where an electric pulverizer was used to reduce the bone fragments to ash. Now the grey material looked more like fine cat litter, the sort that Randy always refused to use.

'From a man, we get an average weight of about seven and a half pounds of bone residue, and from a woman just under six pounds,' said Lloyd.

'So gender is reduced to a difference in bone structure, in the final analysis?'

'You might put it that way, I suppose.'

Cooper filed that one away for future reference. It might be something he could point out to Diane Fry at a suitable moment.

'Is it possible for the ashes from two different people to get mixed up, Mr Lloyd?'

The manager shook his head. 'Everyone worries about getting the right ashes. They think more than one coffin might be cremated at a time, but that isn't so. We're not allowed to do that, and in any case it's impossible. The cremator will only take one coffin at a time, and the ashes have to be withdrawn before it's used again.'

'But you have more than one cremator here, don't you?'

'Two,' admitted Lloyd. 'But it isn't often that both are in use, unless we have a really busy day. We need two so we can still operate when one of them is shut down for maintenance.'

Cooper looked into the committal room, where the coffins slid through from the chapel on silent rollers.

'And when you do get a busy day,' he said, 'the bodies must arrive in here faster than the staff can get them in and out of the cremator.'

Now Lloyd looked worried. 'Well, yes.'

'So you must have to store coffins in here for a while before they're cremated. Cremation doesn't happen straight after the service, as people imagine?'

'Well . . .'

'You see, I've always pictured the flames waiting behind an oven door that opens as soon as those curtains close. But actually, the coffin probably just gets put on a shelf for a while.'

'Not for long. The code of practice requires cremations to take place on the same day as the service, wherever possible.'

'The same day?'

Lloyd swallowed. 'Wherever possible.'

'But you could have bodies stacking up in here all day until you get a chance to clear the backlog?'

'It isn't like that. Not in a well-managed crematorium.'

'Is there always someone in here?'

'The cremator should never be left unattended.'

'Is that in the code of practice, too?'

'Yes,' said Lloyd stiffly. 'Is there anything more I can do for you?'

'Two more things,' said Cooper. 'First, I'd like

details of staff members who have access to the cremation suite.'

'All of them?'

'Going back eighteen months, to the beginning of last March.'

'I'll need authority from my company's head office to release personnel information, but we should be able to manage that.'

'Also, I'll need a list of cremations that took place here on Monday the eighth of March last year.'

'It might take some time to produce the lists. We're very busy today.'

'You can fax them to me,' said Cooper. 'The number is on my card.'

He paused at the door of the cremation suite and sniffed the air. 'It's funny, Mr Lloyd, but I expected more of a smell in here.'

Lloyd blinked, as if he'd already dismissed Cooper from his mind. 'There are automatic controls built into the system to maintain a slightly negative pressure in the cremation chamber,' he said.

'What does that mean?'

'It means we make sure any unpleasant odours don't leak out. They're kept firmly on the inside.'

Back at the office, Cooper picked up the phone on his desk and rang through to Scenes of Crime. He was in luck for once – Liz Petty answered.

'Liz, is it possible to identify cremated remains using DNA?' he said.

'Nope. Cremation destroys DNA. The lab can't get anything usable from cremation remains.'

'That's a pity.'

'Well, don't despair, Ben. There's another possibility.'

'Yes?'

'One thing the public doesn't realize about cremation is that teeth stay pretty much intact, even after the bone residue has been pulverized. If you poke about a bit in the urn, you can often find a few teeth, fillings, posts, that sort of thing.'

Cooper raised an eyebrow. 'I think that probably counts as one of the things the public doesn't *want* to know.'

'I expect you're right. But it might be useful, eh? You could get some partial dental mapping done. Artificial teeth are more difficult to destroy than natural teeth, so if your deceased person had crowns or bridgework, you might be in luck. Sometimes, it only needs one tooth.'

'Hoping for another match from dental records?' said Cooper. 'But I need to get a possible ID first.'

'Of course. But you've already trawled through the mispers for that period, haven't you? When you were trying to ID Audrey Steele's remains.'

'A lot of good that will do me,' said Cooper. 'Skeletonized remains are one thing – at least the experts can come up with information on age, height, gender, racial background. And I was lucky that I got a facial reconstruction done, otherwise Audrey Steele would have remained unidentified. But tell me – how do I go about obtaining a biological identity from a few pounds of bone ash?'

The list of cremations was the first to come through on the fax machine. Eight names and addresses, complete with details of next of kin and the funeral director responsible for the arrangements. In addition to Audrey Steele, that meant seven more dead people with bereaved families.

'Maybe that was the point,' said Fry, when Cooper briefed her on his progress.

'What was?'

'Well, somebody was willing to risk Audrey Steele's remains being identified and traced, weren't they?'

'It was a very small risk. We were lucky with the reconstruction.'

'Nevertheless, the risk was there. And the only reason I can think of that somebody might take that risk would be if they were convinced it would be impossible for us to identify the second body.'

'It's not entirely impossible,' said Cooper. 'With time, effort and perseverance . . .'

'Impractical, then,' said Fry. 'You know how many missing persons there are on the files, Ben. You have no way of narrowing them down. And there's always the possibility that it was someone who was never reported missing.'

Cooper sighed. 'You're right. I suppose I might

be able to make more progress if I come at it from another angle.'

Fry leaned back in her chair. 'And what if there never was another body? You might be approaching this from a false assumption, Ben. The explanation could be something much more prosaic.'

'How do you mean?'

'Well, imagine for a moment that something went badly wrong at the crematorium that day, and one or more people took a lot of trouble to cover it up. In other words, a cock-up rather than a conspiracy.'

'No,' said Cooper. 'That's a cock-up *and* a conspiracy.'

'Whatever. But there might not have been an extra body to dispose of at all. Do you see what I mean?'

'So whose ashes would be in Audrey Steele's urn?'

Fry began to warm to her theory. 'Maybe they just shared out the ashes that they already had. How many other cremations took place that day?'

'Seven.'

'Well, that's enough, don't you think? A few ashes from one cremation, a few from another. You'd soon have an extra urn full enough to convince a relative.'

'Ashes from several bodies mixed together?' said Cooper thoughtfully. 'Mr Lloyd admitted himself it's the biggest concern that families have at a cremation.'

'There you go, then. Perhaps he has a guilty conscience.'

But Cooper shook his head. 'Hold on, Diane – the computer records show a normal burn time and a normal weight of residue. I've got a printout in the file.'

'Are you telling me that computer records can't be falsified?'

'If you knew what you were doing, I suppose . . .'

'Well, before you go off looking for a murder victim who never existed, you might want to take a look at those other cremations,' said Fry. 'See if you can track down the ashes and let Forensics do some comparisons. All you need is one match between urns and your body-swap theory goes up in flames.'

Cooper looked at her to see if she was joking, but she wasn't. 'That's going to take time, Diane.'

'I know. But you don't need to get anyone's life story, just their urns – if they still have them.'

'Even so –'

'Ben, it's preferable to the amount of time and resources that could be wasted if we initiate a futile murder enquiry.'

'All right. I'll get on to it.'

'Fine.'

As Fry got up to leave, Cooper asked her: 'By the way, is there any progress on the Birley enquiry?'

She nodded. 'Right now, we've got Sandra

Birley and her supposed abductor sitting in interview rooms downstairs.'

'Mrs Birley is alive and well?'

'Very much so. And she has some explaining to do.'

When Fry had moved out of earshot, Gavin Murfin leaned across the desk. 'It wasn't entirely luck that we got an ID for Audrey Steele, though, was it?' he said. 'It was your persistence that made the difference, Ben. Most other people would have given up, like Miss wanted you to. She ought to have acknowledged that, at least.'

'It doesn't matter, Gavin.'

Murfin sniffed. 'You're too tolerant by half.'

'I can't be bothered about it now. I've got some difficult visits to make.'

Cooper hoped that eighteen months had been long enough for the bereaved families to come to terms with their loss. He might be about to intrude on their grief in a big way.

15

Cooper didn't need prompting this time before seating himself in one of the low armchairs in Vivien Gill's sitting room – he'd already seen the blinds separating across the road. The baby seemed to be either sleeping or being looked after somewhere else, because he wasn't taken through into the kitchen. That didn't mean he couldn't smell it, though.

'Mrs Gill, this is a bit difficult,' he said. 'But you're aware that we found your daughter's remains. The identification has been confirmed from dental records.'

'Yes, I understand that. It's been explained to me.'

'Well, the thing is, the ashes that you have –' Cooper indicated the urn on the dresser. 'Obviously, in the circumstances, they can't be Audrey's.'

Mrs Gill nodded. 'Yes, I'd thought of that. I'm not stupid.'

'We'd like to take them away and analyse them.'

'You think you can find out whose ashes they really are?'

'It might be possible. And that could help us to find out who . . . well, who took your daughter's body.'

Vivien Gill looked at the urn. 'It's funny, but I almost want to keep it, even though I know it isn't Audrey. It's not as if I've spent my time looking at the ashes themselves, just at the urn.'

Cooper held up his hands. 'The urn is yours. But before long, you could have the genuine ashes to put in it, if that's what you want.'

'Oh, take it. I'll think about whether I want it back, and I'll let you know.'

'Thank you.'

Mrs Gill motioned him to stay seated and fetched the urn herself. Before Cooper could speak, she slid off the lid and looked in.

'Strange, isn't it?' she said. 'What we're reduced to.'

'Yes. If I may . . .?'

Cooper took a large plastic bag from his pocket and carefully slipped the urn in, before filling out a receipt. The lid didn't look particularly secure, so he'd have to be careful to keep it upright in the car. The lab wouldn't be happy to get only half an exhibit, with the rest scattered in his footwell or down the back of a seat.

'Mrs Gill, do you remember anything unusual about the service at the crematorium?'

'How do you mean?'

'Well, were there any mourners you didn't know, for example?'

'There were some of Audrey's friends from the hospital that I hadn't met before. Nurses, you know. But apart from that, I knew pretty much everybody. It wasn't a big do.'

'And apart from the mourners?'

'Well, Batman was there.'

'Who?'

'Batman. Bloke with a black suit, miserable expression, travels in a big car with a lot of space in the back.'

Cooper was baffled, until he saw Mrs Gill watching him with a sharp expression, like a bird. He had a feeling he was being tested.

'The undertaker,' she said. 'Melvyn Hudson.'

'Funeral director is the title he prefers, I believe. So Mr Hudson was there?'

'Of course he was there. He had to do all the business, didn't he? Make sure nothing went wrong. That's his job.'

'And *did* anything go wrong?'

She looked away, as if she suddenly had to check on the weather outside the window.

'Vernon Slack was driving the hearse. God, that lad – it's obvious he only got a job with the firm because his grandfather is part-owner.'

'He can drive a car all right, can't he?'

'Oh, cars he's fine with, and he can lift a coffin as well as the rest of them. But that's about all.

He's useless around the mourners. Doesn't know what to say, doesn't know what expression to have on his face, doesn't know where to put his hands. He's a complete embarrassment. Melvyn does his best to keep him out of the way. And out of sight, as much as possible.'

'How do you know Vernon Slack?'

'Everybody knows the Hudsons and the Slacks. They've been in business in Edendale for ages.'

Vivien Gill seemed to be taking everything very well. But Cooper had learned that an apparent calmness could be deceptive. At any moment the grief might spurt out, like blood gushing from a severed artery.

'Please tell me,' said Mrs Gill. 'I don't understand. Why would anyone want to steal Audrey's body?'

'We don't know. It may have been . . . well, incidental to something else.'

'Incidental?'

'Yes.'

Mrs Gill frowned as she turned the word over in her mind. She seemed to be trying to get to grips with the idea that her daughter's body could have been merely an accessory to somebody else's obsession, a minor stage prop in a scene where the spotlight fell on a different star. Audrey had been so central to her life that she would never be able to manage the shift of perspective. Cooper saw her frown fade as she gave up the effort.

'But we'll be able to do everything properly now,

won't we?' she said. 'We can have Audrey back and do it properly.'

'That will be up to the coroner. But since there's no evidence that your daughter's death was anything but natural, I'm sure the remains will be released soon. Have you thought about whether you'll have a cremation again, or perhaps a burial?'

'No cremation,' said Mrs Gill. 'I know what I'm going to do this time. I'm going to go for a green burial.'

'What a good idea. There's a green burial site near Lowbridge, isn't there?'

'That's the one I'm going to use. I've already contacted them.'

'I'm glad you're looking at it practically. That's the best way.'

'I think so. The others aren't so keen, but they'll lump it.'

'The others?'

'I've got quite a big family. Audrey's family.'

Cooper took the urn out to his car. After a moment's thought, he put it in the rear footwell and packed it in tightly to stop it moving or falling over while he was driving. He would have preferred to take it straight back to West Street, but he had some other calls to make first.

Ian Todd sat in the interview room with a duty solicitor. He seemed a little smaller when he was sitting down, but he was still one of the guiltiest-looking people Fry had ever seen. He had the sort of fleshy face that made a man look untrustworthy, like a used-car salesman. If he'd been wearing one of those tight, dark suits cut too high at the lapels, she'd have known to cross the road to avoid him.

'Why is Mr Todd under arrest?' said the solicitor, as soon as the tapes were running.

'On suspicion of the abduction and unlawful detention of Mrs Sandra Birley,' said Fry.

'I didn't abduct anybody,' said Todd. 'That's ludicrous.'

'Mr Todd, we have photographic evidence of you leaving the Clappergate car park on Tuesday night with Sandra Birley, who failed to return home that night. Since then, there has been no word from Mrs Birley, no contact with her husband or anyone else. Today, we find Mrs Birley in your house. Can you explain that?'

Todd leaned forward suddenly and slapped his hands on the table. No one looked nervous, except the solicitor.

'Did Sandra say she was abducted?'

'We're getting a statement from Mrs Birley now,' said Fry.

'Ha! That means she hasn't said she was abducted.' Todd turned to his solicitor. 'She hasn't made a complaint,' he said. 'How can they arrest me?'

'It's a good question, Sergeant,' said the solicitor. 'What evidence do you have to justify a charge against Mr Todd?'

'I've just told you –'

'None of what you said constitutes evidence of abduction or unlawful detention. Unless you have a statement to the contrary from the lady you mention. In which case, my client will dispute it.'

'Mr Todd has some explaining to do,' said Fry calmly.

'Not unless –'

Todd held up a hand. 'It's OK. Let's have it sorted out and then I can get out of here.'

'Go ahead then, Mr Todd. We're listening.'

'Well, far from abducting Sandra Birley, I'd arranged to meet her on Tuesday night after work. But she was late. So I went to the Clappergate car park, and I waited for her. When she arrived, we walked to my car, which was parked in New Street. Sandra came home with me and she stayed for three days. And that's it. Can I go now?'

'What was the purpose of your meeting?' said Fry.

'That's personal. It's none of your business.' He looked at the solicitor again. 'It's none of their business, is it? They can't ask me about that.'

'The officers can ask. But you're not obliged to answer.'

'Were you having an affair with Mrs Birley?' said Fry.

'It's not an affair,' said Todd. 'She was coming away with me. Well, coming to live with me. She's leaving her husband.'

'She doesn't seem to have told her husband that.'

Todd shrugged. 'She would have got round to it.'

The tapes continued to turn in the silence as Fry struggled to contain her anger. For three days she'd been convinced that Sandra Birley had been abducted and murdered by a psychotic killer who was taunting the police with his sick phone calls. She had failed to get in touch with anyone during that time. *She would have got round it* made her angry. She wondered if she could learn some breathing techniques from Melvyn Hudson.

Now, this was an interesting room. On the middle shelf at about eye level was a six-sided terrarium with stained-glass panels and openings for variegated ivy to trail through. Next to it was a less elaborate container with straight sides and less vegetation, sitting among a selection of coffee-table books and Chinese vases. It wasn't until he was sitting on the sofa that Cooper noticed the focal point of this terrarium. It was a small chameleon, vivid green and standing perfectly still.

At least, it *looked* like a chameleon. The only thing he knew about the species was that they were supposed to change colour to blend in with their background. If this one was real, shouldn't it be light grey, like the material covering the floor of the terrarium? Or a dark pine colour, like the varnish on the shelving?

While Cooper watched, it didn't so much as blink. Was it actually alive?

'The ashes came in a plastic urn,' said Mrs Askew. 'We decided to do something a bit different and display them. He would have liked it, I think.'

At first, Cooper didn't know what she meant. Then his gaze strayed past Mrs Askew's head to the bookshelves. He thought the chameleon had moved, perhaps raised a front leg to allow the passage of air under its belly. It might only have been a slight shift that had attracted his attention. Or it could have been the realization that the material on the floor of the terrarium was a light grey, granular material, like fine cat litter.

Mrs Askew followed the direction of his gaze. 'Seven pounds of ashes go a surprisingly long way,' she said. 'There were even a few ounces left over, so I shared them out into a set of little brass boxes that I found in an antique shop near the Buttercross. I gave a box to each of his grandchildren. That's the best way to be remembered, I think – to have your memory passed down through the generations of your own family. Don't you agree?'

'Yes, I'm sure you're right.'

Of course, Cooper had immediately thought of his own father. It was an instinctive reaction when someone mentioned keeping the memory of a family member alive. It didn't seem to trouble him the way it once had. He found he could even think of the practicalities – whether it would have been better if Sergeant Joe Cooper had been cremated, rather than buried in Edendale Cemetery. And how much his ashes would have weighed, if he had. More than eight pounds, certainly. Plenty to have shared out into little boxes for everyone. And then, perhaps, his father's memory wouldn't have weighed quite so heavily on one pair of shoulders.

There were several Venus flytraps growing in the other terrarium. Cooper could see their thick triangular bases and the teeth on their traps. They looked capable of ensnaring something the size of a bumble bee, let alone a fly.

'Do you know anything about carnivorous plants?' asked Mrs Askew, noting his gaze and assuming interest, the way people did.

'No. Do they catch many flies?'

'Each leaf can catch and digest three meals before it dies,' said Mrs Askew. 'Leaves can open and close without catching anything, but eventually they exhaust themselves.'

'Only three meals in their lives? No matter how big they are?'

'If a meal is very large, the effort of digestion can be too much. Then the leaf dies without ever re-opening.'

Cooper had always hated flies, but he found himself feeling sorry for them – especially the ones that ended up trapped and half-digested inside the leaves of a dying plant.

Mrs Askew pointed into the terrarium.

'There's a leaf at the back that caught a fly about a week ago. It's just re-opening now, look.'

Cooper peered between the teeth of the flytrap

into the fleshy mouth, and saw that the plant had finished digesting its meal. All that remained on the leaf was the dried-out husk of its prey. The fly's brittle wings and the shell of its thorax had been left intact, but its body had been sucked empty of its juices. The insect had been digested alive.

'Interesting, isn't it?' said Mrs Askew with a smile.

Cooper turned, hardly daring to look at her face. He felt that sense of unease again, a discomfort in the presence of an unnatural fascination with death.

'Mrs Askew, I have to go now,' he said. 'I have other people to visit.'

She looked disappointed. 'Oh, well, if you must. But do call back if there's anything else you want to ask me.'

'Thank you. I'll do that.'

She waited on the doorstep and watched him leave. As he got into his car, Cooper looked back and waved. He wished Mrs Askew wouldn't keep smiling quite so much. He was starting to find the sight of her bared teeth a bit disturbing.

David Royce had his brother-in-law's ashes somewhere, if only he could remember where he'd put them.

'What's in this cage?' called Cooper as he waited in the sitting room for Mr Royce to search the cupboard under the stairs. The cage was covered completely, so it might be empty. But Cooper thought he could hear a faint clicking of claws.

'That's Smoky. He's an African Grey.'

'You have a parrot?' Cooper tried to remember the last time he'd seen a parrot in a cage in someone's house. There *had* been one a while ago, but he couldn't recall where. And somehow David Royce didn't seem the type to keep a cage bird at all. A large dog, perhaps. A Rottweiler called Tyson or Satan. But a parrot?

'My sister asked me to have it,' said Royce, his voice muffled by the interior of the cupboard. 'It belonged to Jack. But after he died, she couldn't bear to have it in the house. He taught the thing to speak, you see. And it copied his voice perfectly. It has the sound of him off pat, believe me.'

'They're very good mimics.'

'Good? It's bloody frightening. Well, Joan couldn't stand hearing the old man's voice in the house when she knew he was dead. It was tearing her up, poor lass. Every time she came home, she heard his voice. I didn't really want the thing myself, but I couldn't refuse, could I?'

'What does it say?'

'I wouldn't claim it has a wide vocabulary exactly,' said Royce.

He came back into the room and pulled the cover off the cage. The parrot opened its eyes and looked at Cooper.

'Hello, sweetheart,' it said. 'Where's Jack?'

Then it switched its attention to scratching

under its feathers with the claws of one foot, and Royce went back to his search.

'Is that it?'

'Well, I haven't tried to engage it in conversation,' said Royce. 'But sometimes it says "crap" if it doesn't like what's on the telly.'

'And is that often?'

'Yes.'

'They live a lot longer than people, don't they?' said Cooper.

'Do they?' Royce sounded surprised. 'Bloody hell. I was hoping it'd die a natural death before too long, like my kids' hamsters do.'

'Not parrots. They can live to over a hundred. Winston Churchill had one, and it died only last year. It was a hundred and five.'

'I bet Churchill didn't teach his parrot to say *crap*.'

'I wouldn't be too sure.'

Cooper went out into the hall to see what progress David Royce was making. All kinds of stuff had been pulled out of the cupboard: toys, boxes of shoes, a spare TV set, the ironing board.

'I think it might be upstairs,' Royce said.

'Can I help you to look?'

'Yes, take a wardrobe.'

After another ten minutes, Royce decided they must have scattered the ashes in the garden and thrown the urn away.

'Sorry,' he said.

'Don't worry about it.'

Cooper walked back into the sitting room. At least the parrot remembered its owner, even if it had survived him. In fact, if it was a young bird, it might outlast everyone now living in Derbyshire. Winston Churchill's parrot had seen out not only its owner but nine other prime ministers, right up to Tony Blair. To a parrot, people must seem to come and go like flies in summer.

As he passed the cage, the parrot stopped scratching and fixed Cooper with a sharp eye.

'Crap,' it said. 'Where's Jack?'

In the next house, a row of unmatching straight-backed chairs stood in the bay window, as if set out for an audience at a performance. Then Cooper noticed that other incongruous furniture had been crammed into the room between the sofa and the armchairs – a wrought-iron seat from the conservatory, an office-style swivel chair, and a low, squishy object that his mother would have called a pouffe. A long table had been pushed against the far wall and was loaded with plates and dishes covered with cling film or draped in tea towels.

'I hope I'm not intruding,' he said. 'Is it a bad moment?'

'It's my mum's funeral today. But it's OK, we've got everything ready early,' said Susan Dakin.

'People are coming back here after the funeral?'

'Of course. We don't know who's going to turn up exactly. I don't suppose there'll be many.'

It felt as though the Dakins were preparing for

a party. At one time, a death would have meant a silent house and hushed voices. Not here, though. Susan Dakin seemed entirely content that her mother should be joining her father, wherever he'd gone.

Later, Cooper visited a bungalow at Southwoods where two old women with tight perms sat eating Belgian chocolates shaped like sea horses. He called on a Hucklow couple who had lost their child in a road accident and had never spoken about it since scattering her ashes in the paddock where her pony still grazed.

'My grandma used to say we should draw the curtains and cover the mirrors, as a sign of respect,' said one of the old women, licking a coating of chocolate from her finger. 'But I say that's just daft. Life goes on, doesn't it?'

'She still lives in my heart,' said the child's mother. 'Every day.'

In a house on Manchester Road he met a mother and daughter who both wore cropped jeans and ankle chains, and a ring through the right nostril. It was almost as if they were trying to look like sisters. But where the girl had a studded belt and jeans cut low enough to reveal bony hips, the mother had a smooth roll of fat. The daughter was fashionably pale, but her mother was tanned – though it was the sort of tan gained in a cubicle on the High Street at thirty-nine pence a minute.

'It can bring you closer,' they said, almost together. The father had nothing to say. His ashes were in the brass urn they allowed Cooper to sign for.

His last visit was to the Devonshire Estate again, where Maureen Connolly told him that her sister had stolen their mother's ashes.

'She had no right to take them. They belonged to me. Good riddance to her, I say. She was always a tart, anyway. My only consolation is that she'll be suffering for it, wherever she is.'

'She's dead?'

'No, not her. Last I heard, she was living on some council estate in Derby with four snotty kids by two different blokes – both of them in prison. One or the other will do for her when he comes out, unless she drinks herself to death first.'

'When did you last see her?'

'See her? Not for almost a year. Oh, she rang me a few weeks ago. Wanting money, naturally. She must have been down to the last dregs, or she wouldn't have bothered with me. Desperation, that was. I never doubted it, no matter what she said.'

Mrs Connolly pressed her lips together in an expression of satisfaction. It wouldn't do to smile, of course. It wasn't nice to be seen enjoying someone else's misfortune. But her face came as close to a smile as was permissible.

'I don't suppose you have an address?' said Cooper.

'I didn't ask her for it – why should I? Besides, she's probably moved by now. Persuaded the council to give her a different house somewhere, hoping she can't be found. Some hopes.'

'Well, I can see there's no love lost between you and your sister,' said Cooper, ignoring the look of derision on her face at his understatement. 'But aren't you at all concerned about what might happen to her children?'

'Why? They're nothing to do with me.'

'They're your nephews and nieces.'

Mrs Connolly snorted. 'Nephews and nieces?'

She leaned closer, her face communicating a mixture of disgust and triumph.

'Two of them,' she said, 'are black. Almost.'

Cooper was sweating by the time he got back into his car. The effort of remaining polite and sympathetic in Maureen Connolly's house had been almost intolerable. Now he felt more depressed than he had in any of the places where death had been all around him. The professional morbidity of the funeral parlour, the intellectual prurience of Freddy Robertson, the cremated remains as an interior-design feature. None of them had seemed so negative, or so tragic, as the things that people could do to each other in life.

16

'Of course, while we were all feeling sorry for Geoff Birley, what he didn't bother telling us was that Sandra had been threatening to leave him for some time,' Fry said in the DI's office. 'He says he didn't believe she meant it, that she would never really leave him.'

'He was fooling himself, then,' said Hitchens.

Fry shook her head. 'Actually, no. Sandra agrees with him. She says she wasn't planning to leave her husband at all, just to stay away for a night or two to teach him a lesson. In fact, she was planning to phone him today. The Birleys might have been back together by tonight.'

'But what about Ian Todd? He's Sandra's lover, surely?'

'There's certainly more to the relationship than being just good friends, as they'd like us to believe,' said Fry. 'Todd wants Sandra to leave her husband and stay with him permanently. But, as for *her*, well . . .' Fry shook her head. 'Who are we to try to understand other people's relation-ships? A lot of us don't understand our own.'

'So the business in the car park – what was that all about?'

'Sandra had arranged to meet Ian Todd in the pub after work, before they went back to his place in Darton Street. But she was kept late at the office by a meeting that over-ran. Naturally, Todd thought she'd changed her mind. He couldn't get hold of Sandra on her mobile, because she had it turned off while she was in the meeting. So he went to the car park to see if he could catch her on her way home. When he found Sandra's Skoda on Level 8, he decided to wait for her. And by then, *he* was out of contact because there was no mobile signal on his network inside that multi-storey.'

'Why didn't he wait by Sandra's car?' said Hitchens. 'That would have been the logical thing to do.'

'He said he didn't want to give her a chance to get away,' said Fry. 'So he waited by the lift. He felt sure she'd come up that way, and he wanted her to see him as soon as the doors opened.'

'He doesn't know Sandra quite as well as her husband does, then.'

'No.'

'I suppose it all fits. But it's a pain in the neck that people can't sort their lives out without giving us all this trouble.'

'It's not sorted out quite yet. Mr Todd is seriously pissed off at this moment.'

'I'm not surprised,' said Hitchens. 'Not only has he been used as a pawn in a row between the Birleys, but he's been pulled in and questioned by us on suspicion of a serious crime that he didn't commit.'

Fry remembered the snatch of CCTV footage from the camera in New Street, the two figures walking towards Ian Todd's car. She recalled a brief struggle, a woman apparently trying to break free from the grasp of a man much bigger and stronger than she was.

'It won't do him any harm,' she said.

Fry had been away from the DI's office for only a few minutes when Hitchens threw open the door again and shouted for her. When she went back in, he was on the phone. He talked to her while holding the phone to his ear.

'What's happened, sir?'

'There's been another call.'

'From the same man?'

'Sounds like it.'

'Have you got a trace on it?'

'What do you think I'm doing?'

Fry folded her arms and waited.

'Yes?' shouted Hitchens into the phone. 'It's where? OK, yes. I've got it. I want units there *now*. They're to seal off the area around the payphone, and make sure no one leaves.' Hitchens listened, raising his eyes to the ceiling. 'Yes, I realize there'll be a funeral going on. I'm not asking them to wade in with their batons out and lob CS gas at the mourners. They can be as discreet as they damn well like. They can take flowers and hand out sympathy cards, if they want. But no one leaves until we've had a chance to talk to them.'

He slammed down the phone and pulled on his jacket.

'Not another funeral?' said Fry.

'Yes, another funeral,' said Hitchens. 'This time, he called from a public payphone in the visitors' waiting area at Eden Valley Crematorium.'

'You think our man is actually attending the service?' said Fry in the car on the way to the crematorium.

'He'd be conspicuous if he didn't. Have you ever been to the crem, Diane?'

'No, sir.'

'Well, this is quite different from the situation at Wardlow. There's no way you can give the impression you're just passing. Our man will have had to drive through the crematorium grounds to the visitors' car park and then walk up to the chapel entrance. And it's not as if you could pretend you were visiting the crematorium for some other reason. There'd be other mourners there. They might well notice someone who turned up, then went away again.'

'What if he was making a delivery or something?'

'A delivery of what?'

'I don't know – they must bring in supplies of

some kind. Aren't there offices at the crematorium?'

'At the back, but there's a separate entrance. Delivery drivers don't mingle with the hearses and mourners. You'll see.'

The public payphone was in a small foyer on the far side of the porte-cochère from the chapel entrance. Beyond the foyer were toilets and a quiet room containing a book of remembrance.

'We'll have to get Forensics to give it the works. If we're really lucky, they might lift a print to match one from the phone box at Wardlow.'

'The prints were all very indistinct at Wardlow. No one would be willing to swear to a match. There's no way they could find enough points of similarity.'

'We can hope, anyway,' said Hitchens.

'The good news,' said Wayne Abbott when they arrived, 'is that this payphone has been cleaned more recently than the phone box at Wardlow. So we have fewer prints, less overlay, less smudging. We've found a few latents for you already, and we're dusting the walls for more. We may not be able to match anything up with Wardlow, but some of these prints are clear enough to make an ID if you can produce a suspect.'

'It always comes back to us, doesn't it?'

'Hey, it's your job to provide the bodies, Inspector. We're not *CSI: Miami*, you know. We do our bit, then we go and sit in the van and have a cup of tea while we wait for you blokes to make the arrest. That's real life, that is.'

247

'What funeral was going on here?' asked Fry.

A PC was standing nearby with a notebook. 'This was the cremation of a child,' he said. 'A thirteen-year-old boy who was killed in a road accident in Chesterfield.'

'Why didn't they take him to the crematorium at Brimington?'

'I don't know, Sergeant. Perhaps Brimington was too busy. Or maybe this one's cheaper.'

'Don't let anybody hear you making remarks like that,' said Hitchens.

'Actually, I think it might be a space question,' said Abbott. 'This was a big funeral – about two hundred mourners, I'd say. They have a bigger chapel here, and facilities for relaying the service to the waiting room if there's still an overspill.'

'OK. Who was the funeral director?'

'One of the big Chesterfield outfits.'

Fry looked at the mourners waiting in the chapel. This was what the caller wanted. He'd enjoy the thought of the police waiting for a body to turn up; he'd planned to leave them helpless and frustrated. For now, he was in control of the situation. He'd even told them what he was going to do. *Soon there will be a killing.* Some people really got off on playing God, didn't they?

Cooper carried the urn into the CID room and put it down on his desk. Gavin Murfin eyed it suspiciously, dipping his hand into a bag of jelly babies hidden in his desk drawer.

'What have you got there, Ben?'

'About seven pounds of bone ash.'

Murfin gazed at the urn, chewing reflectively on a jelly baby. 'Well, while you've been out collecting ashes, we've had background checks done on the crematorium staff.'

'Did the list come through from Christopher Lloyd?'

'It did. They're all clean, apart from one who had a couple of minor convictions for taking without consent when he was a teenager.'

'Taking cars without consent, presumably, rather than bodies.'

'Yes, I think you can presume that. Also, I found this – a job advert for a crematorium technician with one of the local councils. You know, those blokes are pretty badly paid. A lot of people wouldn't leave the house for this sort of salary, let alone deal with dead bodies all day.'

Bereavement Services are looking for a self-motivated and enthusiastic individual to work alongside our experienced team of cremator operators. The successful applicant will perform cremations in accordance with the Code of Cremation Practice, and will undertake chapel attendant duties, ensuring that services are conducted in a dignified, orderly and caring manner. Applicants must be willing to undertake the Cremator Technicians Training Scheme.

'But this is a vacancy at a local authority crematorium,' said Cooper. 'Maybe operators in the private sector earn better money.'

'I doubt it. No qualifications needed, you see. There aren't many jobs like that these days. The sort of job a kid could go into straight from school, with no A levels.'

'What's this Cremator Technicians Training Scheme, then?'

'On-the-job training, like. You learn the ropes from your workmates as you go along. Maybe there's some kind of NVQ you can get.'

Cooper tried to picture the sort of teenager who'd want to leave school after his GCSEs and become a crematorium technician. There must be some, but he didn't think he'd ever met any. A career spent burning dead bodies wasn't one he'd ever heard recommended by a career advisor at High Peak College.

He studied the advert again. 'It looks as though the cremator operators are the same people who act as chapel attendants. I never realized that. I always thought the men in black coats were the undertaker's people.'

Murfin took a sniff of his coffee and put it down on his desk, where it joined two more cups half-full of cold, scummy liquid.

'Me, too.'

'That's a bit tough, isn't it? I mean, you might get used to the burning part. The bodies would mean nothing, after a while. It would be just a way of earning a living. But before you do the cremation, they make you mingle with the bereaved family . . .'

'What are you getting at, Ben?'

'It seems to me that would make the job quite different. Much more human. It's the human aspects that are most difficult to deal with.'

'I know what you mean,' said Murfin. 'I'd much rather view a dead body at a murder scene than break the news to the victim's family.'

'Exactly. People find emotions in others difficult to deal with. You never know how they're going to react, whether they're going to burst into tears at the wrong word. It would make you see a crematorium job quite differently.'

Now an image was starting to form in Cooper's mind of that elusive school leaver. He saw a tall youth with bad skin, awkward in a black suit that was two sizes too big for him. A bright enough lad, but lacking in confidence and social skills, frightened of other people and their unpredictable emotions. He would be acutely embarrassed among strangers, averting his face and refusing to make eye contact. But the awkwardness would drop from him like a cloak when he found some task that interested him, something he could do well.

'You know this crematorium,' said Murfin, taking the bag of jelly babies from his desk and peering inside to see what was left.

'Yes, Gavin?'

'Do they have such a thing as a deluxe

cremation?' he said. 'What you might call *la crème de la crem.'*

'That's not funny, Gavin.'

Cooper called up his list of missing persons from eighteen months previously. He'd already eliminated those who'd turned up in the meantime, either dead or alive. He didn't have many names left to play with. Seven, in fact. And that was a good thing, he supposed.

His favourite possibility was a woman from Middleton who had failed to collect her seven-year-old from school one day and hadn't been seen since. Two years she'd been gone now, and there had been no confirmed sightings of her, nor any communication with the family, or so they said. The husband had been looked into fairly thoroughly at the time. There were no indications of depression or any problems in her life that might have caused her to do a runner or harm herself. The difficulty was that she'd already been missing for six months before Audrey Steele's funeral. Where could she have been during that time?

The other mispers belonged to different age groups from Audrey, and all but one were male. Not that it made any difference. The cremator made no distinction between genders, except for the amount of bone ash that came out of the pulverizer. Perhaps he should be looking at them by weight rather than by age or gender, and getting an estimate of their bone mass. There were no other clues to follow, as far as he could see.

Losing concentration, Cooper looked across the desk at Murfin. He was calculating his back time. He always kept a careful record in his diary of how many days and hours he was owed. Not that he ever made any attempt to take the time off – he just enjoyed complaining about it.

'Do you believe in Heaven and Hell, Gavin?' asked Cooper.

Murfin didn't look up. 'Have a jelly baby, Ben. It'll make you feel better.'

'No, seriously.'

'What, you mean like the stuff they teach the kids in Sunday school? A lot of flames, and devils with toasting forks? Eternal damnation for having naughty thoughts?'

'Well, any sort of Hell you like, Gavin. And any sort of Heaven, too.'

Murfin chewed for a minute and wiped some white dust off his hands from the bag of sweets.

'The former I believe in,' he said. 'But I've never seen any evidence of the latter. I'm sorry, Detective Constable Cooper, but your unsupported claims of the existence of Heaven would be thrown out of court by any judge.'

'A Hell, but no Heaven? So you reckon the equation is a bit out of balance, then? How did that happen, Gavin? Some kind of design fault in Creation?'

'You shouldn't say things like that,' said Murfin, wagging a sugar-coated finger. 'You'll upset God.'

The phone rang, and Murfin answered it.

'DC Murfin speaking. Oh, hi. Yes, OK.' He held the phone out at arm's length. 'It's for you, Ben.'

'Who is it? God?'

'No, but she thinks she is.'

Cooper took the phone, grimacing at Murfin. 'Hello, Diane.'

'Drop anything else you're doing, Ben,' she said. 'We need the whole team down here for a meeting with Dr Kane.'

'The psychologist?'

'Yes. We're setting up in the conference room. I want you and Gavin here in ten minutes.'

17

Well, have you found the dead place? Or did you lose the scent? Strange, when the odour is so distinctive. Some say it's sweet, like rotting fruit.

Did you know that you don't have to step on a decomposing body to carry away its smell on your shoes? The soil around a corpse is soaked with all those volatile fatty acids produced by human decay. Our soft tissues all decompose, but some more quickly than others. The uterus can last for months – the organ of life surviving intact as the body festers around it. Just one of nature's little jokes.

And then all we have left is the skeleton. The teeth, the skull, the gleaming bones. This is the final revelation. It's the uncovering of truth. To most people, death is a dirty secret, a thing of shame, the last taboo. To me, it's completion, the perfect conclusion. It's my only chance to be free.

I'm close to perfection now, you see. And you're going to be too late. You may never find the dead place at all. You may never meet my flesh eater.

*   *   *

'There was a German psychoanalyst called Erich Fromm,' said Dr Rosa Kane. 'You might be interested in one of his personality theories.'

She stood at the head of the table, looking smart and self-possessed. Fry was reminded of Professor Robertson in a perverse sort of way. Dr Kane seemed to be the modern, more acceptable face of the same school. She hadn't hesitated when DI Hitchens had invited her to take the central role in the meeting.

'Fromm believed that even the most severely neurotic person is at least trying to cope with life,' said Kane. 'He called that type "biophilous", or life-loving. But there's another type he refers to as "necrophilous" – the lovers of death.'

Fry looked around the table, and saw both Hitchens and Cooper writing the new words in their notebooks. The DI looked as though he might be having trouble with the spelling.

'Necrophilous?' he said.

'Yes. These are people who have a passionate attraction to anything dead or decayed. It's a passion to transform that which is alive into something unalive. Fromm called it "a passion to tear apart living structures". Typically, the individual concerned will be comfortable with machinery, but won't be able to cope with people.'

Fry frowned. 'Why machinery?'

'Anything mechanical is unalive, and therefore predictable and reliable. If a machine breaks down, you can figure out why, and repair it. But people aren't like that. We can't always understand why they behave the way they do.'

'That's certainly true of some people around here,' said Murfin. But Dr Kane ignored him. She'd probably noticed that Murfin hadn't opened his notebook. Chances were he didn't even have a pen with him.

'For a subject with this type of personality disorder,' she said, 'machines are vastly preferable. If they're forced to deal with people, that's when problems can arise. Human unpredictability appears threatening. A subject may feel the compulsion to render a living person unalive, to make them safe.'

That was too much. Fry felt the irritation boil over.

'Render a person unalive? What sort of mealy-mouthed expression is that?'

Kane paused, pursed her lips and brushed back a strand of hair. She was silent for just long enough to make it clear she wasn't going to respond to the question. She looked up at DI Hitchens.

'In terms of an individual's own distorted perceptions, such an act might be considered a form of self-defence,' she said.

Fry snorted, and Hitchens glared at her.

'There's another thing that might help you,' said Kane. 'Personality disorders of this nature often become evident in childhood. But it generally requires some kind of traumatic experience to bring it to the surface, producing a child who clings to ritual as a source of security. Such a child will find predictability reassuring, even when it flies in the face of normal logic.'

'Can you give us an example?' asked Hitchens.

'Imagine that you're a child, and your father sometimes beats you when he comes home drunk on a Saturday night. A normal child will keep his head down and hope his father won't beat him this week. But if you're *this* kind of child, it's preferable for your father to beat you *every* Saturday night, rather than not knowing whether he will or won't. Unpredictability is the most frightening thing, you see. A child in that situation might deliberately do something to enrage his father, to make sure that he's beaten. Then he feels secure.'

'Good God.'

Kane nodded. 'It's a difficult disorder to deal with. There are no cures, only ways of minimizing the effects – and then only if the condition is diagnosed before it's too late.'

'Too late?' said Hitchens.

'Well, as a child, this type of individual lacks the power to influence the actions of adults, other than by making himself a victim. But later in life he may realize there's another way to deal with the unpredictability of people.' The psychologist turned her head slightly to look at Fry. 'That's when he discovers the power to make them predictable – by rendering them unalive.'

'The big question is whether he's serious about

his statement that he intends to kill someone,' said Fry. 'Or could his messages be referring to something that's happened in the past?'

'If there *was* an earlier incident, it could have been a practice killing,' said Kane.

'A practice killing?'

'Exercising that newly discovered power over people. This individual may be seeking some kind of perfection. It makes sense.'

'None of this makes sense.'

Kane took off her glasses to look at Fry. 'It does if you take the trouble to put yourself in the mind of the psychotic individual, to understand his motivations and thought processes.'

'But we agree that we do have a killer here, Doctor,' said Hitchens.

'In fact, there's no evidence of that. While we undoubtedly have an individual with a psychotic obsession, his obsession isn't with killing but with death.'

'I'm sorry,' said Hitchens, 'but I don't see the distinction.'

The psychologist replaced her glasses and looked at the DI for a moment, raising her eyebrows. Hitchens squirmed uneasily. Watching her in action almost made Fry wish she wore glasses, just so she could do that.

'There's a very significant distinction,' said Kane. 'In his messages, almost all the details in the confessional passages refer to what happens to the body after death. How many murderers hang around the body? Once their victim is dead, they're only interested in escaping detection or concealing the evidence. But not this individual.'

'Doctor,' said Fry, 'would you say this type of man might gravitate towards an occupation where he was able to indulge his obsession?'

'Certainly.'

'The funeral business?'

'I couldn't be so specific.'

'A pity. We almost had a profile there.'

Cooper raised his pen to get attention. 'What about the references to a sarcophagus and "the dead place"?'

'The references are probably symbolic,' said Kane.

Fry could see that Cooper was getting excited, like a schoolboy whose teacher had prompted a sudden insight.

'So the sarcophagus could be to do with exposing something to the air and light,' he said. 'Perhaps a dark secret?'

'He's certainly demanding some intelligence from his audience. So, yes – think symbolically, rather than literally.'

'And the flesh eater,' said Fry. 'Tell us, Doctor, is the flesh eater symbolic, or literal? It would be very helpful to know.'

After the psychologist had left, Fry found Hitchens in his office, tapping his teeth again. She resisted the urge to snatch the pen from his hand.

'I've just had a call,' he said. 'Instructions from above.'

'Oh?'

'We have to play it cool on the phone messages, Diane. No more chasing around the countryside like rabbits after every report of someone a bit late coming home.'

'We can't sit on our hands and wait for a body to turn up,' said Fry. 'That might be exactly what he wants.'

'It might be. But we're downgrading the priority of the phone calls until we have further evidence.'

'With respect, sir, we have an offender here who's going to kill somebody soon.'

'Strictly speaking, he's not an offender, DS Fry. Not until he actually does something illegal.'

'He's making threatening calls.'

'Who has he threatened?' said Hitchens.

Fry grimaced. 'Nuisance calls, then.'

'He's wasting police time. That's the worst we can say about him at this stage.'

'He needs psychiatric help.'

'Well, I'd agree with you there. He definitely has a problem of some kind. But whether he's actually intending to kill anybody, we don't know.'

'What's the next move, then?'

'We wait. Patrols will check all the possible sites we gave them, when practicable.'

'When practicable?' said Fry. 'That could be never.'

Hitchens continued with a small frown. 'And we hope that Forensics can come up with something at the locations he made the calls from. They have two scenes now, so their chances of finding matching traces are increased with each call.'

'And I suppose we sit here on our backsides and hope he'll call again, just to make it a bit easier for us.'

'Possibly,' said Hitchens. 'But there are plenty of other enquiries to concentrate on in the meantime.'

The DI looked up at Cooper as he came back into the room.

'How is the Audrey Steele enquiry progressing, Ben? I'm thinking we ought to make it a higher priority before word gets out. There could be a strong public reaction to an incident like this, and we don't want to look as though we're not doing anything.'

Cooper hesitated. As one of the lowliest members of the department, there was always a danger of being caught between conflicting instructions from his senior officers.

'DS Fry suggested I should pursue other avenues before considering the possibility that an unidentified body was involved,' he said, choosing his words carefully.

'I know. A mixing of ashes. And how are you getting on?'

'All the ashes I've managed to collect have gone for analysis. I'm not sure if they'll tell us anything, though. Theoretically it shouldn't be possible to mix up bodies at the crem, unless it was done deliberately, so it may still be just the one cremation we need to explain.'

'That's what I'm worried about. We mustn't appear to be ignoring the more serious possibility, Ben.'

'No, sir.'

Cooper waited. The DI's concerns about public perception might well supersede Diane's judgement on the use of resources, but it was a debate he'd prefer to stay out of. Alongside him, Fry was silent, but he could feel her growing tense. He guessed the debate might continue later, when he was out of earshot.

'The funeral directors would have to be at the centre of the business, wouldn't they?' said Hitchens.

'Hudson and Slack, yes. I've got them listed as my next port of call.'

'To sum up, then. We have human remains that turn out to be those of Audrey Steele, who was never reported missing because she died of natural causes and was cremated with the full works. Or so her family were led to believe. Right so far?'

'Yes, sir.'

Hitchens tapped again, then pointed the end of the pen at Fry. She could see a trace of his saliva gleaming on the cap.

'The question is, if the ashes weren't mixed up, who or what was cremated in Audrey Steele's place? You can't just stick an empty coffin in the hearse. Its weight would be a giveaway, for a start. The bearers would notice. The cremator technicians would notice. We'd have to imagine a conspiracy involving at least half a dozen people, if not more. Very risky.'

'We've been over this. The obvious thing to do would be to put something else in the coffin instead of the corpse. But the crematorium staff still might notice, if the ashes weren't right.'

'Mr Lloyd sent through the computer records for the day in question,' said Cooper. 'That was helpful of him, since it never occurred to me to ask for them. There's nothing unusual about the data for Audrey Steele's cremation.'

'Of course, no one would notice,' said Hitchens, 'if you put a different body in the coffin.'

'An actual murder victim, you think?' said Fry.

'What better way to dispose of the body? No victim, no forensics. Perfect.'

'And even if the remains of Audrey Steele turned up, we would never be able to match them to a missing person.'

'Precisely, Diane. Because she was never missing.'

'If it hadn't been for the facial reconstruction –'

'And DC Cooper's persistence,' said Hitchens.

'Well, yes, and that.'

'Have you still got the list of missing persons, Ben?'

'From eighteen months ago? Yes. But there's a

big problem with it, isn't there? We don't know whether we're looking for a male or a female. We have no idea of age, height, skin colour. Nothing. All we have are ashes.'

'Yes, that *is* a problem,' said Hitchens. He paused for a moment. 'So what do we make of Melvyn Hudson? He's the boss at Hudson and Slack, isn't he? So he'd be in the best position to interfere with a body.'

'Would it be possible on his own?' asked Cooper.

'The staff at Hudson and Slack might know something. They could have helped to cover up, at least. It's one of those jobs, isn't it? An "us and them" sort of job. No one else understands or appreciates us, so we have to stick together, no matter what,' said Fry.

'Could be,' he said. Fry might just as well have been describing the police. It was definitely an 'us and them' sort of job. 'You don't think it's any more than that? There couldn't be somebody with a more personal reason to cover up?'

'And we still have the crematorium staff,' said Hitchens. 'They're hidden away in that room at the back of the chapel. It's an ideal situation for the kind of person Dr Kane described just now. Imagine – he sees human beings reduced to dust every day. There's nothing so predictable as ashes.'

Fry stood up, though she wasn't going anywhere. She just needed to move restlessly around the room.

'If you ask me, there's nothing so predictable as the opinion of an expert.'

'Diane, sit down,' said Hitchens.

'You know, I'm not sure about the crematorium staff,' said Cooper. He'd found himself thinking of the terrarium at Mrs Askew's house, with its seashells and Venus flytraps. Nothing predictable about that, really.

'Why?' said Hitchens.

'Well, I think the type of person Dr Kane was talking about would want to see the processes the body went through after death.'

'And that means he'd have to go back to the scene to check on the body. Maybe several times.'

'Yes, I think so.'

'Somebody must have seen him, surely.'

'We could put out appeals.'

'Only if we had some idea what times he went back.'

'Of course. But wait a minute, Diane – does he know we've found this body?'

'What?'

'We haven't issued a statement yet, have we? There's been no announcement to the media?'

'Well, apart from your facial reconstruction splashed all over the papers and TV screens the other day. Getting the attention of the public, remember?'

Cooper's shoulders slumped. 'Oh, that's right.'

'Why, what were you thinking?'

'That he might go back to the body again. To do a final check.'

'Not much chance of that now.'

Hitchens thought about it. 'Let's stick to what we actually know. We've got a positive ID on a body that was entrusted to Hudson and Slack for proper disposal. But instead of being cremated, the body ended up in the woods, ten miles away at Ravensdale.'

'That's about it.'

'Pretty nasty business, if you ask me. Something we should take very seriously.'

'Yes, sir.'

'Let's take some action, then. We've still got to maintain a "softly, softly" approach towards Hudson and Slack. But I think we're justified at this stage in applying for a search warrant and seizing their records.'

'Wow,' said Cooper, sitting upright with a surge of excitement. He looked at Fry to share the reaction, but she didn't seem quite as enthusiastic as he'd expected.

'Can we raid their premises and go softly, softly at the same time?' asked Fry.

But Hitchens was into the flow now that he'd made a decision, and he started counting off on the fingers of one hand.

'Secondly, we need to interview anyone who was working at the firm eighteen months ago, at the time of Audrey Steele's funeral. Any former employees who've left since then will also have to be traced. Background checks on them all, plus any known associates. We have to narrow down the list of names to those who had the opportunity to interfere with the body. A motive would be helpful, too. But God knows what that might be.'

The DI looked at Cooper. 'How does that sound for starters, Ben?'

Cooper had been trying to make notes. 'Great,' he said. 'And what about the family, sir?'

'Audrey Steele's family? That's a bit delicate, isn't it? But one of them might have noticed something, so they'll all have to be interviewed.' Hitchens stopped counting fingers and steepled them, as if praying. 'Handle that yourself, Ben. You've already spoken to the mother, you said? I suppose she's getting on a bit?'

'Yes.'

'Well, treat her with kid gloves and don't upset her too much. See if you can find some other members of the family who might be easier to talk to. You know what I mean?'

Cooper nodded. 'I know what you mean.'

'Diane,' said Cooper when they'd left the DI's office, 'I don't think you're doing yourself any favours with the DI, or with Mr Kessen either. You didn't seem to give Dr Kane's views any respect.'

Fry slapped her notebook down on her desk. 'Have you ever killed anyone, Ben?'

'No, of course not.'

'Nor me,' said Murfin from the next desk. 'I've thought about it a few times, obviously.'

'I didn't ask you, Gavin.'

'What's your point?' asked Cooper.

'My point is, if none of us have ever killed anyone, how can we possibly know what it feels like?'

'We can't. Not really.'

'And Dr Rosa Kane? Do you think she's ever killed anybody?'

'I'll run a check on the PNC, if you like, and see how many murder convictions she has.'

'Don't be stupid, Ben. It was a hypothetical question.'

Murfin laughed. 'Please dispose of your hypotheticals safely, in the interests of the staff.'

Fry glared at him, but he kept his head down. Cooper thought of the legend of the Gorgon, whose gaze could turn you to stone if you looked at her face. Gavin must have read that story. He rarely met Fry's eye these days.

'The point is,' she repeated, 'even the precious Rosa doesn't know what it's like to kill someone. Despite all her theories, she can't actually tell us what goes on in a killer's head, how he feels before and after the act. Let alone during.'

'She must have talked to a lot of convicted murderers,' said Cooper.

'And do you think any of them told her the truth about their crimes? The clever ones will have told her what they thought she wanted to hear. The less clever ones couldn't articulate a complex emotion if their lives depended on it.'

'Which sometimes it does,' said Cooper.

'Yes,' agreed Fry. 'Sometimes it does.'

'And in the meantime, all we can do is rely on the expertise of someone like Dr Kane. Theories may be all we have.'

'But we don't have to take them as gospel,' said Fry. 'Just because somebody once wrote a thesis for their doctorate expounding their own theories, everyone takes that as proof. It may be all we have, but we don't have to assume it's all there is.'

'What do you mean?'

'There may be reasons for killing that no psychiatrist has ever thought of.'

Cooper threw his hands in the air and let his pen fall on the desk. 'Well, if that's the case, we're in the shit, aren't we? A killer we can't identify planning the death of a victim we don't know for reasons we can't imagine. That's just great.'

Fry didn't answer. But Murfin's response was to raise his hand and drop his own pen on his desk with a loud clatter.

'Hey, are we giving up?' he said. 'Throwing in the towel? Does this mean I can go to the pub?'

Fry stood up, her body tense. 'What I'm trying to do here is encourage a bit of independent thinking. It would be nice to hear a few ideas that haven't been borrowed from some so-called expert. I'd like to see open minds from my team, not a ragbag of second-hand psychoanalysis and sociological mumbo-jumbo. Is that so difficult to understand?'

Cooper and Murfin tried to look suitably chastened.

'OK, Diane,' said Cooper.

He watched her leave the room. It wasn't clear where she was going. Probably just to stamp up and down the corridor swearing under her breath.

'There were some big words in that last bit,' said Murfin.

Cooper picked up his pen. 'She's right, though, Gavin.'

'Yes, I know. But it's like telling jokes, isn't it? Some people know how to be right. And others don't.'

Then Fry came back into the room to answer her phone. Her face changed as she listened, and she looked at Cooper.

'That was your idea, too – the new search at Litton Foot,' she said.

'Is there a problem?'

'I don't know whether you'd call it a problem or not. They've just found some more bones.'

18

Fry had expected dense undergrowth, a thick covering of trees on a steep slope, to make the location inaccessible. But the new site was just above the tree line. There were plenty of rocks, though – thousands of them scattered across the hillside in both directions, clustering downwards as far as she could see. There was no pattern to the rocks, no logic to the way they'd tumbled and come to rest. Many had weathered over the years into smooth, hunched shapes. They covered the hillside like a vast flock of deformed sheep lying asleep or dead in the cold shadows of the north-facing slope.

Yes, there were certainly a lot of rocks. Even so, it seemed incredible that a body could have lain here unnoticed for so long.

She looked around for the crime scene manager. Wayne Abbott was there, already watching her. When Fry gestured, he came towards her slowly, picking his way among the stones.

'Yes, it's north-facing,' he said, as if reading her thoughts. 'There will never be enough sun on this slope to show details from a distance. If you were standing across the other side of the valley there, you could look for as long as you like, but see nothing unless it moved. These rocks must create all kinds of deceptive shapes, and a lot of inter-play of shadows. Very misleading to the eye.'

'And would nobody ever walk across the slope itself?'

'Not unless you had a particular reason to. It's difficult going, as you can see. You'd break an ankle very easily.'

'So how the hell did the killer get the body down here?'

'He didn't carry it, that's for sure.'

Abbott was sweating inside his scene suit, though the weather was cool. Fry could see two trickles of perspiration starting at his temples and clinging to the black bristles on his jawline. She wasn't sure why she disliked him so much. She could only explain it as an instinctive reaction. Wayne Abbott certainly wouldn't have been her choice for a supervisor. But he had the qualifica-tions and experience, so here he was.

The CSM pointed up the slope to where the rocks formed a fissured cliff.

'I'd imagine there are two possibilities. One, the victim fell from the cliff up there. Or was pushed, as I'm sure you were about to suggest. If that was the case, we should find structural damage to the bones. But the second possibility is that the victim might have come to this spot – voluntarily or otherwise – while still alive.'

'And died right here?'

Abbott laughed. 'In either scenario, the victim died right here. The question is how they died, and why.'

'That's two questions,' said Fry.

But he took no notice. 'Did they die suddenly, or slowly?' he said. 'Accidentally or deliberately? By misadventure, or . . . with assistance?'

'Are you planning to give us the answers, Wayne? Or do you just like asking rhetorical questions?'

'I suppose you think you know all the answers yourself, Sergeant?'

'No,' said Fry. 'But I do know what the questions are, thanks all the same. By the way, the smallest trace evidence from this location might be crucial, so . . .'

'No, don't tell me – you want us to go over the scene with a fine tooth-comb.' Abbott wiped the sweat from his face. 'Well, I've got news for you lot in CID. We don't get issued with tooth-combs any more, fine or otherwise.'

'OK, OK. Just do your best, will you?'

Abbott began to walk away. 'Do our best? Gosh, I'd never have thought of that.'

Ben Cooper was crouching among the weathered stones, staring at a damp patch of soil. He was out of sight, and he wasn't sorry. He couldn't hear details of the conversation between Fry and Abbott, but he recognized Fry's tone of voice even at this distance. Her rising irritation wasn't directed at him for once, and he was happy to keep it that way for a while.

Unfortunately, it didn't take Fry long to find him.

'Jesus, everybody thinks they're an expert, don't they?' she said.

'Well, that's what they are, Diane. PhDs with specializations in skeletal biology or human genetics. You've got to respect their knowledge.'

'I don't mean the scientists, Ben. I mean the bloody SOCOs.'

'Oh.'

Fry looked around, breathing deeply. 'What are those buildings across the valley?'

Cooper had already checked. But perhaps it wouldn't do for him to look too much like an expert.

'According to the map, the nearest place to us is Fox House Farm, and the one further over is Hunger House. But it doesn't look as though either of them has been used as a farm for a long time. Most of the buildings have been demolished, and the land around them is planted with mature trees.'

'Hunger House? What sort of name is that?'

'A hunger house was a building where cattle were kept before slaughter. The old custom was to starve animals for a while before they were killed.'

Fry said nothing to that. She didn't need to. Her views on the barbarities of rural life were well known.

'They're on the Alder Hall estate,' said Cooper. 'I suppose they were tenant farms at some time, but the landowner must have decided to evict his tenants and plant woodland. Timber was more profitable, I expect. That plantation is marked on the map as Corunna Wood.'

'Corunna? Who was he? Another local hobgoblin?'

'I think it's a town in Spain where there was a famous battle.'

Fry's expression told him he might be showing off too much knowledge again. But she steered rapidly away from history as a topic.

'What are you looking at down there, anyway?'

'This stone,' said Cooper. 'It hasn't been in this position long.'

'How do you know?'

'The grass is still green underneath. It bleaches and dies after a few days if it's covered over like this.'

'How many days?'

'I couldn't say.'

'You're good on observation, Ben, but you always seem to fall down on details.'

'I'm not Sherlock Holmes,' said Cooper. 'We need to ask an expert.'

'An expert in dead grass – why not?' Then Fry sighed. 'A hunger house. God, what next?'

A team from Sheffield University were unloading equipment – shovels and trowels, wire mesh screens for sifting bone fragments from the soil, evidence bags, tape measures and orange markers. One of the students had already used a video camera to record the position of the remains from every angle before the team approached it.

The forensic anthropology group from the university provided services to many police forces in excavating and analysing skeletal remains. Some of the team had even worked for the United Nations, investigating mass graves.

Under the supervision of the forensic anthropologist, the team began sieving soil from around the remains. They would be trying to locate fragments of bone, personal items, anything that had been dropped or didn't belong in the area.

Cooper stood looking down at the tangle of bone and vegetation, half concealed under the edge of a rock. There was no skull visible, but it could be further down, of course. Until the remains were separated from the earth and plant growth, it was impossible to judge the position of the body, or whether it was intact. Some items had already been photographed, bagged and tagged, and he picked up a bag containing a bone. It felt strangely light in his hand.

'Ben, what do you think the "flesh eater" is?' said Fry, breaking into his thoughts.

Cooper waved a hand around the dale. 'Perhaps Professor Robertson was right when he talked about limestone, Diane. This whole area is limestone. The entire landscape could be the flesh eater.'

Fry nodded. 'It's a possibility.'

'What do you bet some of the bones are missing from this body, too?' said Cooper.

'You think the killer might have taken trophies?'

'I don't know. But if we find them in his possession, it's fairly conclusive evidence, isn't it? He does seem to be a very careful killer. Meticulous, even. My feeling is that he won't have made many mistakes, if any.'

Around the place where the body had lain and decomposed were patches of earth stained different shades. They marked where the victim's body fluids had drained out.

Cooper felt a surge of anger, thinking of Audrey Steele lying out in the open in just this way, abandoned to the elements. And now here was another body waiting for a face and a name, another identity to be reconstructed from almost nothing.

But there wouldn't be much more achieved tonight. It would soon be dark, and the activity around him was aimed at securing the scene for the night, ready for an early start in the morning. A vehicle manoeuvring in the woods already had its headlights on.

Then Cooper saw a movement on the opposite

hillside. A figure was walking along the skyline, dark and indistinct against the grey cloud. Maybe there was a public footpath up there, he wasn't sure. The figure kept moving, but Cooper was certain the eyes were turned towards Litton Foot and the unusual activity below. That would be natural, of course. Any passer-by would be curious. But wouldn't it be more natural to stop and look, to puzzle for a while over the white scene suits and the police Land Rover reversing over the ridge? This walker did none of those things, but scanned the area efficiently in a few seconds, before vanishing behind a rocky outcrop.

Fry had seen the figure, too. 'He'd be miles away before we could get to him,' she said. 'If that's what you were thinking.'

'When I saw him, I was wondering if the killer came back here to check on progress,' said Cooper. 'And what about the smell?'

'There was no one here to smell it, Ben.'

'I suppose not.'

He studied the hillside again. In an open location like this, the scent would have travelled. What were those gases produced by decomposition? Hydrogen sulphide and methane? They'd have drifted away from their source on any available air currents, forming cones and pools of scent, like invisible markers of death in the landscape. Depending on the weather, the smell might have lingered for days, or weeks. But wind and rain would have dissipated it quickly, so that anyone passing within a few yards of the remains might have noticed nothing. What a pity this wasn't dog-walking country.

Then Cooper frowned and looked back down the hill towards Litton Foot. Tom Jarvis's house wasn't visible from here. It was in the bottom of the dale, and the woods were thick in between. But Jarvis's dogs had run in those woods before the new fence had gone up, hadn't they?

Or rather, one of his dogs had.

Then one of the SOCOs called Cooper over to the edge of a patch of bracken a few feet from the location of the remains. 'Look at this –'

'What have you found?'

'See for yourself. But don't get too close.'

Cooper moved a little nearer. 'It's a gin trap,' he said.

'It looks a bit rusty. I don't suppose it's in working order.'

'It's meant to look like that.'

'What do you mean?'

'You're supposed to let a trap develop a coating of rust to disguise it. It gives the steel a neutral smell, so as not to put animals on the alert.'

The trap was fixed into position with a chain and metal stake, and a band of spring steel was anchored to the base at one end. Fry walked over to see what was happening as Cooper pointed to the steel plate at the other end.

'See, only the trigger plate is galvanized,' he said. 'That needs to be thin to keep its weight down. And the catch is made from brass to prevent it rusting to the foot plate. But everything else is rusted over. That's just the way you want it.'

'How do you know so much about traps?' asked Fry. 'They're illegal, aren't they?'

Cooper shrugged. 'You learn this kind of thing by osmosis when you grow up in the countryside.'

'So you understand how it works?'

'It's very simple. To set the trap, you compress this spring, which allows the jaws to open, and a catch closes over them. When you release the spring again, the upward pressure of the jaws holds the trigger plate in position, see? An animal comes along and steps on the plate, releasing the catch. The spring snaps the jaws shut on its leg. The whole thing happens in about a twentieth of a second.'

Fry flinched. 'It's barbaric.'

'That's why it's illegal.'

'Obviously, that doesn't stop people using them. How does an animal get out of the trap?'

'It doesn't. Once the jaws close, they're locked in position by the collar. They can't just be forced open – you have to depress the spring again. Animals don't know that, and they're not physically capable of it anyway. That's why they sometimes end up chewing their own legs off to escape.'

'I don't suppose there's any way of identifying the owner of this thing?'

But Cooper shook his head. 'There might be fingerprints, I suppose. But this is quite an old trap. See – it has a bow spring. That type tends to lose its springiness when it's left set for long periods, or if it gets too corroded. Trap manufacturers dropped it years ago in favour of coil springs.'

He hunted on the ground until he found a stick.

'What are you doing?' asked Fry.

'Setting the trap off. It'll be safer. Somebody is bound to get their hand in it, otherwise.'

Cooper pressed on the trigger plate with the end of the stick. Instantly the jaws snapped shut, biting deep into the wood and shredding the bark.

'Jesus,' said Fry.

Though Cooper tugged on the stick again, the trap stayed firmly attached to the ground.

'Nice, isn't it? And now your prey is helpless, all you have to do is come along at your convenience and finish it off. The trap was probably left by a farmer or gamekeeper with a fox problem.'

Fry nodded, accepting the explanation. But Cooper looked again at his shredded stick and the size of the trap.

'Unless, of course, it was intended for bigger prey than a fox.'

'OK, when you've all finished messing around over there, you might want to see this –'

They turned to find Wayne Abbott regarding them with a sour expression. He was holding a couple of evidence bags containing what Cooper immediately recognized as sections of bone, stained brown and splintered at the ends.

'Just as a non-expert opinion, I have to admit that these should put paid to the accidental fall theory,' said Abbott.

'What is it?' asked Fry.

They gathered round him as he held up the bags. 'Here, and here . . . Do you see the marks on the sheath of the bone? They're quite clear. I'd say that it's only the vegetation that was holding this body together at all. Not too long ago, someone dismantled it. And they were using a *very* sharp knife. They took the skin right off the bone.'

That evening, the news from Edendale crown court was that Micky Ellis had been given the mandatory life sentence, with a tariff of fifteen years. He'd be out in ten, or less. The CPS had called to say they were pleased with the result.

But Diane Fry didn't feel like celebrating. Instead, she spent some time listening to the tapes before she went home. Soon, she'd know them by heart.

What she really wanted was to be able to recognize the caller's voice if she heard it. Despite the distortion, there ought to be some characteristic feature of the phrasing or intonation that would identify him, if only she could produce a suspect for comparison. *The application of intelligence should refine the primeval urge.* The pretentiousness alone should be a giveaway. Who spoke like that, unless they'd been given a script to read? *Inside every person, the evil Thanatos fights an endless battle with*

Eros. Who'd ever heard of Thanatos, for heaven's sake?

Fry looked around the office and noticed Ben Cooper hadn't left yet. He'd taken a personal call a few minutes ago, and he was looking a bit subdued.

'Are you all right, Ben?' she called. 'Why haven't you gone home?'

Cooper looked up, unable to hide an expression of surprise. Too absorbed in his own concerns to be aware of her as usual, she supposed.

'I'm not in a hurry,' he said. 'I'm going to the hospital first to visit my mother, and visiting time doesn't start for a while yet. Did I mention she was in hospital?'

'Yes, I think so,' said Fry vaguely. Maybe he had, but she wasn't sure. 'How is she?'

'That was my brother on the phone. He says the doctors think it wasn't just a fall. It looks as though she had a minor stroke.'

'I'm sorry. But only a minor one?'

'The trouble with one stroke is that another is often close behind.'

Fry could see he was worried, but she didn't know what to say to him. Cooper wouldn't welcome any interest from her in his personal life – especially after what she'd said to him about his interference in *her* life, when he'd secretly schemed to reunite her with her sister. Whatever she said now, he would only consider it intrusive and hypocritical.

She cast around for something neutral to say that wouldn't make things worse.

'Well, don't hang around the office,' she said. 'We can manage without you for a while, you know. Go and get things sorted out, if you can.'

She didn't think Cooper was going to respond. But then he got up slowly.

'I'll see you in the morning, Diane.'

Fry put her headphones back on and returned to her tapes. Half an hour had passed before it occurred to her to wonder what Cooper would do after he'd visited his sick mother.

It might happen in the next few hours. We could synchronize our watches and count down the minutes. What a chance to record the ticking away of a life, to follow it through to that last, perfect moment, when existence becomes nothing, when the spirit parts with the physical. The end is always so close . . . I can smell it right now, can't you?

But Cooper had given himself a job to do that night. While he'd been waiting for visiting time to come round at the hospital, he'd driven to the big DIY store on the retail park and bought himself a flat-pack shelving unit. It was something he'd been meaning to do for months. Well, he certainly needed something to distract his mind, to prevent the phrase 'recurrent stroke' from slipping so often into his thoughts, spoken softly and accompanied by a meaningful look or a sympathetic nod at the unspoken implication.

285

Tonight, his mother had been conscious and lucid, though her right side was partially paralysed and her sight impaired. For some time now, she'd been losing her colour and she was paler than he could ever remember her. Looking at her in the hospital bed, it had seemed no surprise to Cooper that the blood had failed to reach the left side of her brain. Matt was right, of course, that she wasn't all that old – still in her sixties, after all. But tonight she'd seemed much older.

Randy's ear pricked up, and a second later the doorbell rang. At this time of the evening, Cooper always assumed that it was somebody ringing the wrong bell. They usually wanted his neighbour in the flat upstairs or his landlady next door.

But when he reluctantly got up and went to answer the bell, it was Gavin Murfin he found standing on his doorstep.

'Ben, you know it's mad,' said Murfin fifteen minutes later. 'They want to get rid of people like me using tenure, but at the same time they can't get anybody else to come into CID. There's no waiting list any more. When did we last have a new DC in this division?'

'I can't remember.'

They'd walked to Cooper's local, the Hanging Gate, a pub sitting in its own little yard off High Street. At least Gavin had insisted on buying the drinks.

'There are vacancies in every section station,'

said Murfin. 'The only way we can get people into CID is if they transfer for the sake of promotion. They come straight in at senior level from uniform, and they have no idea what detective work is all about.'

'Why don't you take it up with the Federation?' said Cooper.

'Dogberry and his mates? What use are they?'

Cooper smiled at the reference to the Police Federation's cartoon character. He knew Murfin was right, about some of it at least.

'And that's not to mention Dad's Army,' said Murfin. 'Talk about short-term measures. The geriatric brigade won't last for ever, and there's no one to take their place. You can't create an experienced detective out of thin air.'

Murfin drank silently for a while. 'I was thinking about what you were saying, Ben. About Hell.'

'It was nothing, Gavin.'

'But it's obvious, isn't it? Hell is *us*. If there really is a Hell waiting for me when I kick the bucket, that's what it'll be. Just me. Me, messing myself up for the rest of eternity.'

Cooper stared at Murfin open-mouthed.

Murfin nodded. '*You* know, don't you, Ben? Who needs a demon with a pitchfork, eh?'

'Have you talked to Diane about how you feel?'

'What? Why would I talk to her?'

'She's your DS.'

'I'd rather talk to the Yorkshire Ripper. We'd have more empathy.' Murfin suddenly looked tired. 'Sorry, Ben. But sometimes I lose my sense of humour, like.'

'I understand. Do you want another drink?'

But Murfin drained his glass. 'No, thanks. I'm sorry to have bothered you, Ben. I'll go home now.'

'Will you be OK?'

'I'm fine. Hey – what about that date of yours? What happened?'

'I put it off. There's too much happening this week.'

'Pity. Won't she mind?'

'No,' said Cooper. 'She'll understand.'

He waited with Murfin until a taxi came to take him home, and then walked back to his flat. Once away from the town centre, the streets were very quiet. Cooper knew that he'd have to face up to his own death some time. Like most people, he'd always thought he could avoid it for ever. And perhaps he'd read too many stories in which people didn't actually die. Instead, they passed away, breathed their last, or were no more. In polite conversation, death was skated over rapidly, like thin ice.

Sometimes, he could sense that thin ice beneath his feet, and he didn't want to look down. There was too much dark water lying just below the surface.

MY JOURNAL OF THE DEAD, PHASE THREE

So here is the reality. People change shape when they die. The muscles go slack, and gravity drags down the skin. It sinks into the cheeks and pools in the eye sockets. Our flesh forms new contours, like a tide going out and exposing submerged islands. The body cools, our extremities shrivel. Blood settles towards to the ground as the earth begins to draw us closer. Then the skin discolours from red to purple, from green to black. Our final transformation is a Technicolor performance.

When the heart stops pumping blood and the cells have no oxygen, we say a person is dead. Well, the brain might die, but the body doesn't – not really. Our intestines are packed with micro-organisms, digestive enzymes and bacteria, and they don't die with the cells. When there's nothing left for those enzymes to digest, what do our organs do? They start to digest themselves. In the end, we are our own flesh eaters.

Ah, decomposition. The classic two-act play. But the final act is drawn out too long. There's a weathering away of the flesh from the bones, bit by bit, shred by shred. A peck of a beak, the nibble of an insect, a slow disintegration. There's no grand finale, no great denouement. There's no bang in our ending, you see; there's barely a whimper. Only a cry in the night that goes unheard.

19

On the way into Cressbrook next morning, Ben Cooper caught a glint of sun on the cupola of the old mill, where a bell had once summoned labourers to work from their cottages in Apprentice Row. But that was the last glimpse of the sun he would get this morning. Before he reached the mill, the clouds had closed again, and the rain was back.

The roads down here were single track, with passing places cut into the bank where two cars could just get by with care. It called for a good deal of courtesy between drivers, of course. But as long as tourists didn't park in the passing places to take photographs, the system worked fine.

Cooper was pleased to see that both the former cotton mills in this part of the Wye Valley had been converted into fashionable apartments after years of dereliction. The distance between the two mills was only about three-quarters of a mile, a little more if you followed the loops and weirs of the Wye. Upstream, Litton Mill had been notorious for child exploitation in the nineteenth century, when it was owned by the Needham family. Orphans had been brought from London to work in the mill, and beatings and abuse were rife. In fact, so many children had died that the Needhams sent their bodies to other parishes for burial, to conceal the scale of abuse from the authorities.

Yet Cressbrook had been entirely the opposite, a testament to the enlightenment of a self-educated carpenter. William Newton had built his mill like a grand Georgian mansion, with a village school and rows of pretty lattice-windowed cottages for his workers. But could Newton's tenants see the blood of his rival's child apprentices flowing downstream and over the weir? For the sake of residents in the new apartments at Litton Mill, Cooper hoped that the dead slept easy.

There was a hairpin bend above Cressbrook, quite a tricky turning on the way up the steep hill. And a few yards below the bend was the road into Ravensdale. It was tarmacked for part of the way, but only as far as Ravensdale Cottages, the old mill workers' houses known locally as The Wick. The cottages were tiny, twelve of them in two rows facing each other across a sloping strip of earth. They were built of random limestone, with steps up to the front doors, arched leaded patterns in the windows and Russian vine covering the walls.

The road through Ravensdale was still wet, though the rain had stopped hours ago and the sun was out on the higher slopes. The upper end of the dale was so quiet that Cooper could hear the voices of two rock climbers calling instructions to each other as they clung to the face of Ravenscliffe Crag.

Beyond the cottages, a muddy footpath wound its way further north, heading up into Cressbrook Dale as far as Peter's Stone, and over to Wardlow. But on the right a track forked off through the fields and followed the stream. Last year's leaf litter lay in decomposing heaps at the sides of the track, churned into brown sludge by the wheels of passing vehicles.

A group of walkers went by, rustling in their cagoules and waterproof leggings, their boots crunching on the damp stones and splashing in the puddles. All four had their heads down, watching their feet. There was no talking on this stretch. Perhaps they were saving their breath for the climb up the other side of the dale, where the path would be muddy and dangerous.

As Cooper descended the track, the valley sides became lower, the crags disappeared, and the voices of the climbers faded into the background.

In the woods below Litton Foot, the search had resumed. Fry was already there, talking to the anthropologist, but DI Hitchens looked as though he'd arrived only seconds earlier. Swathes of mist hung high in the trees, and water cascaded continuously through the foliage. Before he'd been out of the car long, Cooper's face was cool with moisture.

'What's going on?' said Hitchens, as Fry picked her way towards them over the uneven ground.

'The university team are worried about being able to remove the remains intact, because of the way the vegetation has grown through the bones. They say the roots are too strong, and the bones will come apart if they try to move them.'

'So what are they proposing?'

'They want to dig down a couple of feet and take the whole thing – top soil and surface vegetation all in one lump – so they can take it apart in the lab without damaging any of the bones.'

'Can that be done?'

'They say so. At most, they might have to cut the body in half somewhere along the spine and take it to the lab in two pieces. They're saying they need to distinguish between any injuries to the bones at the time of death and damage caused by postmortem root growth.'

'Which do you think is the least costly option?' said Hitchens.

'Probably the lab will be cheaper, rather than keeping all these people on site.'

'We'll get better results, too,' called the anthropologist, eavesdropping. 'If you're interested in that, at all.'

Hitchens turned away. 'As long as it's in their lab,' he said. 'I wouldn't like to ask the mortuary to take that sort of mess.'

'I think we're going to have to go along with them if we want any results,' said Fry.

'Forensic scientists – don't you think they're sometimes more trouble than they're worth? They play hell with our budgets.'

'Yes, sir. But, unfortunately, they're the people juries believe these days, not us.'

Cooper discovered that a neighbouring force had loaned a special support dog for the search, one that was trained to find human remains. According to rumour, these dogs practised somewhere in the west of Scotland by locating the corpses of pigs buried in police uniforms. The aroma of decomposing pig flesh was said to be the nearest thing to the smell of human decomposition. But the bit about police uniforms was a joke, surely?

He took a chance to get into conversation with the dog handler. Cooper liked to hear about other people's specializations. One day he'd probably have to choose one himself. A year or so ago, he'd been assigned to the Rural Crime Unit, and he'd expected it to be the first step towards a transfer. But the subject hadn't arisen since, and it didn't do to make enquiries, in case it tempted fate.

'The dog's brilliant,' said the handler. 'Nose like a radar. She can detect a decomposing body at the bottom of a lake, just by sniffing the bubbles on the surface.'

'You're kidding.'

Cooper looked at the German Shepherd sitting quietly by its handler's side. He thought what the

dog did with its nose was better than radar, actually – but he couldn't think what else to compare
it to.

'But it's not just managing the dog,' said the
handler. 'Archaeological field techniques can be
useful in this job. We're trained to analyse vegetation and changes to the landscape caused by
burials.'

'How do you do that?'

'Well, above a grave the vegetation is poisoned
at first by too much raw nutrient in the soil. From
the corpse, you know.'

'Yes.'

'But as time passes, the nutrients break down,
and plant growth gets unusually lush. So a very
green patch in an area of sparse vegetation can
be a clue to the site of a grave.'

Cooper studied the dog handler. The man had
a Scots accent, but that didn't necessarily give
credence to the pig rumour. He wasn't even in
uniform, but was wearing a blue boiler suit.

'That makes sense.'

'It doesn't always work, though. We've been
out to sites where the corpse has only been in
place a few weeks, but the soil and vegetation has
settled back into place. It's incredible how quickly
that can happen. Then you've got a real problem.'

They both gazed down into the woods, where
the university team and the SOCOs were still
working.

'Sometimes, you know,' said the handler, 'it's

as if the landscape just accepts a body and digests it completely, given time.'

Fry walked across and drew Cooper away from the dog handler. 'The opinion of the experts is that any missing bones could simply be a natural result of a body being reduced to a skeleton,' she said, as if he'd asked her the question. 'No skin and muscle to hold it together. But I still think you'd need to physically separate some of them from the skeleton. Don't you?'

'You think someone might have come across the skeleton and decided to take a few trophies instead of reporting it?'

'It's a possibility. But you know perfectly well it could also have been somebody who knew the remains were there, and simply waited until the time was right.'

'Who would do that?'

'It would have to be someone fascinated by the process of death.'

'You're thinking that he might have strangled Audrey Steele after she was dead?'

'Why else would he take the hyoid bone?'

'We don't know that he took it. We know that it's missing, that's all. The anthropologist's report said it could have been carried away by an animal. A rat or a fox. Or a bird – he said it might have been a bird, too. Diane, that bone could be anywhere by now.'

'He's been coming back to the body,' said Fry

firmly. 'If anyone or anything took that bone, it was him.'

'How many people would recognize a hyoid bone if they saw one? How many would even know it exists?'

But Fry wasn't going to give in. 'Anyone with some training in anatomy. In fact, anyone with experience of bodies.'

For a moment, they watched the university team getting back to work with their spades and the dog quartering the ground lower down the slope.

'Diane, I've been thinking abut Tom Jarvis,' said Cooper. 'He has four dogs running loose on his property down at Litton Foot. Well, three now. He's had them a while, too – since they were puppies.'

'So?'

'How come none of them alerted him to the presence of a decomposing body a few yards from the edge of his property? Surely the dogs couldn't have missed the smell, even if he didn't notice it himself?'

'Was the body exposed to the air during decomposition?'

Cooper hesitated. 'When it was found, it was.'

'But it was already skeletonized by then.'

'Yes. The thing is, we've been assuming it was exposed to the air the whole time. That would fit in with the time scale, the rapid rate of skeletonization. But in some of the earlier stages, the smell must have been pretty bad. It would have spread over a wide area, especially if it had been carried on the wind. You wouldn't need a dog trained in locating human remains. Any mutt with a functioning sense of smell would have noticed it.'

They walked on a few steps, Fry silent as she let Cooper think it through. He stopped and turned towards her.

'On the other hand, if the body was originally covered or wrapped in something, the smell would have been confined, but the rate of decomposition would have been slower.'

'There's another implication to that,' said Fry.

'Yes, I know. It would definitely mean that someone returned to the scene – and exposed the body. But the lab didn't report any indication of postmortem interference with the remains. None that might have been of human origin.'

'We could get the SOCOs to go over the scene again.'

'With a fine tooth-comb this time?'

Fry put a hand on his arm. 'With an eye to more recent physical traces, Ben. Last time, they were approaching it as a historic site. They probably thought we were asking them to be archaeologists.'

'Sometimes I reckon they ought to bring back hanging for certain folk,' said Tom Jarvis when Cooper called at Litton Foot. 'Or something worse than hanging.'

Jarvis had been working in a shed at the side

of his house. Among the tools inside, Cooper could see a vice and a lathe. The aromatic scent of fresh wood shavings seeped out of the open door.

'Worse, sir?'

'There's other things they used to do round here, so they say. There was a time when they didn't mess around with murderers and criminals.'

'That was a long time ago, Mr Jarvis.'

Jarvis snorted and beat his hands together to dislodge some curls of pale wood from his work gloves.

'Do you know that big rock on the eastern ridge, near the head of Cressbrook Dale?'

He pointed up the dale. Just visible in the distance was the isolated limestone outcrop that Cooper had noticed a few days before. From here, it looked almost square, like a broken molar, the last tooth in a mouth crumbling from decay.

'Yes, I've noticed it. That's Peter's Stone, isn't it?'

'Well, that's the name it says on the maps,' said Jarvis. 'But Gibbet Rock is what it was always called round here.'

Cooper stared at him as the unexpected words sank in. 'Did you say "gibbet"? It was called Gibbet Rock?'

'And still is, for those who remember.'

Jarvis turned back into the shed, starting to pull off his gloves. He looked up in surprise when Cooper took hold of his arm.

'Remember what, Mr Jarvis?'

'Well, they reckon that's where the last gibbeting took place. That's what.'

Cooper dropped his hand, embarrassed by his own response. 'Go on.'

'Anthony Lingard – that's what the young chap was called. They hanged him for the murder of the toll-house keeper at Wardlow Mires. Then he was gibbeted at the rock, fastened up in an iron cage where everyone could see him.'

'When was this?'

'The year of the Battle of Waterloo, they reckon.'

'That was 1815, surely.'

Jarvis shrugged. The details weren't important, he seemed to say. It might have happened yesterday.

'Well, something like a gibbeting was a bit of a treat in those days,' said Jarvis. 'No telly, you know. So many folk turned out to see Lingard that the local fly-boys set up stalls near the rock. Hotdogs and souvenir postcards, or whatever they had then. It didn't last, of course.'

'Why?'

'When his corpse started to rot, the spectacle lost its novelty.'

Cooper nodded. In Derbyshire, such pieces of history lived on in the landscape, memorialized in features like Gibbet Rock. The execution of Anthony Lingard could almost have been yesterday. For those who remembered.

'Anyway, you came here for something,' said Jarvis. 'I expect you're busy with more important things than me.'

'Mr Jarvis, you told me that you used to let the dogs run in the woods at one time. Why did you stop them doing that?'

'It wasn't me that stopped them. The estate put new fences up. That was what stopped the dogs going into the woods.'

'And when was this exactly?'

'Oh, I dunno. The year before last, I suppose.'

'Can we take a look at the new fence?'

'If you like. There's not much to see. It's only a fence.'

Jarvis led him down the path through the garden and entered the paddock by a side gate. Two of the dogs ran up to them immediately, their tongues lolling and their eyes rolling with excitement. Jarvis held out his hand, though he still wore his work gloves.

'Now then, Feckless,' he said, rubbing one dog's ears. 'That's Aimless you've got there.'

Aimless had his nose practically glued to Cooper's boots. The dog sniffed like a bloodhound, almost inhaling the trailing ends of his laces. Cooper hardly dared to lift his feet, for fear of kicking the dog in its inquisitive muzzle.

'Don't worry,' said Jarvis, noticing his hesitation. 'Where there's no sense, there's no feeling.'

The old fencing on the eastern side of the stream was broken in several places and full of holes, more than big enough for one of Tom Jarvis's dogs to get through, or even Jarvis himself. But a hundred feet above it, near the crest of the

301

slope, was a new fence made of stout timber posts and weldmesh, topped by a strand of barbed wire. It was as if the estate had drawn in its boundaries, abandoning the new access land. In other areas, the national park had been busy putting in new stiles to provide access, but it hadn't been necessary here.

'No way through there,' said Cooper.

'I wouldn't like to try climbing it either,' said Jarvis.

'When they put this up, did they re-fence the whole estate?'

'No. Where the grounds of the hall border on to roads, there are stone walls. Ten feet high, those are. They were built a long time ago, to keep the common folk out. In other spots, there's stock fencing, and the farmers make sure that's in good nick. No, it seemed to be the woods they were bothered about. Didn't like the idea of anybody wandering in and enjoying themselves, I reckon.'

'*Did* people used to go into the woods?'

'Oh, aye. There's a public footpath runs at the top of my land. It goes over the top and back down into Miller's Dale. But if you knew where the fence was down, you could go off into the woods. I saw them now and then. At night time, you know.'

'Poachers?'

'Most likely. I've never asked them any questions. I'm not daft enough for that.'

'Has the new fence kept them out?'

Jarvis snorted again. 'You don't keep poachers

out so easily, not these days. They're professionals. They work in teams, and they come kitted up. No gamekeeper would tackle a poacher on his own these days. He'd likely get his head beaten in.'

'Yes, I know.'

The presence of poaching gangs might explain everything. They'd most likely be from out of the area, so no one would recognize them. They'd be armed, and not happy about someone else's overly boisterous dog interfering with their business. If the estate had noticed poaching going on, it would explain the new fence, too. But what game was available in these woods that would be worth poaching? No more than a few rabbits, surely?

Cooper looked around. Down here, the moss was so thick on the wall that it looked as though someone had knitted a bright green sweater for it, draping it in folds of Arran wool. A hollow in the rocks above the track was completely covered in moss and hung with ferns, like a waterfall without the water – except for the continual dampness seeping through the surface. He wondered if some of these fungi were the kind that excreted acids to dissolve rocks and reduce them to soil. Everything decomposed, in the end.

They began to climb back towards the house. Seen from below, the heavy porch seemed to have pulled the house into an awkward shape. It looked hunched and low, like an animal waiting to spring. Cooper remembered the other thing he'd come here to ask Tom Jarvis.

'Mr Jarvis, you have several dogs on the premises,' he said.

Jarvis looked at the dogs, then back at Cooper. Why did he need to waste words? Cooper had already wasted an entire sentence.

'I've just been watching a special support dog in action.'

Jarvis tugged off one of his gloves with his teeth, then removed the other and put them both into his pocket, like someone preparing for action, or a man who was finding the conversation boring. Cooper felt he was about to lose his attention altogether.

'The thing I'm wondering, sir,' he said, 'is why none of your dogs detected the smell of a decomposing body that lay on the edge of your property for months.'

'I don't know. You'd better ask them.'

'Most dogs would detect something like that. The odour is very strong for a while. In some stages of decomposition, it's quite unmistakable.'

'I don't let them go into those woods,' said Jarvis impatiently. 'I told you, they never go in there. Well, except for the old lass, and look what happened to her.'

'Even so . . .'

'Look, I don't know. Maybe the smell of cack threw them off the scent.'

'The body was lying there for eighteen months,' said Cooper. 'But that bag was left only a few days ago.'

Jarvis scowled across the valley. 'There's a lot of shit in the countryside.'

'Maybe.' Cooper realized he wasn't going to get any further without antagonizing Jarvis. 'By the way, what did you do with the excreta you found?'

'What did I do with it?' said Jarvis in amazement. 'What do you think I did with it?'

'I can't imagine.'

'I chucked it on the compost heap. There's no point in wasting good cack.'

'And it's still there?'

'Of course it is. Unless some bugger snuck in during the night and nicked it. You never know these days.'

'I wonder if I could ask you to leave it where it is for a while, sir.'

Jarvis stared at him. 'It'll just rot down,' he said. 'That's the point of a compost heap.'

'I'd like to get someone to take a sample. Just in case we get the chance to do a DNA profile for comparison.'

'A DNA profile?'

'Yes, sir.'

But Jarvis continued to look sceptical. Cooper couldn't blame him. He didn't rate his own chances too highly, either of getting it approved or of persuading a SOCO that it was high priority. Somebody was bound to list the request under 'shit jobs'.

'I don't know much about DNA,' said Jarvis

finally, 'but it has to be taken from cells in the body, doesn't it?'

'Any cells with a nucleus,' said Cooper 'That's right.'

'Well, cack . . .' Then Jarvis paused, as if amazed that he was having to explain it, even to Cooper. 'Cack is waste stuff, undigested food. It's from whatever rubbish you've been eating. If you tested that crap, you'd likely get the DNA profile of a Big Mac and large fries with chicken nuggets. Not that there aren't plenty of those walking around the streets of Edendale on two legs, but what good would it do you?'

'We'd be hoping for some cells that might have sloughed off the gut lining as the material was passing through the intestine,' said Cooper patiently.

'You reckon?'

'But we'd have to get to it pretty quickly. I'm not a hundred per cent sure, but I think the DNA in excreta will degrade within a couple of weeks. In this case, it hasn't been exposed to the sun, which is a good thing. Ultra violet degrades DNA faster than anything.'

'Bugger all this,' said Jarvis. 'What are you doing about the bastard who shot my dog?'

Cooper looked across at the woods. 'We're visiting Alder Hall this afternoon to see what's going on over there.'

'Bloody hell, action. Well, I've got more spare timber – I'll start setting up the gibbet, shall I?'

20

Vivien Gill wasn't alone this time. The first hint Cooper had of company was the number of cars parked in the street near her house, not to mention the cluster of motorbikes. He had to leave his Toyota almost at the corner and walk down, wondering if there was a wedding taking place somewhere. Or a funeral, of course.

The door was opened by a big man in his late thirties, with a beer belly and the shoulders of an ex-boxer. Cooper was unavoidably reminded of Billy McGowan. It was that sense of a man who was out of place in his occupation, a man who ought to be doing something more physical than opening the door to visitors. Preferably a job that involved hitting things.

'Are you the bloke from the police?' the man asked, with instinctive suspicion.

Cooper produced his warrant card. 'Detective Constable Cooper, sir. I'm here to see Mrs Gill.'

'She's waiting.'

'Thank you, sir. And you are?'

'Family.'

The word was barely a grunt, delivered as though he was imparting more information than he normally gave to the police. Cooper's instincts began to prickle. He felt sure that if the man were to give his name, it would be one he recognized from a charge sheet or a magistrates' court list.

He held the door open, and Cooper squeezed past him into the hall. Maybe death and funerals were too much on his mind at the moment, but this person smelled as though he'd already died. Some time around last Monday, probably. Perhaps they hadn't been able to schedule his funeral yet, and he was returning to the earth bit by bit as his body sloughed away.

'Do I know you?' said Cooper.

'No.'

'I think I might have seen you around. Where do you work?'

The man shut the front door and stared at him. He was only an inch or so taller than Cooper, but he carried a few extra stone in weight and most of it was in his belly and shoulders.

'At the sewage works,' he said. 'I'm a shit stirrer.'

Cooper turned as the door of the sitting room opened behind him. A woman he didn't recognize was studying him. She had hair dyed deep red, and she squinted her eyes against a trickle of smoke from the cigarette in her mouth.

'Is he the bloke from the police?' she said to the man.

'So he reckons.'

Cooper showed his ID again. 'Detective Constable Cooper.'

'All right,' said the woman. 'She's in here.'

He could tell from the rumble of noise that the sitting room was full of people. The furniture had been pushed back against the walls, leaving a space in the middle of the carpet, as if in readiness for a performance. For a few moments, Cooper could hardly breathe from the smoke and the heat of so many bodies crammed into a small room.

When he entered the room and was pointed towards a seat in front of a small forest of hostile stares, he realized exactly who was being expected to give a performance.

Gavin Murfin offered the DI a miniature chocolate bar from a box of Cadbury's Heroes, rattling it temptingly. Hitchens shook his head abruptly.

'Sir, DC Murfin has been checking on Melvyn Hudson's former business partner, Richard Slack,' said Fry.

'This is old Abraham's son,' said Murfin. 'And father to Vernon. Richard was the second generation of the family on the Slack side of the business, so to speak.'

'He and Melvyn Hudson were contemporaries?' said Hitchens.

'If you like. Their fathers set up the firm, but both retired and left their interests in the business to their sons. Old Mr Hudson died, but Abraham Slack is hanging on – he just doesn't play an active part in Hudson and Slack any more.'

'So what happened to Richard?' said Hitchens.

'He was killed in a car crash last year.'

'You know, I remember it,' said the DI, leaning forward in his chair. 'There was a lot of stuff in the local paper about him. But it didn't happen on our patch, did it?'

'In C Division,' said Murfin. 'It was a bit ironic, actually. He was on a late-night call at the time, collecting a body from a house near Holymoorside. He was driving one of those unmarked vans with blacked-out windows.'

'Was this before or after Audrey Steele's funeral?'

'After, by nearly two months.'

'Well, I suppose funeral directors have to meet their end the same as the rest of us,' said Hitchens.

Murfin shrugged. 'Also, Dad's Army have been helping me make some enquiries into the state of business at Hudson and Slack. It seems they're almost the last family-owned funeral directors in the valley. All the other independents have gone. Most of them belong to the big chains now, though they often keep the old names to make people think they're still locally owned, like. A couple of them are run by American companies.'

'Has this affected Hudson and Slack?'

'The word is that they've been struggling for a while,' said Fry. 'Apparently, they've lost a lot of business over the last few years to the big boys. I suppose it's a question of advantages of scale, like any other business.'

'The larger players will always push out the small men, if they're allowed to,' said Hitchens. 'That's the way it goes.'

'From what we hear, they can be pretty ruthless. They put the word about that a small funeral director is likely to turn up for a funeral with vehicles that don't match, or a bunch of staff in badly fitting suits who've never been nearer to a funeral than the bar of the Cemetery Inn. Everybody wants a funeral to go off without a hitch, and they're making decisions under stress anyway.'

Hitchens looked from one to the other. 'Hudson told us that business was good, didn't he?'

Fry shook her head. 'What he told us was that there's an increasing demand. Changing demographics, and all that. That doesn't mean all the new business is coming his way, does it? It depends what inroads the competition are making in this area. I wonder how his partner fitted in? Was Richard Slack a modernizer or a traditionalist? Which of them was the real driving force behind the business? It would be interesting to know the relationship between them.'

Fry tapped her teeth with a pen for a moment, then stopped suddenly and looked at the end of the pen in horror.

'There's one other thing of interest,' said Murfin, sounding a bit smug.

'Have you been saving the best for last?' said Hitchens.

Murfin smiled. 'A few months ago, Hudson and Slack reported a break-in at their premises in Manvers Street. Among other items, the thieves took a plastic drum containing twenty-five litres of embalming fluid – some stuff called Chromotech.'

'What use is that to anybody?' asked Hitchens.

'It provides a new drug experience, if you're into that kind of thing. Apparently, the latest trend is to mix embalming fluid with cannabis for a special high. Another idea imported from the USA.'

'That sounds ridiculously dangerous.'

'You're not kidding.'

Fry leaned forward across the DI's desk. 'The medical advice is that this stuff is highly corrosive if exposed to skin or taken orally. Mixed with cannabis, it makes users violent and psychotic. It causes hallucinations, euphoria, increased pain tolerance, and produces feelings of anger, forgetfulness and paranoia. In extreme cases, it can result in blindness or even death.'

Hitchens raised an eyebrow. 'Interesting. Were drug users blamed for the break-in? Was anyone charged?'

'There were no charges,' said Murfin. 'But the theory was that someone read about the idea on the internet and decided to experiment. They took some other stuff at the same time, property worth about ten thousand pounds in total. Anything small and easy to dispose of for a few quid.'

'What sort of stuff?'

Murfin looked at the incident report again. 'Oh, you know – scalpels, hypodermic needles, medical supplies. Anything that looked like pharmaceuticals, I suppose. There's a whole list of items. Including a set of trocars, whatever they are. And don't tell me – I don't think I want to know.'

'Hold on,' said Fry. 'Let's have a look at that list.'

She took the report and scanned through. Gavin was right, the list was a long one. Many of the items were things she'd never heard of and couldn't imagine a use for. Eye caps, canulas, a mouth former . . .

'What is it?' asked Hitchens.

'It was just a break-in, Diane,' said Murfin. 'All right, it's never been cleared up, but it seems obvious it was addicts looking for kicks and some quick money to pay for their next fix.'

'It was just a thought,' said Fry. 'I was wondering if there's enough stolen equipment on this list for somebody to perform their own private embalming.'

When Cooper returned to the office, he found an urn had been left on his desk for return to Susan Dakin. According to the report, the cremains had been weighed in by the lab at eight pounds five ounces. It was strange to think that Mr Dakin probably weighed about the same reduced to ashes as he did when he was born.

But the urn would have to wait a little while yet before it was returned to its shelf. He and Diane Fry had an appointment with a property agent later this afternoon at Alder Hall. And later he hoped to attend Audrey Steele's second funeral.

'Gibbet?' said Fry when he reported his visit to Tom Jarvis. 'Are you saying there's a place called Gibbet Rock near Wardlow and Litton Foot?'

'Yes,' said Cooper. Fry was starting to look flushed with excitement.

'This is it, Ben. "Follow the signs at the gibbet and the rock, and you can meet my flesh eater." This rock will be limestone, right?'

'Yes.'

'His second message is starting to make sense at last. Let's have a look at the map.'

'Where's the transcript?'

'I don't need it,' said Fry. 'It starts "All you have to do is find the dead place. Here I am at its centre, a cemetery six miles wide." This Gibbet Rock is within three miles of Wardlow church, I presume?'

'Easily.'

'"See, there are the black-suited mourners, swarming like ants around a decaying corpse." No problem there – he was at a funeral when he made the call. "Lay them out in the sun, hang their bones on a gibbet." There's your Gibbet Rock –' Fry stabbed a finger at the map. 'Moving west from Wardlow.'

'OK.'

'"They should decay in the open air until their flesh is gone."'

'Audrey Steele?' suggested Cooper. 'It fits.'

'Could be.'

'That's Litton Foot, there.'

Fry nodded. '"Or, of course, in a sarcophagus."'

They were both silent for a moment.

'I don't know,' said Cooper.

But Fry finished reciting the message to the end, as if it was programmed into her memory.

'"It's perfectly simple. All you have to do is find the dead place."'

'I still don't know, Diane.'

'All right. Then we have to follow the signs at "the gibbet and the rock". Let me make a few phone calls, and we'll go.'

'Are you sure of this? There could be other interpretations.'

Fry glanced at him as she picked up the phone. 'Yes, I'm sure. I'm starting to get inside his head here, Ben. Isn't that what you said we should be able to do? Well, I'm doing it.'

'The DI said no more chasing around the countryside –'

But she was already speaking to someone on the phone. Cooper looked at the urn on his desk and the missing persons files. Oh, well. For once, he couldn't be accused of going off and doing his own thing. It was Fry's decision.

And she might be right. He hadn't learned the messages by heart the way she had, but Cooper could recall the one line Fry had missed quoting from the second call. *You can see it for yourself. You can witness the last moments.* They might not have a lot of time to waste.

Half an hour later, Cooper found himself driving back towards Wardlow. It was Matt who'd reminded him that the road between Wardlow and Monsal Head had a local name – *Scratter*. 'Scrat' was a dialect word for scratching or clawing, and horses had to 'scrat' up the hill. But some said the name came from *skratti*, the Scandinavian word for a demon. The Devil himself was called Old Scratch in local folk stories.

The Vikings had left quite a legacy in these parts. Derbyshire had once belonged to Denmark, with an invading army stationed in the next county, in the caves under Nottingham Castle. Those Vikings had been superstitious folk, and had peopled the landscape with demons and monsters, entire swarms of them lurking in every dark place and at every unfamiliar spot on the map.

Over the centuries, their descendants had been reluctant to give up the most sinister stories, even in the face of all that new-fangled religion and rationality. Some of those legends had taken such a powerful grip on the hills and shadowed valleys that they would never be dislodged. Demons hid in the very place names.

'Ben, this Professor Robertson,' said Fry as they drove through Wardlow. 'He's definitely weird, isn't he?'

'He's all right. He's just a bit . . .' Cooper hesitated, struggling for the right word. 'Well, perhaps a bit obsessive. Look, he has this specialized interest, a subject he thinks he's the world greatest expert on. He loves showing off his knowledge. That makes him appear rather . . .'

'Weird?'

'Just because he's slightly eccentric and obsessed with the rituals of death doesn't mean he goes home every night and acts out necrophiliac fantasies on the bodies of his victims.'

'Has he talked to you about necrophilia?'

'No.'

'So that one came from your own imagination, did it?'

Cooper sighed. 'You've obviously made your mind up about Freddy Robertson on no evidence. Is this some kind of intuition, Diane?'

'Intuition, bollocks. This is experience. I've met enough weirdos to know one when I see one.'

'Fair enough.'

'So is the professor married?'

'I don't know. He's never mentioned a Mrs Robertson.'

'Can you find out?'

'I suppose so.'

Cooper's assumption had been that Robertson was a bachelor, or divorced. Men with obsessions were difficult to live with. But you could never be sure – it was remarkable the compromises people could come to in their relationships.

'Oh, I forgot to tell you,' said Cooper. 'I had a really bad time at Mrs Gill's. All the family were there, getting ready for the funeral this afternoon. Audrey Steele's second funeral, that is. They interrogated me about how we were doing with the enquiry.'

'What did you tell them?'

'There wasn't much I *could* tell them. They weren't very happy with that. I was glad to get away before they formed a lynch mob.'

'These jobs have to be done.'

The outcrop called Peter's Stone or Gibbet Rock stood towards the north end of the Cressbrook Dale nature reserve, an area of limestone grassland, with ash woodlands further down the dale. There was a path along the stream into the dale, reached through a tiny, spring-loaded gate and a gap in the stone wall that was just wide enough for a slim person not wearing too many clothes. Cooper thought he would probably manage to squeeze through, as long as he was trying it before lunch and not after.

'There must be another way,' said Fry, looking at the fields full of sheep. In the bottom of the dale, the rushing stream looked impossible to cross.

318

'Yes, I think there is.'

Right at the junction of the Wardlow road, they found a gateway in a farmyard, just wide enough for Cooper's Toyota to scrape through, past a mildewed hawthorn tree. The gate was secured only by a length of orange baler twine looped over the stone gate post. The four-wheel drive managed fine on the track until they came to a point where the swollen stream had breached the field wall and swamped the ground on the other side. Cooper stopped and looked up at Peter's Stone, still two hundred yards away.

'We're going to have to walk, I'm afraid.'

Fry opened the passenger door and looked down at the water lapping gently against the wheels. 'I'm not getting out on this side.'

'It's deep, but clean.'

'I'm not getting out.'

'I can lend you some wellies,' said Cooper. 'They're in the boot.'

'OK.'

The path had been liberally sprinkled with droppings by the sheep that watched them pass, their eyes unblinking, their jaws moving rhythmically. The ewes had recently been shorn, and the red splotches of their owner's mark showed clearly on their sides. Some still had lambs with them, a few months old now, but not yet ear-tagged.

'Make sure you stay on the path, Diane,' Cooper called as Fry began to lag behind.

'Why, are the sheep dangerous?'

'No, the ground is.'

Cooper smiled to himself as he climbed another stile. Fry had at least remembered him telling her how dangerous cows could be when they had calves with them. But sheep were different.

'The signs are warning about dangerous mineshafts. There must have been lead mining around here. The shafts get covered over, and sometimes you don't see one until you're right on top of it.'

Cooper realized he was talking to himself. He turned to see Fry still near the last stile, with an expression of disgust on her face.

'What's the matter?'

She was looking at her hand in horror, as if it had turned into an alien object on the end of her arm. She bent over and began to wipe it vigorously on a patch of damp grass.

'Oh, God, it's sheep shit,' she said. 'There's sheep shit on the top of this wall, and I put my hand right in it.'

'Sheep? Are you sure it isn't bird shit?' said Cooper.

'I don't care what kind of shit it is. It's on my hand.'

Cooper waited for her, wondering whether he ought to offer her a clean handkerchief or something, like a gentleman in a Jane Austen novel. But he didn't carry a handkerchief. He might have a few crumpled Kleenex tissues in his pocket. He started to look for one, but Fry had already found her own and was gingerly stepping over the stile, without using her hands.

'I was just saying . . .' he began.

'Stay on the path. I know.'

Cooper walked carefully through the grazing sheep and reclining cattle, not even looking at them as he passed. They glanced at him and went on cudding. But Fry shied away from the first ewe she came near, and the animal did the same, scrambling away and panicking its neighbours. The cattle slowly got up and moved away from her.

'Diane, stop bothering the animals,' said Cooper, turning to see what was going on.

'I'm not – they're bothering me.'

She turned at a rattle on the slope behind. An old ewe was peering over the ledge at her.

'See, that one threw a stone at me.'

Finally, they crossed a small ridge and found themselves at the foot of Peter's Stone – Gibbet Rock, as Tom Jarvis had called it. Cooper wondered if Anthony Lingard had been gibbeted on top of the outcrop, or from the side of the rock itself. Or perhaps from the slope below it? There was nothing to indicate which.

On this side of the rock, there was a scree slope, an unstable mass of tiny, loose stones. Scree was notoriously difficult to climb, so a path had been worn towards the eastern side, where the gradient was steeper but more stable underfoot. Cooper looked up at the limestone outcrop. It was full of nooks and crevices.

They were breathing heavily by the time they had scrambled to the top of the outcrop. Cooper helped Fry up the last stretch, and stopped to get his breath back. From here, there was only one farmhouse visible on the skyline further down the dale. The opposite slope was formed of limestone terraces and more scree. Lumps of stone dislodged by the sheep lay around it like giant hailstones.

A few minutes later, Cooper lay half-hidden between two rocks, his head down in a deep crevice. He began to inch back towards the air, and when he emerged, he was clutching something in one hand.

'What have you got there?' asked Fry.

Cooper was panting, and red in the face from the blood rushing to his head while he was upside down.

'Well, it looks like a Tupperware box,' he said. 'It was tucked away out of sight in this fissure. And there's something inside it, see –'

'Let's have a look.'

The box was about nine inches long, with a tight yellow lid. It wasn't actually Tupperware but something similar, made of tough translucent plastic. It had two handles that hinged on to the lid and held it in place, making the box pretty much airtight and waterproof. It had been hidden deep in the crevice, and concealed from casual view by a lump of limestone. Fry brushed off some dirt and eased open the lid.

'Lord, what's all that junk?' she said.

Cooper leaned over her shoulder. Among a lot of other stuff in the box, he glimpsed a small toy dog, an England badge, a set of coloured crayons and a pair of sunglasses. There was even a Matchbox Land Rover Freelander that he would have loved as a child.

'I can see a notebook, too,' he said, reaching to lift the crayons out of the way.

Fry held up a hand. 'Get it back to the office and let scenes of crime go through everything. If he's left us a clue here, we don't want to miss it.'

'We've got an appointment,' Cooper reminded her.

'Yes, I know.'

Fry looked at her hand and sniffed her fingers, checking for traces of sheep droppings.

'Don't worry,' said Cooper. 'The dress code is casual. The Duke and Duchess won't be at home.'

He took a last glance at the plastic box before they piled all the stuff back in. There were stickers and pens in a plastic Waitrose bag, a pencil sharpener, dart flights, sweets, and cloth badges advertising something called *Les Randonneurs Mondiaux*. A label inside the Waitrose bag said: *Congratulations! You've found it!*

21

The White Peak could boast very few celebrities, apart from some ageing pop stars and TV personalities. If Cooper racked his brains, he could only recall the singer Long John Baldry, who'd been born in Bakewell, Buxton's Tim Brooke-Taylor of *The Goodies* and DJ Dave Lee Travis. Great writers had passed through the area and moved on. Charlotte Brontë had created Jane Eyre while staying with a friend in Hathersage; Jane Austen had written part of *Pride and Prejudice* at a Bakewell hotel; and D.H. Lawrence had found his real-life inspiration for Mellors the gamekeeper living on the Via Gellia, near Matlock. So even literary links tended to be a bit tenuous.

As a result of the celebrity shortage, local people had to make do with the aristocracy. The dukes of Devonshire and Rutland had once owned the whole of this area between them, and large chunks of it still bore their names. The Devonshires' home at Chatsworth House was a major tourist attraction, more spectacular and more opulent than Buckingham Palace, and containing a substantial share of the nation's art treasures. Or so it had seemed to Cooper when he'd toured the house as a child.

Alder Hall had been one of the Devonshires' smaller properties, so insignificant that an early duke had presented the estate as a gift to a less affluent cousin. The present hall had only fifteen bedrooms and two hundred acres of private grounds, so it would hardly have been missed.

The walls around the estate were high and festooned with ivy. Here and there, water gushed into stone troughs from drainage holes designed to relieve the pressure that built up behind the walls after heavy rain. The main gates were open when they arrived, so presumably the agent had got there before them. Cooper turned into the gateway and rolled the car slowly on to the gravel drive.

Well, there had probably been gravel here at some time. Now, it was hidden by the grass and weeds that had encroached from the shrubbery on either side. If the hall ever did get new owners, it would take quite a few doses of weedkiller to get this lot under control. Cooper could hear the stems of the couch grass scraping against the underside of the Toyota as he inched his way towards the first bend in the drive. He didn't know how far the hall was from the road, but he expected a good view of it at some point. What he got instead was the sight of a figure standing in the middle of the driveway, waving madly.

'What the heck is he doing?'

'I don't know. Is that the agent?' said Fry.

'I presume so. It looks as though he's trying to tell us something.'

The man was signalling as if he wanted Cooper to go to the left. There was nowhere to turn off the drive, except into the bushes, so he skirted as close as he could to the edge.

'Maybe there's a pothole or something. I can't see for this long grass.'

But it wasn't a pothole. As they drew closer to the gesticulating figure, Cooper could see the decomposing body of a sheep lying on the driveway, its clean-pecked ribcage showing clearly through ragged tufts of wool.

Cooper wound down the window. 'Mr Casey?'

'Yes. Sorry about that. I didn't want you to do what I did – I'm afraid I ran over the animal's head before I'd noticed it.'

'Don't worry. We'll not be charging you with anything. We can see the injuries were inflicted postmortem.'

Casey laughed nervously. 'I don't know how long it's been lying there. It's rather embarrassing, really. We're supposed to be keeping an eye on the place and sorting out any problems, in case a prospective purchaser comes along. But we've been rather short-staffed, you see, and the place hasn't been checked as often as it should.'

Cooper looked at the sheep again. He could see the remains of the crushed skull where Casey's tyre had gone over it. But the animal was almost completely skeletonized, and the fleshless jaw bones and teeth grinned back at him knowingly. No one had checked here for months. Or, if they had, they hadn't bothered to move the dead sheep. He could understand how that wouldn't be too enticing for a buyer with a couple of million pounds in his pocket, looking for a smart country retreat.

'Are there sheep grazing in the grounds of the hall, then?' he said.

'There aren't supposed to be,' said Casey. 'This one probably belongs to a neighbouring farmer.'

'Your fences must need some attention, then.'

'The boundaries are stone wall mostly. But they're rather old. I'll have to get someone to check the wooded areas to see if there's a collapse.'

'That would be a good idea, sir.'

'Come on up to the house anyway. The rest of the drive is OK.'

Cooper eased the Toyota over the last few yards of weed-covered gravel and parked next to a black Range Rover near the front entrance to the hall. Casey walked up behind them, sorting a ring of keys from his pocket.

'I hope the house is more secure than the rest of the property, Mr Casey,' said Fry when they'd introduced themselves. 'Or are we likely to find sheep grazing in the reception rooms?'

'No, no. I assure you, Sergeant, it's perfectly secure.'

But Casey didn't look entirely certain of that. And no wonder, if the property hadn't been checked for a while. The decomposed sheep had been a bad omen. Cooper could imagine some of the scenarios now going through Casey's mind. He'd be picturing himself opening the front door of the hall and confronting the unmistakable signs of large-scale theft or vandalism.

The front elevation of the hall itself wasn't particularly impressive. It was built of limestone blocks, with sandstone corners and lintels in the local style. Its eighteenth-century mullions were its most attractive feature, but a jumble of awkward gables, mock battlements and nine-teenth-century alterations had destroyed any symmetry it might once have had. Cooper could see why the dukes never thought of leaving the grandeur of Chatsworth for this.

There was a short flight of steps up to the door. Much of the mortar had disappeared from them, leaving gaps where dirt had collected and moss had darkened the stone. Casey seemed to hesitate before putting the key in the lock.

'There's a burglar alarm,' he said. 'The keypad is just inside the door.'

'Presumably you know the code number?' said Fry.

'Of course.'

Cooper looked up at the yellow box tucked into

an angle of wall formed by the addition of a Georgian wing.

'Who would have set the alarm last?' he asked.

'Whoever had the task of checking inside the house,' said Casey. 'We're supposed to inspect the property at least once a month, unless the weather has been particularly bad, in which event we'll come down to see if there's any structural damage.'

Casey looked a little embarrassed as he waited for Cooper to ask him when the last inspection had been, in view of the company's staff shortages. In fact, Cooper didn't need to say anything. As Casey put the key into the lock, he answered the unspoken question.

'I'd have to look at the records back at the office,' he said, 'if you need details of previous visits.'

'We'll let you know, sir.'

Casey held the door open, and looked relieved when an electronic beeping started. Cooper realized that an even worse scenario might have occurred to the agent – the possibility that a member of his staff had forgotten to re-set the alarm.

'How many people have access to the alarm code?' asked Fry.

Casey clicked the cover of the keypad closed. 'We're not a big company. Half a dozen, at most.'

'We might need their names.'

'Yes, anything you like.'

The agent flicked a switch, and lights came on.

Thank goodness Casey's company was at least remembering to pay the electricity bill.

Cooper turned slowly. The hallway wasn't large for a house this size, but the stone-flagged floor gave it a cold feeling. It also explained the way their voices had begun to echo from the moment they stepped over the threshold. The walls were almost bare, with pale expanses of plaster where pictures had been removed for storage. But the furniture had been left in place – several small tables, an empty display cabinet, an oak chest covered with a lace cloth. Directly facing the door were the main stairs, with square balustrades and a worn red carpet. Despite the lights, the door-ways looked particularly gloomy, especially those that lay at the back of the house, in the shadow of the stairs.

'It's a bit cold in here, isn't it?'

'We keep the heating turned down to a minimum in the summer,' said Casey.

Cooper wondered if there was a ghost here. Almost certainly. Didn't every house of this age have at least one? Probably the rooms were haunted by some young kitchen maid who had drowned herself, but still appeared to answer the bell now and then in the deepest hours of the night. Not that anybody was left to ring the bell now the Saxtons had departed.

He heard John Casey's footsteps on the flags behind him, moving to the right towards one of the doors. The agent was anxious to get on with the inspection, to reassure himself that none of his scenarios were true. He was praying there was no theft, no vandalism, no squatters.

But then Fry stopped him with another question. She was still standing near the keypad for the burglar alarm, and Cooper could tell by the tone of her voice that she wasn't satisfied with Casey. He'd been slipshod, less than professional in his responsibilities. He didn't come up to her high standards. Very few people did.

'Mr Casey,' she said, 'why has your company been short-staffed?'

'Oh, we had a couple of employees leave earlier this year. Experienced people, too. They're difficult to replace, you know. We're in a position of trust here, so we have to be a bit careful who we take on to replace them.'

'And did those employees have access to this alarm code?'

Cooper was still staring up at the ceiling, trying to make out the pattern in the plasterwork, when he heard Casey's response.

'Only Maurice Goodwin,' said the agent. 'He was the man who spent most time out here.'

'Goodwin?'

'He was one of our employees who left a few months ago.'

'Why did he leave?'

'Oh, the usual. A personality clash.'

He moved on through the rooms, and they had to follow him. Without a guide, Cooper was afraid he'd be lost in a moment in the labyrinth of corri-dors and doorways.

'Of course, this isn't the original house,' said Casey. 'There was a property here from Tudor times. Alder Hall Manor passed from the Greys to the Cavendishes, who gifted it to the Saxton family. It was Jeremiah Saxton who built the present house in 1740. At the gates, you might have noticed that he set up his crest of two goats rampant in place of the Cavendish stag. I believe the house is featured in Volume One of *Old Halls, Manors and Families of Derbyshire*.'

'Oh? Is that a selling point?'

'Very much so.'

'Was this place never opened to the public?' asked Cooper. 'A lot of people have done that to help pay for the maintenance.'

'The Saxton family never liked to encourage sensationalism. On a few occasions, they opened the house up to the public, but visitors were never shown the crypt, or even told of its existence.'

'The crypt?'

'It's one of the reasons this property is looking for exactly the right purchaser. It wouldn't suit everybody.'

'But surely a crypt is found under a church?'

'The northern wing of the house was originally built as a chapel. That was some time in the late eighteenth century. Sir Oswald Saxton was a deeply religious man and engaged his own personal chaplain to pray for his soul.'

'Did it do him any good?'

'I couldn't possibly say.'

'But it didn't remain a chapel?'

'Times changed,' said Casey. 'Sir Oswald's successors weren't so devout. And perhaps they couldn't afford to employ their own chaplain, either. Whatever the reason, the chapel fell into disuse. A later owner of the hall converted it into a guest wing. Apart from one or two surviving stained glass windows, you would never know its origins.'

'And the crypt . . .?'

'When the alterations were done, the crypt was sealed. Guests of the Saxton family probably had no idea what they were sleeping over. But then a Victorian Saxton decided to open it up again. Supposedly, he was persuaded to do so by a group of his friends, who were interested in such things.'

'Such things being . . .?'

'Bones. Skulls mostly. I suppose I could show it to you. But it's not for public consumption, you understand. If certain sections of the population knew of the crypt's existence –'

'Don't worry, we're not journalists, you know.'

'Of course.'

There were steel shutters on all the windows, and only tiny cracks and spears of light penetrated the rooms they walked through. Some of the furniture had been covered with dustsheets, so that mysterious shapes stood all around them in the gloom, pushed back against the walls and shrouded like corpses.

'Are you selling the house furnished?' asked Cooper, stumbling against the corner of what felt like a dining table.

'This is a little different from the normal house sale,' said Casey. 'Some of these items have great historic value in the right context.'

'You mean they belong here and nowhere else?'

'I suppose you could put it that way. The vendors were concerned that some of the rooms should stay intact, if possible. Of course, it raised the price a little.'

'Most people like to stamp their own personality on a place when they move in,' said Cooper. 'They want to change everything.'

'Not here.'

John Casey stopped in front of a door. It might have led to a boiler room, or a furniture store – some aspect of the behind-the-scenes activities in a large house. There was no outward clue to the stone steps that were revealed when the agent produced the key from his ring and eased open the lock. The steps were deeply worn in the middle, as if many feet had passed up and down them over the centuries.

Casey went first, after finding the light switch. Cold air greeted him as he descended – the coolness characteristic of a cellar, a chill caused by being too close to the damp soil pressing against the walls.

Cooper was glad that the lights were working. He wouldn't have welcomed walking into this room in the dark, even if he'd known what to expect. The problem was the skulls. Hundreds of them grinned from shelves and niches cut into the stone walls. Some of them had fallen apart, their jaw bones slipping and sitting at awkward angles, their teeth loosened and lying in the dust. Some had gone beyond grinning, and had deteriorated into expressions of slack-mouthed, manic laughter.

Beneath the skulls, hundreds of bones had been stacked in ragged piles. Among a jumble of tibias, fibulas and femurs, Cooper distinguished the shape of a pelvis and a few ribs. They'd been heaped together with no regard for their original owner-ship. Not unless the pile of bones nearest to him had belonged to a man with three legs and no hips.

'Quite impressive, aren't they?' said Casey. 'Not everybody's cup of tea, of course.'

He reached out a hand to stroke the cranium of a large skull occupying a niche of its own near the bottom of the steps. The bony plates over its eye sockets were smooth and shiny, gleaming with a pearly luminescence in the reflected light.

'This one is supposed to bring you luck, if you rub it,' said Casey. 'He's called the General.'

Even with the lights on, it was impossible to estimate how many skulls there were. The long shelves were packed two deep, and shadows in the niches made it difficult to see right to the back. A hundred? Two hundred? Cooper wouldn't have liked to make a guess.

'Where did they all come from?' asked Fry. 'Are these all ancestors of the Saxton family?'

'Good heavens, no,' said Casey. 'The Saxtons themselves are either buried under the nave of the village church, or in a rather elaborate family tomb in the churchyard. I believe there are several quite fine effigies in the church, if you're interested in such things.'

Fry pointed at the rows of skulls. 'So who are *they*?'

'The story is that they were Royalist soldiers, ambushed and killed by Parliamentary militia on their way to help raise the siege of Wingfield Manor.'

'The Civil War?' said Cooper, bending to look closer at the skulls. 'Seventeenth century, then.'

'That's right.'

'But that's before the hall was built, let alone the chapel.'

'The remains weren't found right here, but somewhere on the estate when forestry work was being carried out. As I said, there was an earlier house on this site, and the Saxtons are known to have been Royalist sympathizers, so perhaps the soldiers were billeted here. Certainly, the original house was severely damaged by the Parliamentarians and had to be demolished. A punishment for supporting the wrong side, I suppose.'

Cooper had never heard this story, though there were many others like it in Derbyshire, where the English Civil War had split local sympathies. At Chapel-en-le-Frith, the church had become known as 'Derbyshire's Black Hole' after it was used to imprison fifteen hundred Scottish troops captured at the Battle of Ribbleton Moor. The Parliamentary army had left them crammed in the church for two weeks and forty-four of them were dead when the doors were opened.

'Has anyone ever had the bones authenticated? I mean, to confirm that they actually are from the Civil War period?'

'I'm told it was done some years ago,' said Casey. 'But the findings were never made public.'

'So there must be a record of how many skulls and bones are in the collection?'

'Yes, of course. But again . . .'

'It hasn't been made public. I see.'

Cooper found a torch in his pocket and shone it into the dusty corners. Large black spiders scuttled away from the light. Their webs stretched from skull to skull and filled the eye sockets like pale cataracts. Powdered stone from the walls coated the shelves. In the curious silence typical of cellars, he thought he heard a faint scuttling movement. But it was only Fry, edging back towards the steps, restless to move on.

They walked back upstairs to inspect bedrooms complete with dusty four-poster beds, and bathrooms with ancient plumbing and stained ceramic baths. The roof must be leaking in places, because some of the ornate plasterwork on the ceilings was crumbling and in danger of collapse. Cooper found it sad to see history mouldering away. He'd rather a hotel or conference centre moved in and restored the place, installing en-suite bathrooms and a fitness centre.

Many armies had marched across Derbyshire over the centuries, and not just in the Civil War. It struck Cooper that Alder Hall would have been newly built when Bonnie Prince Charlie led his Jacobite rebels south as far as Derby in the winter of 1745. Wasn't it the Duke of Devonshire's regiment, the Derby Blues, who abandoned the city ahead of the advancing Highlanders? But instead of pressing on to London and overthrowing King George II, the Young Pretender had begun the retreat to Scotland. A major turning point in history had happened right there.

Cooper wondered whether the Saxtons had been Jacobites in those days, or loyal to the king. Catholics or Protestants, Royalists or Parliamentarians. There were times when everyone was expected to take sides.

In one of the bedrooms, he heard the sound of an engine, and looked out of the window. Down below, a small blue car was turning in the driveway, making a slow three-point manoeuvre that barely caused a crunch of gravel. From two storeys up, he could make out that the driver was a woman in a short skirt. He could see her legs, and one arm on the steering wheel, but that was all. He wasn't even sure of the make of the car – a lot of those compact models looked the same. And he was at the wrong angle to get a view of the number plate. The vehicle had moved out of sight to Cooper's left before he could glimpse a single letter.

'Will you want to inspect the grounds?' asked Casey, without much hope of escaping just yet.

'We'd like to see the woods near the eastern boundary.'

'Ah, yes. Well, in that case, we could visit Fair Flora.'

She stood on a pedestal in a high clearing, deep among rhododendrons. She'd been named after the Roman goddess of flowers, and she held a garland in her left hand, clutched across her breast.

'The statue is said to have originated at Chatsworth House,' said Casey. 'But she was given to the owner of Alder Hall a long time ago by one of the dukes.'

'It's a strange place to stick a present from the Duke,' said Cooper. 'Shouldn't she be in the house?'

'She was originally. But the arrival of Fair Flora coincided with a period of ill fortune for the family at Alder Hall. Hauntings, too, they say. Anyway, they decided Flora was to blame, so she was banished to the woodlands.'

Cooper smiled. 'Is that the official story, or the local tradition?'

'Oh, the local tradition is different,' said Casey. 'As you might guess. The older residents will tell you that the statue is a memorial to the daughter of one of the Saxtons who owned Alder Hall. She was a young woman who either died at the hands of a jealous lover, or drowned in the river as she was eloping – depending on which version you choose to believe.'

'Tradition loves a romantic tragedy.'

'Yes. Well, either way, the legends agree on one thing – Flora attracts the spirits of the dead. Through her beauty and innocence, they're drawn to wherever she is. So as long as Flora stands out here in the woods, the spirits of those dead Civil War soldiers won't return to their bones.'

Cooper shivered a little, thinking of the cobwebbed skulls in their damp crypt.

'Anyway, this part of the estate is owned by Alderhall Quarries now,' said Casey. 'They've worked the quarry just above the road there since the beginning of last century. Alderhall sandstone used to be highly valued for some purposes, but not any more. Still, the company allows Flora to receive visitors.'

'She doesn't get many, judging by the state of the footpath,' said Cooper.

'No, it isn't exactly well used, is it?'

The grounds of Alder Hall had been sculpted into a panorama of gently sloping lawns. But beyond the parkland successive Saxtons had planted trees. Cooper could see trees and more trees, marshalled into plantations that Casey told him were named after major battles of their day – Corunna Wood, Ladysmith Piece, Sebastopol Carr.

Their management had been neglected for years, and now the orderly rows were ragged round the edges, like frayed carpets.

Where the grass slopes had been left unmaintained, tides of bracken had encroached from the hillside. Jeremiah Saxton would be upset to see how far his property now failed to match the grandeur of the Duke's estate further down the Wye Valley.

Cooper looked around for Fry. She'd taken a call on her mobile, and was standing a few yards away so she was out of earshot. Now she caught his eye and started making winding-up signals.

'Someone has left flowers here,' said Cooper. 'Recently, too.'

John Casey looked at the spray of flowers in the grass at the foot of the statue. 'Well, as I said, Flora does get visitors occasionally.'

'Why would anyone leave flowers?'

'I've no idea.'

'They're white chrysanthemums, too.'

'Yes? Does that mean something?'

'Ask any florist, Mr Casey. White chrysanthemums are for a death.'

'Oh, really?'

'There's a card, too, inside the cellophane.'

Cooper brushed drops of rain off to read the message. Then he stood up as Fry strode across the clearing, putting her phone away.

'Could you take us back to the hall please, sir?' she said.

'By all means,' said Casey.

Before they got in the car, Cooper showed the card to Fry.

'What do you think it means?' she said. '"Watch over the bones. They must forget."'

'I've no idea, Diane.'

She looked around the clearing, staring at the statue and the dense plantations of trees.

'Ben, do you think he's been here? Our mystery caller?'

'Someone certainly has.'

'Well, it'll have to wait. Everything's set up for the execution of a search warrant at Hudson and Slack.'

'When are we going to do it?'

'The DI's putting things together right now.'

'This afternoon?' said Cooper.

'As soon as we can get there.'

A few minutes later, Casey dropped them off on the gravel in front of the house. He didn't look sorry to be seeing the back of them.

'If you want to find out any more about Alder Hall and the Saxtons, you ought to ask Fair Flora herself,' he said.

Cooper frowned. 'We've just seen her, sir. But I'm not sure that talking to her would do much good.'

The property agent laughed. 'I didn't mean the statue.'

'Didn't you?'

'No, of course not. I meant the real person.'

22

Melvyn Hudson glared at Diane Fry with barely restrained fury. For a funeral director, he had quite a temper below that dignified exterior.

'I have no idea what all this nonsense is about,' he said. 'But you can't hold up our work. We have a funeral to do in ten minutes' time.'

'Everything you need to know is on the search warrant, sir,' said Fry coolly. 'And we have no intention of interrupting your business for a moment. Please carry on as normal. Our people will try to cause the minimum of disruption.'

'Minimum of disruption? With police crawling all over our premises? How do you think this looks to our clients? There's a family coming here this afternoon to bury their loved one.'

'Let's hope so, sir,' said Fry.

'What do you mean by that?'

Hudson was starting to get very loud. Fry looked at the team assembling outside the doors.

'If you'll show these officers where records of

your funerals are kept, we'll get on with the job as discreetly as we can,' she said. 'The sooner we get started, the quicker we'll be finished. And then we can get out of your way, sir.'

'It's an outrage,' said Hudson, starting to go red around the ears. 'Damn it, it's an outrage. This is not the sort of scene a bereaved family expect to see when they deal with Hudson and Slack.'

Fry knew that various members of staff would be able to hear their conversation. They were standing in the middle of the general admin office, and doors were open nearby. She could see what looked like a staff room to one side, with a table, kitchen chairs and a sink unit. Behind the office, she glimpsed a filing room with a row of metal and wooden cabinets.

'With respect, sir,' she said, 'the only person causing a scene at the moment is you. I suggest that might not be what a bereaved family expect to see from their funeral director.'

'Very well,' he said. 'But I insist on being here while you're doing whatever you need to do.'

'That's your privilege, sir. But what about your funeral?'

'My wife's in the chapel. I'll ask her to conduct it.'

'Fine.'

Fry looked round and saw a woman watching from a doorway. She was dressed in a smart black suit, a sort of female equivalent to Hudson, though her hair was dark and tied neatly back. Barbara

Hudson, presumably. Her expression wasn't too friendly.

Instead of facing her, Fry turned towards the workshop. There were all kinds of smells coming from these back rooms that hadn't penetrated the public areas. She wondered how they achieved that. She might like to use the technique in her flat, to keep out the whiff of the students.

'Does your warrant extend to the workshop, Sergeant?' said Hudson behind her shoulder.

'Do you mind me looking around, sir?'

'As a matter of fact, I do.'

'Surely you've nothing to hide?'

'Of course not.'

'What's at the end of the corridor?'

'The preparation room.'

'And what do you do in there?'

'We perform miracles, that's what we do,' said Hudson. 'People have no idea what goes on in the preparation room. And they don't *want* to know.'

'But I'm asking, Mr Hudson,' said Fry politely. And *she* was being polite, too, as far as she could manage. 'Could we take a look?'

'I'm sorry, but there's a case on the premises at the moment.'

'There's a what?'

Hudson inclined his head slightly towards her, as if acknowledging a rebuke. 'A deceased person under preparation. Without the express permission of the family, I'm afraid . . .'

'I understand.'

He turned suddenly and shouted over Fry's shoulder. 'Vernon, you can leave that car alone now. Go inside and give Billy a hand with the flowers. Then get yourself changed. You're driving.'

Vernon must not have responded quickly enough, because Hudson started to go red again.

'And get a move on, you lazy bugger!'

Fry turned in time to see Vernon slam the bonnet of one of the limousines and wipe his hands on a cloth. He had a sullen look on his face, like a teenager who'd been told to clean his room.

'That lad,' said Hudson when Vernon had wandered off. 'He drives me up the wall. But I can't get rid of him.'

'Because of his grandfather?'

'Old Abraham, yes. He says we should give the lad a chance. But Vernon's away with the fairies half the time. Look at him. The wheel's still turning, but the hamster's dead.'

'How long has he been with you?'

'A couple of years now. It seems like a lifetime.'

'Old Mr Slack doesn't play a part in the company any more?'

'He's in his seventies now. Abraham and I still own equal shares of the business, but I draw a salary as general manager on top of that.'

'I see. So you pretty much have sole control of the company.'

'On a day-to-day basis, I suppose I do.'

'And your partner died, didn't he? Vernon's father?'

'Richard was killed in a road accident last year. I expect you know that, Sergeant.'

'And this other gentleman is Mr McGowan, if I remember rightly?'

Hearing his name, McGowan looked up at Fry. Then he edged past to get through the door. Back in the office, Fry looked at the row of filing cabinets.

'You seem to be busy, Mr Hudson,' she said.

'We get about a hundred and fifty calls a year.'

'A hundred and fifty funerals?'

'Yes.'

'And your job is to make all the arrangements?'

'We serve the family's needs,' said Hudson. 'That's how we like to put it.'

'Mr Hudson, we're concerned with one particular family at the moment. The family of Audrey Steele, whose funeral arrangements were handled by Hudson and Slack eighteen months ago. On the eighth of March last year, to be exact.'

'I can't possibly remember one funeral out of so many,' said Hudson.

'Unless there was something unusual about it, I suppose.'

'Well, yes.'

'Do you remember Audrey Steele's funeral?'

'No. Look, let me check the diary. It might ring a bell. We record the main details in there.'

'All right.'

'Last year? March, you said.'

'Yes, the eighth.'

Hudson leafed through the pages of a large desk diary, the day to a page type. 'Ah, yes. Steele. Yes, we did that job. I can't remember it, but the details are here.'

'Would you have seen Audrey Steele's body before her funeral, sir?'

'Not personally. It was a morning funeral. The deceased would already have been prepared and casketed when I came in.'

'You mean the body was in the coffin?'

'Yes. Somebody else would have done the set-up. I mean, they'd have dressed the body and prepared it. Sometimes we do cosmetics and arrange the body with flowers for viewing by the grievers.'

'Did the family want to view the body on this occasion?'

'No. It was a closed-casket funeral. It's a lot better that way. No matter how good the preparation, there can still be a little purge.'

'Purge, sir?'

'A release of body fluids.'

'Ah. Not very nice, I presume?' said Fry.

'No. It's rather unpleasant for the grievers. When their loved one has been interred or cremated, we like our clients to go away with a sense of satisfaction that the whole thing has been done properly.'

'Would it have been possible for Audrey Steele's coffin to have gone to her funeral empty?' asked Fry.

'No, no, quite impossible.'

'What if the body had been removed, and the coffin weighted with something to disguise the fact that it was empty?'

'You don't understand,' said Hudson. 'That trick might work for a burial. But Audrey Steele was cremated. If there was no body in the coffin, it would be immediately obvious to the operators at the crematorium.'

'I see.' Fry looked around the office. 'What's security like here?'

'We had our security system upgraded earlier this year,' said Hudson.

'After the break-in?'

'Yes. Look, Sergeant, are you going to tell me what this is about?'

'While we're collecting the files, you might want to dig out the rest of the information we need,' said Fry. 'We want a list of all your staff, including anyone who was working here eighteen months ago but has since left.'

'That will take some time,' said Hudson.

'Your personnel records not up to date, sir?'

'Of course they are.'

'Then it shouldn't be any trouble.'

Hudson sighed heavily, but went to speak to the secretary.

Fry moved back towards the door, and found

Cooper at her shoulder. 'Why can't we seize the personnel records as well, Diane?' he said.

'They aren't specified on the search warrant.'

'Why not?'

Fry looked at him 'Softly softly, remember? Someone decided on a compromise.'

Before they left, Cooper took a peek into the workshop. Three men were working inside. One of them was Vernon Slack, another the thick-necked Billy McGowan he'd seen helping to carry the coffin at the crematorium. This morning, McGowan had his jacket off and his shirt sleeves rolled up as he lined a coffin with satin-like material and tacked a name-plate on the lid. He had so many tattoos on his arms that his skin looked like blue cheese. He might as well have had two rolls of ripe Gorgonzola hanging out of his sleeves.

A line of coffin trolleys stood to one side of the workshop. Along the walls, cupboards and shelves held rubber tubing and jars of red fluid, a stock of handles, linings and name-plates. Past the trolleys, Cooper could see a series of lockers. He supposed the staff must need several sets of clothing – formal funeral wear, something smart for collecting bodies, casual clothes for jobs in the workshop or mortuary. One of the lockers stood open; a black leather jacket hung on the door.

Cooper thought they ought to go carefully with Melvyn Hudson and his staff. Hudson and Slack was the sort of business that survived on reputation. It could suffer badly from gossip and unfounded rumour. Besides, these were people of guarded emotions, practised at putting up a façade. It was difficult to judge whether Hudson did it out of habit, or was trying to conceal some emotion that you wouldn't want to see on the face of your funeral director.

McGowan looked up and noticed Cooper. He smiled and flexed his muscles. One of his tattoos moved as the skin stretched. A dragon spread its wings, its mouth opening and flickering with blue flames.

As he was leaving the building, Cooper saw Vernon Slack jog past towards the compound where the hearses and limousines were parked. Vernon's bony wrists protruded from his cuffs as he tried to adjust the knot of his black tie. But doing it while he was running only made things worse. The way he moved reminded Cooper of Tom Jarvis's dog, Graceless. He looked the sort of clumsy innocent who'd end up getting hurt, simply because he knew no better.

The tree that had been planted over the body was no more than six feet high – a weeping willow sapling with slender, whippy branches and bark that looked almost yellow in the afternoon sun. Below it, the ground was barely disturbed. The earth would soon grass over and blend with the surrounding area, becoming a natural part of the young woodland. Only a small plaque wired to the trunk of the tree marked the spot as a grave.

Fifteen yards away, Fry turned from the fence and walked back across the grass. As always, she looked curiously out of place among trees. She instinctively hunched her shoulders to avoid them, as if their leaves might bite her. Cooper suspected that Fry and nature existed in two different worlds, with no points of contact.

'Is there no security of any kind in this place?' demanded Fry.

The woman in the black suit was one of the managers of the green burial site. She raised her eyebrows at Fry. 'Security? We don't need security here.'

'Oh, really? Perhaps you should think again. We'll send someone out to advise you.'

The woman scowled and went to Vivien Gill, who stood in the middle of a small group of relatives and friends.

'It's bizarre, isn't it?' said Fry when she got Cooper alone.

'Why?'

'Well, after what happened to her daughter's body, abandoned in the countryside like that? Why would Mrs Gill want to plant Audrey here? She might as well have left her where she was.'

'It makes sense to me.'

Cooper was starting to find the idea of a green burial appealing. Since all those things that happened to the body after death were inevitable, why not turn them into something positive? Here, a corpse would be giving back life.

According to the manager of the site, they were getting a number of celebrity green burials around the country now. Dame Barbara Cartland had been buried in a cardboard coffin next to an oak tree in her own garden. It was a new alternative for farmers, too. All they needed was a bit of land that wasn't used for anything else, and planning permission from the council.

Cooper hoped Matt didn't get to hear about that idea. He already had enough to say about diversification as it was. Golf courses, holiday cottages, fishing lakes – and now burial grounds.

'Very unhealthy, isn't it?' said Fry.

'Don't you see?' Cooper gestured around the burial site. In the middle, the weeping willow stirred its slender branches as it drooped protectively over the grave at its roots. 'Audrey Steele's tree isn't just a memorial to her. In a way, it *is* her. It's a continuation of her life in a different form. People buried here will never be dead. Not *really*.'

'Well, I suppose that's one way of looking at it.'

They began to walk back towards their car, parked out of sight beyond the trees. Then Fry stopped at the sight of one of the black-suited figures.

'Ben, is that one of Audrey Steele's relatives?'

Cooper followed her gaze. The suit didn't really

fit him at all. It was far too tight over his shoulders and belly. But it was certainly the man who'd let him into Vivien Gill's house that morning.

'Yes. Why?'

'I recognize him from crown court.'

'I thought he looked familiar, too. You must have a better memory than me for names.'

'Well, it was only on Wednesday,' said Fry. 'He was sitting in the visitors' gallery with the defendant's family at my murder trial. I'm pretty sure he's Micky Ellis's brother.'

23

When they got back to West Street, scenes of crime had inventoried the contents of the plastic box. In addition to the crayons, sunglasses, toy dog and Matchbox Land Rover, they'd found a Magic Tree air freshener, a Beatrix Potter book, a Digimon tiger, a Nike ski-pass holder, a London Zoo eraser, a glow-in-the-dark skeleton key-ring, three tungsten dart shafts, a magnifying glass, and a miniature screwdriver set.

'Oh, and a purple plastic grasshopper, with a metal tag attached to it,' said Liz Petty. 'Here it is. I thought you might like to see this item, in particular.'

Cooper picked up the transparent evidence bag. He held it up to the light and turned it slowly. He could see that the tag pointed out by Petty carried a six-figure code number on one side, and identified itself, or the plastic grasshopper it was attached to, as 'The Travel Bug'.

'What does it say on the other side?' said Fry.

355

Cooper spun the bag. 'It says: "I go from place to place, picking up stories along the way."'

Fry shook her head in frustration. 'What about the notebook that was in the box with all this stuff?'

'It's just an ordinary spiral notebook,' said Petty. 'You can buy this kind of thing anywhere. As far as we can tell, it seems to be some kind of log book. The first page is headed "Petrus Two", and various individuals have made entries at different dates.'

'Such as?'

'Such as "Itinerant Maggie". She says: "Great location – another spot I'd never have visited, if it weren't for the cache – many thanks."'

'It means nothing to me.'

'Nor me.'

'Sounds like some kind of treasure hunt, doesn't it?' said Cooper.

'Does it?' asked Fry. 'A treasure hunt?' She looked at the bagged items taken from the box. 'That is *not* treasure, Ben. Not by anybody's standards. It looks like the debris from the back of somebody's kitchen drawer.'

'I meant treasure in the loosest sense, Diane. The fun of a treasure hunt isn't the value of what you might find, but the excitement of the hunt. It's a quest. People are always figuring out ways to take part in quests.'

'Really?' said Fry.

'If it helps,' said Petty, 'there's a website address on the Travel Bug tag.'

'So there is – www.groundspeak.com. Anyone heard of it?'

There were shrugs all round the table. Fry looked across at Cooper.

'Ben, you're getting to be a bit of a whizz on the internet, aren't you? See if you can find out what this is all about.' She picked up the skeleton key-ring and spun it thoughtfully in its bag. 'We need to know who's been messing around up at that rock, when they were there, and why. If the people involved have no connection with our enquiry, then we need to eliminate them.'

'OK.'

Fry put the key-ring back on top of the Beatrix Potter book, covering a quaint illustration of a fox wearing a coat and scarf. 'Anyway, we've got some more news this afternoon. The forensic anthropologist had a toxicological analysis conducted on a sample from the first set of bones.'

Cooper looked at her. 'Bones?' he said. 'You mean Audrey Steele's remains?'

'Yes, Ben. The old bones the walkers found.'

Normally, Cooper wouldn't have reacted to something so minor. He'd heard far worse from Fry. In fact, he put up with rudeness and insensitivity from her all the time, because he genuinely believed she had other qualities. But something in the way she spoke so casually about the remains of a human being triggered a response, tipped him over his tolerance threshold. Perhaps it was the personal involvement Cooper felt with Audrey

Steele, ever since he'd seen her reconstructed face in the lab at Sheffield. Or maybe it was because he was about to start all over again with another unidentified victim whose remains were even now being recovered from a hillside in Ravensdale. But for once, he couldn't take it.

'For God's sake, Diane, she was a person with a name, you know. A human being. Not some heap of old bones thrown out for the dog.'

Fry looked up in astonishment. 'What?'

'Audrey Steele. That's what she was called, remember? She deserves to be talked about with a bit more respect.'

'Oh, you think so, do you?'

Cooper was fighting the quickening of his breath, the tendency for his hands to shake when he got angry.

'Yes, I do.'

'Well, thank you, DC Cooper. I'm sure we'll bear that in mind.'

Fry had gone faintly red around the ears at being spoken to like that in front of the SOCOs, and Cooper knew he'd suffer for it later.

'Anyway, be that as it may,' she said, 'someone at the lab pulled their fingers out and got us the report through, even though it's Saturday. They found traces of glycerine, phenol and formaldehyde.'

'What does that mean?' said Cooper, trying to steady his breathing and appear calm. 'Audrey Steele had been working with chemicals? Or

358

would they have been used in her hospital treatment before she died?'

'Neither. Apparently, those are the common constituents of embalming fluid, the sort used in the preparation room of a funeral parlour. Such as the one at Hudson and Slack.'

'Who does the embalming there?'

'I don't know.'

Cooper got up and walked over to his PC, where he called up Melvyn Hudson's details.

'OK, Mr Hudson is accredited with the British Institute of Embalmers,' he said.

'So probably Hudson takes care of the embalming, when required,' said Fry.

'And the break-in they had – the stuff that was stolen . . . Chromotech? That was embalming fluid.'

'The theft was too late to have any connection with Audrey Steele, Ben.'

'It means they probably have routine access to that kind of material at Hudson and Slack, though.'

'Of course.'

'And what about the second set of remains from Litton Foot?' said Cooper. 'Any more news there?'

'I rang earlier this afternoon. The van was just arriving at the lab in Sheffield.'

'So when can we expect some results? Tomorrow, perhaps?'

Fry sighed. 'I had a long conversation with the anthropologist. But we're dealing with the academic world now – and tomorrow is Sunday.'

'Damn.'

'We'll just have to try not to be impatient. Still, there are plenty of other things to do.'

'Such as looking a bit more closely at Melvyn Hudson?'

'I don't think much of Mr Hudson,' admitted Fry. 'Apart from anything else, he treats Vernon Slack like shit. You'd never think he was the grandson of one of the owners.'

'He treats Vernon like what?'

'Shit. You know what shit is, Ben.'

'Yes,' said Cooper thoughtfully. 'You mean cack.'

'What on earth are you talking about now?'

'Just a call I forgot to make. It was something Tom Jarvis said to me when I was up there last.'

'The man with the dog that got shot? What's the latest on that business?'

'No further developments,' said Cooper guiltily. Of course, he'd had no time to do anything about finding the person who shot Graceless, but that didn't stop him feeling guilty.

'"No further developments" is what we tell members of the public,' said Fry. 'It doesn't work on me. Ben, I'd have thought you'd be more interested in it, being an animal lover and all that.'

'It got put on the back burner a bit,' admitted Cooper.

'Well, take it off and stir it occasionally, will you? It creates a better impression. By the way, did you manage to make an appointment with what's her name?'

Cooper looked at his watch. 'I'm setting off now.'

'Good.'

'By the way,' said Cooper. 'Professor Robertson – he's a widower.'

'Oh?'

'Don't get excited – there were no suspicious circumstances. His wife died of cancer.'

As soon as Fry had gone, Cooper made the call he'd forgotten.

'We'd be wasting our time,' said the forensic scientist, when he'd stopped laughing. 'All right, it might not have been exposed to the sun, but one thing you'll definitely get inside a compost heap is bacterial activity. Any DNA present in cells from the gut lining will be degrading away in there and disappearing like – well, like shit off a shovel.'

In the background, his colleagues began laughing again.

'It was just an idea,' said Cooper.

'Tell you what, DC Cooper, let us know when your suspect has produced some fresh evidence.'

With deliberate tenderness, Madeleine Chadwick reached out a hand to the rose and cupped it in her palm. Its petals were still damp from the dew, and it glittered against her fingers, blood red on her white skin.

'Fair Flora,' she said. 'Yes, it's what my grandfather used to call me as a child. Flora is my middle name, you see. It's an old family name, but I've

361

never liked it very much, so I don't use it. Besides, nobody understands the classical reference these days. It's the name of some kind of margarine, isn't it? I'm sure my parents didn't know that when they christened me.'

Mrs Chadwick was tall and straight-backed, dressed in old jeans and a baggy sweater that would have made anyone else look shabby. But she carried herself so well that on her it hardly mattered. Cooper guessed she might be in her early forties, though it was difficult to judge. She had good bone structure, and skin that had been expensively cared for.

'Your grandfather was Sir Arnold Saxton, is that right?' he said.

'Yes. And my father was James Saxton. He died recently, which is why the estate is being sold.'

'So your father didn't inherit the title as well as the estate? Wasn't he the eldest son?'

'He didn't inherit the title because my grandfather was a knight, not a baronet. There's a difference.'

'Ah.'

Cooper tried not to look embarrassed, and Mrs Chadwick turned away, as if to help him. He imagined she'd wear a hat to protect her skin if it was sunny. Something with a broad brim that shaded her eyes. But today had been merely bright and overcast, no danger from the ultra violet.

'You must have been very sorry to leave Alder Hall,' he said.

'Devastated. When you've grown up in a house like that, it's very hard to leave. Fortunately, this cottage is mine. The old barn has been converted into two holiday homes, so the property brings in some income.'

Cooper looked at the house she referred to as a cottage. The views were what an estate agent would describe as 'panoramic'. The gardens alone were extensive, and there were also several acres of paddock around a modern stable block.

'You have horses?'

'Yes, but they're not kept here at the moment. They're in livery.'

'The house must be listed, I suppose?'

'Grade Two, I believe.'

Through a window he glimpsed oak beams and a spiral stone staircase, fringed lampshades and a carved horse mounted on a rosewood base. Pathways meandered through lawns and flower borders, stopping now and then at seats. An in-and-out driveway led to two double garages. One of the garage doors was open, and Cooper could see an internal WC. Who had a toilet in their garage?

There had been a gold-coloured Mercedes standing on the drive near the house. And in the depths of the garage, he thought he could also see a small blue Peugeot. He wondered if the engine was still warm, but could think of no excuse for checking.

'I visited Alder Hall earlier today,' said Cooper. 'You're familiar with the statue, I take it?'

'I used to visit her regularly when I lived at the hall. When I was very small, my grandfather took me to look at her. I recall that I was bit scared of her at first. Grandfather told me I'd be a beautiful lady just like her when I grew up. But I didn't want to be a statue and stand alone in the woods all day. I thought she looked rather unhappy. But I got to know her better over the years.'

'Have you been back since your family left the hall?'

'To see Fair Flora? No, I haven't.'

'Not at all?'

She turned cool grey eyes on him in silent reproach. 'I just said so. Why do you ask?'

'I'm sorry, Mrs Chadwick. But somebody has been leaving flowers at the statue. I wondered if it might have been you.'

'Why on earth would I do that?'

But Cooper didn't answer. He was looking around her garden. It was too big to see everything from one spot. There were more flower beds beyond the trees and alongside the lawns.

'Do you grow chrysanthemums?' he asked.

Mrs Chadwick gave a faint smile. 'White ones, perhaps?'

'Yes. How did you know I was going to ask that?'

'Come this way.'

She began to walk towards the lawn. For a moment, Cooper paused to admire the way she managed to move so elegantly despite wearing sensible flat shoes and jeans worn and baggy at the knees. Then he followed her down a short flight of stone steps into an arbour, where white and yellow chrysanthemums grew in profusion.

'Mrs Chadwick, how did you know it was white chrysanthemums I was interested in?' said Cooper.

Madeleine Chadwick laid a finger alongside the tight, curved petals of a chrysanthemum head, not quite touching it as she had the rose. The colour of the flower almost matched her fingers. But the petals were stiff and brittle, like clusters of fragile bones.

'White is for death,' she said. 'I do know that. White chrysanthemums are the flowers you order for a funeral.'

She smiled at him again, expectantly this time. Cooper sensed a hot prickling on the back of his neck. The sun was warm in this sheltered arbour, and he wasn't dressed for the heat. Besides, he was starting to feel at a disadvantage, and he wasn't sure why. He was used to dealing with people from all backgrounds, but Madeleine Chadwick's air of secret knowledge unsettled him. Her superiority seemed effortless. It was nothing like the smugness of Freddy Robertson, who worked so hard at trying to be superior.

'I don't think I ever explained what enquiry I'm working on,' said Cooper.

'I don't believe you did.'

'Then how . . .?'

But he began to flounder, unsure what question he could ask her. Luckily, she took pity on him, and turned to mount the steps again, back into the cooling breeze.

'John Casey phoned me,' she said. 'He keeps me up to date with anything relating to the hall. So I know about your visit there.'

'Ah. I see.'

It was a relief to have the mystery explained. He should have guessed that Casey would have talked to her. But Mrs Chadwick had manipulated him so expertly that he hadn't thought of the obvious.

'But I can assure you that whoever left white chrysanthemums for Fair Flora, it wasn't me,' she said. 'That's what you came to ask, isn't it?'

'Yes.'

'I haven't been back to visit the hall since we left, two years ago. I don't want to see it empty and abandoned, the furniture sheeted up like a mausoleum. I'm happy to leave everything in Mr Casey's hands. The place doesn't belong to me, you know. It reverted to the Devonshire Trust on my father's death.'

'Yes, I'm aware of that.'

'So I have no claim on it, other than an emotional one.'

Madeleine Chadwick stopped by the rose bush again. She couldn't seem to keep her hands off the deep-red blooms. Their petals were a little less damp now as they moved slowly in the breeze, but their colour was so dark that they looked almost black as they turned away from the sun.

'John Casey told me that you and your colleague were particularly interested in the crypt,' she said. 'The bone collection.'

'Yes.'

'Well, the Alder Hall bones are centuries old. Surely they're of no interest to our busy present-day police force. So I'm surmising there must be rather more recent bones somewhere that you're looking for. Human remains, a victim of violence?'

'It's possible,' said Cooper. 'I can't say any more than that.'

She stroked the petals of the rose, releasing a rich scent, like port wine.

'Black Prince,' she said. 'Do you know anything about roses?'

'I'm afraid not.'

'Roses are very remarkable things. No wonder they've been revered so much through the millennia. People have regarded them with awe and reverence – and quite rightly. The plant itself isn't very prepossessing, is it? Rather ugly, in fact. And it has these sharp, cruel spikes that can draw blood in an instant. Yet suddenly, at the right time of year, this plant blooms into the most exquisite flowers, and a delightful scent fills the air. It's magical and mystical. It's a symbol of the triumph of good over evil. The idea should interest you, as a police officer.'

Cooper nodded, but said nothing. He felt

ashamed of the cynical thoughts that sprang into his mind.

'A man came here a few weeks ago,' she said. 'He wanted my permission to visit the crypt and look at the bone collection.'

'Who was he?'

'I didn't get his name. I just sent him away. The nerve of the man, he simply appeared without warning, and he didn't come up to the cottage to knock on the door. I saw him standing over there, on the entertainment area.'

Cooper looked to see where Mrs Chadwick was pointing.

'Oh, on the patio?'

He heard her sigh deeply. Apparently, a patio ceased to be a patio when it was big enough. Cooper wondered if he should ask Mrs Shelley's permission to build himself a patio. Then he could invite his friends round for a barbecue next summer. If he still had any friends left by then.

'Could you describe this man, Mrs Chadwick?'

'Really, I didn't take much notice of him.'

'But surely you must have noticed something. His age, height, build, the colour of his hair? What he was wearing?'

Cooper was surprised to see Madeleine Chadwick looking faintly embarrassed. It was the first suggestion of a crack in her confident demeanour.

'All I can tell you,' she said, 'is that he wasn't the sort of person I would invite into my home.

One often knows these things instinctively, without the need for noticing details. I hope you understand what I mean.'

She seemed to avoid looking at him as she pinched off a dead bloom. After a moment, Cooper felt a blush starting from somewhere deep in his boots. With perfect delicacy, he'd just been told that he, too, was a person Madeleine Chadwick would forget as soon as he'd removed himself from her property.

Then she suddenly seemed to relent. 'There was one thing . . .' she said.

'Yes?'

'He gave off a strange scent. I didn't get close to him, of course, but I noticed it after he left. It must have lingered, and I'm so familiar with the scent of my flowers that it was incongruous.'

'What sort of scent?'

She extended her tongue slightly between her lips, the way some people did when they were thinking. On Madeleine Chadwick, it looked as though she were tasting the air, testing for a scent. For a second, Cooper was reminded of the chameleon in its tank.

'Not a particularly unpleasant smell, but it didn't seem quite right on a man of his kind.'

'Could you describe it?'

'Oh, you know how a smell fades from your memory once it's gone. In any case, I couldn't identify it at the time. I felt as though I ought to, but I couldn't.'

'And this man hasn't bothered you since?'

'No, thank goodness.'

Cooper took the card from his pocket in its plastic bag. 'Do these words mean anything to you, Mrs Chadwick?'

She squinted slightly to read the card. She was probably one of those people who ought to wear glasses but didn't for some reason.

'"Watch over the bones. They must forget." Was this found with the flowers?'

'Yes.'

'I suppose it might have something to do with the bones in the crypt. Is that your conclusion?'

'It's possible. I don't suppose you recognize the handwriting?'

She gave him a regretful smile. 'No.'

Cooper said goodbye to Mrs Chadwick at the gate and crossed the drive to his car. He took one look back at the garden, and saw her already bending over a plant, her hair catching the sunlight, her elegant fingers no doubt smelling of port wine.

He shook his head, trying to clear his thoughts. Madeleine Chadwick might be right about the triumph of good over evil. But the petals of a rose lasted barely a few days before they wilted and fell. Their triumph was short-lived. The thorns of the rose were different. Their cruelty lasted for ever.

24

Cooper tried not to look at Professor Robertson differently next time they met. He was making an effort to keep Diane Fry's comments out of his mind, not to mention his own reference to necrophilia. That was definitely one thought to re-bury in whatever hole it had come from.

When he arrived at the house in Totley, the professor was in his garden, spraying ant powder on the flagged path and against the back wall. This evening, he was wearing black wellington boots. Yet the trouser legs of his pinstriped suit were flapping outside the boots, which rather defeated the object of wearing them, surely?

'Come in, come in,' said Robertson. 'The blasted insects have seen enough of me. I'm sure they must have grasped my intentions by now.'

They entered the house through the back door into a utility room. The refurbishment had revealed pine floorboards in many of the rooms, and even the kitchen units were built in

Edwardian style, with beech and granite work surfaces.

When the professor passed close to him, Cooper caught a whiff of odour from his clothes. He felt sure it was from his clothes, though he couldn't quite name the smell. It made him think of old garments draped on wooden hangers in a mahogany wardrobe – especially the clothes at the back, the ones that were never worn any more.

Robertson sat with his hands clasped together as Cooper delivered the information he was allowed to share.

'Glycerine, phenol and formaldehyde?' said the professor when he'd finished. 'An unholy trinity, if ever I met one.'

'They're used in embalming fluids, I believe.'

'Exactly. Formaldehyde slows the rate that proteins degrade, so muscle tissues become fixed. That's why it's so difficult to move the limbs of an embalmed body. They no longer have the flexibility of living muscles.'

'Oh?' Cooper hadn't expected to be presented with such an immediate image of the professor handling a dead body.

'Glycerine softens the tissues and reduces fluid loss. An antibacterial substance like phenol prevents breakdown by micro-organisms.'

'It delays decomposition, in other words.'

'Indeed. What embalming really does is co-agulate the body's proteins, temporarily hardening and preserving. The work of the embalmer is the art of denial, the creation of an illusion. The body is drained, stuffed and painted for its final performance.'

Drained, stuffed and painted. Cooper filed that expression away in his memory.

'I wonder if you know a place called Alder Hall, sir? It's in the Wye Valley, not far from Edendale.'

'I believe I know the name. Now, in what connection would I have heard of Alder Hall?'

'There's a collection of bones. Below the hall, in a crypt.'

'Ah. Civil War relics?'

'Yes, sir. Have you ever visited?'

'No, I don't believe so. What's the name of the family?'

'Saxton. What about a lady called Madeleine Chadwick, then? She's the last of the Saxtons.'

Robertson shook his head. 'I don't quite see . . .'

'What can you tell me about ossuaries?' said Cooper. 'Is that the right name for places where bones were kept?'

'Yes, but the Alder Hall crypt isn't an ossuary, is it? As I recollect, the bones were found elsewhere.'

'Yes, sir.'

Robertson waited for him to explain, but Cooper remained silent. He was anticipating that the professor wouldn't be able to tolerate silence, and would feel obliged to fill it with the sound of his own voice.

'A lot of ossuaries came about where there was a shortage of suitable ground for burials,' said

Robertson, sitting back in his chair. 'When you died, you might only be allowed to occupy your grave for a year or two, then you'd be dug up so that someone else could have your spot. The remains could mount up in vast numbers. Families would sometimes visit the bones of their dead relatives each year and wrap them in fresh cloths as long as they retained some flesh. Of course, decomposition takes place four times faster in the air. Burial simply slows the process down.'

Cooper thought of the first messages from their mystery caller. He'd referred to decomposition several times. *The scented, carnal gardens of decomposition.* He knew all about the processes of decay.

And now Robertson was watching him. Not for the first time, Cooper felt the professor might be able to read his thoughts.

'But what about the smell?' he said.

Robertson looked pleased. For a moment, Cooper thought the professor was going to nudge him in the ribs, like a bar-room comedian. Wink, wink, say no more.

'It's the transition from black putrefaction to butyric fermentation that causes the main source of odour. If you ever smell it, you won't want to eat blue cheese again for a while. The body is drying out by then, and the exposed surfaces turn a little mouldy from fermentation. Just like your cheese will, if you leave it in the fridge too long.'

Cooper remembered he had some Blue Stilton in the fridge at home. He'd better throw it away, because he didn't think he was going to eat it now. He'd only be thinking of a combination of Billy McGowan's tattooed arms and butyric fermentation.

His attention beginning to stray, Cooper picked up a book that had caught his eye.

'Do you collect antiquarian books, sir?'

'Well, it's hardly antiquarian. The book has no intrinsic value. It simply relates to my field of interest.'

'I see.'

Cooper opened the book to the title page. What field of interest exactly? He knew the name of the author – everyone did, if only by reputation. But he'd never met anyone before who admitted to reading his books, let alone having one in the house. He flicked through the pages cautiously. He felt as though he might be corrupted by something if he read the words. He'd half-expected to find illustrations – dark, shocking pen-and-ink drawings between the chapters. But there weren't any.

'Yes, the Marquis de Sade,' said Robertson, watching him with that smile again. 'But not one of his, er . . . more celebrated titles, I'm afraid. It isn't terribly easy to find.'

'I've never heard of it,' admitted Cooper, turning back to the cover. The book was called *La Marquise de Gange*.

'One of his very last works,' said Robertson. 'It was published a year before de Sade died. The

Marquis was seventy-three years old by then, and had been locked up in an insane asylum for the past ten years.'

Cooper put the book back on the shelf.

'Don't you want to know how *La Marquise de Gange* relates to my interests?' asked Robertson.

'Do I need to ask? I'm sure you're going to tell me.'

Robertson laughed and put a hand on his shoulder.

'Dissection,' he said.

Cooper felt the pressure of the professor's fingers on the layer of muscle that covered the bones of his arm. The fingers moved slightly, as if parting the sinews and blood vessels to touch the deepest part of him. He had a momentary realization that the professor really could see inside him, and knew what his body looked like from the inside out.

'Dissection became remarkably fashionable among the nobility of Europe in the eighteenth and nineteenth centuries,' said Robertson. 'Some of those self-appointed scientists set up their own dissecting laboratories at home, just as you or I might have a billiards table. They took great pleasure in inviting their friends round for the evening whenever the grave robbers had delivered a fresh corpse. Can you imagine that?'

'No,' said Cooper. But then, he couldn't imagine fitting a billiards table into his flat in Welbeck Street either. Presumably an Edwardian gentleman's residence had its own billiards room, if not a dissecting laboratory.

'And de Sade wrote about this?' he asked, moving back slightly to free himself from the professor's hand.

'Yes, in *La Marquise de Gange*,' said Robertson. 'What a subject to be occupying a man's mind when he's seventy-three, eh? But then, he obviously wasn't afraid of death.'

Cooper followed Robertson with his eyes as he moved around the study, passing backwards and forwards in front of the window, his bulk creating flashes of light and dark as he talked.

'Earlier this week, we visited a place called the Infidels' Cemetery,' said Cooper.

'Oh, really?'

'You've not heard of it?'

'No.'

Cooper was surprised, given Robertson's interests. But perhaps the graves were too ancient for him.

'It's near Monsal Head,' said Cooper. 'Just an old graveyard. But there was an inscription on one of the gravestones that I've never seen before. I think it was in Latin. I wonder if you'd know what it means.'

'Try me,' said Robertson, almost glowing with pleasure at another chance to show off. 'A memorial inscription, you say?'

'Yes. I *think* it was in Latin: *caro data vermibus*.'

'Ah yes, very interesting,' said Robertson.

'I thought it would be.'

'Cadaver.'

'I'm sorry?'

'It's an example of an acronymic derivation. The word "cadaver" was believed to derive from the initial letters of your Latin expression *caro data vermibus*. Literally, it means "meat given to worms". A perfectly apt phrase – in the case of burial, at any rate.'

Cooper was starting to feel a bit detached from reality as he listened to the professor. He'd come to think of it as a weakness that he could so easily slip into someone else's world and share their obsession. Most of the obsessions he came across were the kind he'd rather not have in his head, and it looked as though Robertson's would count among them. He might have to watch some mindless TV tonight to push it out of his mind.

'Is this your wife, sir?' said Cooper, at last finding the photograph he'd been looking for. It was tucked away on a lower shelf of the display cabinet, nestling in the gloom between two willow-pattern plates. The glass of the cabinet was smeared, as if someone had touched it with dirty fingers and not cleaned it since.

The professor himself was easily recognizable in the photo, though he was ten or fifteen years younger and dressed to the nines in a dinner suit and red bow tie, with a matching handkerchief in his top pocket. The lady with him was tall and elegant, and equally well dressed in a red gown that exposed smooth, white shoulders. The couple stood close together as they posed for the photographer. Their manner didn't seem artificial – they looked genuinely happy and affectionate.

Robertson moved over to the cabinet and bent to look at the photo as if he'd never seen it before.

'Yes, that's Lena. We were attending some academic bunfight somewhere.'

Cooper wasn't quite sure how to ask the next question. 'Is she . . .?'

The professor watched him for a moment, almost seeming to enjoy his discomfort.

'Lena died five years ago, shortly before I retired.'

'I'm sorry.'

'It was cancer, of course.'

'Of course?'

'Cancer is rather like the ancient mariner, isn't it? You remember the Samuel Coleridge poem? "It is an ancient Mariner, And he stoppeth one of three."'

'I'm sorry,' said Cooper. 'I don't –'

'One in three people in this country suffer from cancer at some time in their lives.'

'Ah.'

Robertson turned away from the cabinet and walked to the window. He gazed out at the new houses in the crescent below him. Cooper caught that faint smell again. It made him think of mothballs, too. But he didn't know what mothballs smelled like, or even if they were used any more.

He associated them with grannies and antimacassars. He'd have to call in Boots the Chemists and ask for some, to see if he could put a name to the smell. Otherwise, it would remain permanently elusive.

Finally, the professor stopped moving and turned to face him. 'Modern society has mismanaged death, don't you think? Most people would say they want a quiet, dignified death. Yet the majority of us die in hospitals, surrounded by respirators, dialysis machines, naso-gastric tubes, undergoing endless sessions of chemotherapy and cardio-pulmonary resuscitation procedures. Death is converted into a mechanical spectacle, the weapons of technology lined up against the processes of nature. A miniature Armageddon fought in the veins.'

'It must have been a very difficult time,' said Cooper. It was a phrase he'd heard people say in these circumstances. He'd never thought it meant very much. And it didn't now, when he said it himself.

'My wife taught me that there are two stages of dying to go through,' said Robertson. 'First, you're afraid that you'll die. And then you're afraid that you won't. There's a point when death becomes a thing to be welcomed, the event you desire most in the world. Some of us reach that point before others.'

Cooper began to button his coat. He knew when it was time to leave.

'One in three,' said Robertson. 'Why should we be surprised when it affects us, or our loved ones? Yet still we ask the question.'

'What question is that, sir?'

'"By thy long grey beard and glittering eye, Now wherefore stopp'st thou me?"' Robertson smiled sadly. 'We never expect it to be us, do we?'

Cooper didn't know what to say. He was starting to feel very uncomfortable, and slightly queasy. He wasn't sure if it was the tea or all the talk of decomposition.

'Thank you for your help, Professor,' he said. 'I have to go now.'

'A shame. You never did explain your interest in the sarcophagus. Does it relate to your enquiry into the human remains found at Litton Foot?'

'No, it was something in one of the messages.'

Robertson had his back to him at that moment, pouring himself another drink. But Cooper saw his shoulders stiffen, his head come up with sudden interest. For a second, their eyes met in the mirror over the TV set. Cooper felt himself being probed again, as if the professor had found more depths in him than he'd anticipated.

'Messages?' he said.

Robertson turned, raising the glass of whisky to his face, but not drinking – an old trick to hide the expression, or to distract attention from the eyes.

'I probably shouldn't have mentioned them,' said Cooper.

'That sounds intriguing. Do tell.'

'I'm sorry, sir, I can't. It's not really relevant to my present enquiry.'

'Oh, a different enquiry altogether? Something I can help you with, though?'

'I don't think so, Professor. Thank you.'

For the first time, Robertson had lost his affability. He couldn't hold the glass to his lips any longer without taking a drink, or it would have looked odd. He gulped a half-inch of whisky, and put the glass down. Cooper caught an irritable gleam in his eyes, a downwards curve of his mouth, as if the malt had turned sour in its bottle.

'Well, I really must be going,' said Cooper.

Robertson was still thoughtful as he accompanied him to the door and on to the gravel drive.

'Tell me, those questions about Alder Hall – were those related to your messages? And decomposition. Why did you ask me about decomposition?'

'Professor, I'm sorry –'

'You haven't been entirely honest with me, have you?'

'I wish I could share everything with you, Professor, but I'm working under certain limitations.'

'Limitations, yes,' said Robertson. 'We all work under limitations, don't we?'

25

On his way home, Cooper called at the old cemetery in Edendale. The rain had stopped, but a cold wind was blowing across the grass and funnelling through the avenues of stone memorials. The gates were kept padlocked at night, but on the darkest edge of the cemetery there were gaps where the iron railings had been pulled apart. The damage had been done by someone going in, rather than coming out. Or so he hoped.

It was six forty-five and there was still half an hour to go before the cemetery closed. But Cooper could see no one in the grounds, except a woman walking a cocker spaniel on a lead. The dog's ears were blowing backwards in the wind, like the ragged ends of a woollen scarf. As he watched, the dog began casting from side to side with its nose to the ground, sniffing for interesting odours among the lines of gravestones.

The sight made Cooper think of one of the traditional beliefs that still clung to rural burial grounds – the deadly graveyard miasma. Buried, decomposing bodies were supposed to give off a noxious gas that made its way up through the soil and formed an invisible fog. It hung over the graveyard and tainted the air, poisoning anyone who came near. But surely that was just another superstition to justify keeping away from graveyards and avoiding the presence of death.

Cooper shook himself to dismiss the morbid thoughts. These occasional quiet moments at the end of a shift were usually the time when events of the day ran continually through his head. All the most uncomfortable moments would repeat themselves, nudging him into worrying whether he could have done things better. Today, there had been several such moments. He thought he understood Tom Jarvis pretty well, at least. But he couldn't help wondering whether Fry would have handled Madeleine Chadwick better, or if she'd have been able to deal with the steamroller technique of Freddy Robertson.

He could clearly remember the first time he'd met Diane Fry. He could see her now, walking into the CID room at West Street. She hadn't met his eye at first, but had glanced from side to side as if searching for evidence of his faults, traces of any weakness she could exploit. Though she'd been leaner than Cooper had grown up expecting women to be, it was clear from the start that Fry was no weakling.

He only wished she would smile sometimes. A

smile would relax her face and erase those dark shadows that always lurked in her eyes. Even in life, people could transform the look of their faces.

Earlier today, Melvyn Hudson had talked about performing miracles in a funeral parlour. And, in a way, it was true. They took in a dead body, with its sunken face and wrinkled fingers, and they pumped in a pink liquid that mixed with the remaining body fluids, like a shot of champagne in a cocktail. And gradually they transformed a shrivelled corpse back into someone's granny. A miracle.

In the mortuary, too, the pathologist could restore the fingertips of corpses by injecting tissue builder, allowing the dead to be fingerprinted. You could even buy a ready-made kit for the job, complete with syringes, needles and tissue builder. Who said the dead couldn't communicate from beyond the grave?

Then Cooper thought of Audrey Steele. Audrey had surely been trying to communicate from beyond the grave. Somewhere, she'd be getting annoyed that he still wasn't listening.

We turn away and close our eyes as the gates swing open on a whole new world – the scented, carnal gardens of decomposition. We refuse to admire those flowing juices, the flowering bacteria, the dark, bloated blooms of putrefaction. This is the true nature of death. We should open our eyes and learn.

Diane Fry looked up at the sudden noise. She'd hardly been listening to the recording, had been miles away, carried by her memories, out of Edendale and way beyond Derbyshire. She realized that the room had gone dark. There was just a desk lamp still burning as the voice played over and over. *Killing is our natural impulse.* Fry hit the 'pause' button, and the voice died.

'Diane, are you OK?'

It was Liz Petty, passing CID on her way out of the building from the scenes of crime department. It was an odd direction to take. But Fry did that herself at night sometimes, choosing the route that felt safe rather than the logical one.

'I'm just on my way home,' said Petty.

'Working late?'

'I couldn't leave the evidence until morning. But it's all logged in and securely stored now.'

'Good.'

Petty looked at the single lamp and the tape player.

'You're working a bit late, aren't you?'

'Like you, there were just a few things I had to do.'

She hoped the SOCO would leave, but instead she came closer, letting her bag rest on the floor.

'You were listening to the recordings of his phone calls again, weren't you? I recognized the sound of the voice changer.'

'So?'

Petty didn't seem to notice her tone, but kept moving closer. Fry felt herself being observed. Too close, she was. Too close.

'Diane, why do these calls upset you so much?' asked Petty.

'Upset me? They don't upset me. What do you mean?'

'Well . . . disturb you, then. They disturb you, don't they? More than they do anybody else here.'

Fry couldn't meet her eye. She was fighting the urge to confide in Petty. She had never talked to anyone about it before, had never found anyone she thought she could talk to, or who would understand.

'It's what he says in his calls. It makes me think of a child,' she said.

Petty frowned. 'He doesn't mention a child, does he?'

'No, not really.'

'Children are always the worst . . .' But Fry could tell from her voice that she hadn't understood.

'Not children – a child,' she said. 'It was my first murder case, back when I was serving in Birmingham. I was still in uniform, only twenty-three years old. But that doesn't protect you.'

'No.'

'She was eight years old, and she'd been reported missing. It was the summer, during the school holidays. We were told she'd been playing outside and had disappeared. I was sent to the house with CID and some other uniforms. The parents were absolutely distraught. But the DI insisted on searching the property. I kept thinking,

387

"Why are you treating the parents like this when their child has been taken from them?"'

Petty pulled up a chair and sat next to her. She was too close, but Fry didn't care right now.

'You found the little girl?'

Fry nodded. 'She was in a shed, covered over with some old sacking tied up with garden twine. Her skin was already turning black, and her face was covered in maggots. The pathologist said she'd been dead for at least three weeks. Her parents had killed the child and left her to rot. Then they panicked when a social worker rang to make an appointment to check on her. The child was on the "at risk" register.'

'Jesus, how awful.'

'And you know what? Forensics said that the body had been disturbed several times.'

'Disturbed?'

'Someone had been going back to take a look on a regular basis. They could tell by the pattern of staining from her body fluids on the sacking, and from the fact that the twine had been retied several times. We weren't able to use it in court, because we had no way of telling which member of the family had been doing it. It could have been the father or the mother – or maybe even the twelve-year-old son.'

'And that was your first one?' said Petty.

'That's why I remember it so well. I remember the sound that the maggots made as they moved on her face. And I remember the smell in that shed. Stagnant water and vinegar. Sweet, but not like the scent of flowers. Sweet like rotting meat.'

'So when this guy talks about decomposition . . .?'

'Yes, that's what it means to me: an eight-year-old child decomposing in a shed in her parents' back garden in Balsall Heath, with someone gloating over her corpse every day, as if it were some sordid little game. And you don't know how much that makes me want to kill him.'

Cooper woke in the middle of the night, convinced he could hear the sound of bones breaking, a skull crunching under pressure. With his heart thumping from the sudden wrench out of sleep, he rolled over on to his side and opened his eyes. Two green spots glowed in the darkness of his bedroom.

'Oh God, Randy, that's disgusting. Take your mouse somewhere else, if you're going to eat it.'

The cat blinked at him inscrutably and swallowed the remains of the rodent's back legs in one gulp. There would be a small patch of blood left on the carpet, and the mouse's tiny internal organs, shiny and green, cleanly separated from its body by the cat's teeth.

All his life, Cooper had been used to cats bringing their prey indoors. They'd done it at the farm, too – rabbits and small rodents, sometimes unharmed ones they turned loose in the house. He supposed it was only nature. But it could take days to get nature out of the house, once it was in. Sometimes, the only clue that something had got into the house was the smell it caused when it died.

He blinked at a couple of memories from his childhood at Bridge End – a barn owl breaking its neck by flying into their sitting-room window one night, a vole that fell down the chimney while the fire was lit, dying in seconds as it twisted silently in the flames.

And then there was that problem with the rats.

Cooper's bedroom suddenly seemed to fill with the smell as the details of the incident rushed back to him, vivid and overpowering. There had been a particularly bad year when guns and dogs had failed to control the rats on the farm, and his grandfather had resorted to putting poison down in the outbuildings. Matt and Ben were given the job of checking the bait sites each morning and disposing of the corpses.

But one morning they had been late and in too much of a hurry. Matt had put two dead rats into the airtight plastic bucket that the poison came in, intending to dispose of them later. Two weeks had passed before they noticed the bucket and remembered what it contained. Holding their breath, the boys had prised off the lid. Inside, the two corpses had been black and glistening, sunken in on themselves, like slowly deflating furry toys. Slopping around in the bottom of the bucket had been a quarter of an inch of dark, evil-smelling liquid that hadn't been there before. Where had it come from? Matt had wanted to look more closely, but the smell had been unbearable and Ben had felt sick, so they'd slapped the lid shut again.

After that, the stink had hung around the shed for weeks. Every time he went past the door, it had reminded Ben of the rats they'd killed but failed to dispose of properly. Their resentment still haunted the place, as thick and nauseous as the muddy liquid that had drained from their bodies.

Even now, Cooper felt sick as the smell seeped out of his memory. He closed his eyes, but soon realized there would be no more sleep tonight. He sighed, rolled out of bed and fetched a cloth from the kitchen to clean up the blood.

MY JOURNAL OF THE DEAD, PHASE FOUR
But it doesn't have to be like that. The Aztecs believe that life is a dream from which death awakens us. Mexicans celebrate and honour their dead on All Souls Day. The Tibetans believe a dead body mustn't be buried, as the spirit goes to Hell. So they take corpses on to a mountainside and feed them to the birds. Everything must go, including the bones. Sometimes priests have to mutilate a corpse to make the job quicker and easier for the vultures.

The Jews waited for putrefaction to start before they disposed of their bodies. At least that way they could be sure of death. They kept their bodies in unsealed sepulchres, and went to check on them every day. That was what the followers of Jesus were doing when they found him alive. They were observing the progress of his decomposition. They knew he wasn't really dead until the last of his flesh was gone.

The bones had to be perfectly clean, purified of all traces of our earthly corruption. And there is something pure about bones, isn't there? Yet we recoil in horror at the thought of the slightest scrap of decomposing flesh. Consider the skull beneath the skin – the ultimate symbol of inner perfection.

26

'Groundspeak run a sport called geocaching,' said Cooper next morning. 'It seems to be a high-tech form of treasure-hunting.'

'Full marks, Ben. That's what you predicted, wasn't it?'

He looked at Fry in surprise. 'Yes. Well, the way it works is this: somebody places a cache of items in a hidden location, and other geocachers set out to find it, using handheld GPS units and the location's co-ordinates, which are on the website. They get a few clues, too, if they need them.'

'Right.'

'People put all kinds of things in caches – maps, books, software, CDs, videos, pictures, money, jewellery, tickets, tools, games . . .'

They looked at the inventory provided by scenes of crime. Many of the items from Peter's Stone had been in plastic bags, or in clear zipped plastic envelopes of the type used in offices. Cooper watched Fry run her pen down the list, looking for some kind of meaning. Crayons, sunglasses, and a Beatrix Potter book, *The Tale of Mr Tod*. Her pen stopped at the skeleton key-ring.

'There are scores of other caches,' said Cooper. 'Some of them quite close to Petrus Two.'

'I'm not interested in the others, Ben, just who might have been at this one.'

'OK.'

'Hold on, though. Did you say there's a website with the GPS co-ordinates of all these caches? They give clues how to find them?'

'That's right.'

'And do these locations have names?'

'Yes. The person who sets up a cache gives it a name,' said Cooper. He pointed at the contents of the cache from Peter's Stone. 'This one is called Petrus Two – "Petrus" is the Latin form of Peter, I suppose.'

'Latin again?'

'It may mean nothing. Nearby there are locations called Tunnel's Mouth, Tidza Treat, Magic of Monsal, Jonah's Journey. I counted twenty caches within five miles of Peter's Stone.'

'It's the names I'm interested in,' said Fry.

'The names? Why?'

'Look, people choose whatever name they like for a location, then they give clues how to get there. It's all a big game. They like to set each other a challenge. Is that right?'

'That's what I said, Diane.'

'You still don't get it, do you?' Fry leaned a

little closer and recited a line that she didn't need to read from any notes. 'And all we have to do,' she said, 'is look for "the dead place".'

Cooper shifted uneasily. In the past, he'd been accused of developing obsessions. And he had to admit that it was true. Sometimes he got an idea into his head and couldn't get rid of it, yet found it difficult to explain the rationale to anyone else. He was aware of the danger. But in this case, it seemed to be Fry who was developing the obsession, not him.

'What have you got planned for us this morning?' he said, fearing some chase around the countryside looking at graveyards.

'We're going to visit a few people at home. If any of them were involved in what happened to Audrey Steele, we're going to make them feel a little bit more uneasy.'

Fry saw straight away that Christopher Lloyd's home was a modern detached house that was pretending not to be. Cooper turned the car between two carriage lamps on to a cobbled parking area, and they came to a halt near an imitation village pump. It was Mrs Lloyd who let them in and led them through the house.

'Naturally, it's all reproduction,' she said. 'But it's very well done, don't you think?'

'Yes, very convincing, madam.'

'It's a great advantage to have something that looks old, but is actually new. You don't have the same maintenance problems.' She laughed. 'Not to mention the insurance premiums.'

'Of course.'

'And if an item gets damaged, you can simply replace it with a new reproduction, and it'll look just as old as the original did.' Mrs Lloyd beamed proudly at them. 'The house itself is period style, so it's very appropriate.'

Period style? Fry wondered briefly what that meant. Probably whatever you wanted it to mean. Despite the coffee table and the TV in the corner, there was something about the mock Victorian mantelpiece and tiled fireplace, the framed hunting prints and the mustard colour of the walls below the dado rail that made her feel she was in the back room of a pub.

Christopher Lloyd himself was outside, sitting on a stone slab at the edge of an ornamental pond. In the background, water gushed from the mouth of a large ceramic frog. Fry had vague memories of a foster family in Halesowen who'd kept fish, and had given her the job of feeding them for a while. In this pond, she recognized several red-blotched koi carp and a few tench scavenging on the bottom. There was also a single, paler fish about two feet long, which she thought might be an albino sturgeon.

'I hope the records I had faxed to you were what you needed,' said Lloyd.

'Very helpful, sir.'

'So you'll understand that our procedures at

Eden Valley Crematorium are beyond reproach. Nothing can go wrong in our system. Nothing did in this case.'

Cooper and Fry stood by the side of the pool, drawn by their reflections and by the sight of the albino fish ghosting through the water. A few feet away, it broke the surface, and Fry glimpsed a long snout and dead eyes.

'Are you interested in fish?' asked Lloyd.

'Not really,' she said. 'I was just being a police officer and wondering how much they're worth. We've had some thefts of koi carp reported recently, and I was surprised at the value claimed for them by their owners.'

Lloyd grunted. 'The real enthusiasts pay thousands and thousands of pounds for koi. Some of them fly out to Japan to buy direct from the breeders. I can't see the point in it myself. These fish didn't cost anything like that. The sturgeon is worth a couple of hundred, perhaps.'

'An albino, isn't it?'

'Yes,' said Lloyd. 'But unfortunately the albinos don't like direct sunlight. They're dusk-to-dawn creatures, and much prefer the dark.'

Fry glanced at him. 'I know quite a lot of people like that.'

'I'm sure you do. In a way, a police officer is a bit of a fisherman, I suppose. You know where the fish are, but you can only catch them when they come to the surface.'

'That's an interesting comment, sir.'

Lloyd laughed. 'I think I read it in a novel once.'

Fry shivered involuntarily.

'Perhaps it's getting a bit cool out here,' said Lloyd. 'Come into the house. Have a cup of tea or something.'

'No, thank you,' said Fry. She didn't intend to get too friendly with Christopher Lloyd, but wanted him to feel uncomfortable if possible. Lloyd seemed to read the message, too.

'You want me to tell you I was involved in this business in some way, don't you?' he said.

'We don't want you to tell us anything unless it's true, sir.'

Fry turned away from the fish pond and leaned towards Lloyd, until she was close enough to smell the dampness and decay from the weeds he'd been pulling out of the water.

Lloyd shook his head. 'I think this may be the point where I insist that I'm not saying anything else until I have a solicitor present.'

'Certainly, sir. In that case, we'll ask you to come with us to the police station, and we'll wait there for your solicitor to arrive. We must follow procedure, mustn't we? No matter how embarrassing and inconvenient some of us may find it.'

She watched Lloyd swallow nervously and glance towards the house. 'I didn't . . . I wasn't involved in anything. Not really.'

'So what *did* you do? Really?'

Lloyd gulped again. 'I told a lie. I was asked by

a friend to tell a lie to help him out, and I did it. That's all.'

'*All?*' said Fry. 'There's a great deal more to it than that, isn't there, sir?'

'I don't know. I just did what I was asked. No more than that.'

Fry glanced at Cooper. He hadn't taken his eyes off Lloyd while she'd been talking to him. If he'd been following her line of thought, he should be ready with the next question, the one that would unsettle Lloyd that little bit more.

'This friend that you told the lie for, sir,' said Cooper. 'That would have been Melvyn Hudson, I expect?'

Lloyd's eyes flicked nervously to Cooper, and back to Fry again. He wasn't sure now which of them to worry about most.

'If you're thinking of lying again, sir,' said Fry, 'I would strongly advise against it.'

He looked down at the water of the pond for a few moments, then at the house. Whatever he was thinking, it was making him uncomfortable. Then a calculating look came into Lloyd's eyes. He turned his head away towards the water, trying to avoid Cooper seeing his face. But Fry was on the other side of him, and she saw it.

'Actually, it wasn't Melvyn, it was Richard Slack,' he said.

'Really?'

'He wanted me to sign some paperwork. He said there had been a bit of an administrative

399

mix-up at the firm, and he thought I'd be willing to help him out.'

'And did you?'

Lloyd shook his head. 'Normally, I would have helped him out. Richard was a friend, and we should be able to feel we can call on each other. But this would have been highly irregular. The rules are very strict on the documentation. He put me in an embarrassing situation, and I had no option but to refuse. I could have lost my job.'

'What exactly did he want you to do?'

'He wanted me to sign off a job without the disposal certificate.'

'Is that the certificate that's issued by the registrar?'

'Yes. We can't do a disposal without the formal authorization. It's the funeral director's job to make sure it's presented. Richard said it had been lost. He tried to blame Melvyn, actually, but I'm not sure I believed that.'

'And you refused?'

'Certainly.'

'So the cremation couldn't go ahead?' asked Fry.

'Obviously.'

'What happened to the funeral, then?'

'There wasn't one. Well, not as far as I was concerned. I don't know how it was resolved, and I didn't ask. In any case, I understood there wasn't to be a funeral service in our chapel, just the cremation.'

'I don't understand. No funeral service?'

'It isn't all that unusual. Sometimes the family don't want to come to the crematorium. They have the service elsewhere, then the funeral director conveys the coffin for cremation.'

'In that case, there would be no one to witness the arrival of the coffin?'

'Just the driver of the hearse, and perhaps a colleague to help deliver the coffin. It comes straight into the cremation suite, in that case. But we still need the paperwork, obviously.'

'Yes.'

'Now and then we have a job where there's no service of any kind. No family, no mourners. Those are the homeless people, the sad cases where someone has died and their identity can't be established, or where no relatives can be traced. The local authority meets the cost of those disposals. Everyone is entitled to proper disposal.'

Fry looked at Cooper. It was his turn.

'Mr Lloyd, do you remember the name of the person Richard Slack wanted you to sign the documentation for?'

'No, he never told me that. And I didn't ask.'

'There was a lot you didn't ask.'

'Sometimes that's the best way.'

'Shouldn't you have reported this incident to someone, if you were being completely scrupulous?'

Lloyd sighed. 'It was very difficult. But Richard was a friend, as I said. I suppose I thought that if I didn't co-operate with his scheme, he would have to do the right thing and take the blame. I know it's a problem for a funeral director to get a bad reputation, but he must have bitten the bullet and owned up.'

'When was this exactly?' asked Cooper.

'Well, I'm not sure, but it can't have been many weeks before Richard died.'

Fry closed her notebook. 'Thank you, sir. You've been quite helpful.'

Before they left, she looked into the pond for a last glimpse of the pale fish, but it was being too elusive.

'I wish I could afford to breed these sturgeon,' said Lloyd. 'Somebody told me their eggs are where Iranian Imperial Caviar comes from. That's the caviar with a golden colour, not black like the Russian stuff.'

'I wouldn't know.'

Lloyd leaned over the water and stretched out a hand. Fry thought at first that he was reaching to scoop out one of the fish. But instead he skimmed a handful of dead leaves off the surface and flicked them on to the stone paving.

'I'll need to net the pond soon. You mustn't let leaves lie on the water in the autumn. When they decompose, the oxygen level drops, and your fish die.' He looked at Fry as he stood up. 'It would be a stupid way to lose your fish, wouldn't it?'

'What do you think, Diane?' asked Cooper, on the way to the Hudsons' home. 'Is Christopher Lloyd telling the truth?'

'I think it's very convenient for him that Richard Slack is dead. He's useful for taking the blame, isn't he?'

'What do you mean?'

'Well, what if Mr Lloyd was telling us part of the truth, but not quite all? What if it was Melvyn Hudson who approached him, not Richard Slack? By telling us that story, he might be hoping we don't question Hudson too closely about it.'

'But it was Richard Slack who was his friend, not Hudson.'

'Was it? That's only what Lloyd tells us.'

'And if it was Melvyn, then . . .'

'Then Lloyd might actually have agreed to sign off the job. He could be hoping to put us off the scent by shifting attention to Richard Slack.'

Cooper nodded. 'You know the other thing that's worrying me about what Lloyd said?'

'The cremations that take place without a service in the crematorium chapel?' guessed Fry.

'Right. There must be a period of time when the coffin is in the sole charge of a couple of funeral director's men, en route between the church and the crem.'

'Giving them the chance to swap the body?'

'Exactly.'

'What about Audrey Steele's funeral? Was it at the crematorium chapel?'

Cooper thought back to his interview with Vivien Gill. 'You know, I don't think her mother ever said. And I never thought to ask.'

'You'd better ask her, then.'

'Won't a detail like that be in the records we took from Hudson and Slack?'

Fry looked at him. 'You'd still better ask her.'

The Hudsons had a marble fireplace, but no fire. They had brass candle holders without any candles. And they had pine bookshelves, but very few real books nestling among the ivory paper-weights and Chinese vases.

The house reminded Cooper of a flat he'd once visited in North London. The place had belonged to a friend of a friend, someone who worked in the hotel business. As soon as he walked in, he'd found himself open-mouthed with astonishment at the size of the kitchen. It had been tiny – even smaller than the bathroom. Big enough to brew coffee and make toast in, perhaps, or to heat something in the microwave. But far too small to cook a proper meal. To Cooper, it hadn't been a kitchen at all, but some other room that no one had thought of a name for yet.

Barbara Hudson was in jeans and a sweatshirt, with her hair loose, and she couldn't have looked less like a funeral director.

'Do you need me?' she said. 'If not, I've got things to do.'

'We'll let you know, Mrs Hudson.'

She disappeared and left them waiting in the hall. Cooper noticed a large, ornate mirror hanging at the foot of the stairs. It was in an odd position, not where you'd readily see yourself in it. He stooped to look at the edges of the glass. There were no fingerprints, not a single smear or smudge. It had either been polished to within an inch of its life, or just never used. He wondered if this was the sort of mirror that stood reflecting life silently to itself, like a camera without a subject.

Cooper straightened up, and found Melvyn Hudson standing in the doorway. He ushered them in silently, with a practised gesture of his right hand, as if inviting them to view the deceased. In his case, the casual clothes didn't seem to make any difference.

'Mr Hudson,' said Fry, 'we've been talking to Christopher Lloyd, the manager of Eden Valley Crematorium. You know him?'

'Of course. Well, in the way of business, you know.'

'He tells us that your partner, Richard Slack, asked him to do something illegal, but he refused. Do you know anything about that?'

'No. I have no idea what Lloyd means. But Richard knew him better than I do. They were both members of the Rotary Club.'

'This would have been shortly before Mr Slack was killed in the road accident.'

'Yes, that was last May.'

'How exactly did the accident happen?'

'He ran off the road late one night, on his way to do a removal. There was an inquest, so you can read all about it, if you want to.'

'He was alone at the time?'

'So it seems.'

On the surface, Hudson seemed composed and relaxed. But the look in his eyes didn't match either his voice or his manner. It was more difficult to control the expression in the eyes. Ben wondered if Fry had noticed it.

'Where were you at the time, sir?' asked Fry.

'Here at home, with my family. Why do you ask?'

A door closed somewhere in the house, and Hudson seized on the distraction.

'Excuse me,' he said. 'That will be my daughter. I must have a word with her.'

'He's going to lie to us,' said Fry when Hudson left the room. 'Just like Christopher Lloyd did. But he's buying a bit of time to decide on his story.'

'Yes, I know.'

'Probe him. But gently.'

'You want me to do it, Diane?'

'He'll take it better from you.'

'OK.'

But it wasn't Melvyn Hudson who came through the door. A dark-haired woman of about thirty hovered on the threshold.

'Hello. Dad asked me to tell you that he's just had an urgent call. He'll be back in a few minutes. Can I get you anything while you're waiting?'

'No, but you can stay and talk to us,' said Fry.

'Oh, well, I'm not sure Dad would like that.'

'Sorry, your name is . . .?'

'Natalie.'

'Do you work with your father?'

'No, I'm an aerobics instructor.'

'You're not interested in the family business, Miss Hudson?'

Natalie shuddered. 'Certainly not. The very thought!'

'And there's no son to follow in your father's footsteps?'

The woman hesitated. She took out a packet of cigarettes and lit one, not bothering to ask whether they minded, or to offer them one. It was her home, after all. She could do what she liked. But Cooper noticed her fingers trembling slightly as she used the lighter and took the first drag of nicotine into her lungs.

'There *was* a son,' she said.

'Oh?'

'David. My younger brother. *He* would have followed in Daddy's footsteps, all right. That's exactly what he was born for. It was all planned out.'

'What happened?'

'He was killed.'

'Do you mean he was killed, or that he died in some other way?'

'He was abroad, travelling in Indonesia,' said Natalie. 'They think it was bandits. A robbery that went wrong – that's what you'd call it here, isn't it? But I'm not sure it would apply to David's death. I think they probably intended to kill him. He was twenty-two.'

'I'm sorry.'

'The worst thing was that he liked to send postcards from wherever he got to. David thought in images, and he always chose the picture carefully when he sent one. His postcards took a long time to arrive from the countries he visited. They kept arriving for weeks after David died. They were postcards from a dead person. At first, it was wonderful, and I cried to think that he was still communicating with me. It was as if he was still out there somewhere, thinking about me. But then I began to pray for them to stop. I think we all did. We needed an ending.'

'How long ago did this happen?'

'Ten years, four months. Dad was devastated when it happened. For a long time, we thought the loss would kill him. That's the phrase everybody used: "The loss will kill him." Ironic, really, for a man who spends his life dealing with other people's grief. The consummate professional. The person to call on in your hour of need.'

Natalie's voice had become more bitter. When she blew out a cloud of cigarette smoke, her mouth was twisted into a sardonic smile.

'The truth comes out at times like that, doesn't it?' she said. 'Dad made no secret of the fact that he thought the wrong child had died.'

Natalie released more smoke and watched it

drift in a lazy cloud before dissipating in the breeze from the open window.

'You have no other brothers or sisters?'

'No.'

'Then presumably you'll inherit your father's share of the business some day.'

Natalie laughed. 'Will I? I doubt it somehow. I don't know if my father has made a will or not, or who he intends to leave his half of Hudson and Slack to when he dies. Probably my mother will take over the reins herself. Female funeral directors are becoming quite fashionable these days. I don't know what will happen when the old man dies, either.'

'Abraham Slack?'

'Yes. There's Vernon, of course. But Dad doesn't think much of Vernon, as you might have noticed.'

'I got the impression that he doesn't regard Vernon as a potential business partner,' said Cooper.

Natalie laughed. 'You have a way with understatement, don't you? It's quite sweet.'

Cooper felt himself starting to blush. He'd never hear the last of this from Fry.

'I must try to get the chance to talk to Vernon himself some time,' he said, as he began to put his notebook away.

'Good luck. He isn't very communicative.'

'He fits in OK at the firm, though, doesn't he?'

Natalie shrugged. 'On his own terms. Nobody goes out of their way to make Vernon feel as though he belongs. Especially not my dad. If

Vernon ever had the idea that he might become a sort of substitute son to my dad, then he soon got a rude awakening. Dad didn't see things that way. Once David was gone, he was gone, and nobody else has ever mattered to Dad. Yet you ought to hear him sometimes, when he's talking to bereaved families. All the stuff he spouts about families turning to each other for support in their time of need. Oh, he's full of advice then, all right. It's enough to make you feel sick.'

As if on cue, the door opened and Melvyn Hudson came back into the room. He looked surprised to see his daughter still there, and then surprise gave way to anger, which was rapidly controlled and disappeared from his expression.

'I'm sorry to have kept you waiting,' he said. 'Death happens at the most inconvenient times, as I'm sure you know. Has my daughter been keeping you entertained?'

'Yes, we've had a very interesting conversation,' said Fry.

'Oh? Well, Natalie probably has other things to do. So if there's anything else I can help you with, I do have a few minutes.'

Fry stood up. 'Actually, I think we have all that we need for now, Mr Hudson,' she said.

Cooper was caught off guard and was a bit slow getting to his feet.

'Are you sure?' said Hudson.

'We'll be in touch, if necessary. But there are quite a number of other enquiries to make.'

Hudson followed them to the door. Cooper had a sudden, irrational urge to walk past the big ornate mirror in the hallway with him, to see if Hudson was reflected in the glass.

'Just one thing, Mr Hudson,' he said. 'Have you ever been to Alder Hall?'

'No, I don't believe so.'

'Or visited the grounds for any reason?'

'Not that I can recall.'

When they got to the car, Cooper turned to Fry. 'Why did you do that?' he said. 'Hudson hadn't told us anything at all. We never got round to asking him the important questions.'

'Do you think he would have told us the truth?'

'Well, no.'

'So what was the point? Now we've left Mr Hudson with the impression that his daughter may already have told us what it was we wanted to know. It's obvious they don't trust each other an inch. I'm going to leave him worrying about that for a while, and he might be more forthcoming when we tackle him again.'

'That's sneaky.'

Cooper started the car and they drove back towards West Street.

'How does inheritance law stand?' he asked. 'What if Melvyn Hudson hasn't made a will – who would actually inherit?'

'I think it would have to go to probate,' said Fry. 'There's some complicated formula the courts use to share out any part of the estate that isn't willed to a specific individual. There are probably other beneficiaries entitled to a share.'

'But Natalie Hudson would be a principal bene-ficiary, wouldn't she?'

'Yes, I'm sure she would. But she doesn't want the business. She has no interest in it.'

'She might want the money,' said Cooper. 'If there's one of the big American corporations lurking in the wings to snap up Hudson and Slack, Natalie could find herself suddenly very well-off.'

'Mmm. Especially if Abraham Slack could be tempted to part with his share, too.'

'Well, *his* beneficiary would be Vernon, surely? I wouldn't fancy the idea of Vernon Slack running my business, would you?'

'No.' Fry looked thoughtful. 'I wonder if that's what it says in Abraham's will.'

'These family-owned businesses do produce a lot of problems. It's the way feuds start. Bad enough when it's all within the same family, must be worse when there are two families involved. The founders may have got on together perfectly well, but it doesn't mean subsequent generations will.'

Ben Cooper's phone was ringing as he walked into the office. He snatched it up, his head still full of images of furtive funeral directors and unidenti-fied coffins slipping into the flames.

'At last,' said a voice. 'I didn't think anybody was going to answer. I thought you must all be out fighting crime.'

'Who am I speaking to?' asked Cooper.

'My name's Mead. David Mead.'

'What can I help you with, Mr Mead?'

'I thought it was you lot that wanted help from me.'

'Was it?' Cooper frowned. A lot of names had accumulated in the enquiry already, but he was sure he hadn't heard this one before. He wrote it down on his desk pad, but it didn't look any more familiar. 'David Mead, did you say?'

'That's right. But you might know me better as Dangerous Dave.'

27

'Petrus Two isn't actually my cache, you understand,' said David Mead. 'But I know it well. And I've got a few of my own in this area. Some of the best, if I say so myself.'

Dangerous Dave wasn't quite what Cooper would have expected. He was a tall, athletic man in his thirties, with his hair cropped very short. He could have been a police officer, but he explained that he was a fireman based in a station on the outskirts of Sheffield. He liked to spend his off-duty time walking in the Peak District, and had been fascinated to hear from a friend that there was a sport where he could use his GPS unit as well.

'But you do know the person who left this particular cache, Mr Mead?' asked Fry.

'Oh, yes. He's OK. He's been a geocacher for years. I've met him a few times, but I think he's on holiday at the moment.'

'All right. And what about these other people?'

She passed Mead a list of names transcribed from the log book left in the cache. He looked through it, nodding occasionally. 'They're all familiar names. Some of them I've met. The rest I've seen posting their reports on the website, or signing in other log books.'

'You'd say they were all genuine, er . . . geocachers, then?'

'Yes, I would. It's quite a small community in the sport. We tend to know each other.'

'What about the items that people put into a cache? What's the protocol?'

'We do have some rules. Common sense, really. No explosives, ammunition, knives, drugs or alcohol. Nothing illegal. Oh, and food items are always a bad idea – animals will chew through the box and destroy the cache. So most people leave small toys, novelty items, perhaps a CD or a book, stuff like that.'

'And what is this exactly?' asked Fry, holding up the bag containing the purple grasshopper with its metal tag.

'A hitchhiker.'

'A what?'

'Or, if it has a Groundspeak tag, a Travel Bug.'

'Yes, it does.'

'Well, a hitchhiker is an item that you can move from cache to cache,' said Mead. 'There's a candle that has travelled from Australia to Arizona, and a Mr Potato Head that hops from cache to cache all over the place. With a Travel Bug, you can track your hitchhiker's travels through the website.'

'And all this is done with the help of GPS?'

'A good GPS unit can give you an approximate location within around six to twenty feet, as long as it isn't located somewhere really inaccessible where you need specialist equipment. But you don't need to know all the technical jargon. All you need to be able to do is to enter a waypoint.'

'And when you reach the co-ordinates and locate a cache, you open it up to make an entry in the log book?'

'Sometimes you have to wait for muggles to get clear of the area,' said Mead.

'Muggles?'

'Members of the public. Non geocachers. Usually hikers or mountain bikers, just passing by on a footpath or trail. But now and then they can do something infuriating, like settling down near a cache site to have their lunch. You can't open a cache while they're there, because it gives the location away to muggles. You either have to sit it out and wait for them to go, or move on to another site.'

'Aren't muggles the non-wizards in the Harry Potter books?' asked Cooper.

'It's the same sort of thing, really.'

'People who aren't in the know and have to be kept out of the secret?'

'Exactly.'

Fry sighed. 'And in addition to making an entry

in the log book, do I understand that the normal practice would be to take an item from the cache?'

'Only if you put something else in to replace it,' said Mead. 'That's the rule. Otherwise it's TNLN.'

'I'm sorry, sir, you'll have to explain that.'

'TNLN: Take Nothing, Leave Nothing.'

TNLN. Cooper liked that idea. It was a good motto for anyone visiting the national park, where the number of wild flowers picked illegally was exceeded only by the amount of litter left behind. Visitors were constantly urged to take only photos and leave nothing but footprints. If only it were so simple.

'Would you be able to find out for us who left these items?' asked Fry.

Mead pulled a face. 'Some of them. Maybe not all.'

'If you could try . . .?'

'OK.'

'Particularly this, sir,' she said, holding up one of the bags.

'A skeleton key-ring. Glow in the dark, is it?'

'I believe so.'

'Anything else?'

'Yes, we'd like a list of caches in the area. Their names particularly.'

'Well, that's easier. But what area? There must be sixty caches within ten miles of Petrus Two.'

'Within three miles,' said Fry, 'will be fine.'

*   *   *

'You know, I've been thinking about this body-swap scenario,' said Cooper, after David Mead had left. 'It doesn't make any practical sense, does it?'

'What do you mean, Ben?'

'Well, think about it. Put yourself in the position of an individual who's ended up with a body on his hands, for whatever reason.'

'A murderer, you mean?'

'Not necessarily. It could have been an accident.'

'Oh, yes?'

'Well, whatever. But you have a dead body on your hands, right? You have to find some way of disposing of it.'

'And your friend the manager of the crematorium won't play ball?' said Fry. 'If we believe what Christopher Lloyd told us, that conversation with Richard Slack could well have been the first attempt at disposing of the body. But when Lloyd said "no", some other means had to be found.'

'Exactly. And you're someone who has access to the chapel of rest at the funeral director's, where you know there's another body already casketed up, ready to be cremated next morning.'

'OK.'

'So you take your body back to the shop and you do the changeover. On your own, that would be a difficult thing to achieve, but perhaps not impossible. I guess they have trolleys and so on. It would take time, though, and a lot of physical effort. You'd have to tidy up and make sure everything looked in order for the funeral next morning. And then you'd have to put the legitimate body back into your vehicle, wouldn't you?'

Fry frowned. 'Yes.'

'Well, what have you achieved with all that work and effort? Not to mention the risk? The fact is, you still have a dead body to dispose of. In practical terms, you're back to square one.'

'You think he went to all that trouble for nothing?'

'It seems like it, doesn't it?'

'I think he's far too clever to have done something like that for no good reason.'

'Well, he had a different body, that's all. Why didn't he just dispose of his original victim in the woods instead of poor old Audrey Steele?'

'One good reason – there was something about the other body he needed to conceal. Probably some evidence of the way the victim died, a clue that would lead directly back to him. He put that evidence permanently beyond retrieval, by means of cremation. On the other hand, Audrey Steele's body bore no evidence that could incriminate him.'

'But surely he must have known that once we identified her remains, it would take us straight to the doors of Hudson and Slack?'

Fry nodded. 'I think he was relying on two things. Firstly, that we might never be able to identify her, even if she was found. The longer she remained undiscovered, the more remote our chances. If it hadn't been for the accuracy of the facial reconstruction –'

'And a bit of persistence,' said Cooper.

'OK, OK – and your persistence.'

'What's the second thing?'

'Well, we might have been led to the doors of Hudson and Slack, but after all this time, how can we possibly hope to prove which member of staff was responsible for swapping the bodies? Any forensic evidence is long gone or contaminated beyond recovery. And the more time passes, the fainter the memories of potential witnesses.'

'And some of them might have left in the meantime. We're going to have to track them all down,' said Cooper.

'It'll be difficult to justify the time and resources for an exercise like that, Ben, when there are more pressing cases to be dealt with.'

'I was afraid you might say that.'

'If we had an easier, quicker lead to follow up, it would be different. Possibly our only real hope is that a member of staff noticed something wrong at the time. Or had their suspicions, at least.'

'And that they're willing to share what they know with us,' said Cooper. 'Which isn't exactly a given.'

'No. But without that, he might well get away with it. Suspicions are nothing without evidence. And in this case, we have no evidence at all. You know, sometimes you hear of a murder enquiry with no body. This is the first case I've ever known where we have a body – but it's the wrong one.'

'It's got to be that way, hasn't it? Too many people would notice if there was no corpse in a coffin sent for cremation.'

'Yes.'

'So someone removed Audrey Steele's body and put another in its place. Dangerous Dave would approve of that.'

Fry stared at him. 'What?'

'If you're going to take an item from a cache, you must leave something to replace it. Those are the rules of the game.'

'The rules of the game. Right.'

Cooper thought of the mourners standing round the green burial site the day before to say farewell to the remains of Audrey Steele. Many of them had looked baffled to be attending another funeral for the same person, as if they'd just discovered that a human being could die twice over and everything could be even worse the second time round.

'Some game, though,' he said.

The Slacks lived in Miller's Dale, among the winding loops of the River Wye. Cooper knew that these middle stretches of the Wye could be surprisingly remote. From Lees Bottom, the route of the main A6 swung away from the river for a few miles before the roads converged again near Topley Pike. In between, the limestone dales were accessible only by narrow back roads or by hiking through the woods on riverside paths.

A railway line had once skirted the valley sides, in the days when the mills had been working. Now, apart from some disused tunnels, all that was left of the line in Miller's Dale was a double viaduct rising high above the road. It came as a surprise to Cooper every time he saw it. The bridge and its massive iron supports seemed to leap suddenly out of the trees cloaking the narrow valley.

A sharp turn opposite the church took him past the back of the Angler's Rest and into a dark lane alongside the Wye. Cooper drove beneath limestone cliffs and negotiated a flooded stretch of road to reach the hamlet of Litton Mill, where he found Greenshaw Lodge. It had been an engine house once, part of the mill complex. But progressive demolition of the older mill buildings had left the house isolated on the lower slopes among the trees.

As Cooper pulled up in front of the Slacks' house, he saw a man standing on the doorstep. He was in his seventies probably, tall and lean, with the same slightly ungainly look that Vernon had. The old man didn't seem to be waiting for anybody, just standing looking at nothing in particular. When he heard the engine, he turned to stare at Cooper's car with a bemused expression.

'Mr Abraham Slack?'

'Come in,' said the old man without even asking who he was. Cooper thought of giving him some security advice about identifying visitors before he let them into the house, but decided it wasn't the time.

One wall of the sitting room was exposed stonework. Two arches led to the dining room and a breakfast kitchen with Shaker-style wall units. Outside, three steps led to a gravel path which went all the way down the garden. A neatly mowed lawn was broken by recently clipped hedges.

'I sold my own house and moved here to be with Vernon,' said Abraham, putting the kettle on to make tea in the automatic way of local people. 'He looks after me now.'

'You have no other family left, sir?'

'Oh, I have two daughters. Both married with families of their own. One lives in London, and the other in Canada. They both suggested that I might want to go and live with them, but I couldn't face the idea of moving away from here at my age. This is where I've always been, and I'll stay here until I die. I have my grave plot already paid for, of course.'

'Well, of course – considering your profession.'

Abraham smiled. 'Not that either of my daughters would actually welcome having me living with them, I'm sure. They have their own lives to lead. Looking after children is a full-time job in itself, and nobody wants the responsibility of an old person as well, do they?'

Cooper looked away. But he wondered if the old man really was looked after by Vernon, or whether it was the other way round. Abraham looked healthy and sturdy enough not to need any nursing just yet.

'You say that you sold your own home to come here, sir? So was this the house where your son lived?'

'Yes, that's right. Richard and Alison lived here all their married life. But it's Vernon's house now.'

'He's made a nice job of it.'

Cooper glanced around the room. The place was very neat. In fact, the lack of decoration had a rather minimalist feel. But finally he found what he'd been unconsciously looking for. Everyone had family mementos in the house, even Freddy Robertson. Here, a framed photograph stood on a shelf in an alcove.

'Is this yours, sir?'

'Yes, it's my family. My wife and I, with our three children. Vernon grumbles about it, but he knows how much it means to me. Richard would have been about twelve at the time.'

'He looks very solemn,' said Cooper.

'He was the eldest of the three, and he made it his job to look after his little sisters. Richard took the responsibility seriously.'

'What age was he when he was killed in the accident?'

'Forty-six.'

Cooper did a quick mental calculation. The photograph must have been taken around 1970: the year that flower power died, the summer of love already a distant memory. You would never have known from this family group that the sixties had ever happened. The adolescent Richard had the suggestion of an unruly fringe to his blond hair, but no more than that. The whole family looked respectable and well dressed, as if they'd put on their Sunday clothes specially for the photograph. They were posed like a Victorian group, the dignified patriarch with his wife and children gathered around him.

'You must have been proud of him, sir.'

'Oh, yes. And he made a very good funeral director, you know. The firm was in good hands with Richard there.'

Cooper looked up. Was he mistaken, or had he detected a hint of criticism of Melvyn Hudson? It would be understandable, in the circumstances. The old man must deeply regret that his own son wasn't still there to play his part in running Hudson and Slack. Abraham must be reminded of his son's death every time he heard the name of the company or saw it on the letterhead.

'Are the books yours, too?'

'No, those are Vernon's. I brought a few books and knick-knacks with me, but I keep them upstairs in my own room mostly. It's Vernon's house, after all.'

Actually, Cooper thought the room could have done with a few knick-knacks. The shelves could have taken a few more books. In fact, it felt really sparse, a stripped-down room. Perhaps this was the way Vernon liked it. It was, after all, a male household.

'That's my chair in the corner, though,' said the old man. 'I brought a few bits of my best furniture with me. The display cabinet is mine, too, and the grandfather clock.'

As Abraham pointed out his possessions, Cooper wondered what the room had been like without them. There must hardly have been anything in here at all. No woman would have tolerated such a lack of interior decoration.

'When did you retire from Hudson and Slack, sir?' asked Cooper.

'Strictly speaking, I haven't retired,' said Abraham. 'I still own a half-interest in the company, so I attend meetings occasionally. But I haven't been active in the business for more than seven years now. I was lucky enough to be able to retire at sixty-five.'

'Because you had your son to pass the mantle on to?'

'Yes. But Richard . . . he died, you know.'

'That must have been a great blow.'

'We come to terms with these things after a while. But that's why there's just me and Vernon now.'

'What about Vernon's mother?'

'She and Richard were already divorced when he died. She re-married and lives in Shropshire now. Vernon phones her, and he's visited them in Oswestry a couple of times, but he doesn't like her new husband, so he doesn't see as much of his mother as he'd like to.'

'So, Mr Slack, you weren't actively involved in the firm at the time of your son's death?'

'No.'

'Or in the period immediately before that?'

'Seven years ago, I passed day-to-day running of the company over to Richard. And Melvyn, of course. Is there something wrong?'

'We're investigating an incident that may have happened shortly before your son died.'

'May have happened?'

'Sorry, I should say it *did* happen. And someone at Hudson and Slack may have been involved.'

'We have a very high reputation,' said Abraham stiffly. 'We can't afford any irregularities. None at all. It's a very sensitive business we're in.'

'Nevertheless, there was a body which didn't get cremated as it should have been.'

'I know nothing about that. Neither Richard nor Melvyn ever mentioned it. I'm sure you must be mistaken.'

'No, sir.'

Abraham shook his head vehemently. 'No, I would have known about it. There are too many regulations and double checks. Something like that couldn't be concealed. And why, anyway?'

'Sir?'

'Why on earth would anyone do a thing like that?'

The old man glanced out of the window, and

Cooper followed his gaze. He saw a car drawing up in the yard, an old Escort with a rattling exhaust. Vernon Slack got out, looked at Cooper's Toyota and fiddled nervously with his keys, as if he might get back in the Escort and drive off again.

'That's handy,' said Cooper. 'I'll just have a quick word with your grandson on my way out, sir.'

'Don't bully him,' said Abraham suddenly.

'Now why would I do that?'

Vernon had seen him coming. He looked nervous, but then he always seemed nervous. He remained standing in the yard while Cooper came out of the front door. His eyes flickered to the window, so his grandfather was probably giving him some kind of signal, telling him how to behave or what to say. Maybe just a finger to the lips, enough for Vernon to understand: *Say nothing.*

'Just home from work, sir?' said Cooper.

'Yes, I finished a bit early. We were quiet today.'

'I suppose that's bad for business, but good in a way, too.'

'What?'

'It means fewer people are dying,' said Cooper.

'Oh. Yeah.'

Looking past Vernon, he noticed an access to a cess pit concealed below flags between the hedges. It was well designed, almost invisible. There was a workshop attached to the house, with strip lighting and power points. On the other side, a garage contained an inspection pit, shelves full of tools and a large roof space used for storage. The only thing in a state of disrepair was an ancient stone-built privy in the corner of the garden.

'Do you enjoy the work at Hudson and Slack?' asked Cooper.

Vernon shrugged. 'It's OK. I don't do anything too difficult.'

He looked at the window again, but the old man had disappeared. Vernon started to look anxious.

'What were you talking to Granddad about?'

'Mr Slack, I wonder if you remember doing a funeral about eighteen months ago for a lady called Audrey Steele?'

'I wouldn't remember anything like that. You'll have to speak to the boss,' said Vernon.

'The service was at the parish church in Edendale, St Mark's, and it was followed by cremation. Did you drive the hearse that day?'

'I've no idea. Mr Hudson has the records. He makes all the arrangements.'

Cooper looked at him. 'Don't you ever know whose funeral you're assisting at?'

'Why would I need to? I just drive and help carry the casket.'

'What about when you collect a body?'

'I might get told the name. But I don't know any more about it than that. There isn't any need for it, you see. We do the job and look after the grievers, and then we go home. The boss sees to everything else, and he tells us when we're wanted.'

'You're not the least bit curious?'

Vernon shrugged. 'Sometimes, you don't even know the details of a call until you turn up at the house to do a removal.'

He began to edge past Cooper towards the house. Even walking slowly, his movements were a little awkward. Cooper was reminded of Freddy Robertson. But the professor must be nearly forty years older than Vernon, and it was understandable if he was showing his age. Vernon was a young man. He looked like someone who'd suffered recent bruising.

'So you don't remember Audrey Steele's funeral, sir?' said Cooper, trying to keep Vernon from disappearing altogether.

'We do a lot of funerals. We do them every day. How would I remember?'

'Tell me, do you work with Billy McGowan often?'

'Obviously.'

'You get on with him all right?'

''Course I do.'

Cooper was about to press him further about the funeral of Audrey Steele, when he saw Vernon's nervousness and remembered how Diane Fry had left Melvyn Hudson to stew for a while. Even if the trick didn't work on Hudson, it should work on Vernon Slack. In any case, he was keen to be back in the office to hear the geocacher's news.

Then his attention was drawn by the jingle of car keys, and he noticed Vernon's hands.

'How did you get those burns on your hands, sir?' he asked.

'They're not burns, it's just a rash.'

'A pretty nasty rash, Mr Slack.'

'I was doing some gardening, and I must have touched something I was allergic to.'

'Perhaps you ought to see a doctor.'

'No, it'll go down in a day or two.'

'Is that why you've been wearing gloves?'

'Yes, it looks better in front of the grievers.'

Cooper raised his eyes and looked at Vernon Slack steadily. But Vernon shifted his gaze. There was no doubt he was frightened of something or somebody. And it wasn't Ben Cooper.

28

The office was deathly quiet when Cooper returned to West Street later that afternoon. Only Diane Fry was in the CID room, working her way through a stack of reports she'd been neglecting. One of the reports was waiting for Cooper on his desk. It was an initial forensic report on five sets of cremains. No points of comparison.

'I wonder if Vernon has ever told the old man how badly Melvyn Hudson treats him,' said Cooper when he had Fry's attention.

'Why?'

'Sometimes people who're bullied on a regular basis feel ashamed of it and don't tell anybody. It's a particular problem with children in schools. And Vernon still seems to be a child, in some ways. He might be afraid of admitting to his grandfather that he's too frightened to stand up for himself.'

'Especially as he's in a position of the carer now?' said Fry.

'That's it. Vernon will know that Abraham wants to see him as somebody strong. Besides, what could the old man do, except have a row with Hudson?'

'I wonder if Vernon could afford to give up his job at the firm?'

'It depends how much money he was left by his father. He has the house, but that's not worth anything unless he sells it. He may have no other income.'

'The old man is probably worth quite a bit, given his half-share in the firm.'

'You think that's what Vernon is hoping for, to inherit from the old man too?'

Cooper looked at her. 'What do you think?'

'They certainly sound an odd pair. Some bond is keeping them together.'

'They're family. That's enough for most people.'

But Cooper was thinking about his last visit to Vivien Gill's house, and the family gathered in the sitting room. People held together by that kind of bond weren't always good news for everyone else.

'Oh, of course,' said Fry. 'Family.'

A phone was ringing somewhere down the corridor, but no one was answering it. Cooper felt a strange sense of isolation, as if the whole building had been evacuated, except for him and Fry.

'Diane, last time I saw Vernon Slack, he had red weals on his hands. They looked to go part way up his arms, too. They were so bad I thought

433

at first they were burns, but he said it was an allergic rash.'

'So?'

'I'm wondering if they might have been formaldehyde burns.'

'An accident at work?' said Fry.

'Possibly. But why wouldn't he have said so? Why lie about them? And why did he seem so frightened? He was moving stiffly, too, as if he was bruised.'

'You think somebody beat him up and shoved his hands into formaldehyde – what, as a warning? "Look, Vernon, this is what will happen to you if you don't keep quiet"?'

'Something like that.'

'But who would do that?'

'Two people spring to mind. For one thing, I don't believe Melvyn Hudson could have been entirely ignorant of what was going on. But he doesn't seem the type for direct intimidation either. He's a bully all right, but his bullying is psychological, not physical. He's quite capable of scaring Vernon without throwing formaldehyde on him.'

'Agreed.'

'But then there's Billy McGowan.'

Fry flicked through the files on the Hudson and Slack staff. 'Yes, I remember him. A nasty-looking customer, all right – I wouldn't want him handling *my* dead relative. But we shouldn't make assumptions from the way a person looks, should we?

434

Mr McGowan could be a PhD in Nuclear Physics, just filling in time between Nobel Prizes.'

'I suppose so.'

'Mmm. He has a handful of convictions for assault and affray, according to the PNC. Suspended sentences and probation, so he's never actually been inside. Intelligence links him to organized theft from industrial premises, but only as casual labour on heavy jobs. He's a smash-and-grunt man. It's all pretty low-level stuff, Ben.'

'Well, I didn't suppose he was the brains behind the operation.'

'You think he's doing the dirty work on behalf of Hudson?'

'Well, that's basically what he's paid to do at Hudson and Slack, isn't it? How big a step is there between what he does with a dead body and what he might feel capable of doing to a living one?'

Fry seemed not to have heard him as she turned a page. 'And no educational qualifications, to speak of. So I don't suppose he's won any Nobel Prizes, after all.'

'I'd like to look into McGowan a bit more, Diane.'

'OK, you do that.'

She was silent for a moment, deep in thought. 'Speaking of Nobel Prizes,' she said finally, 'this Professor Robertson of yours – how did he come to be involved in this case, exactly?'

'He knows a member of the police committee.

Wasn't that who recommended him? I'm sure Mr Hitchens said it was.'

'Yes, but was Robertson *asked* to help out? Or did he volunteer?'

'Meaning what, Diane?'

'Look, we all know there's a certain type of creep who'll commit a murder, then go to any lengths necessary to get himself involved in the investigation. That's so he can watch what's going on and laugh at us getting things wrong. It's usually the creep who thinks he's much cleverer than the rest of us.'

Cooper shook his head. 'You've just got it in for Freddy Robertson because he rubbed you up the wrong way the first time you met.'

'You can't deny that he fits the profile, Ben,' said Fry. 'Let's face it, as smug, arrogant creeps go – he's the smuggest.'

'It's just his manner.'

'OK. So you think it's a coincidence that he knows all about the same subjects that interest our killer?'

'Professor Robertson is an expert in Thanatology. That's the point. That's why he's involved.'

'I called the anthropologist at Sheffield University,' said Fry. 'He said there's no evidence for any of it.'

'For what?'

'All that stuff about sarcophagi. He said archaeologists have never established clear evidence of burial rites from that time. Excarnation just seems to have been one variant. At some sites skeletons have been found separated from their small bones. But, as we know, those are the bits most likely to fall off if a body is moved after skeletonization. The rest of it is conjecture.'

'Well, experts disagree sometimes,' said Cooper. 'Anyway, Professor Robertson seemed to know all the details.'

'You know what these enthusiasts are like – they develop their own theory from selective evidence, and then there's no hope of convincing them they're wrong. They carry on riding their hobby horse no matter how many times it's shot from under them.'

'Would you describe Freddy Robertson as an enthusiast?'

'Probably. If only to avoid a slander charge.'

'What do you mean?'

'Well, there's a very fine line here, isn't there? A fine line between enthusiasm and obsession.'

'And you think Robertson might have crossed that line?'

Fry shrugged. 'It isn't always easy to tell. He might just have been having a joke with us.'

'A *joke*?'

'There's one other thing I've been thinking about, in relation to our caller. It concerns educational qualifications.'

'You don't need any to be a crematorium technician. You don't need GCSEs to carry a coffin or drive a hearse either.'

'Exactly. But we're looking for somebody well educated, aren't we?'

'Are we?'

'You heard the tapes. Eros and Thanatos. The life instinct and the death instinct. Even without the Freud references, he talks like an educated man. Someone who needs to show off his education, in fact. I think this is a man who likes to feel superior to everyone else.'

'So who qualifies, by your definition?' said Cooper reluctantly.

Fry dropped a file on the desk. 'Melvyn Hudson is a graduate. He studied at Hallam University in Sheffield.'

'What subject did he take?'

'Media Studies.'

'Oh, what? Another thwarted TV presenter? I can't see him as a chat-show host, somehow.'

'Nor me.' Fry looked up. 'Do they study Sigmund Freud in Media Studies, do you think?'

'I've no idea, Diane. But the tone of the messages is certainly pretentious enough to fit some of the media students I've met.'

'It's all part of an elaborate act, isn't it? The caller is putting on a bit of a show – and we're his audience.'

'You could say that. And Hudson is ideally placed to do it, at first glance.'

Fry perched herself on the edge of Gavin Murfin's desk. It seemed to be one of her favourite places to sit, because she could look down at

Cooper in his chair. She was close, without being unreasonably close. She must have known that he found it uncomfortable.

She placed a second file on top of the first. 'So what about Christopher Lloyd? He has an Open University degree in English Literature.'

'You're kidding.'

'I'm perfectly serious.'

'People are full of surprises.'

A memory was triggered in Cooper's mind, a voice quoting Shakespeare to him in a church-yard a few days ago. *Oh that this too, too solid flesh would melt.* Hamlet, of course. But it hadn't been Christopher Lloyd doing the quoting.

'Some of the same things apply to Lloyd,' he said. 'I take it he knows the Hudsons.'

'Certainly. They must have met professionally many times. I wonder if they have any contact socially. Well, that's one possibility to follow up,' said Fry. She covered the two files on the desk with a third. 'And then there's Barbara Hudson.'

Cooper shook his head. 'The caller was a man. No doubt about that.'

'Ben, when Liz Petty demonstrated the voice changer, she proved to my satisfaction, and the DI's, that the voice could equally be a woman's.'

'All right, but it seems unlikely. And Barbara Hudson –'

'– has a doctorate in Sociology. The subject of her PhD thesis was the study of social influences on styles of moral reasoning.'

'Really? How do you know that, Diane? Did you ask her?'

'No, I enquired at her former university in Nottingham.'

'A PhD?' said Cooper. 'So she's actually Dr Hudson. She doesn't use the title.'

'Very few people do. Not in this country. They know that members of the public assume you're a medical doctor and want to tell you about their chronic piles at every opportunity.'

'OK. Any more?'

Cooper didn't really have to ask. He knew perfectly well there was one more. He could see the last file clutched in Fry's hand. Without a word, she placed it on the desk with the name face up, so that Cooper could read it for himself.

'Well, what a surprise,' he said. 'Professor Freddy Robertson.'

'You made enquiries about him yourself,' pointed out Fry.

'I was curious.' Cooper turned back the pages in his notebook. 'Look, he does a lot of work for the Rotary Club, Eden Valley Hospice, Cancer Research.'

'So? Public charity and private iniquity?'

He looked up from his notebook. He wasn't sure if Fry was quoting or not. But he was growing used to it from the time he'd spent with Robertson, so he didn't bother asking.

'Since he retired, he's developed this interest in Thanatology.'

'Yes, but . . .'

'I'll make the call, shall I?' said Fry.

Cooper could tell that Freddy Robertson answered the phone almost immediately. Perhaps he spent his time waiting anxiously by the phone for someone to ask him for his advice. All he wanted was a chance to share his knowledge.

'Oh, Sergeant . . .' said Robertson when he answered his door a little while later. 'I'm sorry, I've already forgotten your name.'

'DS Fry, sir.'

The professor smiled. 'DS Fry, yes.'

Fry stood in the hallway and looked at the coat rack, listening to Robertson's chatter about his Edwardian gentleman's residence without really hearing a word. It was Robertson himself she was interested in. And his voice. Particularly, she wanted to listen to his voice.

'Thanatology,' she said when he'd finished. 'What does that mean exactly?'

'It's named after Thanatos, the personification of death. In Greek mythology, he's the son of Nyx, the goddess of night. His Roman counterpart is Mors.'

'Oh? Is that Inspector Mors?'

'No. The Latin Mors, the Roman god of death, from whom we get *mortality* and *mortuary*.'

'I was joking,' said Fry.

Robertson inclined his head. 'I apologize, Sergeant. I don't always appreciate other people's

441

humour. You were making a reference to a well-known television programme perhaps?'

'Yes.'

'That sort of reference always goes over my head, I'm afraid. I'm rather out of touch with popular culture.'

He walked on ahead into the house. Fry looked at Cooper. 'Was he apologizing just then?'

'I think so, Diane.'

'So why do I feel as though I've been insulted?'

In the professor's study, the atmosphere was cool. No drinks offered, no pleasantries, no invitation to take the most comfortable seat. Fry pulled a chair close to Robertson's desk and rested her elbows on it, forcing the professor to lean backwards to avoid appearing too confrontational.

'In your discussions with Detective Constable Cooper, you've been very helpful over the past few days, sir,' she said.

'I'm gratified to hear it. I do my humble best.'

He looked towards Cooper, beginning to form a smile. But Fry wasn't going to let his attention drift, or the mood soften.

'You might be able to assist us even more, sir.'

'Oh?'

'Looking at the facts we've gathered in our enquiries so far, it seems rather strange that you've been able to cast light on almost every aspect.'

'Strange? Why should it be strange? This is my area of expertise, Sergeant. My role is to cast light where it's needed.'

442

He was trying to keep his tone breezy, but Fry knew she'd needled him.

'Yes, sir. But I find it particularly interesting that you've several times managed to cast your light *before* you were asked the appropriate question.'

'I have no idea what you mean.'

'The sarcophagus, for example. The "flesh eater". You were very keen to tell us all about that. So keen, in fact, that you mentioned it to DC Cooper before he had any idea of the relevance himself.'

Robertson tried for another conspiratorial smile with Cooper, but it wasn't working. For once, Cooper was obeying the instructions she'd given him and was staying detached.

'The same applies to some of the other references in the messages,' said Fry.

'Ah, the messages.'

Fry felt a surge of surprise and excitement. 'You admit that you know about the messages?'

'I know nothing about any messages,' said Robertson. 'Except that your colleague mentioned them to me yesterday.'

And now the professor smiled. Fry heard a squeak of leather, and sensed Cooper shifting uneasily in his chair. So she knew it was true. But she had to press on.

'Professor Robertson, I think you already knew about the calls that have been made to us during the past week. I believe you're familiar with their exact content. Do you own a device called a voice changer?'

'Sergeant, this is quite intolerable. When I agreed to put my time and expertise at the disposal of the police, I didn't expect to be treated in this way.'

'May I see your car keys, sir?'

She'd struck home this time. Fry saw the professor's eyes widen and his nostrils flare as his expression tensed. He jerked forward in his chair as if she'd prodded him with a sharp needle.

Fighting to control his anger, he opened a drawer and tossed a ring of keys on to the desk between them. Fry didn't touch them, but separated the keys one by one with the end of her pen. Robertson's face suffused with blood as if she'd uttered the most deadly insult.

There was no device of the kind that Liz Petty had showed her, nothing like a garage-door remote with a tiny built-in microphone that would disguise a caller's voice. But Fry wasn't entirely disappointed. She pushed the keys to either side and left the keyfob lying on the desk on its own. It was a piece of ivory about two inches long, beautifully carved in the shape of a human skeleton, the skull and ribs smooth and shiny where they'd been rubbed by someone's fingers. It wouldn't actually glow in the dark, but to Fry it shone with significance.

'Now, that *is* strange,' she said. 'To carry a reminder of death around with you wherever you go. What do you gain from that, Professor? Does it make death feel closer? Does it give you a greater understanding of it?'

'I already know about death,' snapped Robertson. 'I know *all* about death.'

'Yes, I'm sure you do, sir.'

The professor's hand was shaking as he looked at the bottle of whisky on the shelf. But before he reached for it, he glared his anger at Fry.

'In the final analysis, Sergeant, I'm just like everyone else – it's life that I don't understand.'

When Melvyn Hudson had put on his protective clothing, Vernon helped him get the body on to the stainless-steel table. They stripped off the shirt, jeans, underwear and shoes, and Vernon shoved everything into a bin liner. They removed the watch and glasses, and taped over the wedding ring. Vernon handed Hudson the disinfectant spray, and he sponged the body down, looking for infestations in the groin and around the face. He disinfected the mouth and nose with cotton swabs, then noticed some fluid in the back of the mouth.

'Help me roll the body, Vernon,' he said.

'What's up?'

'A bit of purge from the stomach. I might have to tie off the trachea and oesophagus when I open the neck.'

Hudson massaged the limbs, then stretched them out, letting the forearms hang off the edge of the table so the blood would drain into them

445

and expand the vessels. He rolled a thin film of superglue on to the inside of each finger and closed them together. Then he lifted the head and slid a block underneath to keep it above the level of the body. If blood ran into the head, it could discolour the tissues.

After Vernon had brought the bucket of bleach solution, Hudson washed the body again, cleaning under the fingernails and looking for staining on the hands and face. He thought about using super-glue on the eyes, too, but instead he placed two plastic eyecaps over them and closed the lids so that they were held shut by the little knobs on the caps.

He looked up at Vernon. 'Did the police talk to you today?'

'Someone came to the house. Detective Constable Cooper.'

'Did he talk to Abraham?'

'Yes.'

'What about, Vernon?'

'I don't know. He was already in the house when I got home.'

The face looked a bit tense. Hudson massaged the forehead and the area around the eyes to relax the dead muscles, then stood back and examined the effect. The upper lids of the eyes had to meet to the lower lids about two thirds of the way down to get the peaceful look. Too high or low, and it made the deceased appear to be in pain, or squinting.

'Vernon, I know you'd be careful,' said Hudson. 'But do you think your grandfather understands?'

'Understands what?'

'The importance of appearances.'

Hudson packed the throat with gauze, put the dentures back in and slid a mouth-former over them, so that its ridges of plastic knobs would keep the lips closed. He shut the mouth permanently by stitching the lips together with a needle and thread, checking that the line of the mouth wasn't too tight before tying the thread off. Then he tilted the head slightly to the right, so it would face the grievers when they viewed it in the chapel of rest.

'Does he look OK?' he asked.

'Fine.'

'I think he looks ten years younger,' said Hudson, and laughed. It was exactly what the grievers always said.

Finally, he packed the anus with cotton wool soaked in cavity fluid and rubbed a light coating of grease on to the face, neck and hands.

'OK,' he said. 'Now the fun starts.'

Hudson used bruise bleach to remove a couple of blackened areas, spread more superglue to close the small wounds, and replaced the missing tissue with putty and hardening compound. He remembered one occasion when he'd been given a body that had been decapitated. He'd had to insert splints to stop the head sagging to one side, then he'd trimmed the edges of the skin and sewn the head back on with dental floss. The suture line had been hidden by a high collar and a tie when the time for viewing came around.

Behind his respirator mask, Hudson was doing his best not to breathe in the vapours from the body cavity fluids and formaldehyde. The preparation room was claustrophobic and sound-proofed to prevent the noise of the pump or the splash of fluids from reaching the public rooms.

'I noticed those burns on your hand earlier,' he said.

'It's nothing.'

Hudson looked at Vernon over his mask. 'As long as it wasn't an accident at work. We wouldn't want that.'

'I know,' said Vernon. 'Bad for the image.'

Then Hudson made the first incision. He'd decided on arterial embalming for this job. But the decision had been an easy one, really. Cavity embalming took such little skill that it gave him no satisfaction. The belly punchers and the throat cutters – there were always derogatory terms for every speciality.

The scalpel felt cool and familiar in his gloved hand as he incised the skin over the left carotid artery and lifted a section clear of the surrounding tissue. Carefully, he inserted the canula into the artery, then attached a drain to the femoral vein in the groin and let the tube hang off the table into the guttering. For a body this size, he'd have to pump in about seven pints of formaldehyde solution, so there'd be a lot to drain away. As the fluid circulated, the muscles would firm up. In about ten hours' time, they'd be so hard that he wouldn't be able to alter the body's position any further.

'Just remember, Vernon,' he said, 'there are a lot of things around here that can be dangerous, if you don't watch your step.'

'Yes, Melvyn.'

Hudson took a grip on the trocar and thrust the sharpened point through the skin and into the belly with one firm stroke. He was pleased with his ability to do this. So many embalmers jabbed and lunged, as if they were spearing fish. All it took was the confidence to make a firm thrust through the abdominal wall, and the assurance to leave the trocar in place as it began to release the gases and liquids that had built up in the body's cavities.

He infused about sixteen ounces of preservative into the abdomen through the trocar, and the same amount into the chest. He examined the genitals in case they needed a thrust of the trocar too, but decided his technique had been good enough for the formaldehyde to reach all the small blood vessels.

Then he thought about the skull. How much gas and fluid might have collected in the cranium? It was possible to pass the trocar up through the nose and into the skull through the thin bone at the top of the nostrils. He could instil cavity fluid and pack the nose with cotton wool to prevent leaks. But he looked at his watch and decided it wasn't necessary. Instead, he used a series of trocar buttons to close up the holes he'd already made.

Then Hudson realized that Vernon was watching him across the corpse, his eyes wide and anxious over his mask.

'Well, Vernon,' he said, 'that's a good job done. Let's get it back into the freezer. This is one corpse that won't decompose in a hurry.'

29

'Don't forget to send us the bill for your services, sir,' said Fry, as she reached the bottom of Professor Robertson's gravel drive.

It had been a protracted interview, long on talk and short on information. Highly unsatisfactory, from Fry's point of view. Worse still, once he'd recovered from his momentary show of temper over the key-ring, the professor had seemed entirely unperturbed by her visit.

'Ah, you don't know, then?' said Robertson. 'I'm giving my time entirely free and gratis. As a favour to my friend, Councillor Edwards. And in the public interest, of course.'

'Very commendable, sir.'

Fry watched the professor walk up the drive towards his house. Even from the back, he looked smug. But entirely free and gratis. She sighed. So that was it. Who could resist the services of an expert when they were provided for nothing?

*　　*　　*

As he waited by the car for Fry, Cooper recalled the professor's distaste for what he called the mechanical spectacle of death, the intrusion of machines into the natural process of dying. He'd sounded sincere. But had it all been an act?

'At least he didn't quote the Bible to you,' he said as Fry walked towards the car. He was hoping she'd forget to ask him why he'd let slip to Robertson about the phone messages.

'Why do you say that, Ben?'

'He did last time I was here.'

'Robertson quoted the Bible? He didn't strike me as religious. Not Christian, anyway. Quite the contrary.'

'Well, it was a passage from the Old Testament. Everyone uses the Old Testament for their own purposes.'

'What part of the Old Testament was he quoting?' asked Fry.

'Why?'

'It might be relevant. What was he trying to tell you?'

Cooper cast his mind back to the conversation with Robertson. 'Something about death.'

'Naturally. But what?'

'Ecclesiastes, he said it was. That's right. Ecclesiastes 3.'

Now Fry looked interested. 'The famous part?'

'Famous part? I suppose so. It was the bit about "dust to dust", but it wasn't quite worded like that in the quote.'

'Oh.'

'That wasn't what you were thinking of?'

'No. Something a little earlier in Ecclesiastes.'

'Diane, I didn't know you were so familiar with the Bible.'

'It must be a sign of my misspent childhood.'

'Really?'

'It's due to one of my sets of foster parents. Everybody has their obsession, and theirs was the most depressing, pessimistic book in the whole of the Old Testament. But everyone knows the verse I'm thinking about. Even you, Ben.'

'What do you mean, "even me"? I went to Sunday school.'

'"To everything there is a season, and a time to every purpose under the heaven,"' said Fry.

'Ah. The Pete Seeger song, "Turn, Turn, Turn". Some hippy sixties band had a big hit with it, didn't they?'

'I don't know about that. The words are from Ecclesiastes. Don't you remember the next part? "A time to be born . . ."'

Cooper remembered. Whether from his Sunday school lessons, or from the old pop song, he couldn't be sure. But the words came almost unbidden into his head. *A time to be born . . .*

'". . . and a time to die,"' he said.

Fry paused at the passenger door and studied Cooper across the roof of the car.

'Professor Robertson is enjoying himself too

much, don't you think? This is the way he gets his kicks.'

'There's nothing wrong with enjoying your work, I suppose. Some of us do.'

Cooper got into the car and started the engine. Fry fastened her seat belt and turned to him.

'Will you turn into a Freddy Robertson when you're retired, Ben? I can just picture you constantly hanging around the door at West Street, volunteering your services free and gratis in the public interest.'

'I'll probably be glad to get away from the place by then. Won't you?'

'You bet,' said Fry. 'Besides, what special expertise would I have to offer?'

Ben Cooper didn't possess a Bible. At least, he hadn't brought one with him to the flat when he moved out of Bridge End Farm. There had been one he'd won as a prize for regular attendance at Sunday school when he was ten years old. But that had been a children's edition, with illustrations of a handsome, golden-haired Jesus walking on water and feeding the five thousand. Cooper wasn't sure it had included the Old Testament. Probably not. There was far too much begetting and Sodom and Gomorrah for the trendy curate who'd been in charge then.

The only other copy he could remember was the old Cooper family Bible, presented to his great-grandfather and great-grandmother when they married in 1921. It had all the family's subsequent births, marriages and deaths recorded on the first few pages, just ahead of Genesis. But that one lived in the sideboard at Bridge End, wrapped in tissue paper and preserved like a sacred relic.

Cooper left his flat, went out on to Welbeck Street and knocked at the door of number six, where his landlady lived. Yes, Mrs Shelley had a Bible she could let him borrow. It was the King James version, of course. No Good News nonsense for her.

She invited Cooper in while she fetched the book, and he stood in her hallway, trying not to make too much noise. He could hear his land-lady's Jack Russell terrier whining and yapping at the back of the house. If the dog realized someone was on the premises, it was likely to explode into full-blown hysteria. Best not to make any care-less movements. Also, he couldn't afford to get involved in conversation with Mrs Shelley. Discussions with her were likely to get compli-cated and bewildering, and he didn't have time for it tonight. He was finally going on his date – a table for two was booked for seven forty-five at the Raj Mahal. Just one of the reasons he hadn't been keen to eat there with Gavin Murfin.

But Mrs Shelley wasn't gone for long. She came back wiping a layer of dust off a heavy black volume before offering it to him.

'I hope it helps, Ben,' she said.

To Cooper's embarrassment, she seemed to be

about to burst into tears, despite the smile she gave him. She even patted his arm. OK. So Mrs Shelley thought she'd just been instrumental in saving his soul. What had given her that impression?

'How is your mother, by the way, Ben?' she said.

Ah, so that was it. He should have known that his landlady would have her ear to the grapevine. Mrs Shelley wasn't saving his soul, but bringing him comfort in a time of need.

'I phoned the hospital this evening, and they say she's stable. Thank you for asking.'

'If there's anything I can do . . .'

'No, everything's fine. Thank you, Mrs Shelley.'

Cooper held the book up in front of him, not sure whether he was using it to ward off his landlady, or acknowledging that he already had what he needed.

Back in his flat, he got himself a beer and sprawled on the old sofa with the Bible. Then it struck him that drinking beer might not be appropriate while reading the Old Testament. He hesitated for a moment. Nobody would ever know, surely? But he had a clear vision of himself spilling Corona in the middle of Ecclesiastes. With his luck, the stain would form an image of a horned goat leaping across the pages, and Mrs Shelley would evict him from the flat as a disciple of Satan.

He sighed and put the beer to one side. Randy positioned himself on the rug, intrigued by the unusual behaviour.

'It's the Bible,' said Cooper. 'You ought to read it – you might learn something. Thou shalt not kill, for a start.'

The cat blinked sceptically, and began to wash his whiskers with concentrated relish. They probably still bore traces of blood from his last victim.

And here it was – Ecclesiastes 3:1. Cooper read the first few lines quietly to himself, while Randy cocked an ear in case food was being mentioned.

To everything there is a season,
And a time to every purpose under the heaven,
A time to be born, and a time to die;
A time to plant, and a time to pluck up that which is planted;
A time to kill, and a time to heal;
A time to break down, and a time to build up;
A time to weep, and a time to laugh;
A time to mourn, and a time to dance.

It was appropriate, of course. But had Professor Freddy Robertson really been trying to draw his attention to this verse with his reference to the Book of Ecclesiastes, or was that simply Diane Fry's unreasonable prejudice against him? If it *was* Robertson's intention, it had proved a little too subtle. It meant the professor had assumed a greater knowledge of the Bible than Cooper possessed. And then, there was that discussion of body snatching they'd had in the churchyard. Robertson had thought that his comments about superstition had offended Cooper, though they hadn't. The professor knew a great deal about a lot of things, but he wasn't a terribly good judge of people, was he?

Cooper looked at the verse from Ecclesiastes again. A time for everything. So what was the time for right now? A time to kill? A time to die?

He suspected it was neither of those. Not yet. The mystery caller would be thinking of another part of the verse as he sat smug and satisfied in his lair somewhere. He would be considering the possibility of another message, something to keep the police on their toes, to point them subtly in the right direction, or in the wrong direction altogether. Or perhaps he'd be deciding whether he should keep quiet for a while longer and let them stew.

Cooper could almost read his thoughts now. There was a right time for all things, he would be thinking. As it said later in the same verse of Ecclesiastes 3:1:

A time to keep silence, and a time to speak.

Diane Fry watched Angie getting dressed. The flat was too small for her to avoid it, and in any case her sister had never bothered about modesty.

They'd been like that with each other as teenagers, so Diane knew she must be the one who'd changed in the last decade and a half. What was it that had changed her most, she wondered.

Which aspect of her life had made her incapable of the closeness with her sister that she'd fought so long to recapture? She knew which it was that gave her the most nightmares and ruined her sleep, even now. Moving away from Birmingham couldn't wipe out that pain; it had followed her in her dreams.

'Where are you going, Sis?'

'Out.'

'But where exactly?'

'Just out.'

Diane was aware that she sounded like a possessive parent, but she couldn't seem to stop herself. And she knew that her sister's answers were deliberately designed to make her sound that way. Angie had always been clever like that. As a child, she'd been the manipulative one who knew exactly how to drive the most patient foster parent wild with frustration.

'Who are you seeing?' asked Diane, trying not to sound too desperate.

Angie pulled on a clean T-shirt. 'Somebody nice, maybe.'

'And will he still be as nice after he's met you?'

Her sister laughed. 'Who said it was a "he"? You can't catch me out, Mrs Detective.'

Diane started to lose patience. 'Come on, Angie, what's all the secrecy for?'

But Angie headed for the door. 'If you speak to me a bit better, I might tell you all about it tomorrow.'

Throwing herself on to the settee and folding up her legs, Diane settled down for another evening on her own. After so many years of restraint, she couldn't believe how often she now found herself saying things she regretted. But there were thoughts that forced themselves into her mind and heart so forcibly that she could no longer hold them in. Even Liz Petty had put her hand instinctively on a tap that had been waiting to be turned on, ever since Diane had read the transcript of the phone calls and visited Melvyn Hudson at the funeral director's.

The one thing she hadn't told Petty about the Balsall Heath case was the most shocking fact of all, in its way. The parents of that dead and decomposing child had attended her funeral, and sent the largest floral tribute. They had made a great show of mourning their own victim. What was the meaning of all that? She would never figure it out. Never.

The Raj Mahal restaurant in Hollowgate was quiet on Sunday nights, which suited Ben Cooper fine. He'd arrived first – a little early, in fact. But a waiter moved in quickly.

'Mr Cooper? Yes, a table for two, wasn't it?'

'Thank you.'

The first thing he did when he'd settled at his table was check out the other diners. Anywhere in Edendale, there was a dangerously high probability that he'd know somebody, or they would know him. If he was sitting a few feet away from a felon he'd once arrested, it could sour the atmosphere badly. Admirers of his father, or friends of Matt's, could be just as embarrassing.

But tonight, he was in luck. There were few customers, none of them familiar, and they all seemed too wrapped up in each other to pay him any attention. Cooper made sure his mobile phone was on, and set it to vibrate. 'Stable' was all very well, but he couldn't afford to be out of touch if the hospital called.

Then he fiddled with the menu for a while, knowing he'd have difficulty choosing what to eat. It was one of those menus where he could happily order any of the items and be confident he'd made a right choice. And on a first date there was always that awkwardness of trying to keep a conversation going to break the ice, making it impossible to concentrate on the menu at the same time.

He looked out of the window, but couldn't see much on the street. The lights from Hollowgate and the windows of the Market Square pubs reflected off the wet pavements and refracted through the drizzle that had started falling just before dusk. Eight o'clock, and the centre of Edendale looked deserted. The car park by the town hall was almost empty.

Cooper knew all the warnings about forming a relationship with another police officer. When it was someone of a different rank that you worked with closely, it was definitely a problem. But this wasn't another police officer. Close, though, in a way.

Finally, the door opened and the waiter hurried over. She looked around the restaurant, saw him immediately, and smiled. Cooper waved. He put down his menu and stood up as the waiter brought her to the table. They kissed chastely on the cheek. Her skin was cool and slightly damp from the rain.

'I'm not late, am I?'

'No.'

She was wearing tailored cream trousers, but he was used to seeing her in trousers. She looked a lot better than when she was bundled up in one of those thick blue sweaters the SOCOs wore, or a white paper crime-scene suit. Very unflattering.

'You look great, Liz,' he said.

The back wall of Hudson and Slack's vehicle compound bordered the railway line where it ran through a cutting between Fargate and Castleton Road. Later that night, after the last train had passed through Edendale, three figures in hooded sweatshirts made their way along the cutting. They moved confidently, as if sure there would be no one to observe them from the industrial units on the other side of the line.

When they reached the compound, the biggest of the three men used a pair of bolt cutters to open a gap in the weld-mesh fence, and they clambered over the wall. Within a few minutes, they had jemmied open a rear door of the funeral director's, with only a splintering of wood and the occasional grunt of effort. Then the company's new security system activated, and the burglar alarm began to scream. But no one was interested in committing burglary.

No one spoke as they entered a store room. Two of them kicked open inner doors, while the third swilled petrol from a plastic container on to the floor and furniture, drenching a stack of chairs and a spare desk, spraying fuel into the adjoining rooms as far as he could reach. Then he lit a petrol-soaked rag and tossed it through the doorway as his companions ran out.

With a dull roar, a blaze flared instantly. Flames engulfed the store room and burst from the open door to lick at the stones of the outside wall. Windows cracked as air was sucked in and drew the blaze deeper into the building. Paintwork scorched as the building filled with billowing black clouds. A smoke alarm burst into life and added its noise to the security system. The three men moved with sudden urgency as they raced back across the compound towards the wall.

But one of the figures paused as he passed between the rows of black vehicles. The other two turned, gesturing to him impatiently. With a ferocious swing of his arm, the biggest man brought down the blades of his bolt cutters and smashed the windscreen of a hearse. The toughened glass crazed, and he jabbed at it until it fell in fragments. Then he tossed the plastic container and the remaining petrol on to the driver's seat and dropped in a lighted match. He laughed at the heat and shock of the explosion as he ran to join the others at the gap in the fence. They clambered over the wall and sprinted back the way they'd come along the railway cutting. A car was waiting for them in a back street near Chesterfield Road.

By the time the first fire appliance turned off Fargate, the three men were long gone. In the street, people who'd come out of their houses to watch the flames had to cover their mouths as the wind changed direction, blowing acrid smoke and flakes of ash into their faces. Something was burning well at Hudson and Slack.

Despite his best efforts, it was inevitable they would end up talking shop. The current point of contact between them was the mystery caller.

'Diane Fry is taking these calls very seriously,' said Cooper. '*Very* seriously.'

The lamb curry he'd chosen was good, not too hot. With a few side dishes, the meal was living up to expectations.

'The tapes have really upset her, you know,' said Petty.

'They're pretty awful. Nobody likes listening to them.'

'It's more than that with Diane.'

'Is it? Why?'

464

Petty hesitated. 'I can't say. She told me in confidence.'

'Oh?'

Cooper was surprised by a surge of jealousy. There had been occasions when Fry had confided in him. But very few occasions. It was some time ago now that she'd told him about her childhood in foster homes in the Black Country, about her older sister who'd been a heroin addict by the time she ran away from home and disappeared from Diane's life. She'd talked to him about Angie again recently, too, but only because she had to. Cooper had somehow got himself involved in events that were nothing to do with him.

But that was really all he knew about Fry's life. Most of the time, she seemed to be trapped inside a bubble of her own, a little capsule of isolation that no one could penetrate. Had Liz Petty managed to penetrate that bubble?

Cooper looked across the table at Liz as she scooped up her curry with a poppadom.

'Do you get on well with Diane?' he said. 'How long have you been friendly with her?'

'Ben –'

'I didn't think she had any friends at West Street. What does she talk to you about?'

Petty put down her fork and gave him a quizzical smile.

'Ben, could we talk about something other than Diane Fry?'

Cooper felt his face start to grow warm. Perhaps the curry was too hot for him, after all.

MY JOURNAL OF THE DEAD, PHASE FIVE

Tonight I went back for the last time. Moonlight filtered through the trees, glinting on steel as I crouched in the grass and took the scalpel from my pocket. I lowered my head to pray. God, give me what I need. I know it's wrong, but please take this soul.

When I placed my hands in the damp grass, I could feel the grittiness of the soil under my fingers, the hard, knotty lumps of the roots. I was able to savour the closeness of the earth, and draw in the power I could sense below the ground.

But then I looked at the sky. I was facing north, and I wasn't sure if that was right. The feet of a body should be pointing to the east, and the head to the west. But which direction should you pray to? Where is God? North, south, east or west? Where does a soul go when it's released? Does it flicker upwards into the sun, like a swirl of mist vanishing at dawn? Or is it absorbed into the earth's atmosphere, drawn into the aurora, where it dances for ever in the flames of the north?

I brought my face lower, until I could hold it close to the bones. I sniffed, tilting my head to catch the play of light and shadow. A skeleton is a remarkable thing. Seen up close, it could be a soaring architectural structure – a cityscape or a cathedral. I saw the ribs curving in graceful arches, the skull a mysterious dome with dark recesses where moonlight glittered on something cold and wet.

Slowly, I allowed myself to follow the grain on the outer sheath of the scapula, to enjoy the planes and angles. I smiled with pleasure at the pure, white smoothness of a joint where once there had been gristle and black strings of tendon. I was so close to the bones that I could see my breath condense on their surfaces. I inhaled the faintest of scents – the scent of a perfect death, pure and clean, and irresistible.

Then I flicked open the blade. I began to work my way inch by inch, brushing at a bit of dirt with a cloth, teasing loose a spider's web. With the edge of my scalpel, I scraped at a dark encrustation on the lower pelvic plate, until the paler surface of the bone appeared. It was still slightly stained, but it'll weather like the rest, given time. I wasn't wearing gloves tonight, but I held my hands at an angle, tilted at the wrist, so that my fingers were clear of the surfaces. I felt like a musician fingering the keys of a delicate instrument.

The thought makes me smile again. In a way, I'm rather like a musician, because music requires a certain kind of skill that comes from practice and dedication. You have to be single-minded, if you're seeking perfection.

Tonight I wasn't disturbed. So this time I wasn't meant to stop. When I was finished, I put away the scalpel with a feeling of satisfaction. I wanted to do everything possible to reach a point as close to perfection as I could achieve. I might not have the chance to go back again. This was probably my final visit. My last hour in the dead place.

30

Fry hadn't really been watching for Ben Cooper to come on duty that morning. A prisoner had come into the cells overnight, and she'd been consulting the custody sergeant about interview arrangements.

As she passed through the security door from the custody suite to go back to the main building, she paused and pulled up her collar against a flurry of rain. Then she glanced across at the staff car park. Her attention had been drawn by a flash of light from a windscreen as a car backed into a parking space. She recognized Cooper's red Toyota, and she hesitated, intending to wait for him so they could walk up to the CID room together. She saw Cooper get out, but he didn't look round.

Then the passenger door began to swing open, and Fry realized he'd given someone a lift to work. He was the perfect Good Samaritan. Probably Gavin Murfin's car had broken down, and Cooper had stepped in to help.

She was about to move away when she caught a glimpse of blonde hair and a navy-blue sweater. Cooper's early-morning passenger was entirely the wrong shape to be Gavin Murfin. Entirely wrong. The image of a broken-down car vanished from her mind, to be replaced by a different scenario altogether.

Fry found it difficult to concentrate as she made her way back upstairs. She was trying to remember what else she had to attend to that was urgent before she went out. There was definitely something. Probably several things. But one thing she wanted to do was get those skeletons in the Alder Hall crypt checked out. John Casey had said there had been an earlier inventory of the bones, which should help a lot.

'Alder Hall? Oh, I think I can help you here,' said Dr Jamieson when Fry rang him. 'The study you're referring to was carried out by one of my predecessors. The records will be here in our archives.'

'That would be wonderful. But are you sure?'

'I can soon check. I'll get back to you ASAP.'

As soon as Cooper entered the room, he sensed something was wrong. There was one of those atmospheres, a vague uneasiness that was difficult to put his finger on. He looked at Fry, and saw her putting the phone down. The tightness of her expression confirmed his suspicion.

'There was an incident at the funeral director's

during the night,' she said, without bothering to say 'good morning'.

Puzzled, Cooper looked at his watch. It wasn't as if he was late for duty or anything. He was a bit early, in fact. He felt a surge of irritation at her rudeness.

'An incident? At Hudson and Slack, you mean?'

'Where else?'

'Well, I don't know,' he said. 'There are plenty of other funeral directors in this division.'

Fry gave him a cool stare. 'Yes, at Hudson and Slack. A person or persons unknown set fire to the place in the early hours of the morning. The fire service reports extensive damage. I haven't been out there yet. I thought you might want to come along – if you're not busy with something else, that is.'

'What would I be busy with?'

'Well, I don't know. There are plenty of other ongoing cases in this division.'

Cooper sighed. 'OK, Diane. Was that what the phone call was about?'

'No. Believe it or not, that was a helpful anthropologist. With a bit of luck, he might be able to produce records of the bone collection at Alder Hall.'

'That *is* a bit of luck.'

'The first one so far.'

'I have to say, those bones looked pretty old to me,' said Cooper. 'If there was a recent human skull from those remains in Ravensdale, it would stand out, wouldn't it?'

'An expert, are you? Learned a bit more than we thought from your friend the professor?'

Cooper shook his head, trying to shake off the irritation. 'It might mean we don't have to bring Dr Jamieson's team in to look at the bones, if the records tally. So we'd save on the budget, too.'

'And, hey presto, everyone's happy,' said Fry.

But Cooper looked at her thoughtfully. Happy was far from how she looked.

'According to John Casey, those bones were found somewhere in the grounds of the hall,' she said. 'Do you think Mrs Chadwick would know where exactly?'

'She might do.'

'Ask her, then.'

'Sure.'

He looked down at his desk. Work was waiting for him. If anything was really urgent – well, it was hard luck, unless he could snatch a few minutes. But Fry hadn't finished yet.

'Ben, you don't believe the Alder Hall crypt is what he means by "the dead place", do you?' she said.

'It's just a feeling. You might not understand.'

'Try me.'

'I felt . . . Well, when I was down there, it felt as though the place had been dead for too long. Does that make sense?'

Fry stared at him, as though she might actually

471

be trying to understand him. 'It's no more than that?'

'Sorry.'

Cooper put his jacket back on, and they headed out. He didn't like to admit to Fry what he was actually thinking. It was something Freddy Robertson had said to him, when he'd been explaining the purpose of a sarcophagus and the charnel house, and the rituals that went with them.

The memory had come back to him as he stood in the crypt at Alder Hall. For a moment, Cooper had felt a hint of what his ancient ancestors had instinctively believed. The bones piled in that crypt had been perfectly clean and dry, free of the last shreds of flesh that had once clung to them. If it was the fragments of a physical structure that held a soul to its body, then the spirits that hovered around those bones had long since departed.

'By the way,' said Fry in the car, 'I've started making enquiries into John Casey's background.'

'The property agent? Why?'

'Well, those two sets of remains were found on Alder Hall estate land. Admittedly, they were much nearer to Mr Jarvis's property than to the hall, but that's only because of the size of the estate. Casey is the man immediately responsible for the site, and he has the opportunity for unrestricted access, too. Once you're inside those gates, anything you do is entirely out of public view.

472

That doesn't apply to anyone approaching from the Ravensdale side, where there are residents in the cottages, and walkers on the footpath.'

'Not to mention the Jarvises and their dogs.'

'Exactly.'

'Well, John Casey may not be the most efficient property agent in the world. But he struck me as vaguely incompetent, rather than criminal.'

'Didn't you think he was a bit quick to draw our attention to Maurice Goodwin and his role at Alder Hall? That was too convenient, I thought.'

'Did you?'

'Look, Goodwin left the company three months ago. And Casey just happens not to have made arrangements for somebody else to check the hall regularly since then? And he just happens not to have found a replacement for Goodwin. Why not? What's so special about the job that he wasn't satisfied with any of the applicants?'

'I don't know. Diane, what are you suggesting?'

'I'm wondering if Casey had Maurice Goodwin lined up as a scapegoat to take the blame if things went wrong. In any case, I'd like to know why Goodwin left the job in the first place.'

'A personality clash, Mr Casey said.'

'That usually means a blazing row with the boss. What if John Casey deliberately manoeuvred Goodwin into a position where he'd decide that he'd had enough and walk out?'

'Leaving Casey himself with free run of the estate?'

'Yes.'

'But a free run to do what, Diane? Dump dead bodies in the undergrowth?'

'Or provide the opportunity for somebody else to do it.'

'It'd be a bit risky,' said Cooper. 'What if a buyer came along to inspect the property? He could have ended up with surveyors and builders swarming all over the estate.'

'Not without plenty of warning. Casey is the man with the keys, remember. Besides, the hall has been on the market for two years. I'll bet he exhausted the supply of potential buyers a long time ago.'

'Two years, that's right . . .' Cooper worked the timings out in his head. 'I bet whoever dumped Audrey Steele's body was hoping the hall would never find a buyer, and the estate would stay neglected. He overlooked the fact that "right to roam" would give walkers free access.'

'I wonder if Casey ever suggested bringing the price of the property down,' said Fry.

'Why?'

'Well, that's what an agent would normally do if he couldn't find a buyer. He'd advise the seller to come down a bit. If you refuse to lower the price, it looks as though you're not serious about selling.'

'You seem to know a lot about the property market all of a sudden, Diane. I thought you'd never owned a house of your own. You rent a flat, like me.'

'I haven't always lived in Derbyshire. I had a life in civilization before I came here.'

Fry turned away and looked out of the car window, as if her thoughts had started to stray.

'Well, if Alder Hall is "the dead place",' said Cooper, 'then John Casey was right about one thing, at least.'

'What's that?'

'It's a little different from the normal house sale.'

He laughed, and glanced at Fry. But her face never changed. She'd drifted off somewhere, to a place where there wasn't much to laugh about.

The car park at Hudson and Slack was empty, except for the fire investigator's van and two police vehicles. There appeared to be no damage to the building at first, as Cooper and Fry drove down the street. The sign over the entrance was intact, and still claimed Hudson and Slack to be a dependable family business. It was only when they parked next to a patrol car that they saw the blackened walls and shattered windows. The parking area was running with water, but it was difficult to tell how much of it was rain and how much was from the firefighters' hoses.

'The damage is serious, but confined to the offices and a store room,' said the fire investigator, brushing soot off his fluorescent jacket. 'Luckily, the internal doors are all pretty solid and fitted with automatic closure mechanisms. They resisted the flames long enough for the first appliance on the scene to get the fire under control within half an hour or so.'

'There's no doubt it was started deliberately?' asked Fry.

'None at all. The back door has been forced, and there are indications of accelerant all over the store room. The fire ignited within five or six feet of the doorway. Similar story with the vehicle.'

'Vehicle?'

He gestured towards the compound behind the building. 'There's a burnt-out hearse. Your arsonists smashed the windscreen, chucked accelerant in and torched it. I found the remains of a plastic petrol can on the front seat.'

'That might be useful.'

The investigator smiled. 'Plastic doesn't hold up well in a fire, so it's just a molten lump. But you're welcome to it. I doubt Forensics will tell you much, except that it's green.'

'Green? What does that mean?'

'Well, if they were following regulations, the petrol should have been unleaded.'

Two lines of crime scene tape stretched from the building to the fence, and a uniformed officer in a waterproof jacket stood by with a clipboard, guarding the perimeter. There was a cough and a shower of rubble, and a scenes-of-crime officer emerged from the damaged doorway. Cooper saw with pleasure that it was Liz Petty. Well, given current staffing levels, it was a fifty-fifty chance she'd have been called out.

Petty smiled, then looked at Fry and ducked her head to wipe a smear of soot from her face with a gloved hand.

'No secret about what happened here,' she said.

'So we hear,' said Fry. 'But no doubt you've got a contribution to make.'

The SOCO blinked slightly, but carefully avoided meeting anyone's eye. She pointed at the fence. 'That's the way the offenders entered the property. They cut the fence and came over the wall from the railway line.'

Cooper walked to the wall and looked down into the cutting. 'There are some industrial units on the other side of the line.'

'Security cameras?' asked Fry.

'A few, but they're covering their own premises. There's no reason they should have a camera pointing this way.'

'We'll have to see if any of them had a night shift working.'

Petty ran a hand along the edge of the door frame. 'I've lifted some good tool marks from the door. But it was probably just an ordinary crowbar or wrecking bar they used.'

'Why does this door open outwards?' asked Fry.

'Ironically, because it's a fire exit.'

'And there was accelerant used in the store room?'

'Yes, and two inner doors were forced open. By the way, I'd like to get the doors removed and taken to the lab.'

'Why?'

'Well, your offenders were in a hurry, so they didn't bother to jemmy the inner doors – they just kicked them open. I'm pretty sure there are boot prints on the panels. But with the amount of fire damage, we'll need lab facilities to get anything useful from them.'

'You keep saying "they",' said Cooper. 'What makes you think there was more than one person?'

Petty shrugged. 'Well, there's no direct evidence, unless we can get two separate boot prints from the doors. But they didn't hang about here, you know. The fire service say they had a crew on the scene within ten minutes of the alarm. I'd say there were two people, possibly three. Two to break the doors open, while the third spread the petrol. Then they got out of the building quick, chucked in a match or a lighted rag, and left the scene. Apart from the one who wasn't satisfied with what he'd achieved . . .'

'You mean the hearse.'

'Yes. That wasn't really necessary. It looks like spite. It must have delayed their getaway by a couple of minutes.'

Without crossing the tape, Cooper moved to where he could see the compound and the scorched paintwork of the hearse. Curiously, only the front end of the vehicle had been damaged, leaving the rear compartment almost intact, though blackened inside by smoke.

'What happened to the other vehicles?' asked Fry. 'There were several limousines in there, and another hearse, too.'

'The staff were allowed to remove them,' said Petty. 'They had a funeral scheduled first thing this morning, so the uniforms let them get on with it. There was even a body in the fridge. That part of the building is undamaged, but the power's off, so they could hardly leave the poor soul in there.'

'I suppose it was the right decision,' said Fry grudgingly. 'Can we get inside, or are you still keeping the place to yourself?'

'Just walk on the stepping plates and stay close to the wall.'

Cooper hung back as Fry went inside. He looked at Petty. 'Sorry about Diane. She's been like that ever since I came on duty. I don't know what's up with her.'

The SOCO began to strip off her gloves. Her face was flushed and glittering with rain. 'I think I might know.'

'Really? Has she talked to you?'

'I can't tell you, Ben.' She looked at the window of the store room, protected by steel bars but with its glass shattered from the heat of the fire. 'You'd better go, or you'll be in trouble.'

Cooper began to move towards the doorway, but hesitated. 'See you later?'

Petty nodded. 'Yeah.'

*   *   *

Diane Fry stood in the burnt-out building, her nostrils filled with the stench of smoke and charred furniture. Water still sloshed around on the floor from the fire crew's hoses, black and floating with ash. She was aware of Cooper talking to Liz Petty outside, but she couldn't hear what they were saying, and she didn't want to. She moved further away from the window, in case she overheard her name. Deep inside, she was holding on to a tide of anger. It felt too strong to resist for ever, or the dam would burst. She had to channel it in some way.

She looked around the storage area. A doorway straight ahead of her led into what she remembered as the staff room, used by the bearers and office staff for their lunch breaks. There were a couple of tables and some tubular steel chairs, a sink, a cooker, a fridge. Paper had been seared from the walls and hung in shreds, like burned skin. The vinyl flooring had melted and bubbled into twisted shapes, lunar contours that swallowed the shadows from the crime scene lights.

To the right, a second door stood open. Fry moved cautiously across the room, following the aluminium stepping plates. She was irrationally afraid of touching anything – not in case she left fingerprints, but for fear that the scorched surfaces would leave black marks on her skin and clothes. She felt as though they'd somehow contaminate her, bring out on her body the dark stains she could feel growing in her mind ever since she'd listened to those phone calls.

Everywhere she'd gone during the last few days, she'd been wondering if she was in the dead place. She'd been expecting to find a body at any moment, as if a decomposing bundle of bloodied sacking lay behind every door, or the rustling of feeding maggots waited somewhere on the edge of her hearing. But now she wasn't even supposed to be looking. No more chasing around the countryside.

Hardly realizing she was still moving, Fry found herself in the next room. What place was this? At first, she couldn't interpret the sea of black pulp at her feet, sodden heaps rising several inches out of the water. A row of grimy shapes ran along one wall, stained metal drawers gaping open. Filing cabinets. She was in the room behind the main office, where the records were kept.

'Oh, God.'

Fry turned and saw Cooper behind her in the doorway. He reached out a hand to one of the filing cabinets and rubbed the soot off a laminated label.

'Personnel files,' he said. 'They've burned the personnel files.'

31

Later that morning, Cooper finally got a chance to catch up on the files filling his pending tray, refreshing his memory of them in case there was anything important he'd forgotten. He didn't achieve much. But handling the files made him feel a bit better, as if touching them might keep an enquiry alive.

He looked up to make sure he could get Diane Fry's attention.

'I think some of Audrey Steele's family were responsible for that arson attack,' he said. 'Revenge on Audrey's behalf.'

'Revenge for what? We don't know what happened to her yet.'

'It would be an emotional response, not a logical one. But they were understandably upset, and they had to find someone to blame. I think they heard all they really wanted to hear last time I visited Mrs Gill.'

'I saw some of the family at the woodland

burial,' said Fry. 'I bet a few of them are known to us. One of them was Micky Ellis's brother, for a start. Let's see if we can find any violent offences on their records.'

'This is the Devonshire Estate we're talking about,' said Cooper. 'If they didn't carry out the arson attack themselves, they're bound to know people who'd do it for a few quid.'

'You're right. But we need to put some effort into it. I'd like to feel sure in my own mind that Audrey Steele's family were responsible. Otherwise, I might start suspecting that someone at Hudson and Slack did it.'

Cooper nodded. 'It could turn out to be very convenient for somebody that the personnel files were burned.'

'Exactly. I've asked Forensics to recover as much as they can. But the fire and the firemen's hoses did a pretty good job between them, from what I saw.'

'That's an odd thing, actually,' said Cooper. 'Those filing cabinets were steel. They're designed to be fire resistant, as long as you keep the drawers closed.'

'Those drawers looked as though they were open when the fire started.'

'Yes, I think they must have been, for the contents to burn like that.'

Fry looked at him. 'No, it means nothing. The arsonists probably opened the drawers and threw the files on the floor to get a better blaze going, that's all.'

'Confidential files? The cabinets should have been locked, surely?'

'We need to ask the office staff.'

Cooper looked at his watch and began to put on his jacket. 'Well, let me know if there's anything you want me to do, Diane.'

'Where are you off to?'

'I want to speak to Vernon Slack again. He's frightened of something, and I'm going to find out what. And then I might tackle Billy McGowan.'

'McGowan? Not on your own, you don't. Do you hear me?'

'OK.'

'And, Ben – what about the dog?'

'I talked to one of the officers working with Poacher Watch. According to local intelligence, lampers often operate on parts of the Alder Hall estate, but there have never been any complaints from the owners.'

Fry smiled. 'How strange. What do you bet that Mr Casey is making a bit of money on the side by giving them access?'

'Taking a cut from poaching gangs? It's possible.'

'It would explain why he wants to keep the place to himself.'

'Maybe that ex-employee would have something to tell us.'

'Maurice Goodwin, yes.'

'The thing is,' said Cooper, 'I reckon it was probably lampers who shot Tom Jarvis's dog. They could have mistaken it for a fox, or a small deer.

But Jarvis doesn't seem to want to believe that. He's assuming someone did it deliberately. In fact, I suspect he might even have a name or two in mind, but he's not saying who they are.'

'You'll have to find a way of getting him to open up, Ben.'

'I'll try.'

'By the way,' said Fry, 'David Mead called. You remember the rambling fireman?'

'Of course.'

'Well, Mr Mead has done a good job for us. He's tracked down the people who left items in the Petrus Two cache – all except one. There's just a single item on the list that no one is owning up to.'

Cooper studied her face, detecting the frustration she was trying to restrain.

'Just one?' he said. 'Let me guess – the glow-in-the-dark skeleton key-ring? The classic symbol of death, a clever reminder from our caller.'

'Actually,' said Fry, 'the key-ring was left by a twelve-year-old girl from Hathersage who goes out walking with her grandmother every Sunday. She bought the thing as a souvenir in Whitby.'

'The Dracula Experience?'

'Probably.' Fry sighed. 'As a matter of fact, the one unidentified item from the Petrus Two cache is the bloody Beatrix Potter book.'

Cooper sat watching his windscreen wipers as he waited for the funeral cortege to pass. Then he turned the Toyota round. He eased out into the road, cutting in front of a delivery van and raising his hand in a conciliatory gesture when the driver glared at him. He soon caught up with the last mourners' car and stayed close behind it as the cortege wound its way through the wet streets. The limousines were so distinctive that he'd spotted them coming towards him before he got within three hundred yards of Hudson and Slack. There wasn't much chance around here of staying unnoticed in a Daimler with personalized number plates, even without the oak veneer coffin in the back.

When Cooper arrived at the crematorium, Melvyn Hudson was already standing in the porte-cochere talking to Christopher Lloyd. Hudson seemed to recognize the Toyota. He lost interest in what Lloyd was saying to him as he watched Cooper park behind the mourners' cars.

But Cooper didn't approach Hudson directly. Let him worry for a few minutes. It was a good tactic, and he intended to exploit it. So he walked through the car park, past the floral tributes and the metal stakes with the day's name cards on them. Many of the people cremated here were commemorated by rose bushes in the garden of remembrance. There were long, circular beds of them, separated by neatly mown grass. Cooper recalled Madeleine Chadwick's enthusiasm for roses. The triumph of good over evil. The scented bloom and the eternal thorns.

The garden wasn't as peaceful as he'd expected. Traffic on the ring road created a constant background to the sound of birdsong. The traces of mercury emitted from the crematorium chimney would be battling against exhaust fumes in the pollution stakes.

After the funeral party had gone into the chapel, Cooper looked around for the Hudson and Slack bearers. Having taken in the coffin, the bearers had left the chapel and were taking the chance to have a break until the service was over. They were standing in their black suits in the shelter of a wall near the cars, smoking cigarettes and chatting.

'Mr McGowan? Could I have a word?'

'Melvyn won't like you turning up at funerals like this,' said McGowan, watching Cooper with a thin smile. 'It might be bad for business.'

He had a cocky waggle of the head when he spoke. Cooper had seen it before, usually in people who had experience with the police and thought they knew their rights.

'Where's Vernon today?' he asked.

'He called in sick.'

'What's wrong with him?'

'No idea.'

'Had he mentioned that he wasn't feeling well?'

'Not to me. Come to think of it, he's not usually the type to be sick, or skiving either. Vernon's the most reliable bloke we've got, in his way.'

'Perhaps he had a hard night,' said Cooper. 'I don't suppose it's the best thing in the world to turn up at a funeral with a hangover.'

'Well, I don't know,' said McGowan. 'A few pale faces and sunken eyes would probably suit the occasion. A touch of the undead, if you get what I mean? As long as you don't actually throw up in the hearse.'

Cooper smiled politely. He'd heard worse comments at scenes of violent crime – the ghoulish humour of people who had to laugh in the face of death, because they met it every day.

'Anyway,' said McGowan, 'Vernon doesn't drink.'

Ironically, it was something Vernon Slack had said that was bothering Cooper. And that puzzled him. After all, it wasn't as if Vernon had actually told him anything – certainly nothing he didn't already know. But he did see Melvyn Hudson and Christopher Lloyd and the others on a day-to-day basis, when they were off guard. Perhaps they weren't too careful about what they said when Vernon was nearby with his head under a bonnet. In a way, Vernon might be the very person to see through the façades and know the truth.

Cooper went back over his conversations with Vernon. They'd been limited and brief. Awkward and unhelpful, in fact. He shook his head. There was nothing jumping out at him. So maybe it wasn't anything Vernon had said, but the way that he'd said it. If he hadn't registered it at the time, he'd probably never recall it now.

'There isn't any need for it, you see,' Vernon had said. 'We do the job and look after the grievers, and then we go home. Sometimes, you don't even know the details of a call until you turn up at the house to do a removal. The boss sees to everything else.'

Cooper's pace slowed a little as the memory came to him. He could hear Vernon saying it now, word for word, yet he hadn't taken any notice of it at the time. It was probably nothing, of course. But it was something to mention, when the moment was right.

Gavin Murfin collapsed into his chair with a sigh, threw a paper bag into the bin and ripped open a plastic sandwich box.

'Getting these names was like pulling teeth,' he said.

Fry looked up. Was this an early lunch or a late breakfast? She could never tell with Gavin.

'What names?' she said.

'The staff who worked at Hudson and Slack eighteen months ago.'

'The *what*?'

Startled by her tone, Murfin stopped with a sandwich halfway to his mouth. 'What's up?'

'Did you say you had a list of staff who worked at Hudson and Slack?'

'Yeah. You asked me to get the background on Richard Slack's RTA. Well, some clever bugger at the time thought it was a bit funny that Slack was doing a call-out on his own. What with that and the woman who thought she saw someone running off, this DC decided to check with everyone at the firm, in case Slack had contacted them before the accident. A waste of time, as it happens, but you've got to admit it's thorough.'

'Gavin, you're wonderful.'

Murfin bit into his sandwich with satisfaction.

'Cheers. Do you want to phone my missus and tell her that? She'd appreciate it.'

'We lost Hudson and Slack's personnel records in the fire last night,' said Fry. 'Very convenient for Mr Hudson, it seems. He tried to make out his records weren't comprehensive, because some of his staff were casual workers.'

'Presumably he must have known who they were, though. He had to pay them, after all.'

'Well, I suppose that might have been the problem. Cash with no questions asked.'

'And nothing going to the tax man, like?'

'Well done anyway, Gavin. Is there anyone we know on the list?'

'Not that jumps out at me. But I'll get them run through the PNC and do an intelligence check.'

'Let me see.'

Murfin passed across the list. Fry was glad to have it in her hand before any more crumbs landed on it. She glanced quickly down it, noting a few familiar names, but several that were new to her. Eighteen months wasn't all that long ago, but there seemed to have been quite a turnover, particularly among the bearers and drivers.

'Oh, wow,' she said.

'What's up now?'

'That's one name I didn't expect. Thomas Edward Jarvis, Litton Foot. This is the man with the dogs, isn't it, Gavin?'

'You're right,' said Murfin. 'Didn't one get shot?'

Fry put down the list. 'Who would have guessed that Mr Jarvis once worked for Hudson and Slack? Not his friend Ben Cooper, I bet.'

'Are you going to tell him, Sarge?'

But Fry only stared at him again as he finished off his sandwich.

'Gavin,' she said, 'what do you mean "the woman who thought she saw someone running off"?'

This morning, the bereaved had opted for traditional music. Cooper could hear the sound of an electronic organ playing the first mournful notes. He was watching the previous party of mourners file past the flowers in the rain when his mobile rang, and he recognized Fry's number on the caller display.

'Yes, Diane?'

'Thomas Jarvis. Did you know he worked at Hudson and Slack eighteen months ago?'

'No, I had no idea,' said Cooper.

491

'He's never mentioned that when you talked to him?'

'No. Well, there's no reason why he should have done – the subject of Hudson and Slack never came up. But you're sure he worked there? Eighteen months ago?'

'He was listed as an employee during the enquiry into Richard Slack's crash.'

'It's certainly an odd coincidence, isn't it?'

'Coincidence? Ben, you do like to give people the benefit of the doubt, don't you?'

'What do you mean?'

'We wondered why none of Jarvis's dogs detected the presence of a decomposing corpse while it was lying in the woods close to his property,' she said. 'Remember?'

'Yes, but there was a possible explanation for that. Somebody might have returned to the site and exposed the remains fairly recently, after they'd already become skeletonized and the odour had dissipated.'

'But there's no evidence to support that theory, is there?'

'Well, no.'

'So we should consider an alternative scenario.'

Cooper didn't like the sound of that. In Fry's vocabulary, an alternative scenario usually meant bad news for somebody.

'You have a scenario in mind, do you, Diane?'

'Of course. What's more likely than that one of Jarvis's dogs *did* detect the decomposing corpse?

Maybe all his dogs knew the corpse was there and made a fuss about it – barked or pointed at it with their noses, or whatever dogs do.'

Cooper laughed. 'And don't you think Tom Jarvis would have realized?'

'Yes.'

There was silence on the other end of the phone as Fry waited expectantly. Cooper knew he was supposed to reach the same conclusion that she had, without having to be prompted. In this case, there was a conclusion he didn't want to come to. But she'd lose patience if she had to wait too long.

'For God's sake, Ben,' she said. 'What if Jarvis didn't take any notice of the dogs' behaviour for one very simple reason – he already knew perfectly well that the body was there.'

Cooper began to pace up and down, aware of some of the mourners for the next funeral watching him.

'Yes, I understand what you're saying, Diane.'

'You've got to make Jarvis talk. I know what you're like when you get together with one of your rural soul mates, Ben. You communicate in manly grunts and meaningful silences. But make sure you ask him some tough questions.'

'I'll do it today. But I have one other visit to make first.'

'OK. And there's another thing you need to know . . .'

Cooper had already started heading back to his

car. He swapped the phone to his other hand to reach the pocket with his keys in.

'What's that?'

'Do you remember that Mr Slack was on his own when he died in the car crash?'

'Yes?'

'Well, I wondered about that. How likely is it that a funeral director would go out to a call on his own? There's no way one person can shift a dead body easily, unless it's a small child's.'

'Maybe someone was going to meet him there?' said Cooper.

'Well, it's possible. But Gavin had a look at the inquest report.'

'And?'

'There was some question over the testimony of a witness – a female motorist who was first at the accident scene and called 999. She told the traffic officers she'd seen someone about half a mile back, before she came on the crash site, which was just around a bend. She saw somebody jogging near the side of the road. It was pitch dark, of course. Unfortunately, she had no reason to take notice at the time – it was before she knew there *was* a crash. She was just struck by the fact that the individual was running. And, most importantly, he wasn't running along the verge but *up* the banking, as if he was heading across the fields away from the road. She had the impression he'd done that because he heard her car coming.'

'Definitely a man?'

'She was fairly confident about that.'

'It's very vague, Diane.'

'That's what the coroner thought. There was no convincing evidence that anyone was in the van with Richard Slack. The staff at the firm were interviewed, but they all said the same thing – Richard hadn't asked them to go with him on the call.'

'What are you saying?'

Cooper was still standing by his car when the organ started up in the crematorium chapel. Not 'Abide With Me', but something else that he couldn't identify at first. The voices of the congregation coming in on the opening lines disguised the tune, rather than making it clearer.

'It was a very late call,' said Fry. 'Three o'clock in the morning. I think Richard Slack wouldn't have wanted to call out one of the casual staff. A family firm like that, I think he would have phoned his partner to do the job.'

'Melvyn Hudson.'

'Of course.'

'Diane, even if your theory is correct, a passenger leaving the scene of an accident isn't a major crime. If Hudson *was* in the van, he might have been injured himself. He might have been in shock or something.'

'Like I said, this was a really late call. Early hours of the morning, in fact. There was no traffic around on that road at three a.m. The lady who found the crash was only on the road because she had to catch an early flight from East Midlands Airport and it was a shortcut from her home to the M1. As the coroner said, the absence of traffic was unfortunate. Because Richard Slack wasn't killed immediately. He died from loss of blood, and from choking on his own vomit, as a result of the position he was left in after the crash.'

'Oh, God.'

'Exactly. The medical reports said he would most likely have survived, if only somebody had been on hand to put him into the recovery position and phone for an ambulance. But nobody was. And so Richard Slack died.'

At last, Cooper recognized the hymn drifting from the chapel: 'The Lord's My Shepherd'. Two lines floated clearer than the others across the garden of remembrance. 'Yea, though I walk in death's dark vale, Yet will I fear no ill.'

A few minutes later, Cooper drove on to the Devonshire Estate. He went a few yards past Vivien Gill's house, checking the number of cars on the street, before he parked at the kerb and walked back to her front door.

'I thought you'd finished with me,' said Mrs Gill. 'It's all over and done with now, as far as I'm concerned.'

'You're not interested in finding out who stole your daughter's body?'

'That's up to you. The general opinion is that you won't get anywhere.'

'The general opinion? Do you mean among your family?'

'We talked about it after the funeral on Saturday, obviously.'

'I'll bet you did,' said Cooper. 'A few drinks in the pub and the talk got a bit heated, I imagine?'

'Some of my family were upset. I was upset, too. We can't believe what happened, and you people aren't likely to do anything about it, are you?'

'I see. So you decided to take matters into your own hands.'

'Me?'

'Oh, not you, Mrs Gill. But I've met some of your relatives, remember.'

'I don't want to hear you talk about my family like that.'

'Are you related to Micky Ellis?'

'Yes, but only by marriage through my eldest daughter. What of it?'

Cooper sighed with exasperation. 'Mrs Gill . . .'

'I think you'd better go now,' she said.

'I need to know –'

'You're wasting your time. I'm not going to tell you anything about them. Not even their names or where they live.'

'We'll be able to find out, you know.'

'Do it, then. Arrest me, and lock me up. I still won't tell you anything. Nor will anyone else.'

Cooper nearly swore with exasperation. The woman gazed at him defiantly, her chin lifted, her

mouth turned down in an expression of stubborn-
ness, verging on contempt.

'And if you're not going to do that, I want you
to go,' she said. 'If I ask you to leave my house,
you have to, don't you?'

He stood up, and turned angrily on his heel.
'Mrs Gill, don't you realize what they've done?
They've destroyed the records that could have
helped us to find out who stole Audrey's body.'

Her expression slipped a little then, revealing a
flicker of doubt. But in a moment her face closed
again, and she walked to the door.

'I'll say goodbye,' she said. 'And that's all I've
got to say.'

DI Hitchens called Fry into his office and asked
for an update. He listened with interest while she
ran through the possible scenarios.

'Have the media shown any interest in this
enquiry yet?' he asked.

'They used the appeals we gave them with the
facial reconstruction, and a bit of stuff on Sandra
Birley. But nothing else seems to have leaked
out.'

'Good.'

'It's odd, really.'

'Why?'

'Well, I'd have put our man down as the type
who badly wants publicity. Needs it, even. He must
have realized by now that we aren't going to share
what we have with the press. Wouldn't you expect

him to do something to get the attention of the media? A call to a journalist or something.'

'Wouldn't it be a bit risky?'

'Not as risky as his calls to us. He obviously doesn't mind taking a bit of a risk.'

'You're right, Diane. Let's think about that for a minute. It might give us a lead on him. What sort of person would take the risk of communicating directly with the police, but avoid the press?'

'Sir, we don't know that he *has* avoided the press,' said Fry. 'What if he's phoned one of the newspapers or the local radio station, and they've done nothing about it or haven't taken him seriously?'

'He wouldn't be very happy about that.'

'No.'

'Is there any way we can enquire discreetly of our media contacts whether they've had a call?'

'Discreetly? No, there isn't. No matter how we approached it, they'd sniff out a story. We'd be defeating our own object, unless we can put pressure on them to keep it to themselves.'

'OK. Maybe it's not worthwhile. But make sure the press office is briefed on how to deal with the issue if the media do get a call from him.'

'With discretion?'

'Exactly.'

'From our point of view, it's possible that a lack of response from the media is the best thing that could happen. If he *is* a publicity seeker, it will infuriate him not to be taken seriously. Then he's likely to go to greater lengths to attract attention. That's when he'll make a mistake.'

'We hope.'

Hitchens nodded. 'Thank God we only have the locals to deal with. The last thing we want is to bring the nationals down around our ears.'

'Amen to that.'

Diane Fry's phone rang. 'It's Pat Jamieson.'

'Oh, Dr Jamieson. Thanks for getting back to me.'

'No problem. I've dug out the records you were interested in – the Alder Hall bone collection.'

'Excellent.'

'But I think I can do better than that. I've asked around, and it turns out my predecessor who did the inventory is still in the area, though he's long since retired. I've even got a phone number for you. You can talk to him directly about it.'

'That's great,' said Fry, though the feeling in her stomach prevented her putting the right enthusiasm into the words.

Dr Jamieson sounded disappointed at her restraint. 'Oh, well, here's the number, if it's any use to you,' he said.

Fry wrote down the phone number that was dictated to her. Then she disappointed Dr Jamieson even more by not bothering to ask him for the name of his retired colleague. She already knew who it was.

'And what about the remains from Litton Foot?' she said instead.

Jamieson coughed and muttered for a few moments, and Fry thought she'd probably offended him. Then he began to prevaricate, like a defendant in the dock when asked a particularly probing question.

'We don't want to make a mistake with this one, Sergeant, so we're not going to jump to any conclusions. There was no skull present, as you know. And in the absence of the skull, it's much more difficult to provide a definite identification of human bones. Some of these remains are fragmentary, so . . . Well, we propose to carry out precipitin tests.'

'Precipitin tests?'

'It's the only way to determine species.'

Fry could hear her own voice getting louder as she lost patience. 'What exactly are you telling me, Doctor?'

'I'm telling you that I can't tell you anything until we're absolutely certain,' snapped back Jamieson.

It wasn't clear which of them slammed the phone down first. When the door of the CID room opened, Fry looked up angrily, ready to take out her irritation on the first person she saw.

But it was DI Hitchens. He walked slowly into the room, like a man suffering a living nightmare.

'Diane,' he said, 'we've got another body. And this time it's a fresh one.'

32

The Ravensdale woods were silent. The damp foliage muffled every sound, except for the rushing of the stream somewhere below. It had been raining all morning, and once he was past Ravensdale Cottages, Cooper found the muddy track covered in stones, leaves, dead branches, and all the other debris washed down by the rain.

At Litton Foot, Cooper walked slowly through the long grass of the paddock and paused by the abandoned car. Tom Jarvis stood at the door of the house, watching him but saying nothing. He was trying to weigh up in his mind why Cooper was here again, and he was taking his time about it.

'Good morning, Mr Jarvis,' said Cooper. Wiping a layer of mould from the glass of the car's windscreen, he peered inside. Then he moved to the boot. 'Is it all right if I take a look, sir?'

'Be my guest,' said Jarvis. 'Don't mind me.'

The dogs had noticed Cooper now, and they

came lumbering around his feet as he lifted the boot lid. Water had leaked through the seals, and the spare wheel sat in several inches of water in the well. He slammed the boot again, and moved on to the chest freezer. It opened with a sucking of rubber, and he knew he'd find nothing inside, except more mould coating the aluminium sides.

Without a word, Jarvis walked towards the old trailer and let down the ramp. The wooden floor had rotted, and the nearest wheel arch was corroded into more holes than a lace handkerchief.

'See anything interesting?' said Jarvis. 'Or is it just routine?'

Cooper held his hand out for the dogs to sniff, and they wagged their tails.

'Mr Jarvis, I understand you once worked for the funeral directors, Hudson and Slack.'

'Aye. Well, get it right – I did some work for them.'

'You mean you were never actually an employee?'

'No. I was a carpenter by trade, see. That was my main job. But I helped out with other work when they were short-handed.'

'You worked on coffins, then? And you were a bearer sometimes, perhaps?'

'If they needed me. What's this all about?'

'You must know Melvyn Hudson?'

'Yes, I reckon I do. Haven't seen Hudson for a long time, though. Probably we'll meet up again when he does my funeral.'

'Did you get on with him all right?'

'Aye.' Slowly, Jarvis walked to the rail of the porch and looked towards the woods. 'A damn sight better than I did with that bastard who was his partner.'

Cooper was unprepared for the vehemence in Jarvis's voice. 'Richard Slack? You're the first person I've heard say a bad word about him.'

Jarvis turned back and looked at him. 'Well, most folk don't care to speak ill of the dead. I wouldn't normally do it myself. But I'll make an exception in the case of Richard Bloody Slack.'

The 999 call had come into the control room half an hour earlier. By the time Diane Fry arrived at the scene, the machinery of a murder enquiry was already getting up to speed. SOCOs in their white paper suits were rustling and squeaking around the house, an inner cordon had been set up across the doorway, and a safe route marked through the garden and past the conservatory. Police vehicles filled the drive and blocked off the street, while officers deterred inquisitive members of the public.

Even worse, a TV crew had arrived and were setting up across the road. They must have been in town on another assignment to get to the scene so quickly. Fry felt a stab of irritation to find herself trailing after the media. The place was already turning into a circus.

DI Hitchens was standing near the crime scene

504

van. He was banned from the house until the senior SOCO allowed him in.

'Well, you got your wish, Diane,' he said, hunching his shoulders against the drizzle. 'This is a murder enquiry now. Mr Kessen has been appointed SIO. He'll be arriving shortly – not that we need him on this one. But at least we'll get our resources. That's what you wanted, isn't it?'

'It looks as though most of the available resources are here already,' said Fry, as a scientific support van backed up to the gate and began unloading equipment.

'It's a walkthrough,' said Hitchens. 'If we let these lads do their thing for a bit, we can all pack up and go home early.'

'It can't be, sir.'

The DI inclined his head towards the house. 'Forget about your phone calls. This is nothing to do with them.'

Wayne Abbott put his head out of the front door and gave them a nod. They climbed into scene suits handed to them from the van, and went into the house.

Sandra Birley's body lay face up in the conservatory. She appeared to have fallen on to the raffia matting from just inside the sliding doors. Blood had soaked into the matting from a serious head wound. Well, at least one wound. Of course, the amount of bleeding from the scalp could be out of all proportion to the seriousness of the injury. But the main source of the blood seemed to be an area just above the left temple, which had left Sandra's hair almost as thick and matted as the raffia she lay on.

'She was in the dining room when she was struck,' said Abbott. 'See the blood splatter on the glass panels of the door? That splatter is on the inside. So it looks as though the victim was standing on the carpet, about here. When she was hit, the blood sprayed in this direction, on to the glass. She staggered back a few steps, probably tripped over the runner, then fell backwards. There's more blood on the wall of the conservatory, see. But it's low down, near the floor. That's secondary splatter – spray from the impact of her head on the matting.'

'Do we have a weapon?' asked Fry.

'We certainly do. A wooden carving of a dolphin. Here we are – it's made of some kind of tropical wood. Very hard, and very heavy. Nicely balanced for a good swing, too. It looks as though the dolphin probably stood on this table right here, near the fireplace.'

'That's right, it did.'

Abbott looked at her in surprise. 'Oh, you've been in the house before? I don't suppose you can tell us if there's anything missing, then?'

Fry gazed around the Birleys' house.

'Yes, there is,' she said. 'The husband.'

When her mobile phone rang, it sounded embarrassingly loud inside the house.

'How's it going down there?' asked Gavin Murfin.

'Don't ask, Gavin. What do you want?'

'I've got some news. I think you might be going to curse the experts again.'

'Oh? Who this time?'

'The anthropologist that we sent the cremains to for analysis.'

'Surely he can't have produced a report yet, Gavin?'

'No, just an initial finding that he thought we might want to know about.'

Fry felt her heart sink. 'What?'

'Well, apparently he sifted the ashes and found a few teeth.'

'But that's what we were hoping for. It gives us the possibility of an identification through dental records, like the one we got for Audrey Steele.'

'Yes, but that's what he was so keen to let us know. A bit too keen actually, if you ask me. Cheerful, he was. Like he wanted to rub it in.'

'Spit it out, Gavin. There aren't enough teeth left intact for us to use, I suppose?'

'Plenty of them. The trouble is, these teeth aren't human.'

Cooper recalled that he had never actually been inside Tom Jarvis's house. He wondered if he was going to be invited in now, to get out of the wet. But he only got as far as the porch, where a couple of old beech carver chairs stood near a window. From this elevation, he could see a small mound

507

of fresh earth to the side of the house, dark from the continuing rain.

'Hudson and Slack was already in trouble by then, you know,' said Jarvis.

'Financial trouble?'

'Aye. They couldn't compete once the Americans starting buying up funeral directors in Derbyshire.'

'Is that what Melvyn Hudson and Richard Slack fell out about? They did fall out, didn't they?'

Jarvis nodded. 'Hudson wanted to compete by being different, selling the firm as local and traditional. He'd worked in the USA, and he knew what the American approach would be.'

'But Mr Slack?'

'He was always the financial brains, so they said. He ran the business side, while Hudson organized the funerals. But as soon as things started to look bad, Slack had only one solution – he wanted to sell up.'

'Sell out to one of the American groups?'

'He'd already been approached, I reckon. No doubt there would have been a nice back-hander in it for him, if a deal had gone through.'

'But I suppose his partner wouldn't agree.'

'Not likely. Hudson cared about the firm, like his father did. And the way old Abraham Slack did, for that matter. Melvyn said he wouldn't see Hudson and Slack end up that way.'

'Was this general knowledge among the staff?'

'Oh, aye. You can't keep things like that quiet

in a small company. It's why some of us bailed out, while the going was good, like.'

'I see.'

'Hudson kept saying that his father and old man Slack had built the firm up from nothing, and he wasn't going to throw it away. It was a family business, and it ought to go on for generations. But Richard Slack thought the firm was dying on its feet. Rotting on the branch, he called it. We all knew what he meant by that.'

'And what did he mean?'

'Well, how could the business go on for generations? Hudson had lost his own son, and all Slack had left was Vernon. Of course everyone understood what he meant by rotting on the branch. The fruit had died.'

'I don't suppose Mr Hudson took that very well.'

'No. Losing David had hit him very hard. But he knew what Slack said was true, all the same. They had a blazing row after that.'

'Did they get on well normally?'

'Not so as you'd notice.'

Jarvis's dogs emerged from the rain and pattered up the steps on to the porch. They shook themselves vigorously, one after another, showering drops of water on the boards. Cooper was just congratulating himself on standing far enough away to avoid being drenched, when two of the dogs brushed themselves against his legs and lay on his feet.

'They've taken a shine to you, for some reason,' said Jarvis.

Cooper nodded. He could feel the water from the dogs' coats soaking into his trousers, as if drawn in by a sponge.

'I gather you didn't like Richard Slack any more than Mr Hudson did?' he said.

'I never could get on with him. Hard-nosed bugger, he was. Ruthless.'

For a moment, Cooper was confused. He wondered why Jarvis was suddenly talking to one of his dogs. Perhaps there had been five of them, after all. Graceless, Feckless, Aimless, Pointless and Ruthless. But no. He meant Richard Slack.

'The old man always had a bit of a ruthless streak, too, by all accounts,' said Jarvis.

'Abraham?'

'Aye. Richard was a chip off the old block, so to speak. Cared for nothing but money. He thought he could pay his staff peanuts, but it wouldn't wash with me. I was a craftsman.'

'Mr Jarvis, you said that Richard Slack was the business brains of the firm. But did he do his share of the funeral work?'

'Oh, if he had to.'

'He was on a removal job when he died, wasn't he?'

'Yes. I left Hudson and Slack not long after that.'

'Did you ever hear a rumour that he wasn't alone in the van when it crashed?'

510

'There was some woman turned up with a tale like that. But it came to nothing.'

'Would it have been normal for him to collect a body on his own?'

Jarvis shrugged. 'That wasn't a side of the job I got involved in much. But I don't suppose it was out of the question if it was an easy removal. They have a trolley they can use. And he might have been expecting someone to be there to give him a hand. Police, or something.'

Cooper watched the dogs at his feet. They were gradually drifting to sleep as the rain dried on their coats.

'Actually, that's a bit odd, isn't it?' he said.

'What?'

'Well, why did you decide to leave Hudson and Slack just when the man you disliked so much had gone?'

Jarvis shrugged again. 'Like I said, the business was already going down the nick then. I'm only amazed it's lasted so long. Slack wasn't much good as a man, but at least he had a head for finance. He was always looking for ways of making money.'

'Unorthodox ways, perhaps?'

'I don't know anything about that. But I reckon by the end of his time, Richard Slack was ready to do anything to line his own pocket. Anything.'

Cooper forgot the dogs and looked at Tom Jarvis more closely. Such a blatant attempt to cast suspicion on Richard Slack seemed uncharacteristic of the man. He looked uneasy, too, as if he was troubled by what he was saying. He kept shuffling his feet and moving a bit across the boards.

Then Cooper felt a trickle of water on the back of his neck, and realized that he was gradually being eased towards the steps of the porch. He was already standing under the edge of the roof, and the dogs were starting to stretch and get to their feet, as if expecting to see him off the premises.

'So . . .' began Jarvis, adjusting his cap.

Cooper looked at the house. The windows were empty, and dark under the shadow of the porch. With a horrible jolt, he was struck by a possible identity for the body that had replaced Audrey Steele's on the way to the crematorium.

'Is Mrs Jarvis home? I haven't had a chance to speak to her yet. If she's home right now, it would save me coming back again.'

Jarvis regarded him silently, frowning with concentration, as if trying to push Cooper towards the path with the force of his gaze. Instead, Cooper held his stare for a moment, then took half a step towards him. The dogs sighed in exasperation and flopped back on to the boards.

'Of course she's bloody in,' said Jarvis.

'Well, could I perhaps . . .?'

Jarvis grunted and turned on his heel towards the door of the house. Cooper took it as an invitation to follow. One of the dogs fell in close behind him, sniffing curiously at his heels as if it had found an interesting scent.

* * *

An extended search found Geoff Birley sitting in his Audi in a layby two miles away, on the edge of Edendale. He looked almost relieved when a patrol car drew up and two officers checked his identity before putting him into the back seat.

When she heard the news, Diane Fry was still in the Birleys' house, watching Sandra's body being prepared for removal. She wondered whether to tell Mr Birley that he'd chosen the Devonshire Estate third option. He'd left his wife exactly where she fell when she died.

At West Street, Fry stood at her desk in the CID room for a few minutes, trying to gather her thoughts. Anxious as she was to question Geoff Birley about the phone calls, it would take some time for him to be processed and ready for interview. They'd probably wait until all the evidence had been collected from the house and statements taken from the neighbours. If he could be placed in the right areas at the times when the calls were made, it might provide evidence of premeditation. The case would be as airtight as possible before they made a move.

There were plenty of other things demanding her attention in the meantime. As always, it was a question of priorities.

Freshest in Fry's mind was the arson attack on Hudson and Slack. A night-shift worker at one of the industrial units had been loading a truck when the fire had started, and he reported seeing three figures running westwards along the cutting. That was lucky, because most people would have looked at the flames and seen nothing else, especially at night. Everyone loved the sight of a good fire. Uniformed officers were following up the lead, and trying to obtain sightings of a vehicle parked in the streets to the west. That would take time, too.

According to a message he'd left for her, Ben Cooper had met a brick wall with Audrey Steele's mother on the arson. But her cousin Ellen Walker had been more co-operative. A phone call to her had elicited details of Audrey's funeral eighteen months ago. The service had been held at St Mark's in Edendale, but the hearse had taken the coffin on to the crematorium afterwards. Mrs Walker had even remembered who the drivers were – Vernon Slack and Billy McGowan. Full marks to Cooper, then. That was exactly what he'd thought might have happened.

An earlier message told her that Cooper had already spoken to McGowan, but not to Vernon Slack, who'd called in sick. Fry frowned at that. Cooper recommended bringing McGowan in for formal interview. She scrawled a big tick and 'OK' on the note, and looked around the office.

'Gavin,' she said, 'set this up, will you?'

Then there was Professor Freddy Robertson. He'd been responsible for carrying out an inventory of the bones in the crypt at Alder Hall. That probably meant nothing, but Fry still had a bad feeling about him. A gut instinct, perhaps, and no more. She shouldn't let it influence her judgement.

'By the way,' said Murfin, 'there's a lady here who says she wants to talk to someone. A Mrs Somerville.'

'Never heard of her. What does she want? Can't you deal with her, Gavin?'

'Well, I thought you might be interested in talking to her yourself, like. She says she's Professor Robertson's daughter.'

Anne Jarvis lay on a sofa in the sitting room. Only her head and arms protruded from the quilt that had been used to cover her, and one hand hung limply towards the floor. The room was very warm, and somewhere a fly buzzed against a window pane.

Cooper halted in the doorway of the room, taking in his surroundings. Almost the first thing he noticed was the quilt's pink floral pattern. It was the worst possible thing for showing up the dog hairs. The atmosphere was stuffy, and the smell reminded him of his visits to the hospital. Where Mrs Jarvis's skin showed, it was white and almost translucent, the light from a standard lamp above the sofa shining through to the veins, as if her body was held together by tissue paper.

With an effort, she turned her head on a pillow and looked at him. 'This is nice,' she said. 'Another visitor. I am honoured.'

'I'm sorry to intrude,' said Cooper. 'I didn't realize . . .'

'That it was a sick room? Yes, I'm afraid so.' Her voice was frail, but still lively. She moved her right hand, but didn't quite complete the intended gesture. 'Don't be shy, whoever you are – sit down and have a cup of tea.'

'I really can't stop, Mrs Jarvis. I just came in to say hello.'

'This is the policeman I told you about, Annie,' said Jarvis, bending over her to lift her trailing hand back on to the quilt. 'The detective.'

'Oh, does he have a name?'

'I'm DC Cooper, Mrs Jarvis.'

'Cooper? I think I knew another policeman by that name once, but I forget what he did. I forget a lot of things.'

Cooper fidgeted uncertainly. He had no idea what was wrong with Mrs Jarvis, and there was no way he could come straight out and ask. It just wasn't done to be so direct. The dog that had followed him into the room sidled towards the sofa and settled itself into position against the edge of the quilt. Feckless, Pointless or Aimless, he couldn't tell. But the animal remained quite still as Mrs Jarvis's hand slipped slowly down and came to rest on top of its broad head.

'It's wet outside again,' she said.

'Yes, it is, Annie,' said Jarvis.

'I'm lucky, then, to get these visitors coming out in the rain to see me.'

Cooper looked round the room. And only then did he see the other man, who was sitting very still in an armchair, partly hidden by the open door. He was about the same age as Tom Jarvis, but smaller and more worried looking, with a green cardigan bunched around his middle and a tweed hat clutched in his lap. He gave Cooper a small, apologetic smile, but said nothing.

'This is my brother Maurice,' said Mrs Jarvis, without turning her head fully.

The effort seemed to exhaust her energy, and she closed her eyes. Her husband hovered uncertainly, and the dog looked anxious. Cooper bit his lip. Every moment he stayed here, he was being reminded more and more of his mother and her hospital bed.

The brother stood up and touched his arm. 'Time for us to go, I think. Annie's tired.'

'Yes, of course.'

Cooper felt himself coming properly alert again as they stepped out of the overheated sick room. He looked at Mrs Jarvis's brother. 'I'm sorry, I didn't catch your last name, sir. Mr . . .?'

The man nodded. 'Goodwin,' he said, holding out a hand. 'Maurice Goodwin. Pleased to meet you, I suppose.'

Lucy Somerville had the air of someone who had never been inside a police station before and was afraid of being contaminated if she touched anything. She sat with her knees tight together and her coat pulled close around her chest, shaking her head when she was offered tea or coffee.

'The thing is, I've been worried about Dad for a while,' she said. 'He and Mum were very dependent on each other. When Mum was gone, he didn't seem grounded any more. His interests started getting more bizarre. Just bit by bit – I don't suppose it was ever any big decision on his part.'

Fry estimated Mrs Somerville's age at about forty-five. She looked comfortable and affluent – the coat was good-quality wool, the scarf silk, though that was all that could be seen of her clothes.

'What sort of things do you mean, Mrs Somerville?'

'Well, until then his research had been factual. It was a specialized branch of anthropology, nothing more than that. Dad studied cultural attitudes to death, the traditions and rituals of burial, and so on. A bit morbid, I suppose, but at least it was an academic interest. Once Mum died, he started drifting into areas that were more . . . esoteric. The internet made it easier. He found all kinds of things that I would never have suspected existed.'

Fry nodded. She could believe anything of the internet. All the most illegal and unpleasant things in life seemed to thrive there. 'Anything specific that you can remember?'

'Oh, I once saw a reference on his computer to something called "Corpse of the Week".'

'What on earth is that?'

Mrs Somerville shuddered a little at the memory. 'I didn't look. The name of it was enough to trouble me.'

'Do you think it was a website?'

'Yes.'

Fry made a note of the name. 'Anything else?'

'Well, Dad once talked to me about a kind of religion called Santeria. He said its practitioners gave themselves power by digging up a body to remove the head, and the fingers and toes. I think there were other bones, too. I forget which. Another time he talked about necromancy. I thought that was just a way of predicting the future or something, like reading tea leaves. But Dad said it was a means of communicating with the dead. There was a ritual to perform. But it had to be within a year of the person's death, because that was how long the spirit hung around the body.'

'Did he go into any more detail than that?'

'No.' Mrs Somerville hunched her shoulders and folded her arms across her body, as if she suddenly felt cold. 'I gave him a piece of my mind then, told him to pull himself together. I said he was getting obsessed and should ask for professional help. He shut up, and didn't mention it again.'

'I don't suppose he ever did seek help?'

'I doubt it. He just shut himself up in his house, with his library and his computer.'

'Mrs Somerville, do you have any reason to believe that your father took his interests further than theoretical research?'

'How do you mean?'

'Do you think he ever tried to put some of those rituals into practice?'

She swallowed, but shook her head vigorously. 'No, no, he would never have gone that far. Dad isn't a practical man, you see. The details would be quite beyond him.'

'But if he used the internet a lot, he might have made contact with people who were more practical – individuals keen to exploit his interests. Did he ever mention anybody like that?'

'No, he didn't talk about anybody else. Do you mean, people who might . . . supply him?'

'There are individuals who'll provide any service, for the right money,' said Fry. 'I presume Professor Robertson is reasonably well off?'

'Yes, he has plenty of money put away.'

'Are you sure he never referred to anybody else? If you remember anything, even the smallest hint, please tell me.'

'No. I don't think he had direct contact with many people, after the courses finished.'

Fry had been about to get up and leave, but she stopped. 'Courses?'

'He had a little group of students at one time who came to him to learn about Thanatology. I think they were a sort of off-shoot from his university work. But they stopped coming when Mum was very ill. Dad didn't want anybody in the house then.'

'They used to come to the house?'

'Yes, he gave private tuition. I don't think there were more than half a dozen of them.'

'Do you know any names?'

'No, I never met any of them. But, please – I haven't explained yet why I wanted to come in and see you tonight. You see, I spoke to Dad earlier today, and he sounded odd, not himself at all. I thought he was ill, but he told me to stop worrying. I didn't believe him, so I arranged to go and visit him this evening in Totley. I wanted to see him for myself and assess his – well, his condition.'

'And what happened?'

Lucy Somerville sighed, and her head drooped. Fry saw now what had brought her into the station. She was feeling guilty. 'I didn't go, in the end. I had to do some shopping this afternoon, and when I got home there was a message from Dad on my answering machine. He said I was not to bother coming to see him, because he'd be out.'

'Did he say where he was going?' asked Fry.

'Yes. That's what worried me most of all. It was such an odd thing to say.'

'What, Mrs Somerville?'

'He said he was going to find "the dead place".'

* * *

Cooper had to drive back through Litton to reach the road in Tideswell Dale. A sculpture trail had been created in the woods here. Thinking about it, he realized it must be barely more than a mile across the hill from Ravensdale, with only a farm and the grounds of Alder Hall lying between the dales.

On an impulse, Cooper pulled into the parking area. There were a couple of visitors' cars under the trees, but no one in sight. The rain was keeping people at home. He collected his waterproof from the back seat and locked the Toyota.

At intervals along the trail were big, deeply-carved figures made from some reddish-brown wood – a sinister-looking owl, a reclining sheep. At the top of the slope, where an abandoned quarry had been converted into a picnic area, he came across a larger-than-life carving of a sleeping lead miner in his boots, muffler and flat cap. The miner's eyes were closed, his right arm rested on his hammer, and his hand clutched a beer mug.

The carving overlooked the road. But when he moved a little higher up the slope, Cooper could see across the fields to the east – a vista of enclosed pasture land with sheep scattered across the landscape like snow. Some of the stone walls looked much too close together. Like the land at Wardlow, these fields retained their medieval shapes, the long narrow strips that were so impractical for modern farming methods. Beyond the Litton road, Alder Hall itself wasn't visible. But its boundaries were clearly marked by the woods, those plantations created by generations of Saxtons.

Cooper remembered one chore he hadn't done yet, and he looked up Madeleine Chadwick's number on his mobile.

'Detective Constable Cooper, Mrs Chadwick. I visited you on Saturday to talk about –'

'Yes, I remember you.'

'Oh, you do? Thank you. Well, I'm sorry to bother you, but there's just one thing I wanted to ask you, about the bones in the crypt . . .'

'Yes?'

'I realize it was before your time, but I wonder if you know where exactly on the estate the bones were found?'

'Oh, it was some distance from the hall, beyond the parkland. I believe one of the tenant farms had become vacant, and it was decided to plant trees on the land. One of my ancestors wanted to take advantage of the demand for timber, I suppose.'

'Would that have been Corunna Wood?'

'Yes, I think so.'

'Thank you, Mrs Chadwick. And I don't suppose you've remembered anything about the man who came asking about the crypt? No? Well, never mind. Thank you for your help.'

Cooper finished the call. The geography and the lack of direct roads in this area were very deceptive. Everything was so close together really, when you could see it – Ravensdale and Tom

Jarvis's place at Litton Foot; Alder Hall and the dense woods on this side of the water; and the austere house where Vernon and Abraham Slack lived, down by the river in Miller's Dale. There was no distance between them at all.

On his way back to the parking area, he caught sight of a sign below the trail: *Stream polluted, don't drink or paddle*. Curious, he made his way down to the edge of the water. He found huge plants growing in the boggy ground, almost choking the stream. Some of them seemed to be a sort of giant rhubarb, but others were the same purple-stemmed monsters he'd seen growing at Litton Foot, the stuff like ten-foot-high cow parsley. He made a mental note to find out what they were some time.

Cooper got his OS map out of the car. It didn't have Fry's six-mile zone on it, but he could remember pretty much where it ran. Did the clues in the phone calls really mean anything? Why had the caller led them to Peter's Stone? Was he trying to mislead them, just having a joke at their expense? Or had they misunderstood his meaning completely?

Fry's interpretation of the second message suggested Wardlow as a starting point, moving west towards the Gibbet Rock and Litton Foot, where Audrey Steele's remains had been found. But the line about the flesh eater remained unexplained.

Moving west? Cooper recalled his first visit to Freddy Robertson's house. The professor had described the traditional funeral procession entering a churchyard from the eastern gate and following the direction of the sun to the grave.

He dialled Fry's number, hoping she was there for once.

'Diane, that Beatrix Potter book,' he said when she answered. 'Did you have scenes of crime check it for fingerprints?'

'Yes, but there's nothing.'

'Shame.'

'One thing I found out, though, and quite by accident. One of the SOCOs speaks a bit of German.'

'German? Are they *all* doing Open University courses down there, or what?'

'I've no idea. But you know the Beatrix Potter book is called *The Tale of Mr Tod*?'

'Yes.'

'Our educated SOCO pointed out that "Tod" is the German word for death.'

Cooper stared at the carved owl at the entrance to the car park. 'Amazing,' he said. 'It fits, though.'

'Unfortunately, it doesn't get us anywhere. As a clue, it's a dead end. So to speak.'

'By the way, I ran into Maurice Goodwin,' said Cooper. 'Remember him, Diane? He's the man who was supposed to have been keeping an eye on Alder Hall until he fell out with John Casey. He turns out to be Tom Jarvis's brother-in-law. It makes sense – he lives nearby, so he was on hand if there were any problems.'

'And were there?'

'Well, Mr Goodwin knows about the lampers. He says he spotted them on the estate a couple of times. He wanted to report it, but Casey wouldn't let him.'

'Is that what they fell out about?'

'I think it started from there. There used to be an ATV kept in one of the outbuildings up there for Mr Goodwin to use, so he could get round the whole estate. But Casey took it off him, so he was pretty much restricted to keeping an eye on the house after that.'

'Interesting.'

'I think Mr Goodwin had his suspicions about Casey,' said Cooper. 'And if he's anything like his brother-in-law, he won't have hesitated to express his opinion. I don't think Casey would have liked that.'

'The old personality clash.'

'Mmm. I wonder whether John Casey is involved in something more than just providing access to a gang of professional lampers.'

'Ben, where exactly are you?' asked Fry suddenly.

'Near Tideswell.'

'Isn't that close to where the Slacks live? What are you doing in that area?'

'I was thinking of visiting the Slacks again. Look, I think Vernon is very frightened. I think Hudson and McGowan have systematically terrorized him until he's terrified of talking to anybody.

That suggests Vernon knows something, doesn't it? Something of interest to us.'

'I agree with the last part at least.'

'I wonder if he thinks they're going to kill him. It could have been Vernon who made the phone calls.'

'It doesn't work, does it? If he wanted us to know he was in danger, why not just come forward and tell us? What's the point of making a mystery of it? Besides, the caller seems to be suggesting he's the killer, not the victim.'

Cooper bit his lip in frustration. 'Vernon hasn't been in work today, you know. McGowan told me he called in sick.'

'Yes, I got your message.'

Then he caught the worried tone in her voice. 'Diane, do you think Vernon's at risk?'

'Yes, Ben. But I don't think the risk to him is from Hudson or McGowan. I think it's from your friend Professor Robertson.'

Cooper listened as Fry told him about Lucy Somerville. Then he finished the call and unlocked the car. He was thinking there were too many dead ends in this enquiry, and not just *The Tale of Mr Tod*. Too many dead people, too, for that matter. Audrey Steele, Sandra Birley, Richard Slack, a set of unidentified remains. Death from natural causes, death by accident. Dead and gone. Dead, and never called me mother.

It was only then that Cooper remembered the sparseness of the rooms in the Slacks' house, and the reason struck him. There wasn't a thing in the place that could have been identified as belonging to Vernon's parents. Someone had removed all traces of Richard Slack from his old home.

33

'You want a search warrant for Professor Robertson's house?' said DI Hitchens, squeaking his swivel chair anxiously. 'What are your grounds?'

Fry reported her interview with Lucy Somerville, while the DI listened with increasing concern, a frown creasing his forehead deeper and deeper. She'd brought Gavin Murfin in with her, too, but he listened without surprise as she related the worries expressed by the professor's daughter.

'And then I got one of the support officers to see if he could find these websites and any indication of Robertson's activities on them,' said Fry.

'What were you hoping for, Diane?'

'I wondered how far Professor Robertson's interest in death goes exactly. How close does he want to get to the real thing?'

Fry remembered Freddy Robertson standing in the churchyard at Edendale, admiring the memorials and telling Ben Cooper that body snatchers had never operated in Derbyshire. It had seemed to mean nothing at the time. But Fry knew the stories about body snatchers, just as everyone did. They'd existed only because they had customers willing to pay for illicitly obtained corpses.

'What are you saying?' asked Hitchens.

'It's incredible, the things you can find on the internet these days.' She looked down the list she'd been given. 'Death Online, The Death Clock, The Charnel House, oh, and something called Corpse of the Week.'

'You're kidding.'

Fry grimaced. 'I took a look at that last one. You need a strong stomach, believe me. It's an archive of photographs – mostly stuff taken from mortuaries, crime scenes, that sort of thing. No details spared.'

'This is a UK site?'

'Yes. But the contributions are from around the world – pictures of Polish autopsies, executions in Afghanistan, the remains of Chechen suicide bombers.'

'Is it legal?'

'I think so. It's not as if you could stumble on something by accident. You have to choose which pictures you want to see. But it depends how the photos have been obtained, I suppose. To me, a lot of them look like scans from official files. Mortuary assistants and crime scene photographers sharing their best work with the world.'

'What's "The Death Clock"?' asked Murfin.

'It's a site that lets you enter your personal details – age, height, weight, whether you're a smoker or not. And then it predicts the date you'll die.'

'Oh, great.'

Hitchens looked at Fry with interest. 'Did you try it out?'

'Yes.'

'And . . .?'

'The eighteenth of April 2040.'

She could see them both working it out, just as she'd done herself. How long she had left, what age she would be when she died. And how many years she'd be able to enjoy her police pension, if she ever made it to her thirty.

'The Death Clock gives you your remaining time in seconds,' she said. 'It counts them down as you watch.'

'It's rubbish, though, isn't it?' said Murfin.

'I suppose you might say it's a bit of fun.'

'Yeah.'

'Anyway, look at these photographs Robertson submitted to Corpse of the Week.'

'Hold on, how do you know he submitted them?' said Hitchens.

'The email address of the contributor is given. The professor left us his card with his contact details on, including his email address. He calls himself *thanatos*, of course.'

Hitchens studied the photos carefully. 'Pretty gruesome.'

'Where would you say they were taken, sir?' said Fry.

'Well, this one is in a mortuary somewhere – not ours, but it could be the Medico Legal Centre in Sheffield. And the next one is certainly a crime scene. The victim has gunshot wounds.'

'Suicide, according to the caption. What about the other two?'

'I can't tell. Not a mortuary, anyway. The lighting's all wrong.'

'I agree. But the body has been carefully laid out, so they're not scene photos either.'

'What do the captions to these say?' asked Hitchens.

'One for the necros.'

'Jesus.'

'As you can see, they show a female corpse, but with no signs of violence. It isn't Audrey Steele, thank God.'

The DI looked at her sharply. 'You think that's something to be grateful for?'

Fry looked down, but said nothing.

'A funeral director's preparation room,' said Hitchens. 'It's got to be.'

'Perhaps.'

'We ought to find out whether Robertson has any connection with Hudson and Slack.'

'We can do that.' Fry took the photographs back. 'Yes, they might have been taken in the preparation room at a funeral director's, but I'm not convinced. I'm wondering if there might be a similar room in the basement of an Edwardian gentleman's residence.'

'A what?'

'Professor Robertson's home at Totley.'

'I see.' Hitchens began to spin his chair again. 'Diane, this isn't evidence. It's speculation. You need something more substantial.'

'Well, we also came up with this –' Fry handed him two pages of closely printed text. 'It's an article written by Professor Robertson and published on one of the thanatology websites.'

Hitchens ran his eye over the pages. 'It looks deadly stuff to me.'

'I've highlighted the relevant paragraphs for you, sir.'

'So you have.'

Fry watched Hitchens read, and saw the recognition dawn on his face. She hadn't been sure whether he'd make the connection immediately. He hadn't listened to the tapes of the phone calls as often as she had. He didn't know the phrases by heart, the way she did.

But, as she watched him, she knew exactly the words that her DI was reading from Freddy Robertson's website article.

Wasn't it Sigmund Freud who said that every human being has a death instinct? Inside every person, the evil Thanatos fights an endless battle with Eros, the life instinct. And according to Freud, evil is always dominant. In life, there has to be death. Killing is our natural impulse. The question isn't whether we kill, but how well we do it. Without a purpose, the act of death has no significance.

For once, the flashing green light on the answering machine gave Cooper a little surge of pleasure as he walked into his flat. He pressed the button and listened to the recording before he even took his jacket off or paid attention to the cat.

'Ah, yes,' said the voice. 'It's Robertson here.'

Cooper stopped quite still in the middle of the room. Robertson? *Professor* Robertson? It must be, yet his voice sounded quite different. He'd lost the heartiness completely. Complacency and smugness had gone. Instead, he sounded weary and dejected. And, somehow, very small.

'I, er . . . that is, I have something I need to tell you,' said Robertson. 'I hope you don't mind my calling you at home, but you gave me your number. And, well, there *is* something . . .'

There was a pause on the recording. Cooper found himself listening for background noises, the way he'd listened to the tapes of the mystery caller. But there was nothing. No traffic, no voices raised in the opening verse of 'Abide With Me'. Only the faint whisper of the professor's breathing, slow and uncertain.

'Strangely, it's the one thing we never discussed,' said Robertson. And now there was a hint of his old self again, the man Cooper had spent so much time listening to. Just a suggestion, but it was there – a sly, ironic taunting that had become all too familiar.

He moved towards the answering machine, thinking the message had ended. But not quite. There was one more thing the professor had to say.

'You don't even have to ask me the right question,' he said. 'This information is gratis. I owe you this.'

Cooper played the recording again. The professor sounded in a bad way. Not just eccentric or strange any more, but disturbed. He had seemed a little too close to the edge.

The call had been made well over an hour ago, when Cooper had been talking to Tom Jarvis. But Robertson hadn't left his phone number. Probably he'd just forgotten, since he seemed so distracted. Cooper dialled 1471 for Caller ID, but a recorded message told him the caller had withheld his number. It was almost as though the professor was still taunting him. *I've got something to tell you. But you're never going to be able to ask me what it is. Ah, what a lark.* He wondered whether Robertson had permanent number withhold on his phone, or if he'd prefixed his call with 141 specially to make life difficult for Cooper.

Never mind. He had the professor's number in his book. It wasn't a problem. But before he rang, Cooper played the message a third time, listening carefully to the voice, trying to judge whether it was sincere, what the underlying emotion was, how unstable the professor might have become. Shaking his head, he dialled the number.

Twenty miles away, in a refurbished Edwardian house on the outskirts of Sheffield, Professor Robertson's phone began to ring. But the oak front door had already closed, a key had turned in the lock, a car started up in the drive. The house was empty.

And now it was Ben Cooper's turn to leave his voice on a machine. He was talking into a void.

Most of the restaurants in the High Street were closed on Monday night. The pubs were open, but full of under-age drinkers. At this time, there was nowhere he could comfortably find something to eat except McDonald's. Oh, well. One Happy Meal wouldn't ruin his arteries, would it?

Cooper didn't immediately recognize the staff member serving behind the counter. Perhaps it was the uniform and baseball cap, the cloak of corporate anonymity, that fooled him.

'You're Ben Cooper, aren't you?' said the young man, after putting through the order and taking his money.

'That's right.'

Cooper looked more closely. He didn't forget faces easily, and this one did look vaguely familiar. Gelled hair with blond streaks, a stubble of beard, a nose that had perhaps been broken once, but mended well. There *was* something about the eyes, now that he took the trouble to look the young man in the face. Perhaps it was an arrest he'd made some time in the past?

'I'm sorry,' said Cooper. 'I know I've met you, but I can't remember where.'

'I'm Nick Summers. My dad's a friend of your brother Matt's.'

'Of course. Your father works for the agricultural merchant's. You've been to the farm a few times with him, haven't you? But I thought I heard that you'd gone away to university.'

The young man looked up as the door opened. But it was only two customers leaving. He relaxed, and leaned on the counter.

'I graduated in the summer. I got a BSc in Environment and Ecology from Leicester.'

'Congratulations.'

Cooper watched the teenagers sitting at the corner table with their Cokes and large fries, and listened to the sound of laughter coming from the kitchen. Inside, he could see two more youths in red baseball caps opening packets of buns.

'So – what are your plans now, Nick?'

'Oh, I'm waiting for the right job to come up. In the meantime, I earn a living as a crew member here. It's not so bad. They wanted to promote me, but I don't really need that. Something will come up before long that suits my qualifications.'

There was a burst of noise as a group of customers came in, straight from the pub across the road. Nick straightened up and moved back to the till. Cooper's food arrived and he moved towards a table.

'Good luck, anyway,' he said.

While he ate his burger, Cooper watched Nick Summers serving customers. He seemed like a natural for the job. It didn't matter what academic qualifications he had or didn't have, provided he could wear the uniform and use the till.

Cooper remembered his own holiday job as a teenager, cleaning caravans with a bucket of soapy water and a long brush. He'd been studying hard at the time, determined to achieve his ambition of joining the police. But he'd still been grateful for the tips given him by the tourists, who'd treated him as if he were the village idiot. He'd never bothered to disabuse them of the idea.

The fries had smelled better than they tasted. Cooper spread a bit of tomato ketchup on them to see if it helped. The sauce was thick and aromatic, and some of it stuck to his fingers.

That was the trouble with preconceptions. They allowed people to pretend they were something else entirely, without even trying.

The thought brought to Cooper's mind an image of the preparation room at Hudson and Slack. He pictured a naked body on the table, the blood draining from a vein as corrosive fluid was pumped in to replace it. He thought of a corpse with formaldehyde flowing through its tissues, coagulating the proteins, fixing the cells of the muscles, soaking into the organs, halting the processes of death like a hand stopping a clock. And yet, in a way, it was still a human being on the table, someone who looked years younger than they did a few days ago. Years younger.

Preparing a body for viewing, the embalmer moulded a face, much like the forensic artist had done to create the impression of Audrey Steele. Dead faces dropped and looked grim, so they had to be pushed into an appropriate shape to please the relatives. Tweak the mouth, brush the hair, apply cosmetics.

Drained, stuffed and painted. That's what Professor Robertson had said. Well, forget the draining and stuffing. A man who could make the dead look alive would surely be able to disguise his own appearance with cosmetics, at least well enough to fool a casual observer. A whole range of liquids, creams and powders had been in stock at Hudson and Slack. A practised hand could easily change colouring, widen or narrow the cheeks, conceal a double chin, firm up the eyelids.

Then Cooper remembered what Madeleine Chadwick had said about the man who'd turned up wanting to see the bones in the Alder Hall crypt, the man whose age she'd been so vague about. Mrs Chadwick ought to have been able to identify his smell. But it had been out of context, a scent that she wouldn't have expected to notice on a man. She'd have associated it more with a session at the beauty parlour, perhaps. It might have been the blend of alcohol, oil, wax and glycerin that came from cosmetic creams and massage oils.

Cooper waited until Nick Summers was free, and went back to the counter. 'Environment and Ecology?' he said. 'I don't suppose you happen to know a plant that looks like ten-foot-high cow parsley with a purple stem?'

When he got back to his flat, Cooper checked his answering machine again, then turned on his PC and did a Google search to see whether Nick Summers' suggestion was a good one. Yes, it certainly appeared to be the plant he'd seen. Giant hogweed. A nasty-looking thing, too.

The cheeseburger he'd eaten was stirring a bit in his stomach when he switched to one of the major online booksellers and looked up Beatrix Potter's *The Tale of Mr Tod*. So 'Tod' meant death in German, did it? No doubt Professor Robertson would have been able to tell him that, if he'd asked. He probably knew the word for death in thirty-five languages.

But when the cover of the book came up on his screen, Cooper stared at it for a second or two, then slapped himself hard on the forehead.

'What an idiot,' he said. 'That's what you get for trying to be too bloody clever.'

The cover showed a classic Beatrix Potter illustration – a fox wearing a long scarf and a poacher's jacket, climbing a stile over a stone wall.

'Wait until I tell Diane in the morning.'

In the absence of anyone else, Cooper looked round for the cat to share his revelation with. 'The German for death, indeed. Of course, it wouldn't mean anything. But this . . .'

He stopped, looked at the screen again, and remembered the call he'd tried to make to Freddy Robertson. The professor wasn't at home tonight.

'Oh, shit,' said Cooper. 'He's gone there now.'

Freddy Robertson's BMW was missing from the drive in front of his house, and there was no answer to the door.

'OK, let's get it open,' said Hitchens. 'Not too much damage, if you can help it.'

Fry watched the oak door being forced. She didn't really mind if it was damaged. In fact, she rather hoped that the mosaic tiles in the hall might get cracked and the mahogany balustrades chipped. Accidentally, of course.

She followed the team into the house as they checked the rooms to make sure no one was inside. She was looking for a cellar, which she felt sure must exist. An image of the crypt at Alder Hall was strong in her mind – the innocuous door off the hallway, the stone steps down into darkness, the smell of damp and earth.

At first she could see nothing, and she began to think she was mistaken. But finally Fry realized she was looking for the wrong thing. She put Alder Hall out of her mind, walked into the kitchen and lifted the edge of a rug laid over the tiles. And there was the trap door.

She called for assistance to roll back the rug, then unfolded the brass ring set into the wood. The hinges worked smoothly, though the door was solid and heavy. When it was fully open, wooden stairs were visible below floor level. She couldn't quite identify the smell that rose from the opening. Not damp and earthy, as she'd been imagining, but something sweet. Sweet and slightly sickly.

Fry looked around. But this time she didn't need to ask. Lights were already being brought. Plenty of lights.

This time, Cooper found no one watching him from the doorway of Greenshaw Lodge. The place was in darkness, and when he drew up near the steps, his headlights showed that the back door stood open.

Taking his torch from the glove compartment, he banged on the front door and rang the bell. Then he followed the path to the back door and knocked on the glass panel. He could see the gleam of white shapes in the kitchen – fridge, cooker, washing machine. But no glimmer of light any further into the house.

'Hello? It's Detective Constable Cooper. Anybody home? Mr Slack?'

There was no response. The Slacks didn't have a dog, so there wasn't any barking, as there might have been at Tom Jarvis's place.

The open door was invitation enough for him to enter the house. Night time, an unsecured property and absent occupiers would justify investigation. But still Cooper hesitated. He groped at the wall inside the door and found two light switches. One of them brought on an outside light fixed to the stonework above his head. He turned quickly, convinced he'd seen a sudden movement behind him. But it was only the light chasing the shadows back into the trees.

For a moment, he studied the garden and neighbouring field. He noticed motorcycle tracks passing through a gate and heading across the field towards the woods.

Cooper turned back to the doorway and tried the other switch again, but nothing happened. The light didn't work in the kitchen. He flicked his torch quickly round the room and caught the glitter of glass on the floor. When he pointed the beam at the ceiling, he saw that the light bulb had burst like a large, pale blister. The remains of its aluminium base were still screwed into the fitting, but fragments of glass littered the tiles underneath. He couldn't tell when it had happened, but surely no one had been in the house since. If the Slacks were here, they would have swept it up. No one left broken glass on the floor, did they?

He still felt he was missing something. He swept his torch over the room again more slowly. And this time he saw it – a rash of black marks on the ceiling and extending two feet down the wall in the corner nearest to the door. It was as if the kitchen had suddenly developed chicken pox. Beneath the marks, a shower of white plaster lay on the work surface and on the top of the fridge.

Cooper pulled out his mobile phone and requested back-up. While he gave the address, he let his torch beam move back across the kitchen. He traced an arc from the scatter of marks on the plaster, past the broken light bulb, and as far as the door leading into the hallway, where it touched the lower banister of the stairs. He let the beam rest there for a moment, imagining the jerky, panicked aim, the deafening roar inside the house, the stink of the powder charge. The foot of the stairs was just about where someone was standing when the shotgun had been fired.

34

It was the smell of wine and whisky. Sweet, sickly and pungent, like the scent of vinegar and stagnant water. Slippery pools of alcohol lay on the flagged floor of the cellar, a dark viscous red spreading to meet a trickle of gold. They were touching but not quite mingling, ruby globules gleaming in the lights. Three bottles of Bordeaux had shattered on the flags, and a fifteen-year-old Glenfiddich lay on its side, a film of whisky trembling on the lip of the neck, ready to spill.

Fry saw that someone had trodden in the liquid before they found the light switch, and his boot had left two sticky red prints. Wine racks stood against one of the walls, but she was disappointed to realize that there wasn't much room for anything else. Freddy Robertson's cellar was tiny.

She took out the photos printed from the Corpse of the Week website. No, they couldn't have been taken in here. The wall in the background didn't match, and the scale of the room was wrong.

Hitchens came down the steps behind her. 'What a mess.'

'Yes, sir.'

He looked over her shoulder at the photos. 'No luck?'

'There could be another cellar somewhere, or an attic room. The garage, maybe.'

'Possibly. We'll find it, if there is.'

He touched the Glenfiddich bottle with the toe of his shoe. It spun slightly in the pool of liquid. The neck turned to point towards Fry, and another drop of golden fluid ran on to the floor.

'What do you think has been going on down here?' he said.

'I don't know. I suppose he was fuelling himself with liquid courage for some reason.'

'We'd better put out a stop request for his car.'

Half an hour later, Fry left the search still going on at the house in Totley and drove back to Edendale. She'd forgotten that she'd asked for Billy McGowan to be brought in for interview, and she was surprised to be told that he was waiting in an interview room. Waiting impatiently, too. But before she spoke to him, Fry had to spend a few minutes readjusting her mind, focusing on a different aspect of the enquiry.

Finally, she faced him across the interview-room table. 'Mr McGowan, you were involved in

546

the funeral of a lady called Audrey Steele, which took place eighteen months ago, in March last year.'

McGowan scratched his fingernails against the table, making a faint scrabbling sound that set Fry's teeth on edge.

'Was I?'

'According to witnesses, you drove the hearse from the funeral service at St Mark's Church to Eden Valley Crematorium. You were accompanied on this occasion by Vernon Slack. Do you remember?'

'No. How would I? There are so many funerals.'

'Oh, I think this one was quite special.'

McGowan shrugged and scraped his fingers again. Fry thought of the mice in the skulls at Alder Hall, scuttling through the eye sockets, curling up inside the cranium, their claws scratching the inner surface of the bone, where the brain had once sat.

'Well, let's see if this refreshes your memory,' she said. 'After this particular funeral, I believe you stopped on the way to the crematorium, and removed the body from the coffin.'

'Wait a minute –'

Fry held up a hand. 'There's no point denying it. What I most want to know, Mr McGowan, is whose body you replaced it with.'

McGowan laughed. 'No one's.'

'It must have been someone's. We have the computer records from the crematorium. They

547

show that the cremation proceeded as normal – the right temperature during the burning, the right amount of residue left at the end. That means bone residue, Mr McGowan.'

'It was no one.'

Fry stared at him hard. 'You must see that we can't accept that.'

'Whatever you say.'

'Let's talk about the body of Audrey Steele, then. You won't claim that was no one.'

McGowan dropped his hands from the table. He looked at Fry, then at the revolving tapes. 'Look, it wasn't really anything to do with me. I was doing as I was told, that's all.'

'Just obeying orders?'

'That's about the size of it.'

'Whose orders?'

'Mr Slack's.'

'Richard?'

'Yes. He was quite a lad for a scheme, was Richard.'

'And this was one of his schemes?'

McGowan licked his lips nervously. Despite his appearance, he wasn't such a tough nut. He seemed glad to be able to get the story off his chest.

'Richard said he'd found someone who'd pay a lot of money for a body, as long as it was in good condition.'

'Who was this person?'

'I don't know. We were never told his name.'

'And why did he want a body? For what purpose?'

McGowan smiled and shook his head, almost apologetically. 'I don't know, and I didn't ask.'

'You just took your share of the money, I suppose?'

'That's right.'

'Mr McGowan, let's get this straight. You're telling us you did what you were told. And you never had any idea who was paying Richard Slack for this service? No clues at all?'

'No.'

'Well, that doesn't really hold water, does it?'

'I don't know what you mean.'

'Let's face it – you must have delivered the body somewhere. I don't suppose you just left it by the side of the road for collection, did you?'

'No . . .'

'So, Mr McGowan – where *did* you deliver Audrey Steele's body?'

Following the motorcycle tracks, Cooper finally came across a building on the edge of a plantation. It was an old building, probably some kind of livestock shed originally. Deep blocks of limestone formed the walls, and the door was of solid oak. Rust was leaking from the nail holes in the timber. But Cooper could see straight away that there was something wrong about this place.

Despite the blue paint peeling from its panels, the door was too solid for an abandoned building.

It ought to be sagging from its hinges, the panels rotten or missing. There ought to be the remains of a broken lock where the door had once fitted securely to the stone lintel. But as Cooper got closer, he could see that the padlock and its hasp were not only intact, but clean and well-maintained. He crouched in front of the door, and sniffed the faint aroma of lubricating oil. Someone had been here within the last few weeks.

He turned his attention back to the door. The lock that secured it was a strong, old-fashioned padlock. Somewhere there would be a large iron key on a key-ring, safe in a drawer or sitting in someone's pocket. But whose pocket? The Saxton Trust owned this land – but what did they know about this disused building standing among the decaying beeches of an unmanaged woodland? Who cared about the overgrown remnants of Fox House Farm?

Cooper walked around the building, careful to place his feet on the dry vegetation rather than on bare ground. He found himself surprised by the size of the place. The side wall extended well back into the trees. Yet nothing had been allowed to root in the mortar between the stones, and no saplings grew in the corners and crevices, as they always did when left unchecked. Birds dropped seeds that would germinate in the least bit of dirt. But not here. Apart from a few clumps of grass in the broken guttering, the building seemed to have resisted the encroachment of nature.

On this side, Cooper could see that all the windows had been filled in with stone and sealed. He gave one stone an experimental shove, and it didn't budge. Maybe there was a double thickness of stone, with mortar on the inside. Or perhaps someone had used breeze block to make a proper job of it.

He moved back a few yards and looked up at the roof. Surely that couldn't have survived in one piece? The weather would have got in and collapsed some of the timbers. But the stone tiles he could see were sound. Sound, like Tom Jarvis had been sound.

But not quite. Where the building was divided by a wall, making a sort of lean-to extension at the back, the middle section of the roof was missing, exposing the interior to the air.

Cooper approached the wall again, found a foothold on the stones and pulled himself up with the help of a branch. He teetered precariously before managing to get high enough to pull himself on to the edge of the roof with one foot where the guttering should have been. He leaned forward but couldn't see down into the building. He shifted his weight a bit further on to the tiles to peer in.

He'd been right about the weather getting in. A rotten timber cracked as soon as it took his weight, and part of the remaining roof tilted inwards. Tiles slithered and cascaded on to the ground, taking Cooper with them. He managed to cling to the branch just long enough to gain some control of his fall, then he landed in a crash of broken stone.

He sat up, patted his pockets to find his torch and shone it around the interior of the building as he brushed the dust off his clothes. Cooper ran the beam along one wall, then the next. He stopped near the opening into the larger room and moved the torch back a few inches, not quite sure of what he'd seen the first time.

'Oh God, how do I get out of here again?'

Inside the abandoned building, the roots of an oak tree had burst through the broken floor like a tangle of snakes. Brambles lay thick on the stones. And blades of grass grew sick and pale through the eyes of the skull.

'McGowan is saying nothing, except he's blaming Richard Slack,' said Fry when she broke off the interview to brief the DI. 'Crucially, he won't reveal where Audrey Steele's body was delivered to. His evidence will be critical in that respect.'

Hitchens had rolled back his shirt cuffs to wipe the condensation off his window. The outside was just as wet, as the rain had been falling again for the past three hours.

'On the basis of the toxicology report, it looks as though the body had been partially embalmed,' he said.

'That might have been done to keep the body fresh. On the other hand, I understand it's becoming more and more common for funeral directors to carry out some cosmetic embalming as routine.'

'So it might not be significant?'

'No.'

'But you think the body went to Professor Robertson, I suppose?' said Hitchens.

'I'm sure of it. Who else could it be?'

The DI squeaked his chair anxiously, seemed about to answer, then changed his mind.

'What's your strategy, Diane?' he asked.

'I'm going to leave McGowan to stew for a bit, then I'm going to let him see that I know he's lying.'

'About what?'

'The body they put in the coffin in place of Audrey Steele's. We know it wasn't human.'

'Not human?'

Fry realized she hadn't told Hitchens about the anthropologist's findings, so she brought him up to date.

'Unbelievable,' he said.

'It seems all too believable in the present enquiry. It's almost as if these experts create problems for us, instead of helping us solve them.'

'No indication what kind of animal?'

'Not yet. They need the opinion of another expert for that, apparently. A different discipline. And more delay while they find someone who's available and the evidence is shuttled around the country.'

'A pity.' Hitchens squeaked again, and Fry decided she'd bring in a can of Three-in-One for him tomorrow, if she could remember.

Then the DI sifted among the papers on his desk for a report.

'What's this?' said Fry.

'The second set of remains from the hillside near Ravensdale. All that fuss about lifting the skeleton and getting it to the lab intact, and it turned out it wasn't intact in the first place.'

Fry held the report in her hand, reluctant even to look at it. 'What do they say?'

'The remains are mostly non-human. Apart from a few small bones, the majority are porcine in origin.'

'What?'

'It was part of a pig, Diane.'

She put the report back on the desk, placing it carefully among the other papers, as if she wanted to hide it, or pretend that she'd never heard of its existence.

'What about Geoff Birley?' she said.

'We're going to let him wait a bit longer, too.' Hitchens hesitated. 'Diane, we can't place Birley anywhere near the locations where those phone calls were made. He can produce witnesses to his whereabouts on all three occasions.'

Fry sighed. 'It doesn't really surprise me. He never struck me as the type.'

'Don't forget to let DC Cooper know about any progress with McGowan, will you?' said Hitchens.

'Of course.'

'Where is Cooper, by the way?'

'He's off duty.'

But Fry realized that it wasn't actually an answer. On or off duty, Ben Cooper could still be working the case.

'Fox House Farm,' said Cooper when he got through to Fry on his mobile. 'Remember it?'

'In the plantation across the valley. What was it called?'

'Corunna Wood. The Beatrix Potter book was a clue.'

'What?'

'*The Tale of Mr Tod*. "Tod" might mean death in German, but look at the cover of the book, Diane. I don't know how I could have forgotten.'

'Forgotten what?'

'"Tod" is also the country word for a fox. That's what Beatrix Potter's Mr Tod is – a fox. And this is where he lives, at Fox House. Or rather, this is where he dies.'

'Ben, I don't really know what you're talking about.'

'Never mind. But I think I've found your dead place.'

'You have? Is there any sign of Freddy Robertson?'

'His BMW is parked near the Slacks' house.'

'And the Slacks themselves?'

'Nowhere to be seen. You've been to Robertson's

place, Diane – have you seen any sign that he possesses a firearm? Maybe a shotgun?'

'No. But, Ben – you say you've found the dead place?'

Cooper looked at the skull. The skeleton lay inside a limestone building, exposed to the air, not so much as a shred of desiccated flesh left on its gleaming bones. Something had picked it perfectly clean. Something that might be called a flesh eater.

'Yes, Diane. I think this is it.'

35

When Fry arrived at Greenshaw Lodge, four uniformed officers had gathered on the steps near the back of the house, their torches playing across the ground. They were wearing yellow jackets with white glowing strips, like figures from a ghost train. One of them was talking into his radio, calling for the medical examiner and specialist support.

'What have you found?' she said.

'A body, Sergeant. Quite a fresh one. Dead no more than an hour or two, we reckon. The clothes are barely wet.'

'Any ID?'

'Not yet.'

Fry stepped to the edge of the pool of light created by the officers' torches. The body lay on its side, the left cheek pressed into the grass, hanks of grey hair tangled and damp on the neck. Life had gone from the face, the eyes were open and staring. But she could see as much as she needed to.

'I know who it is. It looks as though death came a bit closer than he expected, after all.'

'What?'

'The victim is known to us,' she said. 'His name is Professor Frederick Robertson.'

'Are you sure, Sarge?'

'Certain.'

While the officer using his radio relayed the information to Control, Fry looked at one of the other men behind the torchlight.

'Do we have any idea how he died?'

'It looks as though he was shot.'

He directed the beam of his torch on to the ground near the professor's shoulder. Fry saw the oily gleam of congealing blood, the dark stains of a man's life draining into the earth. For a moment, she didn't know what to say. Then a phrase came into her mind, a phrase so appropriate that it could almost have been spoken in Robertson's own voice.

She turned away from the officer's puzzled face and gazed into the darkness.

'*Caro data vermibus*,' she said. 'Flesh given to the worms.'

Ben Cooper thought of the old Datsun in Tom Jarvis's damp paddock, the clumps of grass pushing through its corroded floor. The paddock and this building in the woods seemed to be worlds apart at first glance. But they had a similar atmosphere, forsaken and lifeless, the result of their human use.

Both places had the feeling of somewhere that had been turned into a graveyard.

Then Cooper shook his head. No, not a graveyard. That wasn't right. There had been no attempt at burial here, only prolonged exposure of the corpse to the air, a sacrifice to the destructive effects of the Peak District climate. This building couldn't be considered a graveyard. But it might be called a charnel house. A dead place.

Near the skull lay a large stone, which he'd dislodged when he fell. Cooper remembered the stone on the hillside at Ravensdale. The grass had been pale green underneath it, recently covered over. But the underside of this stone and the ground it had been lying on were swarming with wood lice. Their grey shapes scurried in all directions when he turned it over.

As a child, Cooper had known the tiny crustaceans as coffin cutters. He imagined the name must have originated in one of those rural beliefs around death. Wood lice liked the dark and the damp, they were associated with dead and rotting vegetation. They were like flat little tanks, with legs that protruded from overlapping armoured plates. But he'd been told that the reason wood lice sought the dark and damp was because their bodies weren't watertight. They dried up and died when they were exposed to the air.

Straightening up, Cooper backed away from the skeleton towards the wall. With some difficulty, he located a couple of toe holds where the crumbling mortar had left gaps between the limestone blocks. Stone dust and fragments of mortar cascaded down the wall, dislodged by his boots. He winced, hoping he wasn't doing too much damage to the scene. He'd never hear the end of it, if he was.

Finally he saw the tree branch close above his head and was able to reach it to help himself up to the top of the wall. He scrambled over the edge and slid back down into the undergrowth. Beyond the woods, he could hear the occasional sound of an engine. For a moment, one of them seemed very close, but it stopped and he wasn't sure. Distances could be very deceptive.

Cooper took a few steps away from the building into the overgrown weeds, intending to wait under the trees. But before he'd gone three yards, he felt something give way beneath his foot with a metallic snap. For a split second, he felt only the instinctive fear of an unseen danger. There was no time for his muscles to respond.

Then steel jaws slammed shut on his ankle, biting hard from both sides, their teeth sinking in deep. He staggered, thrown off balance by the sudden loss of use of his right foot. Then the impact was followed by pain, and he could feel the jaws gnawing deeper with the slightest movement. Driven by its powerful spring, the trap had caught him just above the top of his boot, penetrating his trousers and socks and puncturing the soft flesh with vicious ease.

Cooper collapsed in the grass, gasping at the jolt of agony as the metal teeth moved sideways, tearing at him like the blades of a saw. He fumbled desperately at his foot, found the jaws of the trap and felt the rusted metal, already slick with his blood. It was an old-fashioned animal trap, shaped like a clamshell and sprung by his weight on a strip of steel lying in the grass.

After a few minutes of fruitlessly trying to prise the teeth from his ankle, Cooper felt his fingers slipping on the metal, and knew that his hands must be covered in his own blood. He took a deep breath, trying to calm himself so he could think clearly. If he was right about what type of trap he was caught in, it would be impossible to open the jaws without depressing the spring that powered them. Somewhere, there ought to be a chain and metal stake holding the trap to the ground, and a spring lever to force back the jaws.

He wiped his hands on the grass, thinking too late of the possibility that there might be another trap nearby. Then he tried to roll over to bring his arms nearer to the trap, only to be driven back by the agony that shot through his leg. He could feel his foot starting to swell, his boot growing tighter and tighter against the damaged flesh.

After a brief rest, he tried again, but more slowly this time. He edged over on to his side and inched bit by bit across the ground until he could reach the base of the trap. He was sweating by now. When he wiped a hand across his forehead, he wasn't sure whether the slipperiness he felt was perspiration or blood, or a mixture of both.

His mobile phone had fallen in the grass a few feet to the right. He could reach it. It would hurt, but he could reach it. He'd charged the phone up in the car, as he always did. And it had only fallen in grass, so it wouldn't be damaged. He thought he could even see the faint glow of the display.

Cooper nearly blacked out from the pain, but he knew his fingers were almost touching the phone. He breathed deeply, trying to clear his vision of the swarms of black specks, and the dark tide that was creeping in from the edges.

But maybe he'd lost too much blood and he was hallucinating. A slow rumble that he'd been hearing for a few seconds came closer, and stopped. A motorbike? It was followed by a rattle and the creak of a hinge. But then came a long silence, and he almost decided that it was an illusion – until he saw movement in the long grass, and heard a faint swish coming towards him, steadily getting nearer.

Two dark shapes appeared at the edge of his vision, and he blinked to try to make them go away. But that only made the specks swarm more quickly. If they were a pair of feet in black boots, he'd have heard more than their swish through the grass, more than the distant whisper of breath far above him. He'd have heard reassuring words, a call for help, or someone speaking his name. There would have been *something*.

Consciously trying to ignore the dark shapes, Cooper began to edge his fingers further across the grass. He had almost touched the phone, when suddenly it was gone. A movement came down out of the sky, and the phone was gone.

Cooper groaned. And then he lay listening to the swish of someone passing back through the grass towards the trees, gradually moving further away from him, further away with his only means of summoning help.

After all the photographs had been taken, Diane Fry bent over Robertson's body and went through his pockets. She took out his wallet, an address book, an opened letter, car keys and a mobile phone. Finally, she pulled out a blue plastic card with lettering superimposed over a red heart. She showed it to DI Hitchens, who had just ducked under the tape of the inner cordon.

'An organ-donor card. Why did he have this on him, I wonder?'

'You're supposed to carry those things with you,' said Hitchens. 'Otherwise, they're not much use. Who does he give as his next of kin? His daughter?'

Fry turned the card over. 'Well, well. It says: "In the event of my death, contact Mr Vernon Slack." Full name and signature. And it says he wanted his organs to be used for the treatment of others.'

Hitchens studied the body. 'It's a bit late for

that. He's beyond being any use to anybody.'

'But surely he wasn't related to Vernon Slack?'

'You don't have to give the name of a family member. It can be a friend, or a colleague.'

'Just a friend. OK.'

'Bag the card with the rest of the stuff, though. There might have been more to the relationship between them than we think.'

Fry nodded. As she slid the organ-donor card into an evidence bag, she read the slogan in white lettering across a bright red heart: *I want to help others to live in the event of my death*. Well, you couldn't really wish for more than that from your death. No matter what you'd done during your life.

Cooper looked up and saw Vernon Slack standing over him with a rifle. Staring at the end of the barrel, he thought of the bullet wound in Tam Jarvis's dog, Graceless. Tears were running down Vernon's face.

'Who have you killed, Vernon?' said Cooper.

Something moved and glittered in Vernon's eyes. Then it was gone again instantly. It was as if two black beads had rolled over, revealing their glistening cores for a second.

'It doesn't matter now,' he said. 'I might have killed someone, I might not. It's all the same in the end.'

Cooper thought of Abraham Slack. The old man had moved to Greenshaw Lodge so that Vernon could take care of him. But the phrase 'take care of' was open to a different meaning. The house hadn't seemed a welcoming place, not the sort of home you'd expect to rest in and be looked after. Instead, it had felt sparse and cold, more like a house that someone was preparing to leave.

He tried to sit up, forgetting the rifle, or the fact that it might be more sensible to keep still.

'Where's your grandfather?' he said.

But Vernon only stared at him 'You aren't very clever. You're not clever enough, and you're too slow. If you're stupid, you'll get beaten.'

Cooper closed his eyes, trying to make sense of what was being said. There was something surreal about the situation. Maybe it was the pain in his foot or the loss of blood that was making him light-headed and strangely unafraid. But he didn't feel threatened by Vernon, despite the firearm in his hands.

'You told us to look for "the dead place", didn't you?' he said.

At first, Vernon seemed not to hear him. His attention was focused on the building where the white bones lay gleaming in the darkness with a curious fluorescence. He shifted the rifle under his arm until the barrel was pointing at the skull. It was as if he feared the dead more than he did Cooper.

'Yes,' he said. 'But, like everyone else, you were looking in the wrong direction.'

'What do you mean?'

Vernon coughed, and turned weary eyes back to Cooper.

'You're still being stupid. The dead place isn't a building, or a location in the landscape. It isn't in the physical world at all.'

'I don't understand.'

'The dead place . . .' said Vernon, a sudden blockage choking his throat, 'the dead place is in other people's hearts.'

Then the barrel of the gun swung upwards and Vernon turned quickly, his heels squealing in the wet grass.

That was the sound Cooper would remember most clearly for weeks afterwards. It seemed to be the only thing that made sense for a while. In his memory, the squeal went on for a long time, rising to a shrill scream, high-pitched and inhuman. Then there was a loud roar and a flash, and Vernon had disappeared.

In the doorway of the abandoned building, Abraham Slack stood outlined for a moment in the light of the blast, a double-barrelled shotgun trembling in his hands.

36

By morning, crime scene tents had sprung up like mushrooms in the autumn rain. SOCOs, photographers and police officers were finding different ways of getting lost while travelling from the old engine house at Greenshaw Lodge to the ruins of Fox House Farm on the Alder Hall estate.

As a result, the forensic work went slowly, and it was well into the day before the bodies of Professor Freddy Robertson and Vernon Slack were removed. Longer still before recovery work began on the skeletal remains from the abandoned building.

Meanwhile, Abraham Slack wasn't talking. In the interview rooms at West Street, detectives were used to frustrating silences. But the old man, sitting with his solicitor, refused to offer even the beginnings of an explanation for his decision to kill his grandson. The first discharge of the shotgun had torn apart Vernon's torso, and pellets from the second barrel had shredded both his lungs, so he'd died breathing his own blood.

As he listened to Diane Fry reading the description of Vernon's injuries, Slack hung his head and sagged with distress. The interview had to be suspended while a doctor examined him. To Fry, the old man looked as though he'd given up at that point. Perhaps he had. But when they got him back into the interview room, he still wasn't talking.

Fry was relieved when DI Hitchens called her out of the room. She was exhausted, and her head was aching again, worse than ever. Though she'd managed to get home some time in the early hours of the morning, she hadn't slept at all. Whenever she'd started to drift out of consciousness, those steel springs had snapped in her forehead and plunged deep into the nerves behind her eyes, like the teeth of a gin trap.

'Billy McGowan is changing his story,' said Hitchens.

'Really?'

'It looks as though he'd decided that Richard Slack was the perfect scapegoat. Being dead can make you useful sometimes.'

Fry nodded. 'McGowan used to work for Abraham, didn't he? Was he protecting the old man?'

'No,' said Hitchens. 'Vernon.'

'But Professor Robertson – ?'

'The team at Robertson's house found comprehensive records on the professor's computer. It turns out that Vernon Slack was one of his private students. Perhaps Vernon thought he had something to prove to the people who thought he was so useless.'

'A funny way of doing it, sir.'

Hitchens shrugged. 'I don't know. A special insight into the death business? Maybe he intended to defy expectations and take over Hudson and Slack one day. He could have been planning to take the firm in a different direction.'

Fry squinted uneasily at the DI, but realized he was joking.

'He *was* Richard Slack's son,' she said. 'He could have inherited his father's ruthless business streak, but it got twisted somewhere along the way. And instead, everyone ended up feeling sorry for him.'

'Everyone, Diane?'

'Well, Billy McGowan must have felt some sympathy for him. If someone like McGowan was willing to keep quiet about Vernon's arrangement with Professor Robertson, then Vernon must have had something about him that I couldn't see.'

'I suppose so.'

Fry looked at the door of the interview room. 'That still doesn't explain why the old man killed him. Why did he do that?'

On the other side of the door, Abraham Slack sat looking at the triple-deck tape machine with a dead stare, devoid of emotion. Even the tapes had ceased to record his silence.

*   *   *

Ben Cooper was in the kitchen of Greenshaw Lodge when Fry found him later that day. He'd been watching the house gradually become sparser and more empty as the forensic team carried away items for examination. In the sitting-room display cabinet, he could still see the photograph of Abraham Slack and his family, though the SOCOs' lights reflecting off the glass made the individual figures impossible to identify.

'There was something about the way Vernon spoke,' he said, when Fry negotiated the safe path to reach him. Cooper was trying to get his thoughts clear in his own mind, and Fry was the only person he thought might understand.

'Shouldn't you still be in hospital?' she said.

'They've stitched me up and given me a tetanus jab. There was no point in staying there any longer.'

She looked at his bandaged foot. 'No bones broken or anything? I've seen such horrible stories about animal traps.'

Cooper shook his head. 'The trick is to lie still and minimize injury. Animals don't know that, so they end up tearing their own legs off.'

Fry grimaced. 'What do you mean about the way Vernon spoke?'

'When I talked to him, he never once said "I" or "me". It was always "we" or some passive form, like "There's a job to be done". Most people would have said "I've got a job to do". But when Vernon spoke, he made it sound as if none of it was anything to do with him personally. It was as though he was distancing himself from the whole thing.'

Cooper looked at Fry to see if she was listening. She was studying the marks of the shotgun pellets in the wall, where Abraham Slack had loosed off his first, and wildest, shot. The cartridge case had been found in the hallway, near the foot of the stairs.

'It's exactly what Dr Kane said about some of the phrases used in the phone calls,' he said. 'An unconscious form of denial, suggesting underlying guilt.'

'So Vernon made the phone calls?' said Fry.

She was trying to sound as though it was a minor detail. But Cooper knew that the calls were very important to her.

'Yes, Diane. I think they'll find a voice changer somewhere among all that stuff they've taken out of the house. Or maybe in Vernon's car.'

'How can you be sure?'

'He was at the councillor's funeral in Wardlow, you know. That was a Hudson and Slack job, and Vernon was one of the drivers. It might have looked odd for one of the mourners not to go into the service, and someone might have noticed that. But the drivers wait outside the church. Vernon was ideally placed to make that call.'

'What about the call from the crematorium, though? That funeral was being conducted by a

571

firm from Chesterfield. It wasn't Hudson and Slack's job.'

'But the one before it was theirs, Diane. There was a half-hour turnaround at the crematorium. The limousine drivers from the previous funeral were just waiting for the mourners to finish inspecting the floral tributes. They were away out of the gates long before we arrived.'

Fry had been looking at the pellet marks too long now. She couldn't even have been seeing them any more.

'And Vernon was there?' she said.

'I'm sure he must have been driving one of the limos that day.'

She looked at Cooper then with an eager expression, as if there was something she needed from him.

'Ben, he said there was going to be a killing. What killing did he mean?'

Cooper frowned. 'I don't know. There's only one person's death you can fully control, isn't there? There's just one form of dying that has an unambiguous meaning. That's when you take your own life.'

'You think that's what he planned to do?'

'People don't get to choose how they die. With one exception: suicide. It's the only way we can have any control over our own death. The only way we can give the end of our lives any meaning.'

Cooper knew that suicide was often an act of

anger against people who were close to the victim but had failed to recognize their despair. Or it could be aimed at those who caused the despair in the first place. In its way, suicide was an especially cruel form of revenge.

But Fry looked unconvinced. He guessed she might be remembering the words of one of the phone messages: *As a neck slithers in my fingers like a sweat-soaked snake* . . . They would never know whether Vernon had been referring to a real killing or re-living a fantasy. Was that what he'd been thinking as he sat in the wrecked van with his father helpless at the wheel? It was a moment when he might have acted out his fantasy of killing the man he hated.

'You know Vernon Slack studied under Professor Robertson?' said Fry. 'He was the professor's star student, apparently.'

'So he's not quite as dumb as he seems.'

Cooper paused, letting the sentence repeat in his head. It seemed to be accompanied by faint and unidentifiable music.

'Isn't that a line from a song?'

'Damn, you're right,' said Fry. 'What is it?'

'I can't remember. But it'll come back to me later on, when I'm not thinking about it.'

'I hope so. Otherwise it's going to keep going through my head for the rest of the day.'

Cooper stood up with some difficulty, trying not to show too much discomfort. 'You know,' he said, 'I think Freddy Robertson would consider a star student to be the person who took in every precious word and echoed his own views most faithfully.'

'Yes, you're right, Ben. I bet he liked Vernon because he was easy to influence. Faithful is a good word. And loyal, too – like a dog.'

'Why do you say that?'

'Well, he'd kept the professor's secrets for a long time. He stayed loyal, even when Robertson himself started to worry that Vernon would crack and give him away.'

Cooper frowned. 'Is that the way you read it?'

'What do you mean, Ben?'

'I think the loyalty was the other way round. Vernon thought he was doing Robertson a great service by obtaining a real body for him. It was meant to be a special gift, the way a cat brings its kill into the house for its owner.'

'Are you talking about Audrey Steele?'

'Yes, of course. The theft of her body was nothing to do with Richard Slack – it was Vernon's idea. But Robertson rejected his offering. It was a step too far for the professor – it brought death a little bit too close. Perhaps he was completely horrified by the idea.'

'So he was nothing but talk, after all.'

'But he didn't give Vernon away, did he?' said Cooper. 'That's what I meant about loyalty.'

'How do you know all this, Ben?'

He slid a plastic evidence bag across the kitchen table. It contained an exercise book with a red cover, the pages well thumbed and loose. The outside of the bag was stained with a streak of blood. Cooper realized the blood was probably his own.

'It's Vernon's journal,' he said. 'This is what his grandfather found when he started to get worried about Vernon's behaviour and searched the house. You don't need to read much of it to realize why the old man reacted the way he did. He was witnessing the destruction of everything he'd built up. Not only the business, but his family, too. And the cause of it was the one thing that he thought he had left – his grandson.'

'A journal? You mean like a diary?'

'Take a look,' said Cooper. 'Read it.'

Fry accepted the journal with the expression of someone who'd just been handed a ticking bomb. She opened it near the back, as if she hoped to avoid the worst.

MY JOURNAL OF THE DEAD, PHASE SIX

On the day I was born, my bones were soft. So soft that you'd hardly have heard them break. Perhaps, if you'd listened carefully, you might have caught the gentle crunch of a forearm as it fractured, or the crack of my thigh bone splintering. But they'd hardly have been audible, I'm sure. Not above the sound of my screams.

Now, my bones are older and stronger. If I live long enough, they might twist and become brittle, until they won't support my body any more. But deep down, the marks of my childhood would still be there – the tracks of fracture lines, the signs of incomplete healing. They're invisible now, except to an X-ray machine. Invisible, except in the jagged lines of pain etched in my memory. My bones will never forget, until the day I die.

There's magic in our bones. They produce our red blood cells, trillions of them surging through our bodies. I think the magic must lie in the marrow, that pale, mysterious jelly. If only I could suck out enough of it, my blood might be stronger, and my bones might heal.

Yet every time I think about blood or pain, I get a sensation along the nerves in the backs of my calves, an involuntary cringing, a sudden discomfort like the blood withdrawing from my veins, like shallow water dragging over sharp stones. What kind of direct connection is there between my brain and the muscles in my legs? It's one of those peculiarities of the body, a secret that no pathologist will ever bring to light with his knife.

But soon he'll be gone, the man who made me like this. When the last shreds of his flesh are stripped away, his grip on my life will be broken. Finally, his spirit will separate from his body, prised away like a dead snail sucked from its shell, like sewage pumped from a septic tank. His voice will fall silent in my head, the pain of his presence will stop, and the nightmares will be over. No more of those endless memories of beatings, the feel of his neck in my hands, a neck soaked with sweat as he lies helpless and bleeding – but I can't, can't bring myself to kill him.

Just one more day. And then I can be like everyone else. It takes just one more day.

And this will be a real killing. The final, complete

and perfect destruction. By tonight, he'll be gone for ever. Gone from the dead place.

Fry thought the journal had finished. She turned the page at what seemed to be the last entry. But on the other side, there was a final scrawl – two lines in hastily printed capitals:

IT WAS ALL A LIE. HE'S STILL HERE IN MY HEAD. WHO ELSE DO I HAVE TO KILL TO GET RID OF THIS THING INSIDE ME?

'There's an earlier entry that looks identical to one of the phone calls,' said Fry, when she'd finished reading.

Cooper nodded. 'Some of it is borrowed from Professor Robertson. Notes from when Vernon was his student, perhaps? He seems to have taken in every word as gospel. But the professor could be very persuasive. Mesmerizing almost.'

Fry slid the journal back into its plastic bag and took off her gloves.

'And what about the human remains at Fox House Farm, Ben?'

'I think that'll turn out to be Vernon's father.'

'Richard Slack? You think Vernon stole the body of his own father?'

'It would have been easier to achieve than with Audrey Steele,' said Cooper. 'Especially as Richard was due to be buried rather than cremated. There were people already complicit by then.'

'But why?'

'It would make sense, if Vernon took on board some of the ideas that Freddy Robertson was teaching him – the practice of excarnation, the sarcophagus and the charnel house. He left a body in "the dead place" to be sure that all the flesh had gone from the bones.'

'And he was going back at intervals to check on progress?'

'He wanted to be sure that his father's spirit had gone. He was afraid it would linger unless the bones were completely clean and dry. That's what Robertson had told him, you see.'

'And when the bones were finally clean –'

'Vernon thought he'd be free. Free of the nightmares, free of the memory of his father. He seems to have believed that his father was still in his head somehow. Well, you've read it, Diane. He expresses it clearly enough himself in his journal.'

'So perhaps when he called, he knew he was getting close: "Soon there will be a killing." He might not have been talking about his own death at all.'

Cooper sat back, suddenly weary. 'Vernon must have hated his father very much. It appears his father abused him badly as a small child. Vernon bore the pain in his bones all his life. I noticed him moving stiffly, but thought it was a recent beating. It wasn't – it was a very old one. A series of vicious beatings, dating back to infancy.'

'Richard Slack was worth more as meat for the worms than he ever was alive.'

'Yes, you might say that.'

'And if his father was still alive, no doubt he'd

turn up at the child's funeral and send flowers,' said Fry distantly.

Cooper stared at her.

'Diane, are you all right?' he said.

Fry seemed to shake herself out of some reverie. 'Fine. Look, I understand now what Vernon meant about the dead place being in other people's hearts,' she said. 'But there had to be a physical place too, didn't there?'

'Where else for him but his own home? The house he grew up in, the place he associated with his parents, particularly with the man he'd always hated so much. This house was always a dead place for Vernon.'

Fry was quiet for a few moments. Watching her, Cooper knew she'd return to the same subject that had obsessed her all along, though he didn't know why.

'Those messages he sent,' she said. 'The gibbet and the rock, and all that. Do you think Vernon was hoping we'd work out the clues in time and stop him?'

'We'll never know, will we?'

'If he was, Ben, we were too late.'

There was nothing Cooper could say to that. 'Too late' were the saddest words in the language, and they both knew it.

'Was it Rod Stewart?' he said.

'What?'

'That line from a song. "I'm not quite as dumb as I seem".'

'I don't know any Rod Stewart songs,' said Fry.

'Come on, you must do.'

'Well, I hope I don't.' Fry shivered suddenly. 'Bloody Freddy Robertson. He could have saved us so much time. Why didn't he tell us what he knew?'

'This Lucy Somerville, his daughter,' said Cooper. 'I imagine she's an only child?'

'Yes. Why?'

'It means Professor Robertson never had a son of his own.'

'Oh, I see.'

'And Vernon never had a real father. Not one that he cared about.'

'So Robertson became a father figure?'

'Very much so, I think. It's all in the journal, Diane, when you have time to read it.'

Fry glanced at the book on the table. 'I'm not sure I want to read it.'

'Believe me, it's all there. Robertson's big mistake was to come here to Greenshaw Lodge at the wrong time. He chose the moment when Vernon's faith in him had been destroyed. As far as Vernon was concerned, his substitute father had let him down, too. Robertson *was* killed with a rifle, not a shotgun, wasn't he?'

'So the doctor says. A single bullet, close to the heart. Enough to cause fatal internal injuries and major blood loss.'

Cooper felt a sudden stab of guilt. It was quite irrational, and something he could never admit to Fry. But, sitting here in this tragic house, almost surrounded by human corpses, he felt guilty that he'd never found out who shot Tom Jarvis's dog. Now, poor old Graceless would be pushed so far down the list of priorities that her death would lie on the files for ever, and her killer would never face justice. Mr Jarvis would become just one more person Cooper hoped never to meet on the streets of Edendale, in case he was challenged for an explanation.

He looked at Fry. There was something else that needed explaining.

'Diane, there's something about the tapes of those phone calls, isn't there?' he said. 'A personal reason you find them so hard to listen to?'

'How did you know?'

Cooper almost told her, but held his tongue at the last second. Some instinct suggested it wouldn't be wise to tell the truth for once.

'I just guessed.'

But Fry had that look on her face again, the one that suggested she didn't believe him. 'Don't worry, Ben. I think I know who must have told you.'

'No, really –'

'Well, maybe you're right,' she said. 'But it doesn't matter.'

Fry watched the scenes of crime team carrying out the last boxes to one of the vans. There was still a lot of activity around the nearest tent, where Freddy Robertson's body hadn't been removed to the mortuary yet.

'But Robertson could still have told us what he knew,' she said. 'He could have saved his own life, he could have saved Vernon's. What *was* wrong with the bloody man?'

'Do you want my expert opinion?' said Cooper.

'Go on, then.'

'He was just weird.'

Fry caught the look in his eye and saw the joke.

'Oh, that's your view as an expert? You haven't just borrowed that opinion from someone else and used it as your own, I suppose?'

'I'm very experienced in my field,' said Cooper.

'Yes, as long as it's a field of sheep.'

Cooper struggled to keep pace with her as she walked out of the house and headed towards the lane, past the crime scene vans. 'By the way, Diane, what sort of fees can expert consultants claim? Do I send my invoice to you, or to the DI?'

And then Fry laughed. It was the first time he'd seen her laugh for months. It altered her whole face, the way the sun could change the landscape after rain. She looked at him and opened her mouth to speak, and Cooper felt his heart lift, as if she were about to tell him something he'd waited years to hear.

But he would never know what Fry was going to say. Her first words were interrupted by the ringing of his mobile. With an instinctive expectation of the worst, Cooper looked at the number showing on the caller display.

'It's Matt,' he said. 'And there's only one thing he'll be calling me about.'

If life were really a book, it ought to be possible to turn the last page without pain. The way a life ended shouldn't make anyone forget the way it was lived. But Ben Cooper had a deeper fear. It was one that he hardly knew how to acknowledge.

While his sister Claire sat with Matt watching over their mother, Ben waited outside in the trees, reluctant to miss the last shreds of light as the day came to an end. The dusk deepened so gradually that it was only when the air began to chill his skin that he realized he'd been standing in the dark for the last half-hour.

After the past few days, he was afraid that he wouldn't know how to accept death. He wasn't sure that he'd understand how he was supposed to react, what other people would expect of him. When the reality of dying came close enough to touch him personally, he was terrified that his mind would go into denial. How could he face the physical truth of what he had talked about with Freddy Robertson? The slow process of decomposition that began with the final breath, the stages of decay and the mould of fermentation, the swarming bacteria and digestive enzymes that would return the body to the earth.

Surely, when the moment came, it would be too much to cope with. He'd be frozen with fear, terrified to express a thought or emotion, in case it burst a barrier that held back the worms and the demons of the grave. Everyone would think he was heartless and cold, that he was showing no grief. He might not be able to face his family, feeling as he did.

Ben wondered if there was anybody he could explain it to. He thought about talking to Matt or Claire, but he knew they wouldn't understand. It wasn't fair to inflict it on them anyway. Nobody wanted to think about death. Not really *think* about it. He was afraid he might shock them by referring to his mother's body as 'it'. But his perception of dying had changed. He no longer believed that what remained after death would still be the person he'd known and loved.

For a moment, he watched the lights on the relief road. One after another, they flickered and died on the parapet of the footbridge, though the vehicles themselves weren't visible behind the fencing. The hum of traffic reminded him of the garden of remembrance at the crematorium. He shivered, and went back to the ward and let the others take a break.

Ben Cooper held his mother's hand for a long time, until he finally fell asleep in the chair by her bed. He must have dozed for only a short while. Yet he woke feeling as if a long time had passed and the world had changed while he slept. He'd been dreaming about being lost in great, echoing caves where water ran all around him. But the dream slipped rapidly away as he opened his eyes and remembered where he was.

He was still holding his mother's hand, but her fingers felt limp and cold.

'Mum?'

Her eyes were closed – as if she, too, were asleep. He wondered what she'd be dreaming about. Ben put his palm against her forehead. It was smooth – smoother than her skin had been for years. And much cooler, too.

He looked at the unnatural whiteness of her still face, and at first he thought that she must have been replaced with a marble statue of herself while he slept. A beautiful statue, finely sculpted, but lacking the vital spark of life.

'Mum?'

But he'd seen it often enough to know the truth. His mother's stillness was beyond sleep, beyond the slightest trace of breathing.

Ben laid his mother's hand gently on the cover, making sure it was in a comfortable position. Then he patted it twice and looked up at the window. He wasn't quite sure what he was supposed to feel at this moment. He'd expected to go through all kinds of emotions, but none of them seemed to come. There was only a spreading numbness, a sort of emptiness waiting for something to fill it.

Finally, he got up from the bed and opened the door. He turned once and took a last look at his mother. She seemed peaceful, for which he was grateful. And her bed had recently been made, so that she looked neat and tidy, clean and comfortable. That seemed to be important, too.

Slowly, Ben walked the few yards down the corridor to the nurses' station. A young nurse in a blue uniform looked up at him, and smiled.

'Yes, sir? Is there anything I can do for you?'

'It's my mother,' he said. 'I think she's dead.'

37

Although it was two days after his mother had died, Diane Fry was still being unusually attentive. It made Cooper nervous. Like an efficient supervisor, she'd been concerned for his welfare, tentatively asking the usual questions to test his state of mind, his ability to do the job, and wondering whether she should send him home, in case he embarrassed his colleagues. And now she'd left a message asking him to meet her here at the sculpture trail in Tideswell Dale, if he felt up to it. What was all that about?

In the end, she'd even agreed to collect Cooper at his flat, since his foot had stiffened up and was making it impossible for him to drive.

'We've had a busy two days,' Fry said in the car.

'I'm sorry I missed them.'

'We've had a whole mass of interviews to do. Not just Abraham Slack – who still won't talk, by the way. But we've also had Melvyn Hudson in,

587

and Billy McGowan again. And your friend Tom Jarvis. He's a straight talker, isn't he? Mr Jarvis, I mean?'

'Yes, you could say that.'

'I quite liked him.'

Cooper's eyebrows rose at that. Fry never liked anybody.

'And he speaks highly of you, Ben.'

'I don't know why. I never did much for him.'

'They were a mixed bunch, those three. But they had one thing in common. They all hated Richard Slack.'

Fry stopped to fumble for change and put some money in the machine for the car park. The gate was unlocked, allowing them to drive through on to the track that led up to the picnic area above the sculpture trail.

'It doesn't surprise me,' said Cooper. 'They all knew Vernon's history, I suppose. And none of them wanted to put him through any more than he'd suffered already at the hands of his father.'

'Clannish people in the funeral business, aren't they?'

'It's "them and us". Remember?'

'Don't I just?'

Fry got out of the car to close the gate. The choked stream moved sluggishly just below the track.

'Look down there in the water,' said Cooper.

'What? I can't see anything.'

'Look at the plants.'

'The giant rhubarb?'

'That's *Gunnera manicata*, from the South American swamps. But that wasn't what I meant. I was looking at the other stuff, the giant hogweed.'

'Oh, yeah. And where does that come from?'

'The Caucasus, I think.'

'I never knew the vegetation of Derbyshire was so cosmopolitan.'

'Be careful you don't touch it,' he said, as Fry took a step closer to the edge of the stream.

'Why?'

'It secretes a sap that burns the skin and causes blisters. It's a photosensitivity problem, I think. But it can cause temporary blindness, and in some cases serious long-term damage such as recurrent dermatitis. You daren't cut the things down with a strimmer without wearing protective gear. They're a real menace.'

'Vernon Slack had blisters on his hands,' said Fry.

'He got them from touching giant hogweed while he was crossing the stream at Litton Foot.'

'On his way to Fox House Farm.'

'Yes.'

'Apparently, he used to leave his motorbike at Tom Jarvis's, then cross the stream and climb up through the woods. He told Jarvis he was doing a bit of poaching on the Alder Hall estate. He probably left him a rabbit or a pheasant occasionally, as proof.'

'Did Jarvis ever suspect there was more to it?'

'We don't know,' said Fry. 'He doesn't say.'

'No, he doesn't give much away. But it's best to pay attention to what he does say.'

Fry frowned. 'He was clearly being intimidated by someone. I think the poachers must have been trying to warn him away from their territory, don't you? All that business with the dog and the bag of excreta.'

'I never thought Tom Jarvis was the type to be easily intimidated,' said Cooper.

'Maybe.'

Cooper reflected that there had never been any evidence that the bag had actually existed, either. Mr Jarvis might have had reasons of his own for laying a false trail.

Fry parked at the edge of the picnic area, near enough to reach the carved miner overlooking the road. Cooper remembered these carvings from when the wood had been a sort of reddish golden brown. Now they were weathered from exposure and had developed a patina of green mould.

'There must still be some of Audrey Steele's bones scattered across the hillside over there,' said Cooper. 'I don't suppose we'll ever find the last bits of her.'

'We're not even looking for them any more,' admitted Fry.

'So they'll stay there for ever, unless they turn up in a bird's nest some day.'

'What's the matter, Ben?'

'I'm wondering whether it'll make any difference

to her family. They thought they already had all of her once. Then Audrey turns up again, but some of her is missing. I'm not sure how I'd feel about that myself. I'm trying to work it through in my mind.'

'If you really need to know, you could ask them,' said Fry.

Cooper looked at her, feeling a brief pity at her lack of experience in human relationships.

'People never tell the truth about any subject that has to do with death,' he said. 'They only tell you what you want to hear, or what they think sounds respectable. All of it is a pretence. No one can examine their true feelings about death too closely. It's much too frightening.'

'You mean people don't want to admit they're glad someone is dead, because they're expected to show grief?'

Cooper turned away. 'That isn't really what I meant. But never mind.'

On the other hand, he knew it was possible for people to accept death into their lives in unusual ways, like Mrs Askew keeping her husband's cremated remains in her terrarium. It was practical and down to earth, yet her husband was never completely out of her memory. He just hoped Mr Askew had been fond of small reptiles.

'What *did* you mean, then?' said Fry. She sounded as though she was trying hard not to be irritable with him.

But Cooper shook his head. 'You know, I was

591

initially misled by Ellen Walker's comments about the weather on the day of Audrey's funeral. I pictured the family standing outside the crematorium chapel, admiring the floral tributes in the sleet. But they didn't go to the crem, only to the funeral service at St Mark's. They decided not to witness the final disposal – and that was a form of denial in its way, of course. It was a decision that provided the opportunity for what came afterwards.'

'You haven't said that to the family, surely?'

Cooper laughed. 'Of course not.'

Fry took a deep breath, but seemed to change her mind about what she was going to say.

'You know the teeth in the cremated remains that Vivien Gill was given?' she said. 'We were told they were non-human, but we had to wait for an expert opinion on what animal they came from. We just got it this morning.'

'They were pig's teeth, weren't they?' said Cooper.

'How did you know?'

'A dead pig is as close as you can get to a dead person, right down to the smell. The second set of remains at Ravensdale turned out to be from the carcass of a sow, didn't they? From the cut marks on the bones, I bet it was used for practice. And Tom Jarvis used to keep pigs.'

Fry nodded. 'We're not sure how heavily Jarvis was involved. But he's been trying to protect Vernon Slack, we know that.'

'And Billy McGowan was doing that, too.'

'Yes.'

'I saw Vernon's motorbike parked outside the Jarvis house the first time I went there, you know. He might have been watching from the woods when I went down to look at the grave site. The dogs would have been used to him, I suppose. They got used to me pretty quick.' Cooper had a sudden thought. 'I wonder if that was when he tried to cross the stream further down and damaged his hands on the giant hogweed.'

Fry pushed her hands into her pockets and sat on the wooden plinth next to the miner, resting her arm on his knee. From here, there was a wonderful view over the dale, down to Ravenstor and Miller's Dale in the south. They might have been able to see the spire of Tideswell Church to the north, but for the hills in between. Fry didn't seem to notice any of it.

'We traced the owner of the rifle,' she said.

'Oh? The one that Vernon used to kill Freddy Robertson?'

'He got it from one of the gang who poach in Alder Hall woods. Vernon had seen the lampers. And he recognized one of them. When he met up with the man at a funeral, he dropped some hints and was invited to go lamping a couple of times. Then Vernon told him he needed a rifle to shoot rabbits on his own property.'

'Really?'

'Yes, really. And you might be interested to know that we got a match with the bullet the vet took from Mr Jarvis's dog.'

'You've identified the person who shot Graceless?'

'That's why Mr Jarvis thinks so highly of you, Ben.'

'But I didn't –'

'It doesn't matter.'

Cooper looked at Fry. For a long time, she'd regarded him as something to be avoided as far as possible. He seemed to be an irritant to her, every bit as noxious as the giant hogweed that had caused the burns on Vernon Slack's arms.

'Gavin Murfin came to see me, you know,' he said. 'Was it you who told him about something called the Death Clock?'

'Yes. It's a website that lets you put in your personal details, and it predicts how long you'll live. It claims to give you the exact date of your death. Why?'

'Well, Gavin found the website and tried it out.'

'Ah. And did he get an interesting result?'

'Yes,' said Cooper. 'It told him he'd died three months ago.'

'Poor Gavin.'

Cooper couldn't help smiling. 'Actually, I think it did him good. He's decided he might as well enjoy himself as much as possible if he's living on borrowed time.'

'Back to his old self, then.'

'Freddy Robertson was right, you know,' said Cooper. 'It's the unknown we're most frightened of, the things we don't understand. And more than anything else in the world, death is the great unknown. The only way to come to terms with it is to understand it. If you can do that, then death loses its power to be quite so frightening.'

'I hope that's so.'

'He wasn't right about everything, though. Vernon Slack had been listening to him too much.'

'What do you mean?'

'The idea that the soul hangs around the body until the flesh is gone from the bones – that isn't true at all. There's a moment when the personality dies, when the person you loved is gone for ever. In the hospital, I knew exactly when that had happened. There was no doubt about it, none at all. And then nothing mattered any more. I mean, I wasn't worried about what death would mean for Mum, all that business about decomposition and the body digesting itself. Because anything that took place after that moment wasn't happening to *her*. It was just nature tidying up.'

Fry straightened up. 'Have you seen the clouds over there?' she said.

Cooper looked across the valley in amazement. He had never known her to notice the weather in the Peak District before, not unless it was actually raining so hard that she was in danger of drowning. But he saw what she'd noticed. There were banks of dense grey clouds over Hammerton Hill, but they were breaking up as they rose, allowing a glimpse of sky.

He turned to look at Fry. She was gazing past him at the view, as if seeing the landscape for the first time. Over her shoulder, Cooper could see the carved miner smiling as the sun touched his face. The miner didn't care what happened to his body – and why should he? Someone had captured his spirit and preserved it for ever. His memory would never decompose, his soul was intact, his eternity was beyond the need for a physical body. Somehow, from somewhere, he'd found the secret of peace.

But Cooper had one more thing he needed to say. It was something that had been burning a hole in his heart since he'd spent those hours sitting by his mother's bed, with too much time to think.

'Vernon Slack said the dead place was in other people's hearts,' he said.

'Yes?' said Fry.

'But he was wrong about that, too, wasn't he?'

'What do you mean, Ben?'

'Everybody who knew Vernon lied to protect him. Everybody. They tried to shift the blame on to his father, who deserved it, God help him. And his grandfather decided he'd rather suffer himself than allow Vernon to go through the nightmare he'd face if he was arrested.'

Cooper put his hand on the shoulder of the carved miner, testing for a bit of warmth where the sunlight touched the wood.

'In fact, Vernon was loved by everyone around him,' he said. 'He just never knew it.'

'Ben . . .'

Cooper withdrew his hand and looked at Fry. But he wasn't sure who he was talking to when he spoke again.

'We know so little about death. But the fact is, most of us know even less about love.'

One Last Breath
Stephen Booth

Fourteen years ago Mansell Quinn was jailed for murdering his mistress. Now he has escaped and is on the run, hiding amongst the Peak District's many summer tourists. When Quinn's ex-wife is found dead, DC Cooper and his tough boss DS Fry suspect it is only a matter of time before another victim is found. And Cooper – as the son of Quinn's arresting officer – is high on the list.

As they desperately search the case files for clues and the death toll rises, darker possibilities emerge. Are the killings the work of a deranged killer who cannot be found – or a desperate man, wrongly convicted?

'*One Last Breath* underlines Stephen Booth's status as one of our best story-tellers'   *Sunday Telegraph*

ISBN-13 978 0 00 717204 7

Scared to Live
Stephen Booth

An assassination in the night – an open window and three bullets from the darkness – the victim a harmless middle-aged woman. But can she be quite as innocent as she seems? The death of Rose Shepherd swarms with questions – unlike the deaths of a woman and two children in a house fire. A tragedy, yes, but an everyday one.

Then DS Fry discovers a link between the cases, a link that crosses the borders between nations, between right and wrong, between madness and sanity. She and Ben Cooper discover why some people are scared to live – and others are fated to die ...

'Booth's aim is to portray the darkness that lies below the surface... in this he succeeds wonderfully well'

MARK BILLINGHAM, Daily Mail

ISBN-13 978 0 00 717210 8